Nowhere but NORTH

A North and South Variation

Nicole Clarkston

Copyright © 2018 Nicole Clarkston

Cover Design by Janet Taylor

All rights reserved.

ISBN-13: 978-1718087613

Dedication

To all the ones who went before
And who wait ahead. One day
I will hold you again.

Contents

Acknowledgements	viii	Fourteen	202
One	1	Fifteen	215
Two	17	Sixteen	227
Three	32	Seventeen	244
Four	47	Eighteen	258
Five	63	Nineteen	272
Six	79	Twenty	291
Seven	92	Twenty-One	307
Eight	111	Twenty-Two	322
Nine	135	Twenty-Three	336
Ten	149	Twenty-Four	351
Eleven	160	Twenty-Five	372
Twelve	176	Twenty-Six	384
Thirteen	188	Prologue	392

Acknowledgments

Nowhere but North is the hardest book I have ever written. From a technical standpoint, I did what you are not supposed to do: I wove a story in the present tense, while constantly looking into the past. I hope I have succeeded, but only the reader can judge.

However, it was not this challenge that drew out the completion of this book for just over two years. Part of it was personal. Although the griefs of my own life were not precisely the same, John and Margaret Thornton broke my heart, again and again. Perhaps that is why I love this couple so much—they are more than just a literary couple. They are a reflection of *us*, and their tragedies and triumphs are our own.

So many dear friends held my hand and lifted me up through the grueling two years of this book. They watched me follow the rabbit trails otherwise known as *These Dreams* and *London Holiday* and kept encouraging me to come back to this one until the story had been told. It began innocently enough, with a few blog posts celebrating the release of *Northern Rain* in 2016. Rita Deodato of *From Pemberley to Milton* and Janet Taylor of *More Agreeably Engaged* both helped set my feet on this path. Thank you, my dears!

Janet astounded me with this cover. She and her son Jeff crafted it from scratch. As she was so intimately acquainted with the story from the beginning, she was able to create an image that beautifully portrays our couple—the tenderness, the desire to comfort, but also the frustration of disparate needs. I should just stop writing books and tell her what a cover should look like, because she captured it all.

In 2017, Austen Variations held a fundraiser in the aftermath of Hurricane Harvey. Compassionate readers gave generously to the relief efforts and were honoured for their kindness in different ways. Debbie Fortin, a dear friend and already a trustworthy sounding board to me, appears in this book as a cameo. I hope you come to adore her as much as I do.

Joy Dawn King has been indispensable, particularly during the last half of the process. When I was staring at a scrambled manuscript, unsure of an ending and tearing my hair out over the flow and sequence, she pointed me forward and then pushed. *Hard*. Thank you, my sweet friend!

Finally, I have the *best* group of beta readers a writer could ever ask for. Jennifer Joy, Joana Starnes, Jeanne Garrett, Carole Steinhart, Angela Dale, Don Jacobson and Trudy Brasure… just typing that list gives me the chills! They caught typos and inaccuracies that I stared at for two years and never noticed! I could not be proud of the book you hold in your hands, if not for them. I have no words to describe the selfless support of my fellow authors or the enthusiasm of great readers like these. Any writer who can call even one of these amazing people a friend is blessed, indeed.

-NC

One

30 August 1855

"With this ring, I thee wed, with my body I thee worship, and with all my worldly goods I thee endow: In the name of the Father, and of the Son, and of the Holy Ghost. Amen."

John Thornton's throat constricted and his chest hammered. Those words had sealed his future—words he had once desperately longed to speak over himself and this woman standing at his side, but words which seemed unwelcome to her ears. She had not desired his hand.

The rector gave the direction and the register was signed in due course. She laid aside the pen and came to stand beside him. One last tradition remained—a silly, inconsequential deed at that, and one they could have dispensed with, had not he insisted that none should suspect their marriage was anything other than agreeable to both parties.

His limbs quivered with apprehension as he turned to face the woman who was now his wife. Her face was cast down as she, likewise, performed the scripted manoeuvre. The white veil frosting over her features heightened the pallor of her bloodless cheeks and clashed against the black of her mourning dress. She lifted her chin dutifully, waiting for him to complete the required motions.

Swallowing hard, his eyes full of regret, he reached to lift her veil. His fingers brushed only the filmy gauze concealing her countenance, careful not to touch her more than necessary. He would ask nothing more of her after this single public intimacy, but the proper forms and customs must be observed so that no one might murmur.

John dropped the lace behind her back as her eyes, wide with alarm, found his. He drew a reckless breath, steeling his courage, and then bent to inaugurate their union with a quick brush of his lips against hers. No feeling was exchanged, no sweet promise of hope and love shared. It was simply done.

One more had been added to his household. One more to provide for, to extend his name to. For better or worse, Margaret Thornton was his problem now.

~

Eight Days Earlier:

"May I please speak with Miss Hale?"

John Thornton shifted his hat between his hands as he dared to confront the Hales' disapproving maid. Dixon glared up at him, her eyes swollen and red, but her manner no less vigilant over her mistress than it had ever been. In fact, it was a good deal more so.

Dixon's mouth worked. She also seemed to know there was no other recourse, but she did not like letting him to her young lady just now. "This way," she grumbled, apparently not caring that her manners were less than exemplary.

John followed her up the stairs. To his surprise, Dixon led past the small sitting room on the second floor and up to Mr Hale's old study. She stopped before the door, crossing her arms. "You'll take care of her, Mr Thornton." It was not a question.

His eyes, which had drifted to the closed door, snapped back to the woman. "I shall try."

This seemed to satisfy her. With a grunt and a lurch, she worked her way past him to lumber down the stairs, leaving him alone. He turned to the door, clenching his fist. His task was before him, and he would not shrink from it.

For three days now, since his old friend had failed to awaken Sunday morning, Margaret had been without a protector. No concerned family descended upon the little Crampton house, no benevolent godfather came to offer aid, and no valiant suitor had arrived to carry her away from her grief. Her only comfort had been the bitter maid and the grizzled old weaver who first brought him the news of Mr Hale's passing. She had nowhere else to turn.

John eased the door open. He did not see her at first, scanning, as he was, the chair and the desk which had belonged to his friend. The room was dim, lit only by the low afternoon sun filtering through the curtains. At last, his searching gaze settled on her forlorn figure.

She looked to have fallen into her father's worn settee before a dying fire, her tousled head draped over a small end table where a stack of Mr Hale's books formed a pillow of sorts. Her eyes were closed, but her lashes shimmered with sorrow in the glow of the fire's embers. Pity tugged at his heart.

How he yearned to cast himself at her feet and pull her into his loving arms! If only she longed for his comfort and waited only for his voice to release her anguish into his strong embrace. Moisture pricked his own eyes. It would not be so, but at least he could offer her some measure of protection. He owed his friend that much.

John stepped into the room, afraid to disturb her repose, but knowing that he must. He stopped before her, his fingers twitching when she did not seem to hear his approach. "Miss Hale?"

Her head jerked up, blinking as she tried to see him clearly through unshed tears. She straightened without a word. Apparently, she was expecting him, for her face held no questions—only what appeared to be resignation.

Pressing his lips together, he drew one step closer to her, then lowered himself to his knees before her chair. She dropped her gaze modestly.

Now that it was time, and he was nearly assured of her acceptance, he could not form the words. He had spoken them once before, and that memory choked his throat and caused his pulse to drum with uncertainty. He knew she did not care for him and probably loved another. It was no virtue of his own which would require her to accept him, and there would be no affection he could expect once she did. They had little to offer each other, apart from respectability and security. It seemed a paltry consolation.

During his hesitation, Margaret's eyes had travelled up once more. Her voice was trembling and scarcely audible when she spoke. "You have been to the funeral."

He glanced at the black arm band he wore, sorry that its presence might cause her additional pain. "Yes." His mouth went dry. *Get it over with, man!* There was no sense in drawing things out.

"Miss Hale, will you do me the honour of becoming my wife?" he blurted, his voice quavering with hope.

Margaret's stricken eyes met his. She held him for a long, suspense-filled pause, before answering in a broken whisper. "Yes."

John hissed out the tense breath he had been restraining. At least she had determined to be sensible about all this, even if she were not happy. It would spare him the distress of arguing with a woman in mourning for her lost father.

He ought to be overjoyed in this moment, having secured the promise of the one who delighted his heart, but he could not. He had just asked her to commit to a life with a man she did not love, and she had no choice but to accept. Rather than pleasure at her answer, he felt only remorse for her sacrifice.

He gave a firm nod, indicating that he had heard her hushed reply, and that their deal was struck. "I shall make the necessary arrangements. Do you...." He hesitated in distaste for the indelicacy of the questions he must ask. "You will wish to marry without delay? A common licence?"

She looked down, her gaze hovering somewhere near the centre of his waistcoat. Every possible solution would require some breach of propriety. They could not hold a traditional ceremony with the bride in deep mourning, nor decently wait the prescribed period without a chaperoned living situation for her. The best answer was a quiet ceremony, granting her his name and honour—for there was none other to offer it.

She was silent for a moment, causing him to stir in discomfort. At last, another whispered "Yes," reached his ears.

"I will speak to the vicar directly. Perhaps I will ask my mother to assist you?"

Her bodice was trembling with short, shallow breaths. "I think... I think that is unnecessary, sir. There will be little for me to do until...." She faltered, her eyes refusing to lift again to his.

She was correct, of course. The silk mourning gown she wore would suffice for their simple marriage ceremony, and her belongings need not be moved until she came to his home. There would be no cause to disrupt the household until then.

"I dislike leaving you alone here. Are you certain you will be well until we can make other arrangements?"

"I have Dixon. And Mr Higgins promised to look in each day."

He sighed. "Of course." He rose to his feet. She did not follow his movements, and he turned reluctantly away. Within seconds, however, he stepped again to her side. She looked up in swift surprise.

"I will take care of you!" he vowed hoarsely. "You need have no fear, Miss Hale."

Her mouth twitched into a bare approximation of a smile, but it did not travel to her eyes. "I know you will, Mr Thornton."

Margaret Thornton—for that was her name, now—stood in the centre of the spacious chamber. She clutched a satchel of personal items as she took in the opulently decorated room that was to be hers. Her new mother-in-law had offered a brisk tour, then taken her leave—it was likely a relief to them both to part company without delay.

Her marriage that morning had passed with little recognition. In fact, the austere Milton ceremony had borne no resemblance at all to the pastoral simplicity of her father's old church, where she had always assumed she would one day wed. The setting was wrong; the voice leading her in her vows unfamiliar, the sacred traditions empty, and the audience of well-wishers absent. And the groom... she still could not decide about him. Why, *why* had she not objected to that vexing charade of a kiss, as if that little display were sufficient to convince their witnesses that he was not acting out of duty, nor she out of desperation?

It was all so very, very wrong. There was no reception breakfast, out of consideration for her state of mourning, and there would be no wedding tour. It was just as well, for she scarcely knew what she would say to her new husband if they were required to spend days alone together.

Husband. She swallowed.

It had been noble of him to offer marriage. She certainly did not deserve such consideration from him, but she ought to have expected that he would render this one final homage to her father. *Oh, Papa!* The tears flooded her eyes before she could restrain them.

Her breast heaved with the effort of controlling herself. She must not crumble now! Not when her new life and duties spread before her. She could not disappoint her father's memory! She choked on the lump in her throat.

It was for her father's sake that Mr Thornton had overcome his disenchantment with her to offer a home. No other had done so much, so she could do no less than to respond with dignity. She would honour the man who was her husband, regardless of his lost respect. Perhaps, one day, she might find a way to earn it back.

"Do you find the room to your liking?" The low, even tones startled her—it seemed she must now become accustomed to a man's voice in her chambers.

Mr Thornton stood in the doorway, apparently uncertain of his welcome. She made an effort to smile. "Yes. It is a lovely room."

He entered hesitantly, his eyes scanning the sparse but opulent furnishings, and the walls which were garishly papered in gold and brown paisley, making it seem like a grand hall. The room which had seemed much too large a moment ago shrank before his towering presence, and she felt stifled for breath.

"I am afraid the décor may not be to your taste. We will re-paper it whenever you wish. I expect you would prefer your own furnishings as well? I shall have a few articles brought directly. Your own writing desk and dressing table, and perhaps your father's settee to start?"

She was watching his feet as he walked towards her. "There is no need to put you to such trouble."

"Margaret," he voiced her name softly, haltingly.

She glanced up. It was the first time he had spoken thus.

"This is to be your home, and I wish for you to be comfortable. Will you not tell me how I can help you to settle?"

"You have already been more than generous, sir," she breathed. It had not escaped her that she was a married woman, and the man who held claim over her stood not three feet away in her bedroom. She could not know what he might ask of her, nor when he would do so. She only understood that she belonged to him now, just as surely as did everything else in this room.

His lips thinned. "Margaret...." He paused, waiting for her to meet his eyes. "I would have you know that I am sorry. I understand this is not what you desired, nor what I would have wished for you. I hope that one day you might be content here with me."

She blinked rapidly again. "Thank you… John."

He took a tremulous step nearer. "I have sent Williams with a few men for your most immediate belongings. They should arrive within the hour. Miss Dixon has agreed to remain at the house to supervise the disposition of the larger items, but I imagine that once you feel able, you will wish to take part in that process. There is no hurry—I will keep the rent on the house for as long as you need."

She thanked him again, recognising the full kindness of his gesture. She was required to stay here with him, but he would not rip her maidenly home from her just yet. How much was it all going to cost him?

"Well...." He stood a moment more, as if unsure of his bounds. "I have some work to do. Mother is here, should you require anything for your comfort, and her maid Jane or one of the other girls will assist you until your Dixon is installed here permanently."

She remained still and silent as he left her, closing the door carefully behind himself. Somehow, she had never pictured herself abandoned in a strange house while her husband went back to work on their wedding day. She had certainly never imagined greeting this day wearing mourning black, with only Dixon and a tired old weaver and his daughter to pay their respects in her honour.

Margaret forced herself to move methodically towards the bed to begin unpacking the few things she had carried with her. She *would* not cry. John Thornton had plucked her from poverty and solitude and brought her to his home, unwelcome though she felt. Her own family—what was left of them—could not have done more. She was grateful… truly, she was. And those were *not* tears cupping in the corners of her eyes.

Helstone
24 April 1837

"Margaret why are you crying?"

Frederick Hale, a lanky youth at twelve, scooped his sister from her nest in the woodshed. One scruffy kitten clung wildly to her dress, its eyes staring in fright as Margaret fumbled to clutch it to her middle.

"Fred! Helen is falling!" She pushed away from her brother with her free hand once she had gained the relative safety of the shed floor, then bent to croon to the terrified cat.

Fred muttered a colourful phrase he had heard from a local farmer—one which his father had sternly forbidden. "What a ridiculous name for a cat!" he rolled his eyes but softened when a few more tears slid down her cheek. "Tell me, sweetheart, what is the matter?"

Margaret was cradling the kitten to her face to wipe the tears away. "Mamma s-says I can-not take He-Helen to London!" she sniffled. "She s-says Aunt does not l-like animals!"

"Oh, for heaven's sake," he grumbled. "She will be here when we return. We are only going for a fortnight."

"But she will not remember me!" wailed the plaintive voice. "She will be almost grown, and she will forget about me."

"Look, Margaret, cats care little enough for people. They only like being fed. I daresay Helen likes the back door of the house as well as the front. Bring her some milk when you return, I suppose. She will remember you then."

Scandalised blue-green eyes widened at his dismissal, and her lip quivered. "Helen is my f-friend!"

"Oh, come, Margaret, we do not leave for three more days yet. Why all this fuss?"

She scrunched the limp, pliant little creature to her cheek once more. "Edith's nurse won't let her play with me," she murmured into the cat's fur. "She says I am a p—a p...." Another sob shuddered the small child.

"A pest!" Frederick doubled, bellowing with laughter. "Dearest, now I see! Edith's nurse is pretty strict. Perhaps if you stayed in one room, instead of wandering and frightening her."

"She doesn't like me at all," pouted the quivering mouth. "I don't want to go, Fred!"

"Oh, Margaret, you do take it to heart so. Last time was quite a bore, I confess. Perhaps if we are very polite, we may go back to the park, like we did last year. Do you remember the fountain?"

Her sanguine countenance raised to him once more and she nodded. "Will the geese still be there?"

"I think so, but you had best not chase them this year. Remember how angry Uncle was?"

"I did not chase them. I was only looking at the babies." Her face fell. The cat, at last weary of being held against its will, spun about in her grip, and in no uncertain terms exerted its independence. Margaret released it, for she had already encountered unpleasant scratches from this particular feline. When it had gone, she stood grumpy and dejected, watching the crooked tail as the half-grown cat stalked from the woodshed.

"Come, Margaret, cheer up," her brother coaxed. "Let us think of something fun we may do before we leave for London."

Her innocent face gazed up at him, and he warmed with affection. She was adorable, his little sister. Dark, wayward curls sprang for expression beneath her prim bonnet. Clear, intense eyes surveyed him gravely, and soft, pure cheeks rounded to a purposeful chin. It was Edith who always claimed the beauty when the two cousins were together, but if a twelve-year-old boy might have an opinion on the subject, he much preferred his own sister's vibrant personality and the way it shone forth so markedly, even at four years of age.

That determined character sparkled now with renewed inspiration. "What can we do, Fred?"

He made a show of deep thought, chewing the sides of his cheek and holding her in a playful, suspenseful stare. "I know! Let us go peek into the parish charity basket. Do you suppose that ugly green dress is still there? I wager no one has taken it yet."

Her cheek dimpled in boredom. "It is. I saw it yesterday."

"Hmm." He tapped his finger to his lips, as if deliberating a great plot. "What could we do with it? Make a straw man and dress it? We could stand it up on the lawn and frighten Dixon!"

Margaret did not immediately leap at the idea as he expected. She turned away, gazing over the yard towards their mother's rose garden. Frederick chuckled again. She was so serious for such a small girl!

A moment later he realised Margaret's senses had been sharper than his own. Beneath the prickly bushes rooted a brown nose, then Farmer Grady's greying hound emerged soon after. Spotting the children, he wagged his tail and made his friendly way towards them. Children, as any dog knows, are always good for a little petting, and the two Hale children were no exception.

A wicked notion struck Frederick, and he laughed aloud. "Margaret, would it not be funny to put the dress on Dane here? Oh, only think of him running through the church yard tomorrow!" He dissolved into hoots of laughter, imagining the scene. He would never do it, of course, but the shocked faces of the assembled parishioners would almost make up for the punishment he would be sure to receive later.

Margaret had gone still, her eyes bright and wide. She stared up to him in mute astonishment, and if he had to conjecture, he might have feared that she would carry out his suggestion. He almost thought to warn her off of mischief but just then they heard their mother's voice from the house.

He sighed. "Well, come along, Margaret. I suppose it is time for evening tea."

The evening tea had been a silent affair. John Thornton had taken his customary seat at the head of the table, but at the foot was the new mistress of his home.

It was not without some tense disquiet that he had observed his mother starting for her old place, then thinking better of it. Margaret had glanced between them with a look of unease as she had taken the chair which was now hers, but whether it grew from regret over her new circumstances or remorse for his mother's discomfort, he could not say.

His mother had been firmly set against this course. He fingered his silverware as his gaze flitted between the two women at his table. Margaret kept her head bowed and scarcely touched her food, unable to counter the other's frosty reception. His mother, seated halfway between them, looked only straight ahead with a serene hardness to her countenance.

John sighed. He would have to speak with her again. He had offered Margaret a home, and he would not see it become a place of misery for her. Perhaps he might have done better to have asked his mother to stay with Fanny for a few days while Margaret became accustomed to her new surroundings, but to do so now would cause even more discomfort for all.

At last the stilted proceedings concluded, and the Thornton family—all three of them—retired to the drawing-room for a quiet evening. John found his paper, but his eyes were ever lifted over the edge as he watched his new wife in the firelight. Heavens, but she robbed him of breath! Even now, in full mourning as she was, there was a sensual grace about her figure which cried out to him, enticing him in a way he was helpless to deny.

She held a book, but it seemed her mind would not exert itself this evening, for it slanted listlessly as she stared vacantly into the fire. The flames glowed softly over her ivory features, stony and expressionless as her thoughts wandered. He would have given a great deal to know what lay on her heart this night and with what measure of optimism she looked to the future. Perhaps she, like he, was not entirely without hope, but the dream of winning her affections appeared monumental to him.

How long will I be able to bear it?

To have Margaret in his home every day, carrying his name and presiding over his household, was simply too tempting. The lush curves of her figure, the soft ringlets of her hair where her pins had worked loose… she was so *real,* so easily drawn under his power at last! Only a thin door stood between his room and hers, and… well, by heaven, it was his right!

But there, she had sworn only her life and her future. Her heart was not yet his, nor could he force it to become so. To ask what he wished of her when she would respond only out of obligation… he shuddered in revulsion. It was in every way abhorrent to him.

His hands trembled as they gripped the edges of his broadsheet. Swallowing hard, he bade himself to look away from the haunting vision that was his legally wedded wife. If he did not, he would not be able to vouch for his sanity.

He stared unseeingly at the headlines scripted out before him, his jaw clenched. Somewhere to his right, he heard his mother at last setting her needlework aside, and his body sagged in relief. Finally, the uncomfortable evening was drawing to a close.

Margaret had noted the change as well and was looking curiously to Hannah Thornton. He shifted his paper and caught her eye. "Margaret, it is Mother's custom to lead the household in prayers every night before we retire. I hope you will feel inclined to join us."

"Oh. Of course, Mrs Thornton."

His mother lifted a cool brow as she surveyed the younger Thornton lady. It seemed they would have to come to some agreement about what they were to call one another, but she appeared content to keep Margaret in her place as an outsider. John, however, was scowling very faintly in her direction.

The household had gathered, the evening devotional completed, and at length, John rose from his seat. He extended a shaking arm to his wife. "May I see you upstairs?"

Eyes wide, lips pale, she accepted. Small fingers dug painfully into the flesh of his inner arm as she conveyed to him far more tension than she likely realised. Her unease abated only a little as they left his mother behind, and mounting the stairs with her thick skirts required her full concentration.

His heart twisted in sympathy. There seemed nothing he could say or do to alleviate her suffering. He could but grant her space and see to her every want, and perhaps in time, she might grow to be more at home. Drawing up at her door, he moved his arm and her hand slid away.

"Have you everything you need?"

Her throat worked as she gulped nervously and nodded. She was looking at his feet again.

"Jane or Sarah should be in shortly to help you. I..." he stopped, unable to find more words.

It seemed unjust to tell her how his soul leapt for joy that she had come into his life, regardless of the circumstances, but churlish somehow to leave her without some assurances of his felicity in their new relationship. He reached hesitantly for her hand. "I wish you a pleasant evening," was all he could manage.

She lifted curious eyes to him. Round and softly dilated, they studied him for a breathless second. "You... you will wish to..." she paused and drew a gasping breath. "You will knock later?"

His stomach pitted. So, he had not made his intentions clear enough. He released a taut sigh. "Let us speak in privacy."

Her nervous hands fumbled with the door latch, and then they stood together in the dusky room. "Listen, Margaret," he began, his tense fingers kneading his brow. "It is only right... After all, you are in mourning, and... and you know, it has surely been a trying day for you...."

She gazed at him in complete silence, no emotion flickering across her vivid features.

"So, you see, there can be no need, not tonight," he ground out, his teeth biting down on his tongue and his left fist clenching. He must escape soon, or he would make a liar of himself! Her skin looked so soft, and she smelled of roses.... He began to groan in self-pity but covered the sound by clearing his throat.

"I see." That was all. No change in expression, no movement to step back from the door and release him from the confrontation. Her nostrils fluttered, the only symptom to betray her unease.

"I assumed you would be relieved." He rubbed his palms surreptitiously along his trousers. They were positively aching with his need to reach for her!

"I can see that you are."

His mouth fell open. "I only think of you!"

He watched her cheek muscles tighten and her expression harden. "Mr Thornton, we both know I brought nothing to this marriage but myself. I wonder, sir, why you took the trouble if you do not intend to...." She stopped and squeezed a sudden tear from her eye.

"Margaret! You cannot expect that I—"

"Please hear me out, sir!"

He swallowed his protests and waited for her to compose herself.

She seemed to be choking, exerting every shred of her remaining strength to bite out the words before her shattered tones betrayed her. "I am the interloper here, Mr Thornton. Your mother does not welcome me, your staff no doubt wonder what you are about, and my support must have come at a very dear price. I pledged my obedience to you, sir, but if you intend to treat me as a poor relation rather than a wife, I beg you would reconsider before it is too late!"

He stared, flabbergasted. "Too late? It is already so! What would you prefer? That I force you? That I demand your compliance without regard for your own feelings? A fine proof that would be that I truly am the monster you have always believed."

"I neither believed nor implied any such thing! But I am not such a fool as to fail to acknowledge the reality of our circumstances. It is your duty, and your right...." Here, her voice at last failed her, and her features pinched, as she clenched her eyes and covered her mouth with a gasp.

"A duty, you say?" he snarled bitterly. "I should say my duty now is to care for my wife. You speak of rights as though I had hired your services! I know well enough that I am no more than a tradesman, capable of thinking only in terms of buying and selling, but I shall never intrude where I am not welcome. Rights, indeed! You may be pleased to consider yourself the martyr—the noble wife who silently bears all manner of humiliation in the name of feminine dignity—but I would be no better than a beast who takes a woman against her will. I am sorry, but you have judged me wrongly if you thought me capable of that!"

Her body was heaving with restrained sobs, the cords in her neck raised as she sniffled and strove valiantly to remain on her feet to meet his heated gaze. "You would shame me, then?"

He turned away with a furious hiss, raking his sweating hands through his hair. There was no pleasing the woman! He thrust his fists to his hips and paced away from her, taking care to keep his distance from both the woman and the largest piece of furniture in the room, lest he should sweep her to it and kiss her until he could think clearly.

"You and I both know that it will be noticed," she protested through growing tears. "Your mother has a poor enough opinion of me!"

He stopped, narrowing his eyes in tight scrutiny. "Is that what this is about? You fear that my mother will make things harder for you if she assumes you have refused me?"

She made no immediate answer but the continued working of her jaw. He almost turned away in finality, but a desperate whisper called him back. "She could think worse things!"

He spun round, staring at her pale face. This was a difficulty he had not considered. He began to breathe again, deliberating. Refusal... or unchastity. He would tolerate neither disgrace to be attached to his wife—and she was correct in assuming his mother knew intimately all the workings of the house.

He nodded, sighing in resignation. "Very well."

She flinched as he started towards her again, but froze in wonder when he did not go to her, but to the writing desk. He searched the top drawer until he found the pen knife, then rolled up his sleeve. "Sir?"

He glanced at her, pressing his lips, then drew the blade across the hard muscle of his forearm.

"Mr Thornton! What have you done?"

"Pull back the counterpane," he commanded brusquely.

Her brow furrowed, she did as he directed. He pinched the shallow wound until a respectable pool of blood had formed, then bent to create a gory smear across the sheet. Grimacing at the vulgarity of it all, he straightened.

Margaret looked as though she were about to faint. He started in concern. "You are not troubled by the sight of blood?"

She shook her head, dazed. "No, but... I had not expected you to...." Her hands gestured vaguely in the direction of his wounded arm.

He clenched his jaw and rolled his sleeve down once more. The slight cut was already closing up, but he did not wish to distress her further by making her look upon it.

"I cannot ask it of you yet." He completed the task of buttoning his sleeve and looked back to her. Some of the colour had returned to her cheeks.

He drew near and held out his hand. Hesitantly, she received it. "I *am* pleased that you are here. It is not my wish that you should feel unwelcome in any way. My mother... it will take time, Margaret. For all of us. Do you understand?"

She swallowed and nodded blankly.

His expression softened. "I will bid you a good night, then." He permitted a flicker of hope to shine in his eyes as he gingerly lifted her fingers to his lips.

She allowed the intimacy without comment. Only after he had returned her hand did she offer a quiet, "Good night... John."

He retreated to his own room via the hallway rather than through the shared door. There was no need to emphasise to her so early that he would be little more than thirty feet away as she slept... nor did he think he could walk across her chamber again without somehow stumbling and humiliating himself.

He felt like a gangling youth again with her in his house! The intent way she scrutinised his every move, as if weighing him against the ideal gentleman she had not married, wholly unnerved him. Fool that he was, however, he could not help thrilling in the fact that her attention was fixated on him alone, and no man but himself had access to her bed chamber. He fumbled with his own door latch, in much the same way Margaret had struggled with hers.

John stripped down until his chest was bare, then found the mirror at his washbasin. The only relief to be had this night was cold water, and for a mercy, there was plenty of it. He splashed raucously, heedless of the mess he created on the floor and the aching protests of his chilled muscles. If he could not seek divine blessing in the arms of the enticing woman in the next room, he would chastise his own flesh until it yielded in humbled submission! He almost succeeded.

His head finally clearing somewhat, he reached for a hand towel to dry his face. It was in the mirror that his eyes caught the unfamiliar flash of candlelight pouring from beneath the door, and the faint shadow dimming it as a figure moved within. Without the noise of splashing water to distract him, he heard each sound… bare feet… a sigh… the counterpane as it rustled… the groaning of the bed frame.

The towel was shaking in his hands. He stared at it, clumsy and awkward once more as his fingers fumbled to make sense of the damp cloth. Something dulled his vision—perhaps it was the memory of how her sheets had felt against his skin, or the warmth of her mouth still lingering on his lips from that one kiss they had shared all those hours ago.

Numbly, he reached to hang up his towel, but like the novice he suddenly felt himself to be, he missed the hook. He jerked his hand in correction, but his body had quite simply forgotten the mature grace it had known only yesterday. He tried to halt the swing of the towel and the arch of his elbow but was too late. The pitcher, now mercifully emptied of water, shattered into a hopeless pile of shards.

Milton-Northern
10 February 1835

"Did you break something, John? What in thunder are you doing up here?" The voice made its way up the hall and into the room long before its owner did.

Twelve-year-old John glanced up shamefacedly from the odd-shaped contraption in his hands. "I was trying to make it work, Father."

George Thornton lowered himself to the nearest chair. He was a tall, well-built man of five and thirty, with keen dark eyes and a ready smile. "May I?" He held out his hand, and his son passed him the apparatus which had befuddled him.

"Oh, yes!" the father enthused when he recognised it. "Barlow's wheel, the new motor design that I brought home from London. My partner wished me to show this next week to a group of investors. But why is it not working? Was this the crash I heard?"

John reddened. "I dropped it. I am sorry, Father. Now it is misaligned, and I lost some of the mercury."

Thornton fixed his son with a serious expression. "That is rather wasteful, my son, for this was quite costly. You must find some way to repair it."

John straightened. "I have some money set aside. I will go tomorrow to buy more mercury, and I am certain I will have it good as new!"

The elder Thornton returned the wheel with a cheerful grin. "See that you do. I ought to discipline you—what will Wright say if he hears the model was destroyed before the investors even saw it? However," he eyed his boy with a look that made him squirm, "I doubt you will make that same mistake again. Have you thought how to repair the frame?"

John turned it about, then pointed to a weak joint in the design. "If I heat it here, I think I can bend it to allow the wheel to spin easily again without compromising the strength of the metal."

Thornton nodded in curt satisfaction. "That should work. It is a remarkable discovery, is it not?"

The boy's eyes lit. "Father, only think what technology like this can achieve! If it were large enough, we could power anything. We would not need horses to pull our carriages, and perhaps even the steam engine itself will be replaced!"

"That will be a long way off, John, if it ever happens at all. Nothing else could ever produce so much power."

John looked back to the marvel in his hands, unconvinced by his father's scepticism. "I should still like to see it tried."

George Thornton shrugged with an easy grin. "Perhaps someday it will be. Wright, my partner, seems to think as you do. Now, set that aside. I have something of rather great import to discuss with you. Tell me, John, how are you getting on with your studies?"

The boy shuffled in his chair, suddenly looking anywhere but at his father. "Well enough."

"Would you still claim that, if I told you I had spoken with your master?" Thornton queried, his expression searching and hard. Jovial though he could be, his temper was not to be tried, and John knew it.

The lad dared to meet his father's eyes. "I expect I should not, Father."

Thornton's face revealed nothing; waiting, as he was, for his son to confess all.

"I did not complete my report on Constantine. And I did not memorise the third declension irregular nouns."

"Yet your master claims you are the ablest boy in his schoolroom. Your scores in mathematics are perfect, and the master says that even with half the effort applied by the other boys, you excel in your Latin and Greek. Why is it, John, that my son should not be giving his very best, when he is capable of far more than he achieves?"

John stared at the floor, swallowing. He had already grown ashamed of himself, but it needed the convicting humiliation of his father's discovery to galvanise his resolve to improve himself. "I shall do better."

"John—" George leaned back in his chair—"I know you would rather be building machines like this—" he gestured to the wheel—"or working as other boys already do, but I would see you take the opportunity to improve yourself while you are yet young. It is a chance few have had, and I confess, I am envious of you."

A reluctant sigh rose from the lad. "Yes, Father."

"John…" Thornton hesitated, glancing at his son's downturned face, and continued. "I have decided to send you to London for school."

The boy's face jerked up in horror. "Father, I promise I will work harder!"

"It is more than that. I speak of your future advantages. I am afraid it will not be a prestigious school, but Mr Wright's family in Bentinck Street has offered to sponsor you, along with their own boys. With them, you will learn a great deal more than you can here. Many things are within Wright's reach which are beyond mine, and you may even establish some connections which will be useful in your future."

John forced himself to look up from the floor, his incredulous gaze seeking his father's. "Will Mother be very unhappy that I am to go?"

Thornton gave a short, wry laugh. "It has taken me two years to persuade her to it. I wanted to send you to a public school, but she was firmly set against it—even could I have afforded it. At least with the Wrights, she has the comfort that you will be looked after by someone she knows, and people of our own class."

Regret dimmed the boy's features. "I will be sorry to leave her, though, Father."

"Your mother is most occupied with Fanny at present. She is not strong, you know, and your mother fears…." The man's voice trailed off as his cheek flinched in pain.

"She fears losing Fanny as she did Elizabeth," John finished in a hushed tone. "Father, if… if the worst happens, may I return?"

"I expect your mother will insist upon it. She will miss you terribly, John, but I am convinced this is for the best."

The boy lowered his head, then with a firm jaw and a determined glint in his eyes, met his father's gaze once more. "I will not disappoint you, Father."

George Thornton stood, and John followed. He placed a strong, work-hardened hand on his boy's shoulder. "I know you will not. I am already proud of you—although, I do have hopes that your new physical education lessons in London will help you at last become master of this lanky frame of yours! I cannot afford for you to keep dropping my models."

A sheepish smile grew on the adolescent face. "I am sorry, Father. I ought not to have touched it, but…."

"But you found it too intriguing to ignore? That's the Thornton blood, John. We cannot help but dream of the future. Industry needs men like us, and who is to say? Perhaps someday you will turn this mechanical fascination of yours into something truly remarkable. You might even grow to be one of the greatest men in Milton, with a fine house and a business of your own."

John turned adoring eyes to his father. None understood his ambitions quite so well! "Perhaps," he grinned.

"Come," Thornton ruffled his son's hair. "Your mother is waiting for us to join her at breakfast."

Two

London
27 April 1837

She clutched the blankets up to her nose, eyes roving distrustfully about the strange bedroom.

Nothing here smelt the same, felt as it ought, or cast the faintest shadow of welcome. She had been asked to come here, been granted the proper honours and greetings, but the truth was that this was not her home. Even the furnishings seemed ominous in this dark, ponderously decorated space.

Margaret shivered under the coverlet and listened to the sounds from the next room. At least she was not entirely alone—*he* would protect her from the ghoulish shades lurking in the corners of her imagination. She heard a thump, a muttered oath, and then silence. Alarmed, she sat upright, the blankets falling away.

"Fred!"

There was no answer at first, save the pounding of her own heart. "Fred?" she called again—more doubtfully this time.

Her door split open, permitting a narrow vertical crack to the dazzling light outside her cloistered prison. "Margaret, are you still awake?"

She drew the blankets up to her chin and nodded. "I am afraid to fall asleep."

He ambled into her room, nudging the door so that it *almost* closed... but not quite. "Afraid? Whatever for? You are not afraid of the dark, Margaret. Surely not!"

She shook her head and watched as he sank into the corner of the too-soft bed.

"Then what is it? Tell me, my little princess."

She quivered, nibbled the tips of her fingers, and confessed, "I am afraid I will be lost when I wake up."

The second day of her marriage was almost as surreal for Margaret as the first. She had awakened alone in a strange house, and a strange girl helped her to dress. Her husband—was he really such?—had thoughtfully ordered a tray carried to her room so she might breakfast this first morning in peace and privacy.

Margaret touched the food apathetically with her fork, her eyes on the folded note he had left on the tray for her. Dropping the utensil, she plucked up the paper in resignation. His words yielded no sentiment, and he had likely expected to receive none in return.

Margaret,

I have ordered horses for the carriage every day this week. They will be ready by ten o'clock each morning, should you choose to employ yourself with Miss Dixon. I have also asked Sarah, who will have helped you this morning, to accompany you if you desire.

When you are quite decided about matters there, I will send Williams to carry out your wishes. I do not know if you would like my personal assistance with these affairs, but I am at your disposal. You needn't trouble yourself to come to the mill. Just ask Mrs Adams, the cook, to send her boy to bring word and I will come.

You need not feel obliged to go if you do not wish. Whatever you decide for today, I hope you may pass it pleasantly. I will see you this evening.

John

Margaret sighed and dropped the missive beside her plate. At least he was treating her kindly, but she might have wished for a husband who seemed to desire her company. She still shrank in mortification when she remembered the last evening—not at all the wedding night she had expected. What manner of husband would rather shed his own blood than come to his wife? Was she so repulsive to him?

You forget, he caught you in a lie once!

Her teeth set. What manner of husband, indeed? Perhaps he was doing them both a service in keeping his distance, and had determined he ought never permit himself to trust her. No man would wish to humble himself before a woman in whom he could not place his confidence.

She stirred her tea listlessly. She desired his faith, above all else just now. It would have eased her sore, broken heart to have a confidante, even if the only one who might be called upon to listen was… was *him*. She closed her eyes and willed her pulse to calm.

How honoured, how comforted she had been when he had made his second offer to her! The pungent impression left by his first proposal had furrowed deeply into her heart, gradually turning and freshening her brittle antipathy. How could she have been so blind to the pull of her deeper feelings?

He was rigid and hard, yet guided by a deep sense of honour which she had grudgingly learned to admire. And then there was that forceful profession of love, that proclamation that he was but a slave to a newly awakened passion— one which shook him with its very power and depth. No other man made himself so vulnerable, nor dealt with her so honestly. She had not wished to fall in love with John Thornton, but stubborn, impossible man that he was, he had given her no choice.

For no one else could she have faced the mob that day! No excuse for her feminine safeguarding would suffice—not if she were fully honest with herself. She once told Mrs Thornton that she knew not how she should bear up if she were tried, but now she had her answer. At least Hannah Thornton claimed to possess the courage and presence of mind on a similar occasion to save someone she cared nothing about. Margaret, however, felt sure she would have cowered within the house were it not for the identity of the man she had sent into the lion's mouth—the very man who held the power to infuriate her like no other!

How could present circumstances have wrought such a perverse alteration? She dared not confess her wilfull, rebellious feelings to him, for fear of his scorn. She had sullied her dignity miserably enough in his eyes. Far better it was, certainly, to behave the proper and dutiful wife—eschewing, if she could, her inconvenient and erratic responses to his seeming power over her. Provoking, troublesome man!

She picked at her breakfast tray, frowning. It would require a marvellous work to make straight the path laid before her feet. He was a curious man; fascinating in so many ways, yet incomprehensible in so many others. It would take a lifetime to sort him out.

She dropped her fork. It seemed she would get that particular wish, at least.

~

"G'mornin', Master!" Nicholas Higgins tipped his worn cap as his employer strolled by his work station.

John, lost in his own thoughts, halted abruptly and swivelled about. "Oh. Good morning, Higgins."

The weaver gave a tug on the lever of his small loom to disengage it. "'Ow fares th' Mistress this morn', Master?"

John's face jerked in surprise, for he himself had only just considered the title. "The...." His voice trailed off. "I have not seen her today. I trust she is well."

Higgins' mouth worked in sorrow. "'Tis a righ' pity. Th'ould parson,'e were a good fellow."

Thornton heaved a weary sigh. "He was a good friend to me. I am very sorry—and sorrier still for her."

"Aye," Higgins nodded. "She'll be needin' some comfort, Master." His eyes twinkled in fellowship. "I s'pect it's'ard, hoo bein' a gen'le lady an' a'."

Thornton's cheek went rigid. "I imagine that marriage to a cotton manufacturer is not what she desired."

Higgins' brows shot up, and well they might. Thornton had long prided himself on being the most self-assured, masterful man in all of Milton. Now he was but a dejected, fangless swain, longing for a hint of favour from a silent damsel.

He well knew of what was said of him—that his recent displays of humility caused everyone to wonder over his state of mind—and that every single one of those occasions had somehow or another involved the former Miss Hale. Higgins would be right to wonder, for he had seen more of John's weaknesses than any other. The offer of employment, the concessions regarding the mill kitchen... the stunning personal request that he and his daughter attend yesterday's simple wedding, for Margaret's sake....

And now he, the unassailable John Thornton was a pitiful coward, and it must be all too obvious that he feared being found unworthy in the eyes of his wife. Oh, aye, a faithful and true husband would he be, but how could even he aspire to *her*?

"Well, tha's a'." Higgins sighed and dipped his head with a shrug. "Yo'll take care o' hoo', Master. Tha's a' she wan's now."

Thornton's shoulders drooped, and his eyes began to rove beyond Higgins to other parts of the mill. "I hope so." He lingered another moment, having nothing in particular to say, but grateful for the fraternity of one of the few who had been in favour of his marriage. It was to be hoped that those who loved Margaret might have had her best interests at heart when they encouraged her on this course.

At length, John's expression straightened back to his usual, sombre mien. Nodding to his employee, he wandered away.

Higgins watched him go, frowning and shaking his head. No newly minted husband had a right to look so downcast, particularly not with such a treasure now living in his house.

John Thornton made his typical rounds about the mill, and eventually arrived back in his office to stare down a stack of paperwork.

He shed his coat and took a seat at his desk, but his mind would not apply itself to the tasks before him. It dwelt instead on the bereaved woman who would be waking on her first disorienting morning in his house. What a change in circumstance for her! Material possessions she could claim now in abundance, but he feared that her gently bred dignity had suffered by their union. Lowly tradesman that he was, he was not worthy of her—she had been rather candid on that point in the past.

Throughout his life, he had railed against the ceiling of the middle class which limited his advantages. He thought that he had at last broken through that barrier, only to have it cast over him once more when he looked into the eyes of the woman who thought him beneath her. It had always been thus— the very moment he began to take pride in achievement, he would receive a harsh reminder that he was no better than a tradesman's son.

London
September 1836

"John, my boy! By Jove, you are a sight for sore eyes!"

John started, nearly dropping the pen he held. "Father!" He leaped up from his study desk with a practised grace which his father could not fail to note. A year ago, he would likely have caught his foot on the chair leg and spilled the entire ink bottle.

"I had not been expecting you! Did Mother come? How is Fanny? Am I to return home with you?"

"Slow down, son! One question at a time, if you please!"

"Forgive me, Father," the boy laughed sheepishly. "I had your letter only yesterday, and you spoke nothing of coming for a visit."

"It was quite the surprise for me as well, but a pleasant one, I assure you. Wright had sent for me to help him in negotiating this newest speculation he is considering, and I thought it a fine chance also to come see how he is treating my son. Now, let me look at you! Why, you have grown!"

"I think I shall catch you up yet, Father." John stretched to his full height.

"I think you may have already done so. And how strong you are looking! The wrestling is building your arms, I daresay. How are things for you here, John? Have you been keeping up with your studies?"

"The master says I am head of my class," he admitted with a bashful grin.

George Thornton, however, was not the practiced negotiator he was for nothing. "But?"

John tapped his pen, his eyes sliding reluctantly to the side. "I… I am afraid I am not faring quite so well with the *other* lessons Mr Wright has so generously offered," was the diplomatic response.

Thornton crossed his arms and studied his boy with an amused twinkle. "You cannot tell your left foot from your right in the waltz."

"Oh, I get on with the steps well enough. It is dancing with a… a… *partner*. I constantly tangle up!"

"It helps if you breathe while dancing," his parent observed drily.

The boy's face reddened. "You heard about that?"

"I? I am only just arrived. I could not possibly have heard about you nearly fainting and tripping the dance school mistress until she landed in a heap of petticoats. I certainly did not hear of you fleeing back to your room, not to be seen again until the following day. And what was this about a dinner party where you offended a guest by refusing a harmless dance with their daughter?"

"It was not a formal occasion." John's face heated visibly. "Miss Harris was no more inclined to be made a spectacle for her elders than I. Besides, Harold stood up with her in my stead… that time."

"I sincerely hope you will respond better on another occasion."

The lad slumped in mortification. "I do not understand why I must learn to waltz. What benefit will it be? I shall not be a fine gentleman, Father, but a working man!"

"Success in business is about building the right connections," Thornton reminded his son. "Make the right friends, meet the right young ladies, and your ascent up the ladder is all but assured. I wish I had learned that at your age."

"Father, I shall never marry an heiress, if that is your advice. I should not even wish it! It seems... dishonest. Reaping the result of another man's labours by falsely charming his daughter—"

"Who said anything about doing it falsely? I only say to take care to polish your manners and look to your education now, whilst you can. Do not make my mistake, settling too early or too easily. I would not see you caught by a penniless girl."

"Father, I—" but the boy was cut off when his father stabbed a finger at him.

"John! I will not bend on this point!" George Thornton's typically genial face had begun to take on a darker hue, one which his son knew all too well. Thornton may have lacked his wife's sterling force of will or her ironclad character, but he did possess a temper—and with it, a tendency towards drastic swings in humour.

Not wishing to trigger such an episode—particularly not here, in the home of his host and his father's partner—John ceased his objections. "Yes, Father." He chewed his lower lip, a doubtful eye cast on his parent. After a moment, he offered, "My horsemanship is improving."

Thornton rapidly turned from his annoyance. "Excellent! Would that I could afford for you to continue that pursuit when you do return home, for it is a capital means of securing advantageous friendships. Many a promising enterprise has begun on the hunt field."

John sighed, frowning unhappily. Aloud, he only answered, "Yes, Father."

"John," George shifted to an easier posture, his face softening in some little regret at his son's sudden dejection. "It is not my intention to pressure you into a life you do not desire. I hope that is not what you have learnt to believe. There is a threshold above which we mere tradesmen cannot rise. The elite will have their distinctions, but the world is changing, my boy. To hold on to their precious status, they depend more and more on men like us. It is a wise businessman who cultivates strategic relationships where he may. Wright understands that. It is the reason he has found such success, and his motivation for providing his own sons with these same opportunities."

John was sullen, staring at the floor.

"You disagree?"

John pressed his mouth into a thoughtful expression. "I have noticed that Mr Wright is capable of saying one thing and meaning another. I would not model myself after that pattern."

"Explain yourself."

"Well, the reasons he has given you for hosting me here, for one thing. He seemed at first to be genuinely welcoming, eager to do you a service as a friend. However, some things he has said made me wonder if he is not rather intending to obligate you to him, so that he might call on you to support him when you would rather not."

George Thornton surveyed his son with growing shock. "That is rather a serious charge. I must applaud your thinking—that is the thinking of a man of business, and I am glad to see it in you. However, I have the very greatest faith in Wright. He and I studied together as well, you know. Remember what I said about these connections made in your youth, for they can and must serve you well."

The boy's shoulders drooped once again as his father dismissed his concerns. "Yes, sir," he mumbled dutifully.

"Now, see here, John, some are born to privilege and a life of careless ease. They will look down on you if you allow it. You must earn your way, my boy, every tedious mile of it. I hope you are wise enough to make good use of your time and skills now while you do not yet need to labour for your bread. Who knows, John? Perhaps you may, indeed, marry that heiress someday."

Margaret did eventually take John's—or rather *their*—carriage to her old house. The experience of commanding her own driver was novel enough. It was more eerie still to make her way up the steps which had been her home for a year and a half, knowing that yesterday's indifferent ceremony had changed everything for her.

In truth, she would much rather not be facing her dismantled house again so soon, but that cold grey door was simply less intimidating than the available company in her new home. She did not like shouldering this task on her own, but more daunting still was the request she would have had to make of the man who had unwillingly obligated himself to her. No, far better to let him to his work than to remind him of the weight of the duties he had assumed!

With a long breath, she put her hand to the knocker, fearful of what the opening door would reveal. The harmony of her old home was far greater to Margaret's sentimental heart than the sum of fondly remembered trinkets and baubles. This had been her mother's last home. Here was the last place where her touch could be felt, and now, it must all be broken up. Margaret's eyes threatened that familiar hot, prickling sensation as Dixon opened the door to her.

"Oh, it's you, Miss! I feared it'd be the landlord."

Margaret smiled, not even bothering to correct Dixon's old form of address. "No, and you shall not see the landlord, Dixon. Mr Thornton has the matter in hand."

Dixon peered around Margaret's shoulder to the waiting carriage. "Well, that's fine enough, then!" She took Margaret's cape and bonnet at the door, her fond gaze searching her young mistress for any symptoms of either contentment or distress.

Margaret was not insensible to Dixon's scrutiny. "I am well, Dixon."

Dixon harrumphed, a little embarrassed at being caught staring, and led the way to the upstairs sitting room. Margaret suppressed a quiet smile, but it vanished when she entered the room which had once been her mother's domain.

Everything was in shambles. Dixon had been busy, and the room was nothing at all as Margaret would have chosen to remember it. They had boxed her mother's clothing long ago, but now even her little portrait frames and mementos were unceremoniously swept from sight. Though still cluttered, the chamber was already barren.

"Oh, Dixon!" she breathed hoarsely. "I do not think I can do this!"

Dixon heaved a weary sigh. It was likely as hard on her as it was on Margaret, but the old serving woman had not the luxury of an advantageous marriage to lift her from her grief. All was on her broad shoulders, but she would bear up, as she always did. "There, now, Miss. We'll have this settled soon enough."

Margaret sniffed, glancing about the room with sorrow. "Mr Thornton says we need not hurry."

Dixon pouted and turned to wrap a little silver bell for packing. She made no reply, but her opinion was plain.

Margaret stiffened. "Dixon, I can see you still disapprove, but I will not have you thinking ill of Mr Thornton. He has been very good to us."

"Oh, yes," Dixon muttered bitterly. "I'd warrant he has. Caught himself a lady, he has, and now he must think himself quite the gentleman."

"Dixon!" Margaret's ire flashed. "I will not allow you to disrespect my husband. If you continue to speak so, I will dismiss you immediately!"

Dixon turned slowly, her expression all astonishment. She stared, as if trying to determine if Margaret were in earnest. "Beg your pardon, Miss."

"I am a married woman, Dixon," Margaret reminded her, a dangerous edge to her voice which she had never used with Dixon.

"Ma'am," Dixon corrected herself. Her face quivered in confused agitation as she turned to her task again.

Margaret remained frozen to her place, her arms crossed over her breast as a shield against the cruelties of her new trials. She was terrified herself at this path and could have wished for Dixon's encouragement just now. "Dixon, I hope you may come to understand my reasons...."

Dixon looked back up, her face growing red again. "I thought you were set on going to Corfu," she grumbled accusingly. "I wouldn't see you go to Cadiz and be converted, but why not go to your cousin? She'd have had you, to be sure!"

Margaret narrowed her eyes. "I preferred to remain here, Dixon. I do not need to justify myself to you. I had sufficient inducement to stay, and that is all."

Chastised again, Dixon turned back to the tray of curios and trinkets. She said not another word for three full hours.

~

Hannah Thornton did not glance up from her needlework when her new daughter-in-law returned to the house. She did not look up when that same young woman entered the room and assumed the seat opposite her. Nor even did she lift her eyes from her work when she heard her name uttered in polite deference.

She was, however, required to speak. "Yes?" she replied briskly.

After a brief pause, the young lady spoke again. "I was hoping, madam, that I might ask to see more of the house and meet the staff? At your convenience, of course."

Hannah at last dropped her needlework. *Would it be rude to send Jane with the new wife as she surveyed her domain?*

She sighed. *Probably.* Margaret's tour of the house was the next official step to her own imminent discharge as mistress of John's home. Her heart rankled with the indignity of it all.

"I suppose I may spare the time in an hour." She resumed her needlework, casting only an occasional glance up at the girl.

Margaret's face was pale. "I... I see. Thank you." She was silent some moments and then spoke again. "Would it be possible for me to speak with the maid responsible for my room?"

Hannah paused. That seemed an innocuous enough request, but perhaps it was a veiled slight. This was a clever, manipulative young woman, after all. "Is it not to your liking?" she asked sharply. "I looked it over myself, and fresh linens were supplied only this morning. I should be surprised if you found anything amiss."

"No!"

Margaret's face had gone from sheet white to flaming scarlet at the mention of the linens—a sham of a thing if Hannah had ever seen it! The drips of blood on John's sleeve told the rest of the tale; he was not welcomed by his wife, and he did not wish her to know of it. She gritted her teeth and returned to her sewing, wishing she could ignore or at least forget the entire conversation.

The young wife, however, was determined to speak. "I have no complaints at all, madam. I only wished to thank her, for every consideration had clearly been made for my comfort."

Hannah's lips set into a grim scowl. "There is no need to thank the house maids personally. They carry out their instructions, that is all."

Margaret blinked. "I-in that case," she managed a little roughly, "I must extend my gratitude to you, as well. Your efforts are… welcoming."

Hannah dipped her head gravely in acknowledgment. The young lady's countenance had washed quite pale once more, and she put two fingers to her forehead as though it pained her. Hannah gave infrequent glances in the bride's direction. Eventually, Margaret mumbled some excuse and fled.

Hannah breathed out in sweet relief. To think she must now make way for that artful young woman, who only married John to secure a life of luxury! Where was that other man she had seemed to fancy, and why turn back to John, whose faith in her was so misplaced? Loyalty must be a thing foreign to Margaret—and now John, her fine, noble son, had shackled himself to that graceful little pretender for life!

Her cheek twitched as she viciously ripped out a stitch she did not like. Her needlework commanded a devotion this day which it rarely did, and the promised hour was long up before she thought to set it aside to perform her duties to the new mistress. She much preferred instead to remember back to the good, honourable old days, when her John's fidelity had belonged to her alone.

Southport Beach
August 1837

"Mother, may I assist you?" The tall, lanky scamp jogged up the beach, offering her a gallant bow, then his arm.

Hannah Thornton lifted her head. "Why, yes, my young man! I fear my walking shoes are not suitable for the sand. Where is your father?"

He jerked his head to indicate a direction farther up the shore. "He is trying to help Fanny find shells on the firmer sand, near the water."

"Near the water! He is not allowing her to get a wetting, John?"

"No, he is picking her up whenever the waves come close. Really, though, she seems so much stronger than before. She is getting on better, is she not?"

"You only saw her during holidays these past two years. This has been the way with her. She does well enough until she takes a chill, and then the cough lingers for a month."

"But she is making steady improvement, is she not? She recovers a little more easily each time."

"A precious little," she agreed with a reluctant smirk. John always had a way of forcing her to optimism, regardless of her own notions. "I am grateful to have you returned from London, John. Two years was much too long to do without my son."

He offered his most charming grin, which was quite a little *too* charming for his jealous mother's taste. "Too long, indeed. How I missed you all!"

She leaned on his arm more as she laboured over a particularly soft part of the beach. "I should have thought you found amusements enough to divert you in London."

"I learned a good deal, I will confess, but my best day in London was my last. London, with all its fine folk, was not for me, Mother. I was pleased to return home."

She gave a fierce, satisfied nod. "I am glad to hear it. I feared you would be seduced by that city."

"Like Father?"

She sighed and turned to her son, noting again how strange it was to look up to him. "He wants what he believes is best for us. I am afraid it may not lead down the glamorous road he imagines."

The jaunty, fearless smile of youth appeared on his handsome face. "You needn't worry, Mother. He told me only last week how his latest venture is sure to pay out remarkably well. That is how we are affording this holiday, you know."

"Did he happen to tell you where he obtained the funds to invest? He did not, did he?"

His cheer dissolved, the shadow of uncertainty dawning. She had never slighted her husband in John's hearing, but this worry had been tormenting her to the point of anxiety.

"He did not. I assume he borrowed a portion—or all of it. But Mother, surely there is no cause for concern. Mr Wright's speculations pay out nearly every time, do they not?"

"This one was a greater chance, and a much higher investment. Your father has leveraged himself too far this time. He is too prone to make light of such matters. Always dreaming, that man!"

"Mother," he pulled her to a halt with a stubbornly cheerful smile. "I beg you would not worry. You know it is not fitting that we should doubt Father's decisions. It does anger him so."

Hannah gazed blankly at the sparkling waves. "He takes spells of melancholy, when you are not around, and he thinks I do not see. He locks himself in his study and drinks for hours, raging at any who would dare to disturb him, but the next day he appears as merry as ever. Oh, John, I hope you never become a bad one for drink!"

He laughed, as if trying to dismiss her concerns. "The few times I have sampled brandy, I fell almost instantly asleep. I could develop a tolerance for it, I suppose, but I cannot see why I should indulge such an expense when it will only dull my senses."

"If only your father had half your present wisdom on the matter!"

"Come, Mother, all will be well, I am sure of it. Let us enjoy this fine day and not live in fear for the morrow."

She set her teeth and eyed her son. "You are right, John," she grumbled. "It does comfort me that you will be working soon, in case we should face some calamity."

John's chest swelled, and she could almost swear that his buttons would pop with pride. "I start with Mr Hamper as soon as we return! I am honoured that Father was able to find me this position. It is a good place, I think."

"Indeed. I understand that a few boys two or three years your senior desired to train as Mr Hamper's clerk. He was wise to choose the most promising of the lot."

"Mother—" his ruddy cheeks flushed in embarrassment—"he only did so as a favour to Father. Father had convinced him to join in the investment opportunity with Mr Wright, and they have great hopes for future partnerships."

"Mmm," she commented neutrally, but a teasing smile made her dark eyes sparkle in the sunshine. "Tell yourself what you may, but I know you will not disappoint Mr Hamper."

"I hope not!" he agreed fervently.

"And soon, you shall be earning enough to wish for an establishment of your own. What say you, John? Will you be leaving me in a few years to be master of your own house, and perhaps even marry a pretty little wife?"

"*Mother*," he rolled his eyes, and looked to her as though he would dissolve into the sand.

"Oh, come now, John, surely the notion has occurred to you," she chuckled, thoroughly enjoying his mortification. "Your father and I married when I was only seventeen, and he twenty. That is not so very far off."

"You and Father have both said that you ought to have waited until he had gained greater security. Had not I better do the same? Besides, what need have I to marry? What could a wife do for me that my own lovely mother cannot?"

An indelicate noise startled from her and she turned her face sharply away. She sputtered, then cleared her throat and gasped in an effort to regain her composure. "Keep that sentiment as long as you may, son John," she pleaded. "I am in no hurry to be replaced in your heart."

He laughed, and his cheeks darkened again as some of the implications behind her mirth registered in his adolescent mind. "Never fear, Mother, you will always be first. Oh, look, there is Father waving to us! Come," he tugged at her elbow, seemingly eager to change the subject. "He said he wanted ice cream this afternoon. I should enjoy tasting it."

She dipped to the sand in a flamboyant, playful curtsey. "Lead on, kind sir."

"Mother," John drew that good lady aside as soon as he entered his door. "How is Margaret this evening?"

"Well enough, I should think," she answered flatly. "I took her through the kitchen this afternoon, and she has spoken with Mrs Brady as to the management of the maids. She has retired to her rooms now."

"You have thrust household duties on her so soon? She ought to have been given time to adjust."

"It was her idea. She seems eager enough to assume the role of Mistress."

"Mother, I thought we had resolved this!" he hissed. "I wish her to feel welcome, and if it pleases her to make herself useful and to learn her way about the house, I hope you will not speak ill of her."

Hannah Thornton was not of a character which was given to sulk, but sulk she did. She crossed her arms and verily thrust out that dogged jaw of hers—the one she had passed to her son—and glared back in silence.

"Mother," he groaned wearily, "I beg you to give her a chance to prove herself. It would be unfair to expect her to step into this new role without some difficulty. She has suffered much, and she had not the normal betrothal period to anticipate such a dramatic change to her life."

The sullen mouth curved downward still more, if that were possible. "You do not think the lass foresaw marriage for herself? If she did not, it paints a pretty picture of her character."

His eyes flared dangerously, an expression her son had never turned on the woman who had borne him. "*Mother!* That incident was over half a year ago, and since that date, Margaret has ever acted as befits a lady!"

"Has she?" challenged the slighted matron. "There is some great shame connected with that business—nay, I do not ask that you reveal it! You were right to keep it to yourself as a man of honour but take care that you do not trust the young lady more than she deserves."

His limbs were shaking, his countenance startlingly white against the dark hair of his brow. He was breathing in great, sucking draughts through his clenched teeth, and his fists balled as he strove to restrain his fury.

"I do not pretend to know all her affairs! I have not yet gained her trust so far. But I do have faith in her virtue and believe that she must have had some perfectly innocent reason for walking out that night. You know her mother's funeral was only the following day. Many persons might wish to lend the family aid or comfort under such circumstances. The gentleman may well have wished to indulge his charity without fanfare."

"Where is that 'gentleman' now? Why has this helpful soul not come forward at Mr Hale's death?"

He spun away, resting a shaking white hand on the sideboard by which he had been standing. He was still and mute for a full minute as his mother's iron gaze bored into his back. At last, he answered in a weak, faltering voice.

"I do not know. I only know that no other *had* come to offer assistance. My love for her aside, I owed her father's memory the faithful keeping of his daughter. I could not have turned her away, destitute and friendless—not if she had declared to my face that she loved this other man and reviled me more than ever! I can only hope…." Here, his words broke, and his fingers flexed and drummed helplessly over the polished wood he gripped. He cast his eyes beseechingly to the ceiling.

"I only hope," he continued in a whisper, as his voice failed him, "that one day I shall be found worthy in her eyes, and that she may learn to hold some affection for me. I daren't believe she might love me as I do her, but I wish her to be happy here."

He turned to his mother once more, looking faint and doubtful. "Will you help me in that? I quite depend upon you!"

Hannah's face had drained of all colour, even to her lips. She stared, speechless with both horror and pride. There was none to equal her noble son, nor any who could match his faithful heart. That he should throw himself away on one who was incapable of understanding his worth… it was too unjust! Yet, her motherly burden would not be denied, the affliction of her great love for her son could not be forgotten. His cherished face—that of his father, very nearly—pleaded with her to surrender her affronted dignity. There was nothing else for her to do.

She hung her head in defeat. "Aye, John."

Never did her old Darkshire inflexions surface more markedly than when she was vexed, and just now, she was very much so. "I'll do as I can."

He released a long, quaking sigh. "Thank you, Mother."

Three

"Was your day agreeable?" John stopped his wife in the hall as he escorted her to her room. Dinner had been as awkward and strained on this second evening as on the first, and he had exchanged less than ten words with her all day. This was the first opportunity he had found since the prior night to solicit her feelings, and he scarcely knew how to begin.

She met his soft question with hesitation and parted lips. He tugged at her elbow, causing her to turn towards him. "You went to Crampton today?"

"Y-yes" Her brow creased, and she stared again at the buttons of his waistcoat. He determined to examine them when he undressed later, to see if they were somehow out of sorts.

"You had a productive day, then?"

Her eyes flashed up at last. The strange look she graced him with caused him to bite his own lips together. She had probably never in her life been asked if her day was productive! He groped for a gentler expression.

"I meant… did it pass satisfactorily?" He cringed. That question sounded suspiciously similar in intent to the other.

A crease appeared at the corner of her mouth, and for the first time in his memory, an amused warmth lit her expression. "Quite." The light faded once more, and she resumed her inspection of his waistcoat.

He gazed helplessly into her crown of shining dark hair. Like silk… rumpled silk, all the more touchable for the few wayward curls pulling loose near her temples. His mesmerised gaze trailed down to the tender spot where blood had once darkened her hairline, then lower still to where her pulse drummed erratically against the pale flesh of her throat. How her rich hair must curl round that ivory throat when she tugged it free of its pins, and then allowed it to spill over her pillow! What would it feel like to—

"John?" Her head came up sharply, cutting off the outrageous ideas flitting about his beleaguered brain.

"Yes?" He jerked, a little too quickly. Did his voice crack?

"I… I would like to finish the house without delay."

His brows arched in interest. "Have you any particular reason?"

She swallowed, and her head dropped. Again, with the buttons! Daring, he touched the tips of his fingers to her chin to lift her face and made a wild guess at her troubles. "Does it grieve you to linger there?"

Those luminous eyes clenched in answer.

"I see. Do you wish for me to accompany you tomorrow?"

Imploring eyes opened once more, and she gave the barest of nods. "If you can spare the time."

"I ought to have gone with you today. Forgive me for leaving you to your own devices. It was unfair of me."

She lifted her shoulders, her tearful gaze dropping again—this time to his feet. "I would not have wished to trouble you." Her tones fairly dripped with martyrdom.

"Will you be ready by ten?" he asked quickly. He could not bear to argue his duties as a husband with her, not again.

She nodded a hesitant reply in the affirmative. They made plans to meet downstairs in the morning, and he bade her a chaste goodnight. He lingered a long while outside after the door had closed.

~

Half an hour later, he lay flat atop his own bed, not even bothering to toss the counterpane over himself. His room was freezing—as it always was—but he was too restless for slumber. His desperate ears sought every movement, every breath from the next room. Would she cry herself to sleep as she had the previous night?

He writhed in torment. He could not bear to hear her suffering! Surely, he might find *some* way of comforting her even if he dared not go to her as a man went to his wife. His eyes wide open in the darkness, he stared blindly at the ceiling as his other senses reached into the next room.

He heard Sarah leave her, and the creak of the floor as her bare feet stepped softly to the bed. *What would she be wearing?* He gritted his teeth and clawed at his own eyes in a vain effort to banish his imaginings. *Margaret...* she was so temptingly close!

She would not deny him, either. She had a mind of her own, to be sure—his favourite thing about her—but her feminine pride was burned into her character. She would count it a disgrace to turn her husband away if he should ask....

He heaved a moan of agony and tried to smother himself with the pillow.

In an instant, he had snatched it from his face again. He could not miss a single sound! He held his breath, waiting for the sobs he knew were to come. They were soft and muffled, but distinctly hers, nonetheless.

Taking care to make no noise of his own, he straightened from his bed and tiptoed to the door. He pressed his ear to the wood, and the old panels amplified the heartbreak pouring from the other side. Tense with self-doubt, he slid to a crouch, his back pressed to the door. Once or twice silence prevailed in the room, and he thought she might have finally drifted to merciful dreams. The quiet never lasted long.

At last, he could bear it no longer. She was his wife, and he had sworn to take her into his care! Did that not include comforting her in sorrow? He leaped to his feet with predatory grace and gasped for courage. With a rush of forced bravado, he tapped his knuckles on the door.

The sounds within paused, and he imagined her sitting up to determine if she had truly heard a knock. He clenched his fist and knocked again, more firmly this time. "Margaret?"

She did not answer. His heart thundered in the silence, but after an excruciating minute, bare feet pattered across the cold wooden floors. He strained to hear as they stopped, only inches away. Hoping to encourage her, he spoke her name again. His eyes fastened on the latch, then raised to find her through the crack she permitted.

She looked nothing at all like a bride opening the door to her husband—if, indeed, he might be trusted for an accurate expectation on that point. Her plaited hair was disheveled, her eyes swollen and red, and she wore a billowy, unflattering shift of some sort. He had seen evening gowns which were more revealing, save for the soft silhouette of her form set off by the warm light of her hearth. Angels in heaven, she was a goddess!

His mouth ran dry and his heart throbbed in his ears. And, like a bloody pup, he was staring, slack-jawed and hypnotised. He shook himself. Cost him his sanity it may, but he would not embarrass her... or himself. He forced his eyes back to her face.

Her puffy cheeks looked as though she had just scrubbed tears from them, and her mouth quivered. She crossed her arms self-consciously before her breast and silently blinked up at him. He had never seen her looking more irresistible! It was not her crumpled beauty, but her yawning need which called to him, and in this, perhaps, he could offer her what she sought.

"Oh, Margaret!" he breathed, and impulsively held his arms out to her.

Without hesitation, she flung herself into his chest, and the tears came. Her slim body racked with sobs, and were it not for his arms about her, he doubted not that she might have tumbled to her knees. Her cries were soft and keening, inarticulate as she pressed her wet cheeks into the collar of his nightshirt.

John closed his eyes and found tears of his own spilling down his face. He hid them in her hair, all thoughts of her tempting feminine shape banished for now. How he ached for her!—for her multiplied grief, for her isolation, for the terrifying, unwanted new life she had been required to accept. Then he wept for his lost friend, and for memories of his own which whispered once more to him.

John was under no illusion that she had suddenly done away with her mistrust. He simply felt grateful that she allowed him to comfort her when there was no other to be had. He held her until the tremors slowed, and her face pressed into him more out of embarrassment than sorrow. His hand stroked lovingly down her shoulders, detecting their sculpted perfection beneath her shift, and brushing the thick satin braid which fell between them. *Oh, how he would glory in her touch....* Sensing himself in danger once more, he straightened and stepped back.

She occupied herself in turning her face away and wiping her eyes with her bared fingers. "I am sorry," she mumbled. "I did not mean to disturb you."

"Margaret, you do not disturb me. I would wish... it would give me the greatest pleasure to offer you some comfort."

She hugged herself, closing him off once more. "It is..." She choked, and the remainder of her words came out in a harsh whisper. "It is hard!"

He thinned his lips and flicked his gaze to the modest hearth fire still casting its warmth from the corner. "You ought not to be so much alone as you have been this week. I should have never... will you forgive me?"

Her expression fell from sorrow to astonishment and she gazed up at him. Wordlessly, she nodded.

He offered a tight smile, entirely unsure of the wisdom of what he was about to suggest—heaven have mercy, she wore neither corset nor petticoat! He had never even seen a woman without such garments, much less held her as she cried on his shoulder.

His breath staggered in his chest, and he almost backed away in terrified defeat. But no... She needed *someone*, and there was no one else. "Perhaps we may sit by the fire together for a time?" he croaked.

She assented more readily than he might have expected and led the way to the little settee of her father's at the opposite side of her room. As she cautiously took a seat at the far end, he glimpsed her dainty ankles crossing beneath her shift.

He nearly swallowed his own tongue. His eyes flew wide, and he floundered in searching out his place.

Margaret had not missed his reaction. She squirmed, tugging the homely garment down around every breath-taking sliver of skin. Her cheeks were bright red. "I... I forgot to bring my house slippers."

"I will buy you some tomorrow!" he offered quickly, then winced at himself. The last time his voice had creaked like that, he had been thirteen.

"Oh... I am sure there is no need." She shrank from his unexpected energy, hugging a worn brown pillow to her middle. "I may retrieve my own by tomorrow."

He gulped, willing his bounding pulse to be still. "I do not wish you to take a chill, that is all." He cringed again. A smooth one with the ladies, that he was.

She smiled bashfully down at her hands. "You are very kind, sir."

"*John.* You must stop calling me 'sir' and 'Mr Thornton,' at least when we are alone. *Please.* I shall never learn to believe we are truly married if you do not."

Her cheeks flushed still more, and she dipped her head. Was she secretly laughing at him? *Better than tears,* he consoled himself. *Anything* was better than watching the woman he loved cry.

Margaret curled on her side of the furniture, biting her lips together and fastening her gaze on the fire. He tried to do likewise, but the soft haze it cast over her golden skin sent everything else into the shadows. She was inches away—so close he could feel her warmth more distinctly than that of the dying fire. It could do no harm simply to cradle his arm about her....

She was blinking rapidly once more, the crimson stain from her cheeks spreading to her neck. He caught his hand before it moved. Perhaps if he closed his mouth and stopped gaping at her like a lecherous fool... little wonder she seemed uncomfortable!

To bring his own treasonous limbs under regulation, he clasped his hands together and rested them upon his knees. Every muscle quivered with hopeful anxiety. What was he to say to her? He took a deep breath and plunged ahead with the first topic to present itself.

"I wrote to Mr Bell this morning." Before the words even left his mouth, he regretted them. What better way to impress her utter vulnerability upon her again than to remind her of her absent godfather? Had Bell been in England....

He clenched his teeth. Had Bell been in England when his old friend had died, Margaret would not presently be his wife. He could not decide whether he ought to be elated or sorrowful about that fact.

Margaret gave no indication whether she had perceived his repentant thoughts. She turned up to him, her eyes soft. "You wrote about my father?"

He drank in a deep, cleansing breath to restore his mental clarity. "Everything. The last word I had of him was several weeks ago, and he had intended to sail for South America. I have no idea when the letter will reach him."

"He left you his address in South America?"

"I sent it through his agent in London. I expect the fellow will know where to forward it."

She was silent again, tipping her face low to gaze at her folded hands. John watched with ardent longing as a tendril of her dark hair tumbled down from where she had tucked it behind her ear. *Blast.* He was done for.

Hesitantly, and not very gracefully, he lifted his fingers to restore the wayward strands. She jolted in some shock, bumping his hand with her chin.

"I beg your pardon!" She lurched back.

"No!" He was panting. What the devil was wrong with him? "My fault... I surprised you."

Her lips parted, her eyes dilated, and her breathing became uneven. His presence in her darkened bedroom was most decidedly affecting her, though in what way, he could not know. It would be so easy to just lean over... so simple to taste those lips... but to his untrained and willingly deceived eyes, what so closely resembled burgeoning desire could, in fact, be gripping fear. The two passions might be one and the same, given the proper inducements. Surely, such tender expression, such hesitant yearning as his imagination sought to envision could not be for him. He dared not risk it!

He forced his gaze away, snatching back his hand. Margaret, too, had straightened. She held her shoulders squarely and exerted a trembling effort to control herself... and not to chastise him. It was generous of her. She was so young and so exquisite—he was too rough, too unpolished! Surely, she had been taught to expect better from a gentleman... from a husband. He grimaced.

John stared unseeingly into the embers of the fire. There must be some way of salvaging her night, so she might rest. A muffled, quivering intake of her breath brought his eyes back to her. *Not the tears again!*

"Ah... may I stoke your fire for you?" Distraction, that would serve!

Margaret looked to him in mild astonishment. She did not reply, but her gaze shifted over his shoulder to his own darkened chamber. "Why do you have no fire in your room?"

"I seldom do. My hours are not always predictable, and I do not like to trouble the maids to keep it tended."

Her expression softened into something close to a smile, but then cooled again. "You are not often at home, then?"

He hesitated. Did she seem troubled by that information, or relieved? "I usually work late," he supplied cautiously. "I expect that my routine must now change...." He could not keep the hope from his voice as he hungrily sought her response.

"I would not ask you to alter your business day for my benefit."

He frowned in disappointment. Where was the sparkling, regal, haughty young woman who had commanded his actions and stolen his heart? In former days, she would never have quailed at presenting him with her opinions, be they ever so scornful. Did she suddenly fear offending him because they were married? Or had her grief so diminished her spirits that she no longer possessed the strength to challenge him?

"Margaret...." He hesitated, then floundered ahead. He could lose nothing by a little honesty, could he?

"You are my highest concern now. If it should please you to have my company, I will do all I can. If, however, you prefer more privacy—"

"I do not." She held his gaze with beseeching eyes, her breast trembling in uncertainty.

He stilled, but scintillating pleasure quickened his veins and tingled through him. "You... you would like me not to work late?"

"I... I would not wish to impose upon your business."

"But," he probed intently—not wishing to allow her to back away in modesty, if that was all it was—"you might welcome my company?"

Her timid gaze found his face again. She only nodded, very softly, but her eyes spoke volumes.

The whole of his being lit with unrestrained joy. "I... of course! But... I do not wish to burden you. Perhaps if you do not desire to be alone, you might leave the door cracked? I would not then need to trouble you if your wishes are otherwise."

She swallowed, and her cheeks brightened. It was for the husband to request his wife's attentions, not the reverse. His suggestion was rather unconventional, to say the least, and placed her modesty in an inconvenient bind.

He growled at his own brashness. Again, he had unsettled her! He started to apologise—though he still thought the idea a workable one, if she would have it—but she stopped him.

Her hand reached to touch his—the first time she had volunteered such contact—and she was visibly bracing up her courage. "I think that a fine solution, John." Then, she smiled.

She smiled! He would have laughed in relief, but he could not dare to frighten that glorious expression away. His held breath trembled from him, and he caught the hand she offered.

"Then, we are agreed." He was grinning like an idiot, the muscles of his cheeks utterly disobeying any effort of his to restrain their enthusiasm. He had made Margaret smile, on only their second day of marriage! It was an auspicious beginning, indeed!

The moment of elation was not destined to last long. She did not pull her hand from his, and he made no moves to release it, but the melancholy descended over her again like a shroud, blocking out all but sorrow.

"Margaret?" He peered gravely down into her face. "Will you tell me what troubles you?"

She dropped her head, drew a solemn breath, and then met his eyes with a piercing intensity. "Does it get any easier, John? The grief, I mean. Promise me it will not ache like this forever!"

"Easier, with time," he sighed. "I imagine it must be bitter to have lost both your mother and father in so short a span."

Her focus seemed to drift. "Yes," she whispered. "But was it not as bad, or worse for you?"

"I think the two situations cannot compare. The circumstances were… are… very different."

"Will you tell me?" She looked up to him with honest need.

He could not refuse.

Milton-Northern
17 October 1837

"John, I want you to go to the grocer's for me."

Fourteen-year-old John groaned and rolled his eyes. Again, she would interrupt him! He had precious few minutes allotted to himself of late after beginning his new employment. Today happened to be the one day Mr Hamper had allowed him to return home early, on the promise that he would apply himself to this very study and report what he learned on the morrow.

"Mother, I am not yet finished. May I go in an hour?" His tone was not *quite* impertinent, though he would be hard-pressed to call it respectful. She *did* insist on monopolising his time so these last weeks.

Hannah Thornton appeared around the corner of his door frame, her stern brow arched. "I need the flour now, if I am to start tomorrow's bread. You may tinker with your drawing later."

John made a face, but only briefly.

A threatening gleam flickered in his mother's eyes. "Do you have something to say, young man?"

He straightened in immediate regret. No one ever prevailed by harassing Hannah Thornton, and well did he know it. His expression, however, had not gone un-noted, and now he must account for it.

"It is not a drawing, Mother, it is a schematic," he explained calmly. "There is an improved design for the economisers on the steam engines, and Mr Hamper wished me to learn all I could to help him decide if it is a sound investment. He has not the time to investigate it himself. It is quite an honour that he has asked it of me."

"You may do that later, John."

He grimaced sourly but made certain to look at his book as he did so. "I do not understand why you must now do all the baking for us. What happened to Samantha?"

Many other mothers might have brought the house down round his ears for such cheek. Hannah Thornton, however, was subtler. She fixed him with a grim stare, but some cunning spark lurked behind her expression. "What would be convenient for you?"

The lad gulped. Now, he had done it. "I will go now," he amended, setting aside his pen and rising.

"No, no, my son, you must stay. This is important, as you have said. I suppose I may wait an hour."

He hesitated. He knew his mother too well to accept her words at face value, but once she laid down her instruction, she would hold him to it. "Forgive me, Mother. I may do this later."

She lifted her chin and pursed her lips. "No. Stay, John. I shall be content to wait." She swept away, giving him no opportunity to apologise or to capitulate.

She left him to do as he had desired, but as she intended, he was riddled with guilt. He dropped to his seat once more, but the fascinating boiler schematics which had so involved him no longer seemed terribly critical. He tapped his pen on the side of his desk and watched the clock.

Twenty minutes later, his conscience overcame him. Perhaps it was not too late, though he suspected that his mother had already gone to the market herself. He glanced up at the clock again. It was only half past three. Feeling ashamed of himself, he rose and began to silently descend the stairs, his eyes ever searching to determine if she were still there, only waiting on his guilty apology.

The house was perfectly still. The maids had all been mysteriously dismissed the prior week, for what reason he could not accurately discover. His father had been silent and despondent of late, his mother pale and anxious. Still, neither had disclosed more to him than that there were some concerns relating to his own former host, Mr Wright, and that speculation which had troubled his mother.

As John made his stealthy, cautious way down the stairs, a shadow fell across the hall, and shoes whispered softly against the floorboards. He froze. Mother never crept about. Her steps were always firm and resolute, announcing her path with clear determination.

Who could it... he started when his father's tall shape edged into view. Father never came home so early! Perhaps there was more bad news. Surely, he must be searching for Mother to share his woes.

John started forward to explain his mother's absence but stopped in confusion as he watched the furtive manner of his father. The strong, determined face he had known all his life glanced over his shoulder, only once, and John's limbs turned to ice.

There was something dull and lifeless in the haunted eyes—eyes which only a month ago had been bright and assured. The man's countenance was grey and haggard; the firm jaw hung slack. It was as though George Thornton's body had already passed through the valley of the shadow, and the brilliant, carefree soul of the man he knew as his father refused to remain in the hollow shell.

As John watched in growing apprehension, his father slipped inside the door of the study, and the door clicked between them. He heaved a few short, flustered breaths. *What to do?*

He ought to go comfort his father. Whatever troubled him, it could not be so grave that the effervescent George Thornton might not see his way clear to the other side. With the stout faith of his wife, and John's own increasingly able assistance, surely whatever misfortune must have befallen them could not be so ominous as his father seemed to fear! They would face these troubles with a united will. With that resolve, he trotted down the stairs to his father's study.

He had not gone four paces before the gunshot rang out.

A cry of alarm and fear wrung from the boy. *Father!* His knees failed him, and he tripped, stumbling down the bottom steps and landing gracelessly on the floor with skinned shins and palms. He scarcely even noticed, so quickly was he back on his feet. Panicked, and heedless of the unknown dangers, he stumbled to the study.

"Father!" John slammed face-first into the door, expecting it to yield to his touch on the handle. It was locked, and he could not slow his hurtling body quickly enough to prevent dashing his shoulder into it. The pain jolted his frenzied thoughts and crystallised his growing dread.

Sobs of cascading worry began to shake him. He cast about desperately for his mother, who would know where to find the key… but she had gone to the market. Of course, she had, because he had disappointed her!

His hands were trembling, and suddenly, he was hideously relieved that his mother was not at hand. Understanding burst upon him with all the ferocity of denial and fear for what he might discover behind that forbidding, portentous door.

He was already screaming in adolescent torment when he ran back from the dining room with the heavy wooden chair. He slashed with it, over and over, until the chair disintegrated, and the door frame stood in ruin. With one last, frantic kick, the shattered door gave way.

He leaped through the splinters and froze. The room was eerily quiet, but the pungent aroma of metal and gunpowder drilled into his senses. There was no movement to be seen… except the desk chair, which tilted askew, almost ready to topple. John's face was numb as the tears of denial started to trickle down. He panted, wishing to run—but he *had* to know.

He took three cautious steps forward, and that was when his shoes met with the spreading pool of blood from under the desk.

~

"Sit down, son!" Robert Donaldson, the bespectacled, middle-aged surgeon only lately arrived in Milton, fairly shoved the shaking boy into a chair. "You can do no good in that room!"

The dead man's son—John, he had said—looked to be reeling and faint, but he had not vomited again for the last several minutes. Donaldson clucked to himself in pity. The things the boy's young eyes had seen this day would forever be seared into his memory.

When he had first arrived, the boy was still on the floor, his father's ruined head in his hands. He had been screaming disconsolately over the body; then trembling, weeping about the tang in the air, the shattered glass of the window behind the desk… and the spray of blood! So much blood… Donaldson had rarely witnessed such carnage. The entire room was showered in George Thornton's demise, though at first the lad seemed to have been blind to the worst of it.

The wreckage of the study was nothing compared to the last vision the boy would ever have of the man who had raised him. George Thornton was beyond recognition, but for the familiar striped cravat and a prized pocket watch identified by his son. The doctor watched in heartbroken pity as the youth buried his streaked face in his trembling hands, too wrung out to cry more. He only mumbled, over and over under his breath, "I should have stopped him. I could have… I should have stopped him!"

"Son, where did you say your mother went?" Donaldson interrupted. There was a kind urgency in his voice—he hated pressing the distraught young man, but the lady of the house *must* be found, and the news broken gently.

"I don't *know!*" he lashed out.

Donaldson drew back, his hands raised in surrender to the anguished lad. Fury was likely the last emotion left to him and employing it must have infused him with some little strength.

"You asked me before, and I only know she was going to the market!"

Donaldson sighed wearily. He gestured to the neighbour woman, who had been the one to send for him, to remain by the front door. If Mrs Thornton should come home, someone must be ready to apprehend her before she stumbled upon the brutal scene.

"Son," Donaldson tried again, "Mrs Clarence said you have a little sister? How little?"

John quivered and clenched his teeth. He had apparently forgotten about her in all of his affliction. "Two years and a half. She has been ill—I expect Mother left her sleeping upstairs."

Donaldson thinned his lips and scrutinised the lad. If it had not yet dawned on John Thornton, it had occurred to the doctor. This traumatised youth was now the man of the house, with two others dependent upon his keeping. A hideous burden; one he had seen inflicted on far too many mere children. "Why don't you look in on your sister, son? Oh, and take this."

The boy looked up dubiously as the doctor pressed a hot, damp cloth into his hands.

"Your face, son. Your mother ought not to see you so," Donaldson suggested. "You might burn that shirt, as well."

Young Thornton looked down at his clothing. He was covered from his ears to his shoes in his father's caked and drying blood, a testament to the vain efforts at which the doctor had first found him. Whatever made the lad think he could save the man with a gaping hole like that in his head?

A fresh wave of passion seemed to choke the boy. His composure broke, and the tears flowed anew as he crumpled the steaming fresh linen over his eyes. If only the cloth were sufficient to scald that vision forever from a person's memories! Donaldson clucked in pity.

"Go, get yourself to a mirror, young man!" the doctor admonished. Reluctantly, John staggered from his chair, still mopping his eyes with the cloth.

"That's the way, lad," Donaldson encouraged. "Go on upstairs—yes, go to your sister." The white-faced young fellow unsteadily mounted the stairs, gripping the railing as if it were the only thing keeping him on his feet.

As soon as he vanished from sight, Donaldson hurried to the door and gestured to two burly men waiting outside. "Come in, now. The body is in the study, just through here. Be quick about it! I don't know where the widow is, but she may return at any moment."

As George Thornton's body made its final journey from the house he had so proudly secured for his young wife, Donaldson frantically waved to a pair of young washer women. "There you are. Quickly, come. I daren't let the lady see—yes, in there!"

The good doctor did all within his means, calling upon the neighbours for their grudging assistance and putting the room to rights as well as he could. There was nothing a doctor could do for the dead man, and nothing anyone could do for that brave, devastated boy, but he could spare the widow some little measure of the shock she was about to receive.

Donaldson would never see a penny for his trouble, for this family was already in straits enough. He wondered, glancing above his head at the invisible children huddling upstairs, if the survivors had yet heard what was whispered in town today about Daniel Wright and that failed speculation. He had been hoping in vain that he would not see a case such as this after those reports had begun circulating. How many men were now destitute?

The washing women were still hard at work—though the walls were now somewhat improved, and the floor roughly swabbed—when young John made his reappearance. He was cuddling his little sister to a fresh shirt, clinging to her as though she were his comfort rather than the reverse. Donaldson moved to stop him from entering the study again, but the boy's attention was not on the cursed room. Instead, he was staring towards the door, his face utterly blanched. Donaldson's heart sank.

He turned, expecting that the person now behind him would not be seeking any polite introductions. She was a handsome woman, somewhere between thirty-five and forty years of age, with jet hair and dark blue eyes to match her son's. Her sudden deathly pallor, too, was his.

Donaldson tried to intercept her, but the woman never saw him. Her eyes fixed on her son, and the deep, shared empathy of a mother with her child must have imparted to her the whole of the grisly revelation. She dropped her parcel and stumbled forward, only one word on her lips.

"George!"

Margaret's face was streaming with tears of misery. He had offered her the warmth of his arm some while earlier, and she had hungrily draped it round herself, so she might not have to look upon his countenance as he told of his father. What horrors trembled in his voice! She had known the superficial facts, but never considered the gruesome images he still carried, nor the sheer devastation of such a discovery to a mere boy.

"John—" she was staring at his far hand, resting lightly upon his knee. How was it not clenched in anguish, as was hers? "I ought not to have asked. I am sorry!"

He straightened somewhat, drawing her eyes to his. "I have told you too much. Forgive me, I did not intend to cause you any greater distress."

"No! You mistake me. I… I am glad you told me." She twisted under his arm to seek his face. "I cannot imagine what it must have been for you."

The tension present in his manner at the beginning of their late-night encounter had vanished. Somewhere about the time she had begun to shiver with dread at his unfolding tale, and he had hesitantly slid his arm behind her in comfort, he had found the freedom to breathe easily in her presence.

He met her expression with open quietude, despite the pain in his eyes. "It is in the past. I have long since made my peace with it."

Margaret caught her upper lip with her teeth, continuing to blink as the tears pooled. She could not so easily dismiss the complete upheaval of his young life. What calamitous forces had shaped his character, and how had he not succumbed to despair? It was a puzzle she felt unqualified to sort out as yet, but one surety warmed her heart. Whatever sorrows she might claim, the strong man under whose shoulder she now nestled had faced worse. Most curious of all, he seemed generously inclined to offer her sanctuary, whether she deserved it or not.

"Margaret?"

She looked up. Blue eyes gazed softly into her own. She saw him catch himself, but after a brief struggle, he haltingly raised his other hand to touch the backs of his fingers to her cheek. A light caress brushed away her grief, and then his fingers uncurled to hover just under the base of her ear.

Margaret's breath came ragged and shallow. Her lips parted, moistened still with captured tears, and she drew a sharp little gulp when his warm thumb soothed them away. His eyes… *oh*, those beautiful, eloquent eyes! She was hypnotised, swept from her wave of mourning to a tide of awakening feeling.

There seemed only one answer to the yearning growing within her. Her chin wavered and lifted, her neck lengthening with each panting breath. He was closer now—was he drawing near by his own desire, or was it all her own unseemly impulses? What would he think of her if she…? *Oh!* An unbidden gasp jerked her.

John's hand dropped away, and he stiffened back to his own side of their seat. His arm, still looped about her shoulders, tightened uncomfortably. He looked to the remains of the fire, the muscles of his jaw working in the shadows.

Margaret clenched her eyes in regret. Just when he had shared the darkest secrets of his heart and a wavering tenderness had broken down some of their uncertainties, the doubt surfaced once more.

"I… I should allow you to rest." He kept his face turned as he spoke.

She shivered as his arm slid from her. "Yes, that would be for the best," she murmured, almost inaudibly.

He offered her his hand, and she fumbled to accept it—uncertain how a woman was to grasp her husband's hand. In the end, her fingers wrapped clumsily over the back of his thumb, and he lifted her with no visible effort. They stood, then, only inches apart.

Once more, she lost her composure. He was so tall! Her gaze rose only to the hollow of his throat, an intimate view to which she had never before been privy. The warm cleft trembled with his pulse and breath as she stared at his bared skin—soft, yet prickled now by some sudden chill.

Nothing else filled her vision until she straightened a little away. The distance made her thinking no clearer, for her view of him widened and the full measure of his manly symmetry met her fascinated eyes. The thin nightshirt he wore was a poor disguise for the power simmering within his broad shoulders and deep chest, and his scent, now unconcealed by layers of wool and flannel, warmed her heightened senses.

She could still feel, as if she remained yet in his embrace, the warmth and strength of his body through that light cotton. Would that he felt as she and wished to return to that exquisite communion! How readily they might learn the ways of affection if only he could see her as he once had—as a woman he admired and trusted, and who would bear his heart.

Margaret slipped her hand from his and could not help but notice how he still seemed frozen, reaching for her, even after the contact was broken. *Was it possible?* She searched his expression but could not read the complex interplay of feeling inscribed there.

It was John who found his voice first, unsteady though it was. "Good night, then, Margaret."

She offered him a hopeful smile, but shyly ducked her head as she did so. "Good night, John."

He lingered yet another moment, staring in mute indecision. Then, with an impetuous gasp, he touched her shoulder to press a quiet, brotherly kiss to her cheek. He straightened, his fingers kneading against each other as his hand fell away once more. "Rest well, Margaret," he said roughly.

Margaret was gazing blankly at him, her mouth agape. Numbly, her fingers went to her still-warm cheek as she watched him disappear behind the door. He did not close it completely.

Four

Margaret never did sleep that night. It had been nearly one in the morning when John had left her. From the dubious comfort of her bed, she could watch the hands of the clock spinning impassively about its face, indifferent to her despair at finding rest. After well over two hours of futile effort, she returned to the little seat by the fire.

She tried to read, but her thoughts lingered only on the boy she had learned of this evening—the boy whose existence had been wholly unknown to her before. In her mind, John Thornton had always been exactly as he was: an authority to be challenged or obeyed, a force which drove all before him and held lives in his power. But she had seen him now—had seen the stolen youth brimming beneath that controlled mask, and she could never again be ignorant of it.

Her father and her own experiences had compelled her to recognise John as good, but it had taken the stricken horror still evident in his voice for her to understand that he was without equal. That crushing, hideous blow did not break him, as it would any other, but forged him into yet a greater man than he could otherwise have been.

She was absently musing thus over the dwindling fire when there was a soft knock on the door between their rooms. Perhaps he could not sleep, either! She hurried to the door, some lonely hope inspiring the notion that he might have wished to see her.

He was dressed, but for his hat and coat, and smiling timidly as his eyes swept unconsciously over her. "I am sorry to disturb you so early."

"Early? Is it morning already?"

"Five-thirty, or just after. Did you sleep well?"

She blinked and stifled a yawn. "I—" her words cut off as another yawn took over.

He emitted a soft huff, almost a chuckle. "Nor did I," he confessed, then he sobered. "I would not have troubled you, but I am afraid I must break the promise I made to you last night."

Her eyes simply refused to focus, and she could not help rubbing them. "Promise?" she asked blearily. "I do not recall…."

"I said I would accompany you to the Crampton house today, but I have only just received a note from my overseer." He paused, his still-ungroomed cheeks flinching in discomfort.

"Mr Williams? Is there some trouble?"

"He is ill. Williams has been with me for four years, and only twice has he ever been too ill to work, so I do not doubt him. I hope it was merely his dinner which troubled him, and that he will be back to work by tomorrow."

"And you cannot do without him? Forgive me, I do not yet know how matters are."

"I can, but it is twice the work. I could possibly take an hour or two away from the mill today, but a full work day with neither Williams nor myself to oversee matters… it would prove folly."

Margaret nodded, unable to hold back another yawn, and crossed her arms. "I-I see." Mindless of the coarseness of the act, she dug her index finger again into her uncooperative eye. If only she could focus on his face as he spoke!

Her vision did manage to sharpen rather suddenly when he stepped close to her. She was forced to tip her face up, and was shocked to find the deep, almost heartbroken regret etched into his rigid features.

"I am sorry, Margaret! I would not disappoint you, had I any power to do otherwise."

A weary smile pulled at her mouth. "It is quite all right. I fear I would be in no condition today to face what must be done at the house."

"That should not matter. You have asked nothing so far but this, and I am prevented from doing you this small service by my work."

"It could not be helped," she shrugged reasonably, her gaze finding a button at his chest. It was easier, somehow, to face that small, stolid point, than to look into his eyes and allow her hopes to fancy what they might. He was an honest man, after all, and would only naturally wish to keep his word, regardless of his reasons for giving it.

"Margaret…." Once again, his fingers touched to her chin. A secret little thrill shivered down her spine, but she kept her eyes lowered for another heartbeat until she could meet his gaze with composure.

"Margaret—" his voice was low and pleading, and his thumb stroked deliciously over the lower edge of her jaw before his hand dropped away. "I know you never expected to be bound to one such as I. No proper gentleman would find it troublesome to set aside his duties for the day to see to your pleasure. I would not blame you if this incident should serve to heighten your dismay over present circumstances."

Margaret knit her brows. "I think you mistake me. I suffer no such sentiment."

His eyes widened. "Do you not? You do not feel I abandon you during your time of grief?"

She intended to speak no reply which might justify his feelings of guilt, but he would not release her from his scrutiny. "I… perhaps… no, John, I should not think so."

He nodded in resolution. "You do, and you deserve to. I have failed you miserably these two days."

"No!" she objected sharply, then dropped her gaze again as his eyes flashed surprise. "That is… last night, when you sat with me, and the things you told me… I found it very comforting. It was good of you."

"I do not call it 'good' to rob you of sleep, as I have apparently done. Margaret, I've no right to ask, but will you oblige me in one thing?"

She raised her head swiftly, the word "Anything!" trembling upon her lips, but she dared not voice it. Instead, she only waited in earnest silence.

His cheek flinched as he took her hand. "Stay here today. Recover your strength as well as you can, and tomorrow we will go to Crampton together. I would not see you go back there alone."

"Dixon is there."

"Aye, and what comfort did she offer yesterday?" he countered, and Margaret thought she detected a slight edge in his voice. During the week of their "engagement," John and Dixon had clashed more than once over the best means of consoling her and helping to ease her transition to married life. Apparently, he thought little more of Dixon's efforts now than he had a few days ago.

She could not help a shy tightening of her cheek as her head dipped once more. "I will stay, if you wish it."

He narrowed his eyes, regarding her sceptically, but apparently decided to withhold whatever comment he would have liked to make. "I will inform Mother that you will wish to remain within your rooms this morning, so that you need not feel expected downstairs."

The pleasant warmth of his considerate attentions faded when Margaret remembered her new mother-in-law. She swallowed. It would be yet another excuse for Hannah Thornton to think the less of her, but aloud she simply uttered, "Thank you."

~

John managed to plod through his workday, performing the tasks of two men with the mental clarity of half of one. His every pulsing thought was with Margaret. *My wife!*—he reminisced ardently. What delirious completion he found in that simple phrase. He, a married man, after all those years of solitude!

The hours they spent in quiet conversation, with her tempting body curled so invitingly close to his own, had quite positively been the most blissful and tempestuous of his life. Even the emptying of his very deepest sorrows could not dampen the thrill he felt when he remembered the smile which had been for him alone, and the delicate scent that clung to his shirt for the remainder of the night.

He kneaded his eyes as he attempted, for the third time, to tally the morning's numbers. The fragrance of his nightshirt and the tingling fire where she had pressed against his side—throughout his entire body, really—were to blame for his utter lack of sleep. Euphoric disbelief was an apt description for his addled state of mind, but the cumulative fatigue was beginning to tell on him. In truth, he had not slept well since the day of Mr Hale's death, and the awakening of the certain knowledge that he was her only refuge.

He had every intention of wrapping up his duties, then slipping over to his house for an hour in the afternoon. The hands would be gone to their dinner, and Margaret would certainly be down from her rooms in search of some occupation. Perhaps she would not mind a private tour of the modest library in his study.

He rocked back in his chair, smiling as he imagined her studious contemplation of his own sanctuary. Would she be pleased or disappointed by the collection that had taken him years to build? Would it be the same accustomed gravity, or a flicker of kinship which marked her expression when she turned around to him?

John closed his eyes, his heart longing to see the latter in her face. Would that she could come to view him as a friend, possibly an equal! Equals were able to protect and comfort, and friends, after all, were permitted *some* liberties… perhaps even a bit of irreverent playfulness. Would she permit him to wrap her in his embrace, sharing his over-sized leather chair some evening in the library?

What could begin as a comfortable interlude—with her reading to him from one of his old books and tucked close to his side—might well flourish into something more promising. Her body would be supported against his chest, her thigh pressed to his, and her mouth—the sweet breath of her lips as she read aloud—mere inches away.

He swallowed and passed a shaking hand over his eyes. He was getting too far ahead of matters! She was not ready... yet was it his own wilfull imagination, or was she already growing to be more receptive of his company? Was she simply in need of a companion, or had she at last begun to... to like him a little? Whatever her reasons, if she welcomed him, he would deploy every courtly manner and charm at his disposal to encourage her affections. A peaceful evening of gentle conversation and his own comforting arms might be the decisive moment to turn his wife's grieving heart to his.

As he mused on that highly diverting topic, a fist from without pounded upon his office door. He groaned. "Come!"

Higgins peered around the door. "Beggin' yo'r pardon, Master."

"What is it, Higgins?"

"Sir, it's th' second loom. Th' shuttle's 'ung up, and a good bit o' cloth ruined."

"What? Again!" he cried in exasperation. "I thought Thompkins resolved that matter."

Higgins' only reply was a cautious shrug. "I 'ad th' lads from that loom spread o'er th' others, till yo' say what's t' be done, Master."

John snarled in annoyance. There went any hope of finishing his duties quickly. "Come, Higgins, let us see what we can make of it."

Helstone
July 1837

"Where is he, Mamma?"

Margaret stood on her toes, straining to peer over the ledge of the window and up the lane. Papa ought to be home by now, but the sky was darkening, and no lone figure was silhouetted against the setting sun over the fields. She looked over her shoulder, her small brow etched in worry. "Mamma?"

"I told you, Margaret, he has gone to Mrs Grey's," her mother explained patiently. "She is dying, and he must do his duty by her. Goodness only knows when he will return."

"But he has been away so long!"

"And so he always is. Come away from the window and have your tea."

Margaret obeyed, but reluctantly. Her thoughts were all for the door, and she watched it with the devotion of one who believed that a moment of inattention would render her worrisome hopes a vanity. She nibbled from her plate, sipped dutifully from her cup, but whenever her mother's absent-minded gaze should stray, Margaret would again strain her neck to look out the window.

"You may as well put up Mr Hale's plate," her mother sighed to Charlotte. "I do not expect he will return for a long while yet."

In dismay, Margaret watched as Charlotte carried the meal set aside for her father into the kitchen. Her mother was not looking her way, so she stole a bit of bread from her plate to secrete it behind her back. A moment later, a generous slice of cheese joined it, and then the rest of her cake.

Her mother remained inattentive, fussing with the lace at the edge of her shawl and speaking now and again to Dixon of topics that could hold no interest for Margaret. A table napkin had disappeared; swept behind her to bind round the little stash of comfort she meant to save for her father. Last of all—and this would be the most difficult—she filled her tea cup again and dropped two cubes into its amber depths.

"Mamma, may I be excused?"

Mrs Hale glanced over Margaret's plate and dismissed her, but Margaret did not scamper away at once. The napkin parcel she had tucked into her sash, but she could not secure the cup without some distraction. It came in the form of Charlotte, whose task it was to clear away the tea, but she stopped for a moment for some instruction from her mistress. Margaret saw her chance, and the next minute, both girl and saucer had vanished.

Her father was very late—so late that the rest of the house had gone to bed, and only a single lamp was left to greet him. Margaret had slipped from her room to crouch on the steps, and when his dark, stooped figure entered the house, she met him in the passage.

"Margaret! My child, why are you awake?"

She pointed shyly towards his study. "I saved some dinner for you, Papa."

His beloved face softened, and he bent to gather her in his arms. "I could have done very well for myself in the larder, my dear, but it was kind of you to think of me."

She tightened her arms around his neck and he carried her, then lowered himself into an old settee near his desk with her on his lap. "Well, now, you have even saved me some tea! You are quite the hostess, my dear."

She beamed proudly until he lifted the cup, although her pleasure faded when no comforting steam rose from its surface. But her father acted as cold tea were his particular favourite and never betrayed an instant's displeasure, even when she could see that the lumps of sugar had never been properly stirred. Nor did he object to the crumbled, half-eaten cake or the bread and cheese which had dried out. He savoured them as if they were served on the finest settings from her aunt's home in Harley Street, all while snuggling her on his knee and telling her of his day.

Margaret leaned her head back against her father's shoulder. She could listen to his gentle, measured tones without ceasing, whether he preached a sermon or read to her from Homer or simply chronicled all the doings of a country parish. His lap was her favourite place, for nowhere else did she feel so safe and understood.

She never did see him swallow the last drops of his tea, nor have the satisfaction of carrying his empty plate to the kitchen for him. The voice she loved so well was better than any nursery song, and with her ear pillowed against her father's chest, she drifted to sleep.

Margaret could not remain in her seat as her mother-in-law so placidly managed to do. The entire day had passed and ended, with no appearance at all by her husband. The only word she had was a hastily scrawled note apologising that he would be detained through the afternoon, and possibly even the evening meal.

Margaret slipped her hand within a concealed pocket of her gown, and her fingers clasped the note. He was not avoiding her, was he? Her eyes burned with the sum of an entire day of unshed emotion. Spent and weary as she had been of late, it was possible her feelings were not to be trusted, but… she darted a quick glance to John's mother, who, in her dogged application to her needlework, appeared wholly unperturbed by his absence. Perhaps it was not at all unusual for him to be delayed in the evenings, but her lonely insecurities continued to trouble her.

She paced, without realising that she was doing so, until a low noise from the other woman distracted her. "Margaret—" Hannah Thornton did not bother to look up, but spoke seemingly to the work in her hands—"perhaps now would be a good time to discuss some of your duties as mistress of the house."

Margaret tilted her head curiously. She had been requesting such information, but the elder woman had seemed reluctant to divulge. "Is there anything in particular we ought to discuss first?"

"Indeed," was the indifferent reply. "Possibly it has been your upbringing, as the daughter of a country parson, to pay social calls on the working class. You must recognise that you occupy a very different place in society now."

Margaret had turned to gape at the woman. "I do not believe I understand you properly."

Hannah grimly set aside her needlework and deigned to look Margaret in the eye. "I understand you spent the afternoon in the workers' kitchen with the daughter of a Union leader. Even were you not in mourning, it would be unseemly for the mistress to condescend so."

"Mary Higgins is a friend! May I ask why it should be improper for me to take an interest in my husband's workers? I should think you would encourage me to learn more of the mill."

Hannah arched a dark brow over her sewing glasses. "As the mistress, yes. You ought to understand the ebb and flow of the business, so as to make intelligent discourse among John's equals. We do not value a woman who is ignorant of such matters here in Milton, as the fashionable folk in London might," she sniffed. "However, fraternising with the hands, disdaining all our social conventions and appearing to tender your loyalties to the workers, rather than to your husband, will not serve."

Margaret raised her chin. "I thank you for your advice," she retorted crisply. "I shall take it under consideration." She spun back to the window, her fists balled. *The nerve of that woman,* to lecture her about her quest for companionship—as if she should wish to take on the aspect of the bitter, stone-faced matron who could claim no friends at all!

"I should hope so," was the grumbled response, though Margaret failed to acknowledge it.

She continued staring out of the darkened window towards the mill. It was not difficult to pick John's office window out from among the others across the way, for a feeble light still glowed from within—at least it *should* not have been difficult, if not for the prickling moisture clouding her vision.

"I expect that he may be some while yet."

Margaret only glanced over her shoulder, less eager than before to hear Hannah Thornton's thoughts. "Why should you say that?"

The silver needle flashed in the lantern light as the widow's nimble hands never faltered. "He has a deal to occupy him," was the brusque answer. "John has never been a man of leisure. I should think he has even more concerns at present than usual."

"Madam—" Margaret flexed her fingers and then knotted them again into a determined fist—"I quite understand that you find me responsible for John's additional burden. I assure you, I do not fail to appreciate his efforts."

Hannah pursed her lips, and a light flickered in her eye which Margaret had not yet learned to identify. "That is rather an arrogant presumption, Margaret, to believe that your recent arrival could so disrupt the workings of the mill. John has long been accustomed to work late whenever the need arises."

Margaret felt the heat crawling into her face. As she had been earlier in the day, she was overcome with the stifling urge to flee to somewhere—*anywhere!*—else, so long as she was out of Hannah Thornton's glowering presence. Her breath quickened as inspiration struck.

"If he is to work longer—" she lifted her shoulders in a flash of her old resolve—"then I expect he could do with a tray to sustain him. If you will excuse me, madam, I shall see to it."

Margaret swept out of the room, grateful for fresh air over her scalding face. Had she lingered and paid very close attention, she might, perhaps, have noted the crafty smile teasing just the corner of her mother-in-law's lips.

Weston
March 1838

"John, you are going to starve yourself!" Hannah Thornton, the widow of Baker Street, had been hovering near the rear exit of the draper's shop where her son spent his days. She knew it was often one of his duties to tote crates of scraps or empty bolts to the back of the shop, and here, more than once, her patient attendance had been rewarded.

Fifteen-year-old John, coated in sweat and caked in dust, turned in the darkness at his mother's voice. "Another hour and I will have done, Mother. You need not have come so far."

"I came because it is nearly ten. You have not had a bite since five this morning, and that only water-porridge. Take this." She reached for the pocket of his coat and stuffed a small, dense parcel inside.

He felt of it curiously. "The last of the bread loaf? Mother, you must give this to Fanny." He began to tug it free of his clothing, but his mother put a staying hand to him.

"John, you are too thin. A pretty thing it would be if I should let you, who provide for us all, drop at your work for want of a few bites of dinner!"

"I am to be paid tomorrow, and because of the additional shipments this week, Mr Davis has promised me an extra shilling. I shall eat like a king out of that." He flashed her a gleaming smile in the dusky light—charming and carefree, and almost believable.

"John—" the perceptive mother halted him, placing a tender hand upon his cheek. "You need not bear this burden alone."

She felt his jaw tense as he blinked, his breath quickening in his chest. He had not shed a single tear since that harrowing day five months earlier, but she was no fool. The wrenching trauma of all he had seen, and would not tell her of, had never yet ceased to haunt his gaze.

In word and deed, his manner ranged from gentle stoicism to forced cheer, but beneath his maturing exterior simmered a raging torrent of hurt, confusion, and anger. Though he never spoke the words aloud, the guilt he was determined to bear over that day's terror yet darkened his spirits. One day, she feared greatly, it would all be brought to a head by some crisis of the heart. She could but pray and do all within her power to sustain him against that eventuality.

His chin shifted in determination beneath her hand. "I know I needn't, but I would spare you what troubles I can. It is not right that you should have had to suffer so."

"Many things are not right in this world, my boy. That is no reason that my son should hang his head. Whose infinite wisdom has sent us these days of hardship, and who saw fit to first give us many good years of plenty to strengthen our constitutions?"

He swallowed as his face dipped and he nodded in resignation. Her hand slipped from his cheek, and as it did, her sensitive fingers noted the first traces of masculine grit along the edges of his jaw. Her boy was growing to a man, but at the moment, he was a bewildered, tortured one indeed.

"My faith must be weak," he murmured to the darkness. "I cannot think this good Lord you speak of could have permitted all this."

"It is not weakness to doubt, my son," she whispered back, taking his hand. "Mankind has crafted for himself a wretched world, far short of the perfection which was intended—that is what we are to understand. Many things have not been revealed to us, but there is always a reason. You are being shaped for some purpose. I know not if we will ever see it clearly in this world, but you must trust in that."

The pale glow of his eyes in the moonlight eclipsed to blackness. His tall form bent before her in some agony of feeling, and she placed a comforting hand on his shoulder. His head bowed, he reached suddenly to enclose her in a tight hug, trembling all the while.

Hannah rumpled her young man's dark hair; a thing she might seldom, if ever, have an opportunity to do again. She tried to sniffle back a rush of her own tears, but they stubbornly fell as an anointing on the shoulder of her son—the one person who had stepped into the gap between her and despair. "Bless you, my John!"

He drew back, his deepening voice cracking and hoarse. "I am blessed already, to have a wise, strong, faithful mother such as you. I could not do without…." She heard him swallow, saw him turning away in the shadows.

She took his face again between her hands. "John, you are my comfort and my joy. I will ever do what little I can, but you deserve so much more."

He shook his head, then reached to clasp her calloused fingers. "One day, Mother, it will be I who will care for you, and you will not need to smuggle meals to me out in the night. You may do your needlework comfortably enthroned by a warm fire, and we will all retire for the evening with satisfied bellies and contented hearts. I would see you proud and happy, cared for in every way!"

"One day, John," she agreed with a wistful smile. "Until then, carry out your duties with constant fidelity. Become the man I know you to be, my John, for anyone would be proud to call you her own."

"That will be all, thank you, Sarah." Margaret hung the lantern on a small hook just outside John's office and took the tray from the maid who assisted her.

"Are yo' sure, ma'am?" Sarah protested. "Yo'll n'a be for walkin' back t' th' 'ouse?"

"I shall wait on Mr Thornton."

Yes, she most certainly would, for she preferred to sit in the corner of a dirty office watching him work than to return to that frigid drawing-room. John would not object... surely.... Her hands trembling on the tray, she directed Sarah to take back the lantern before she could change her mind.

She forced herself to draw one last calming breath before she knocked. She had no idea what sort of protocol breach she was about to infract—after all, what *did* a mill master's wife do when he was working without meals? What did his mother do when he was hers alone?

She knew what a parson's wife did, she supposed—what Margaret Hale would have done. She must find her new way as Margaret Thornton—whoever *she* was. Gulping in quick resolve, she determined that she would remain true to the woman she had ever been, unless given sound reason to change. Her hand reached for the door.

There was no response to her soft, hesitant knock, nor was there any to the somewhat louder one she dared a moment later. She cast her gaze about the darkened hall. This *was* John's office, was it not? Shifting the tray, she tried the latch and found it unlocked.

The light from the room poured over her skirts and the tray first, and she took a hesitant step inside. There, bathed in the tepid warmth of his own lantern, was John's inert figure, slumped over his desk. He was sound asleep.

She paused. Never had she seen him so unguarded, so completely unaware of her scrutiny. Coming softly near, she set the tray aside to contemplate the resting features of the man she had married. Her stomach quivered, and a halting smile grew on her lips. Absent the austere mien which had tainted her first impressions of him, his face was... *beautiful*. There was no other word which suited, and she gave an inner start at that confession.

She tilted her head. She once declared him not handsome in the conventional way, but his countenance she always acknowledged as remarkable, simply for its quiet power and noble bearing. Now, without the look of the bulldog about him, she saw the man Mrs Thornton claimed to know—the man she had met last night. She saw the boy grown to full strength, yet still possessed of an innocence and a vulnerability he carefully concealed from everyone else.

It was not merely the absence of his usual wariness which startled her. His features, soft in repose and made familiar by two days of living under the same roof, were positively striking. Her admiring gaze travelled from the dark locks of hair, curling defiantly over a brow that was smooth now in sleep, and down the bridge of his nose with its permanently thoughtful little furrow. His brows slanted straight and low over eyes which she knew to be impossibly black at times, and brilliantly blue at others. They were cloaked beneath the thickest, longest lashes she had ever seen on a man. How did she never notice that before?

The next detail to inspire wonder was his unshaven cheeks. It seemed he rushed out so many hours ago without attending to that task, and now a softly dishevelled shadow described his jaw. Margaret's throat tightened. How often he forsook the morning ritual, she could not be certain. In her own experience, he always appeared perfectly groomed—but then he had been calling as a guest at her home during most of those encounters, and naturally would have taken care to present himself properly.

Yet, as he was now, he seemed so… so mortal—a being within her realm, instead of the industrial figurehead she first presumed him for. Perhaps it was rather inelegant of her, but she cherished a hope that he did occasionally skip his morning shave, so she might admire the masculine outline of his face by the evening. What would it be like to touch those short, sandy bristles… to feel them scraping and tickling against her neck, if he should come to her one night?

Her limbs crumpled, suddenly watery and faint. Gasping in shock at her indelicate new ideas, she sought the edge of his desk for some support against the disconcerting spin of the room. Her disobedient eyes, however, soon trailed to his bared arms sprawled over the surface. His hands… she forced her breath to steady.

They were the hands of both a working man and a learned man—smudged with ink, yet calloused here and there with hard labour. Beneath the short, perfectly manicured nails and embedded in the raised prints of his index finger, she thought she detected faint traces of machine grease. Yet, the fingers were long and elegant, well purposed for every gentle pursuit.

Without conscious thought, she reached to trace the back of his nearest hand. His flesh was cool, and she spread her curious touch over the rest of his fingers. In dismay, she found him to be quite cold. This would never do!

As some protective impulse compelled her to warm his chilled fingers, they curled in her hand. His grip tightened reflexively, and his body jerked with a sharp intake of breath. Margaret froze, caught in her guilty indulgence with her hand now trapped in his.

He was blinking, his expression hazy. "Margaret?" He gave an instinctive tug, and before she quite knew what was happening, Margaret found herself pulled bodily into his lap. Her voluminous skirts forced his wheeled chair to swivel and roll away from his desk, and she made a wild grasp for his neck in a panicked quest for balance.

"John!" she cried—more in alarm than indignation.

She felt his shoulder, and the arm he had wrapped about her, go suddenly stiff. "F-forgive me. I was surprised, that is all, Margaret. I meant no offence."

Margaret had, in only a few seconds, decided that this position was quite a comfortable one. She made no move to leap away from him, as his opened embrace seemed to permit. Rather, a bashful smile soon developed into a quiet chuckle, and then blossomed into hearty laughter as John's own expression lightened in relief.

His arm tightened once more as he shifted her weight to hold her more comfortably. "May I ask to what I owe the pleasure of this interruption to my nap?" He grinned, flashing that artless, incandescent smile she remembered from their early acquaintance.

"It is late, and I thought perhaps you might like something to eat." She flicked a meaningful gaze to the tray on the desk.

His brow furrowed in distress. "Late? How late?"

He craned his neck about to look over his shoulder at a clock, allowing her an unimpeded view of his exposed throat. Margaret's eyes widened. Yes, this was a very comfortable seat, indeed.

"Nearly eleven!" he lamented when he found the time. "How can that be?" His free hand pressed into his eyes. "Margaret, I never meant to stay so long."

"I noticed," she smiled down at her lap, pardoning him. "You must be quite weary."

He sighed, then his hand clasped hers. "I had every intention of returning to you this evening. You have been too much alone, and it was not my wish to abandon you once again. I fear that I am proving a disappointment to you."

"Had I known,"—she felt her cheeks heating—"I would have brought you a tray earlier. Perhaps I will remember that in the future, so you might be able to finish more quickly."

A radiance lit his eyes, and a hopeful smile hovered on his lips. "You would do that?"

"If you would like it."

His grin widened. "I most certainly would, but I hope you may not find too many occasions to do so. I do not recall the last time I fell asleep at my desk."

She cast a worried glance at the scattered correspondence and tally sheets arrayed over the surface. "Is there some trouble, other than Mr Williams' illness today?"

He sighed, his far hand nestling ever more comfortably around her waist. "It would be unfair to claim there is not, for you deserve the whole of the matter. Yes, the mill's finances have been strained since the strikes. Our orders have been delayed, which has caused our buyers hardships of their own, and their payments have been slow. I would seek out new buyers to generate more immediate capital, but I cannot in good conscience take their orders when I am still catching up from several months ago."

She stared uncomprehendingly at the stack. "I suppose I do not understand what you can hope to do here. You are searching for some detail you might have missed?"

She looked back to him with the question and found that his face had tipped very near her neck while she was looking away. He pulled back, sucking in a deep breath. "Y-yes," he stammered, then shook his head very slightly as if to clear it.

"Or, rather, not that so much as simply updating all my records, as I must do each day. It is a tedious business, and one in which I cannot dare to fall behind. I am afraid that several unforeseen events today have utterly derailed all my usual routines. Fortunately—" he rubbed his eyes again—"I believe I can safely retire now and make up the rest on the morrow."

"You must be hungry. Had you any luncheon?"

"Higgins brought me a bite around midday, while we were trying to sort out a troublesome loom. Best hire I ever made, Margaret. I owe you my gratitude."

Margaret, modest as she was, came very near to leaning a mere three inches closer to kiss those rugged cheeks in that moment. She had never imagined such a confession from him, and it came so readily! The pleasure of his easy embrace, as she perched upon his knee, and her growing admiration for the man as she now so intimately saw him, swelled painfully in her heart. If she had not already begun to love him before she had married him, he would not have left her long in peace.

It was her own reserve that sabotaged her. Each moment spent in his company made her more thoroughly his, but there remained her own lingering feelings of guilt. He had every reason to doubt her integrity! She could not absolve herself, and would not allow him to do so, in her certainty that a man such as he could never sincerely embrace a woman who had once defrauded the truth. Could he do so, his own honour would become suspect.

Margaret had smiled at his light-hearted quip about Higgins, but her turning thoughts had checked her before she acted upon her audacious impulse. John apparently sensed the shift in her manner. His expression sobered, and he altered his posture to assist her to her feet. Reluctantly, she allowed herself to be removed from his embrace.

John's face was bright red—for what reason, she did not know, but his knuckles pressed to his brows in some attempt to command himself. Margaret, her cheeks burning, busied herself in presenting to him the simple repast. It was little more than a meat pasty and a snifter of brandy, for she had not thought it wise to bring a hot tea kettle or a full meal so far.

John had regained some measure of his composure, accepting the silverware that she proffered and preparing to address himself to the tray. "Would you like to share it?" he asked, his tones once more hesitant.

The astonishment must have been plain on her face, for he rushed to justify himself. "I only thought perhaps you might be hungry as well. Has it not also been some while since you ate?"

"I am well enough, but I thank you." She withdrew to his side and crossed her hands patiently over her skirts.

His eyebrows quirked. "Then, I suppose the sooner I put this away, the earlier we may go to bed." The words were scarcely out of his mouth when the blood drained from his face. His fork dropped with a clatter and he raised his head, an apology already on his lips.

Margaret was turning her face, fearing it must be several shades of pink. She daintily cleared her throat and tried to act as though she had not heard his remark. How was she to respond to such a notion? He had every right, did he not, to make any requests he wished of her, but had not yet seemed inclined to do so. Whatever one might call the budding urges within her own heart, it was more than a little humiliating that he appeared to nurture no similar appetites.

Or... did he? She daringly watched him through slitted eyes as he tried to eat his meal with both haste and good manners. He was casting hopeful glances her way every few seconds. Was it possible that he did, in fact, desire her as he once claimed, but in his doubt would not permit himself to approach her? *Of course.* She dropped her eyes to the floor. That old shame seemed forever between them!

John finished his meal and drained the contents of the brandy snifter. He rolled down his shirtsleeves and reclaimed his coat and hat near the door before she could tidy up the remnants of the meal. "Leave it. It is late; I will see to it tomorrow." He offered his arm and even wrapped his free hand over hers when she took it.

Margaret glanced up at him. "Your hand is still freezing! Are you well?"

He shrugged as they walked. "My office is warm, perhaps a little too warm, during the day, but once the work is over and the boiler cools, it can be like an ice box. I am afraid I was in it for far too long this evening."

"And your room is probably cold, too," she lamented.

"Perhaps I might share your fire again tonight?" he suggested in the darkness. She could not read his expression, but something in his voice sent a prickle down her neck.

"If... if you are not too weary."

"I am, and I expect you are, as well, but if you can bear a quarter hour longer, I should like to enjoy your company for a few minutes, at least."

Margaret's cheeks tugged into an elated, laughing smile, but she made herself answer sedately. Perhaps he might yet be willing to bridge the gulf of misunderstandings between them, and if he were, she resolved to tell him everything—so long as he cared to hear. "Of course, John."

The elder Mrs Thornton was not below when they returned to the house—for which Margaret, at least, was grateful. They separated at their respective doors to dress for bed. John would only require a handful of minutes, and so they agreed he would wait at her hearth while she finished in her dressing room.

Margaret hurried over her typical evening regimen and emerged only a few moments after she had first heard his steps passing through her bedroom. He faced away from her, his arm resting over the back of the little settee. She trod softly, in still bare feet around the furniture to take her place but stopped when she reached the hearth.

He was asleep again. That bristled, dimpled chin nodded to his chest, and with every few breaths she heard a rasping sound in his throat. There would be no waking him easily this time.

She deliberated for a moment, but at length decided that she ought to do as she had last agreed. Gingerly, she eased herself into the seat beside him. The slight jostling to the cushions caused his arm to roll down from the frame of the settee to drop over her shoulder.

He stirred in his sleep. "Margaret?" he mumbled thickly, his eyes still closed.

"Yes, John?" she answered, knowing that exhausted and mellow from his brandy, he would never hear her.

Whether he did register her response could not be certain, but his head rolled towards her, and he nuzzled a firm, very distinct kiss to her temple.

Margaret allowed herself a moment of hope. Somewhere within the gentlemanly, reserved man she had married, still lurked the passionate man who had sworn undying love to her. Perhaps it was not impossible that they might yet discover the sort of marital harmony she craved. Perhaps, if she could bring herself to trust him enough to share her darkest doubts and griefs, as he had done with her, his faith might be restored, and her own heart might find its helpmeet.

Smiling at that last thought, she nestled her head into his shoulder to relish at least the sense of his company, if not his conversation. Neither roused from that warm little settee until dawn.

Five

"Margaret? The carriage is ready."

John had spent a short while that morning at the mill, helping Williams settle in after his day of illness. As soon as it was possible, he had hurried back to his home to keep his promise to his wife.

Nothing, not even the still-recalcitrant loom, nor the mounting stack of paperwork on his desk, could wipe the smile from his face this morning. He had awakened with Margaret's soft cheek on his chest, and her arm draped unconsciously round him. *That*, he had instantly decided, was how he wished to begin every day for the rest of his life—although he could gladly do without the lingering stiff neck.

Margaret rose from her chair to join him in the doorway. "Mother, we shall return before the evening meal," he assured her as Margaret drew near. Hannah's only response was a dry, silent nod.

Dissatisfied, he stared at her. His mother was certainly not making things any easier for Margaret. He sighed in exasperation, but Margaret's fingers slid around the elbow he had offered, and all other thoughts were banished. From that moment on, he could anticipate an entire day with her.

The drive was not a long one, and, indeed, both had walked the very same distance many times. He had, however, desired to preserve her strength, and expected that the completion of the day's tasks would find her quite worn. In addition, he thought with some satisfaction, the carriage ride offered yet another opportunity to wrap his arm about her as a shelter against the cool September morning. She did not appear to object.

Dixon greeted them at the door and led the way through a maze of crates in what had once been the family's drawing-room. "Are these the items to be sold?"

"Everything in this room," she informed him primly. "That fellow Harper you sent is coming for them tomorrow."

"What is left for Margaret to decide?"

Dixon crossed her arms. "The master's room. I won't touch that," she declared stubbornly, with a significant glance towards Margaret's pale face.

John narrowed his eyes. "Dixon, you look as though you could do with some fresh air."

Dixon straightened somewhat, her self-important expression melting, and her arms dropping from their combative stance. "Sir?"

John placed a possessive hand in the small of Margaret's back. "Mrs Thornton and I will manage Mr Hale's personal effects. You have accomplished a deal here, and we are most grateful. Take this," he searched in his pocket for his coin purse and dispensed the contents into her palm. "Just outside, you can catch an omnibus for a six-pence and take a very pleasant ride out to a charming country town. There are gentle fields and a quaint little marketplace where you may purchase anything you like. I think you will find it most refreshing. I wish you a peaceful day of rest, Dixon."

Dixon accepted the coins, for he would not tolerate a refusal, and stood gaping for another half moment towards her mistress. Margaret cast him a baffled glance but made no moves to countermand his will. He almost wished she would, so he might once more behold that breath-taking, defiant beauty who had so thoroughly shattered his complacency.

Instead, Margaret took the woman's hand lovingly in her own. "You do deserve a day to yourself, Dixon. I expect we will want you to join us at the Marlborough house by tomorrow. Mr Thornton is making the arrangements, so you will be quite comfortable."

She tipped a sly glance to him, and he caught it with a pleased smirk. *There she was.* He had not married a mouse after all.

As Dixon wandered away for her hat and shawl, still stunned and confused, he offered Margaret his hand to the stairs. "Your Miss Dixon disapproves of me."

Margaret took his hand but did not follow at once. "Dixon wished for me to make a different choice."

He stared in puzzlement. She had some option other than marriage to him? The only other possible avenue would have been that of a governess. Fortunately for him, she would be dismally unqualified for the post, for her wilfull nature would inevitably have clashed with her employer.

She gave him no opportunity to ask the question. Her eyes flashed back to his and her hand tightened around his fingers. "Please be gentle with Dixon, John. She is grieving as well, you know. Losing Papa meant losing what she had left of Mamma, and she did love my mother so!"

He gave a tug at her hand and drew her into his arms. She came easily—so willingly! He could almost believe she truly longed for him to hold her. He wrapped her into his chest, delighting in the soft clinging of her arms upon his waistcoat. "I will see she is well cared for, Margaret," he promised into her ear. "She will always have a place in our home. You have my word."

A warm smile pulled at the corners of her mouth—the mouth which was just inches from his own. His pulse hammered, as it always did when he touched her, but he reined himself viciously in check… until her eyes lifted to his. Heaven above, was that a fire kindled in those bright eyes? She held his gaze for a breathless second, and then he watched her eyes dip unconsciously to his own mouth.

His resolve crumbled. He edged very slightly lower, and the most miraculous thing of all happened. Her chin lifted. It was perhaps only by a hairsbreadth, but it was enough.

"*Margaret*," he whispered—almost pleaded. There was the barest perceptible nod as her face tipped nearer, and her eyes fluttered closed.

Her breath played over his sensitive skin, and lightly, tenderly, he grazed her upper lip with his mouth. He moved with aching slowness as she trembled in his arms. She shivered, the rhythm of her breath hitching, but she pressed bravely into his embrace.

Her lips parted, and her chin tipped just a little higher, her body leaning into his. Cautiously, she permitted him more, and even reciprocated the gentle strokes of his lips with hesitant brushes of her own. His courage mounted rapidly with his stirring need. Against all his fears, the woman who had been forced to marry him was gradually unfurling her charms… *for him*. He raised his hand to cup her cheek, to draw her more firmly, but Dixon's heavy footsteps plodded back from her room off the kitchen to interrupt him.

Margaret stiffened away, gasping in apology. He forgave her with a slight shake of his head and a weak smile, swallowing the wordless jumble of emotions that poured through his mind and paralysed his tongue.

"Well, I'll be seeing you later, Miss," Dixon grumbled as she secured her hat.

Margaret drew a short breath. "Ahem, yes, Dixon. We shall likely remain all afternoon. I do hope you enjoy your outing."

Dixon scowled, but was careful not to do so while looking in John's direction and saw herself out the door. It rattled closed, and then they two were the only remaining souls in the house.

John peered through the corner of his eye at her flushed countenance, wondering what it would take to recreate the moment he had just lost. He reached hesitantly for her hand, but she did not heed. She was gazing up the stairs, a look of astonishment and inspiration dawning.

"Margaret? Are you well?" He clenched his fist. If he had somehow distressed her, just when she had begun to turn to him, he would never forgive himself!

She jumped and spun towards him. "John, there is something I must show you! Come, it is in Papa's study!"

She scrambled up the stairs without his assistance, leaving him bewildered behind her. There was nothing to do but to keep up with the rustling black skirts. "Margaret is something wrong?"

She made no answer as she reached the third floor. Instead, she hurried to her father's desk and searched in the top drawer until she found what she sought. Snatching it up, she returned to him with heightened colour warming her cheeks. She visibly caught herself; then, as if offering her whole life in the upturned palm of her hand, extended the object to him.

He took it with a quizzical frown. "A portrait?"

She swallowed and nodded tensely. "Do you recognise the face?"

John raised the miniature to study it more carefully. It was of a young man in a navy midshipman's uniform. He looked to be approximately sixteen at the time the likeness was taken, but he appeared a strong youth with a firm set to his chin and roguish hint about his mouth. The nose was perfectly straight, the eyes clear and light. John squinted and changed the angle of his hand, so he could compare the portrait to his wife. "A relative?" he guessed, though the resemblance was plain enough.

She nodded intently, as though only waiting for him to hit upon the revelation. "You have seen him before, though he was much older… do you remember, John?" Her voice pleaded with him to recall whatever she so desired for him to know.

He stared harder at the miniature, then his stomach dropped, and his hands began to tremble. Margaret's eager nod assured him that he had stumbled upon the correct realisation. "The man at the station!" he marvelled under his breath.

"Yes! Oh, how glad I am that you remembered! John, this is my brother Frederick."

"Brother! Why have I never been told of this?"

Margaret took the miniature back and gazed lovingly at the faded image. "Frederick… he can never come home, John. If anyone heard where he was, he would be hunted down and hanged! He should not have come when our mother was dying, but it was my fault. Mamma asked me to write to him, and we both knew he would never stay away."

"Margaret," he shook his head in confusion. "Perhaps you should start from the beginning. Come, sit down, and tell me what you would have me know."

*Helstone
August 1837*

"Margaret? Shh, come very quietly!"

Margaret rolled drowsily, rubbing the sleep from her eyes. At once she blinked, fully alert. "Is it time now, Fred?"

He pressed a conspiratorial finger to his lips and jerked his head towards the passage. "We mustn't disturb Mamma. Come!"

The child, clad in her little white nightdress, tumbled from her bed. Her brother tucked a blanket round her and picked her up—all the better to avoid detection on their nocturnal adventure. This was to be their last time together for some while, and though most twelve-year-old boys did not relish the company of four-year-old girls, familial loyalty compelled the boy to risk this one last outing.

He tiptoed with her through the parsonage, down the steps and out the back door where a splendid apple tree spread inviting branches. It boasted one particularly comfortable crotch where brother and sister had spent many an hour together, and there they were bound on this night. Perhaps neither considered that it would be Margaret's last opportunity ever to climb a tree, but such it was. After he left, there would be none to assist the child, and she certainly could not do so once she became a young lady.

He hoisted her to their branch and nestled his back against the trunk to pull her securely into his embrace. "Comfortable, Margaret?"

She only nodded, her bright, curious eyes already searching out the gravid moon, hanging low in the sky. They had a perfect view from their little place in the tree as a broken limb above their heads made clear a portal through the leaves. "It is full, Fred, just like you said it would be!"

"What did I tell you? The sixteenth today, that is what the calendar predicted."

"How?" she tilted her head in cynical bafflement. "The calendar is only paper. How can it know what the moon is to do?"

"Why, Margaret, do you not yet know how it works? It's a regular thing, do you see. The moon has her rounds to make, lighting sea faerie paths and frightening off the dragons. She must always be right on time, or the sun will set after her."

She frowned and turned back to him. "You made that up."

"Not the bit about the sea faeries."

She set her little mouth, with its wide, full lips, into an intimidating pout, comical on her youthful features.

"Oh," he relented, "Papa taught me all about it. I suppose that's what made me want to go to sea, really. The moon, and the sun and the stars, they all have their courses. Nothing can alter them—they each march to their proper time, and they are always predictable. Papa said once that is the only bit of the future we are always permitted to know. I don't know about that, but I do like being sure of where I am in the world."

"How does the moon tell you that?"

"Oh, why, in that case, it's not so much the moon as the stars. Do you see… oh, bother these branches. Come down, I will show you."

He took the blanket from her shoulders and spread it upon the grass for them both to lie on. He then set the example, sprawling himself out with his hands laced behind his head. Margaret, her childish arms much shorter by comparison, did her best to follow suit.

"Look," he pointed. "Do you see that shape to the north there? It's called the Plough. See how bright all the stars are?"

"Yes, I see it."

"Now, look at the two stars nearest the bottom. See how you can draw a line from them to that other star there, off to the right?"

"That one? It is not very bright." She squinted, grimacing as small children so often do when concentrating very hard.

"Not as bright as others, but it is the most important. We call that one the North Star, or Polaris in Latin. Everything else will rotate, but Polaris always stays exactly where it is. It's how we navigate the ships." He spoke, as boys are wont to do, as one who has already passed all initiations and earned his place among the men he longed to join. His father would have chided him, but his little sister only grinned in appreciation.

"So, you see, Margaret," he continued, "that star always points north—nowhere else. It's like home, if you will—if I know where it is, I can find where I am going. Why, I can even tell how far north or south I am by how high it sits in the heavens!"

She was silent for several minutes, then, in a small, frightened voice; "Will you know where I am?"

He glanced to her in surprise. Her face, bathed in moonlight, cast a worried expression. "Why, of course, dearest little sister! Even on the sea, I shall know which way England lies, and there you will be."

She swallowed, her features settling into a more stubborn frame. "I think you should stay here, Fred. I shall never leave Helstone."

"You will, you just do not know it yet. Papa and Mamma plan to send you to London when you turn nine to take lessons with Edith. Oh, do not look so frightened! You shall be quite old enough, and that little cat of yours will be busy with a dozen kittens of her own."

"I will come back and live here forever when I am finished, then," she announced.

He chuckled at her innocent decisiveness. "I imagine that choice will not be yours to make, but no sense worrying about such things now, dear one."

"How long will you be gone, Fred?"

"Well, it will be two years before I even put to sea. I've some studies to complete, and then I shall be a cadet. After that, I must work another year or two on ship before I earn my midshipman's rank. I hope to make Lieutenant by the time I am twenty."

Her face fell. He supposed that twenty must be ancient, and eight years an eternity to a child of her age.

"Come, Margaret, it is not so bad! I will have leave to come home once in a while, surely. Let me show you a few more stars, so you will always know where to look up. I will be seeing the same stars, do you know. Let me see… ah, there she is. Andromeda, the Chained Maiden—or, as I like to call her, the Northern Princess. Poor girl, she was taken to an awful place to be sacrificed because her parents were vain and foolish. And then, in flew Perseus on his great steed Pegasus… there he is… and he saved her from a hideous fate. Just like St George!"

Wide eyes gazed back in astonishment. "Is that true, Fred?"

"Naturally." He chucked her chin. "Heroes always save the princesses. That is what I shall do someday, Margaret. There is nothing like the navy for adventure!"

~

London
29 April 1847

"Margaret, dear, a letter is arrived for you!" Mrs Shaw, with her prim curls and still youthful looks, breezed into the schoolroom. Edith and Margaret both glanced up from their studies.

"It is from your father." Gifting the letter into her niece's hand, she left the room.

Margaret, ever eager for news from home, tore into it with trembling fingers. "Oh, I hope he is to be early this spring. I am so longing for him to come take me back to Helstone!"

Edith, boasting her mother's bright curls and merry, round cheeks, tilted back in her chair. "If I did not know better, Margaret, I should say you did not like being here in London with us."

Margaret flashed a brief, embarrassed smile to her cousin, but quickly her attention turned to her father's sober hand. Within only a few lines, her face had drained of all colour. Edith emitted a brief cry of alarm as Margaret's eyes grew wide and her lips parted in horror.

"Margaret, what is it? Is Aunt unwell?"

Margaret had leaped to her feet and stood, clutching the letter. Her brow furrowed and rippled in agonised little jerks. "Fred!" she gasped. "No, it cannot be!"

Edith, not yet so mannerly as her mother would perhaps have wished, came to snatch the letter from her. "What is it?"

"Frederick! Papa writes that there has been some terrible mistake. He—" she clenched her fist and buried her face in it to sob. "He has been branded a traitor!"

"Surely not! Frederick is as honourable as anyone. He would never have betrayed his duty."

"Papa does not believe he did." Margaret took the letter back, searching the short missive for understanding which was denied her. "He writes… oh, but he does not know!"

"Know what, Margaret?"

She shook her head numbly. "There has been some news about Captain Reid and his officers being recovered from a boat after a mutiny. Frederick was not among them!"

"But what can that mean, Margaret? Frederick was not a senior officer, there was no reason for him to have been set adrift as well."

"It means, Edith, that Fredrick has been counted among the mutineers."

"No! Why, that means…."

Margaret was trembling, the tears beginning to stream down her cheeks. "There must be justice! They cannot hang him, Edith! Surely, he was acting against some great wrong. I know him!"

Edith shook her head. "Do you suppose he was provoked? That he lost his temper, perhaps?"

"I cannot think but that he was an innocent party!"

"Darling!" Edith drew a comforting arm about her cousin. "You remember how Fred has written of heroism and adventure. Is it possible he thought his captain gravely in the wrong?"

"I think that a certainty. He must have been trying to save another, but what good is it to be right when the law is against him? Oh, Edith, he is under a death sentence!"

"Come, Margaret, there will be an investigation. Frederick is not the man to run after all! He will be seeking to clear his name, and when all is discovered, everything will turn out right! You will see."

Margaret bowed her head and fell to her chair, sobbing. "No, Edith. Father is right! Frederick can never return to England, and we shall never see him again."

John had taken back the miniature, staring blindly at the face of his lawful brother. A brother! And such a man—John could not decide if he thought the fellow dreadfully impulsive or impossibly honourable.

"You say that he lives in Spain now?" he asked in a quaking voice.

"Yes, in Cadiz. He married some months ago—her name is Dolores. She sounds most endearing in her letters."

"What has been done to investigate his case?"

Margaret drew a sharp breath and her gaze fell to the portrait. Sensing her distress, he reached to touch her hand. "Margaret, you do remember that I am a magistrate?"

She nodded, her eyes still low. "I know that it is asking a great deal of you," she whispered miserably. "Please, John, I beg that you would not report him! He is so far away, surely he can do no harm—"

"Margaret! You mistake me, my love!"

Her head snapped up, and she regarded him with open wonder. "Wh-what did you say?"

John's stomach clenched. Had that really slipped from his tongue, so naturally and without precedent? "I..." he faltered and looked helplessly into her beseeching face.

"I said 'my love.' You are my love, you know, Margaret. I thought you should not like to hear it, but I swore to you once that I should love you in defiance of all you might say against me, and indeed, in spite of myself. I have ever done so and shall continue so long as I draw breath."

Tears had started in her eyes. "But you could not have! How could you not hold me in utter contempt? I was so cruel, and then I grasped at a lie to save myself!"

"Margaret, my Margaret," he soothed. He cupped his hands round her face and drew her tenderly close. "I forgave you long ago, for every 'offence' you now claim. How could I do aught but love you? Was I to despise you for my own failings? I knew even then that there must be some justification, for though I doubted at first—though I endured such imaginings as would astound and mortify you, your character was the one thing I found I could be certain of."

"But what you must have thought! You cannot know how I longed to explain it all to you. I knew how vexed, how—"

"Jealous? Aye, I was, I confess it—despicable feeling, and I was sick with it! I would have traded my immortal soul for such an embrace from you, but I loved you all the more, and could see no harm come to you."

"And it was you who saved him—saved me! You, the one man whose good opinion I longed for, knew all my shame and yet did not condemn me. I am unworthy, John!"

"Let us not speak so, for my own sense of unworthiness must be far greater. You must no longer lower your eyes before me, nor speak as if under condemnation. I believed in your virtue even when I would have cursed him who had won your love.

"And now the truth of it—oh, my Margaret, all this time he was your brother! Little wonder you were so desperate to protect him. You were trying to defend an innocent man and had no help or means at your disposal. I promise, love, you shall never have to act alone again! If there may be justice for your brother, I will do all that can be done."

Margaret's fearful trembles had begun to slow in the warmth of his assurances, but present instead was an entirely new sort of shiver. Her eyes, fixed so earnestly on his face, had darkened, and her full lips parted. He stroked the rounded edge of her cheek with tender fingers.

"There is one thing more I must know. Your brother, and this cousin you mentioned—would either have taken you in when your father died?"

Her breathing, quick and shallow under the restraint of her stays, intensified. "Yes," she answered guiltily. "Both surely will be disappointed that I did not go to them. Edith lives in Greece now with her husband—a Captain Lennox. They were expected to have returned to England by last year but matters in his regiment have detained them some while longer. I know she would have wished me to come to her, though.

"Dixon proposed that we sell the furniture and purchase passage to Corfu immediately, even before a letter could arrive. As she says, Edith and the captain are sure to return to England when his commission is up, and when they do, my aunt will return from her own travels abroad. I might have come back with them all to live in London again."

He studied her for a long moment before begging the question which might answer for his every aching desire. "Then why would you settle for me?"

Her eyes widened innocently. "I did not settle! I married you because I wished to—because after coming to know you, I realised I could never esteem another, but I was such a fool! I thought I had lost you forever, and rightly so. When you came that evening, I hoped it meant you might still cherish some little affection for me, unworthy though I was. Oh, please, John, I never meant to take advantage—"

"'Some little affection'!" cried he, his tones broken with both anguish and elation. "Have I been so cold that you were uncertain of my love? I shall declare it every day, over and again until you grow weary of hearing!"

She was sobbing, laughing for joy. "Then you shall be repeating it forever, and so shall I! I love you, John Thornton, and I wish to live out my days by your side."

Had he gone suddenly mad? Was he delirious? For Margaret was there, nearly in his arms, and reaching for him, swearing the love he had believed impossible. His throat seemed numb, his eyes incapable of any action but simply to stare at her, wondering, as her fingers brushed his temples. Her eyes shone, and her fingers slipped to his jaw, so near his mouth.

He could deny himself no longer. His face shining in purest ecstasy, he pulled her against himself and greedily sought her lips. This time, there was no hesitant subtlety in his embrace, nor did Margaret quail in his arms. They reached for each other as though another instant apart might suffocate them, and together, they at last learned to breathe.

He pressed her against the back of the sofa, his hands sweeping over her precious face, tangling in her once perfectly dressed hair, and cradling her waist. He kissed her mercilessly, hungrily, as though in that moment he could devour her sweetness and take forever to himself that spark of hers which had lighted his life. Gone was the wilting lily who had come meekly to his home, uncertain of her welcome and weakened with grief and shame. In his arms now throve the wildly passionate, headstrong woman whose graceful power over him had so many times caused him to defy his better sense. Each brush of her lips, every little gasp and shiver, drove him further beyond his own control.

Her fingers splayed through his hair, twisting and caressing, and drawing him ever closer. He braced an arm behind her back, helping her to shift beneath him, and pressed the full length of his upper body over hers. "Margaret," he sighed into her neck, nipping and nuzzling the tender flesh below her ear. A light, feminine cry of surprise and pleasure rewarded his eager attempts. He lifted his face from that sweet cleft to admire the deliciously hypnotised euphoria diffusing over her beautiful features.

"J—John," she pleaded, "oh, do not stop." She hooked soft fingers under his jaw to pull him lower once more. Groaning helplessly, he covered her mouth, capturing each divine breath for his own.

His free hand began to wander her delicate form, trapped beneath his. Timidly at first, he explored the line of her collarbone, visible now as she reclined against his forearm. He felt her gasp and raised his mouth from hers. Full, trusting eyes gazed openly back to him as soft fingers trailed over his cheek. He pressed another gentle kiss of reassurance to those succulent lips, then lowered his mouth to the untouched flesh, dipping just above the swell of her bosom.

She drank in a breath, her breast rising and falling in little gasping shudders. Only a glimmer of her delicious skin was bared by the modest gown she wore, but it was enough. Intoxicated and utterly beyond himself, he tipped his chin to slip teasing kisses up the ivory column of her neck, then tracing down to the edge of her laced décolletage. Her head lifted from his arm in protest, then fell back again in surrender as she breathed out his name.

How long had this very dream tormented his nights? Banished forever was the haunting nightmare of Margaret in another man's arms, that inglorious Duessa manifested in his tortured imagination! His Margaret, his pure and faithful queen, called out only for him. The heady rapture of this realisation nearly blinded and choked him, and he braced his shaking hand against the curve of her waist to steady himself.

Margaret stilled below him, her breathing tight and shallow. She raised darkened eyes to him, granting the permission she knew he longed for. Full of reverent disbelief, his worshipful fingers followed the sweep of her black gown until his thumb and forefinger cupped beneath the soft mound pressed to his chest. She tensed but did not flinch away. After only the barest hesitation, she arched tremblingly into his touch, her breath whispering into his neck.

John claimed her mouth again, his manner gently seductive now rather than ravishing. His fingers curled, testing the layers of satin and whalebone edging between them. Her warmth and shivering approval of his advances thoroughly crowded his mind! If he continued, without checking himself, a scarce few moments would see him stripping away those last barriers to her feminine secrets and tasting for himself the treasures which had always before remained a mystery.

He swallowed hard as he opened his eyes and forced himself to look on her black gown, and to consider all the reasons for it. Panting and shaking, almost ready to fling away all other cares, he pushed himself back. "Margaret," he choked, "we must not—not here!"

Her eyes closed, and she trapped her lower lip in small white teeth. "You must think very little of my dignity."

"Not of yours, but of my own!" He eased his weight from her. "Forgive me. I am afraid I have quite forgotten all propriety."

Margaret accepted his hand and raised herself to a sitting position. "There is nothing to forgive. You had sufficient encouragement, I think."

He felt a carefree grin overcome his features, the first of such he had known in years. "Margaret! I hope you may ever continue to encourage me so! He is a blessed man whose wife welcomes his attentions."

She blushed, her tousled hair falling rakishly low over her cheeks and her clear eyes sparking with amusement. "It is no disagreeable task, John."

A joyous laugh rumbled in his chest. "Come, we must tend to other matters, or I will surely lose my mind once more—and I make no promises that I will be able to recall myself again." He rose and extended his hand to help her to her feet, then pulled her into his arms. "I only ask one thing."

Margaret sighed and rested her cheek on his chest, closing her eyes and embracing him for one last, sweet moment before they commenced their sad duties. "What is that?"

"Let us finish quickly here, and hurry home," he murmured into her ruffled tresses.

Margaret's arms slid up, round his shoulders, and he felt her slim body shaking in a brief chuckle. "Agreed, John."

~

Almost nothing was settled that day of Mr Hale's affairs. Margaret moved about the study in a sorrowful daze, more often than not with one hand twined through John's fingers as she sought his reassuring touch. Blindly, she stood back from the ponderous bookshelves and glanced unseeingly over the stacks of hand-written sermons. At each point of indecision, John's loving arms would wrap about her, offering solace and a good deal more.

These interruptions always began innocently enough, but after the fourth— or perhaps the fifth—such occasion, when John was giving serious consideration to the fact that Margaret's maiden bedroom stood silent and inviting on the lower floor, he forced his aching hands down from her.

"Margaret," he nuzzled to her ear, "I will send a few men over here tomorrow to crate up everything that is left and bring it all to a few spare rooms in the house. You need not decide in haste, but sort through at your leisure. Let me take you home now to rest."

She sighed in relief. "I would appreciate that, John."

With the very greatest care, he escorted her below and gave notice to the driver waiting outside that he and his Mrs Thornton wished to depart. How well that sounded! He was beaming in pride when he returned to help her into her cloak and bonnet. For the first time, he felt himself the honoured husband of a much-treasured wife—a wife who gladly bore his name and found pleasure in his company. No more blessed man could have existed in all the kingdom; of that, he was quite certain!

"Are you warm enough?" he asked, tucking her under his arm as the carriage pulled away.

She nodded into his shoulder, then straightened. "Oh, dear! I forgot my house slippers again."

He laughed, easily enough, but a deeper timbre to his cheerfulness suggested a heat which he had nearly always before kept hidden from her. "If you can survive but a few moments without them this evening, I will see to your comfort thereafter. That is, if you will permit me."

Her cheeks reddened. "I… that is, I should be glad of… what I mean is—"

Her stumbling attempts at a receptive answer ceased when he slipped his other arm about her and pulled her close. "Just leave the door cracked, love. I will understand what you wish."

She nodded, and he gave her no cause to speak again until they had returned to the house which both could now call home.

~

Hannah Thornton had long been fascinated by the marvellous technology that powered her son's mill. Well did she recall her first visit to a similar factory—the impressive power of the massive engine, harnessed and directed by man's will, was wholly unmatched in their time.

The awesome capacity for strength and creation were nothing to her, however, without the hand-thrown lever which locked all the drive shafts into play. Absent that detail, everything might remain cold and lifeless. Once that small mechanism engaged, a world of possibility expanded for the pulsing, charging beast of the whole industry.

Such were her thoughts this evening as she sat at dinner, gazing at her new daughter-in-law. Someone—none but her son, she realised with humiliation—had thrown that great lever in the former Miss Hale. The young woman who now graced the end of the table—her old place!—was not at all the broken, dejected girl who had first come to it three days prior. Her manner was bright and confident, a blush stained her cheeks, and if Hannah were not mistaken, her lips were softly full and flushed as never before. Her chin she held high and proud, and her dazzled eyes sought only John.

With fearful reluctance, she dared herself to look to her left. What would she find if she looked into the eyes of the boy she had raised? The face she encountered made her blood chill.

He was smiling. It was not the easy, carefree expression she knew from former days, nor was it the masterful gleam she had grown accustomed to as her son found success in life. This was an entirely new light beaming forth from his beloved countenance. He was at peace and overflowing with such powerful feeling that even his mother could scarcely command a second of his attention.

The couple—for such, she could see plainly, they had now become—exchanged tender, silent looks of such warmth and intimacy that Hannah felt herself quite the interloper. Some barrier had fallen during those hours in the old Hale residence. She sighed and dropped her gaze to her plate, unable to look on any longer.

John deserves this, she counselled herself. *How long did he put aside his own joy?* For so many years had he been her sole possession, turning to none but her when life's cares tore at him. He had taken the diligent training in self-discipline she offered at their point of need, and crafted it into something finer, stricter, more purposeful—she did not quite like to call it prideful, yet she found her own pride in his success. He was better than the father who had lent him strength, better even than the mother who had cherished and sent him forth into this life… and he had been entirely hers.

John had suffered an attraction to women as a young man, to be sure—she could not have respected him as she did, had he not proved himself stronger than his flesh. What made the maternal satisfaction flourish in her soul was his utter victory at training his own eyes, mind, and—she had once thought—his heart. Never had women troubled him against his wishes since those long-gone days of boyhood—never, until that one day eighteen months prior when he had approached her with that bashful half-smile and asked her to call on some new ladies in town. Perhaps that was the moment when the dread began its fatal twist round her motherly heart.

She raised sullen eyes to the blushing bride to her right. Oh, yes, Margaret had secured her boy, in almost every possible way a woman could—but how long would the girl's affection last? Had she not already proof that the lass was perfectly capable of a fickle change of sentiment? What would be the catalyst for her inevitable disenchantment; when the vain charm of her husband's attentions faded, and the life of a manufacturer's wife wore down that aristocratic bearing?

How such a girl's pride would suffer, when she awakened one morning to the blast of the steam whistle and discovered her existence to be nothing at all like the fairy tale she had doubtless concocted! There would be no turning back for any of them—Margaret Thornton was to live out her days a middle-class matron. Whether she would find satisfaction in that life remained to be seen.

Hannah prodded her meal listlessly and set aside her fork. John glanced up in mild surprise. In truth, she thought in some annoyance, it was the first time he had looked directly at her all evening. Her John, her light and comforter, was lost.

She closed her eyes, scolding herself. *You knew this day would come!* Was it not the very outcome she had desired, and even perhaps had a hand in setting to motion when she had fairly driven Margaret from the drawing-room and into his arms the previous evening?

The battle was over, and there was nothing left for her to do but to retire from the field and hope for better days. She could scarcely look the victorious young woman in the face, and the thought of hours spent as a superfluity in the company of lovers was unbearable!

"John," she spoke shakily, her eyes on the new bride, "I fear Margaret looks rather flushed this evening."

Margaret traded curious glances with her husband. She looked self-consciously to the backs of her hands, trying to detect this terrifying colour which Hannah attributed to her.

"Margaret—" that familiar name still caught between her teeth—"though our evening regimen has been inflexible these ten years, it is only natural and suitable that in your state of mourning you may wish to seek some time for quiet spiritual reflection. There need be no expectation for you to join the household devotions if you prefer privacy. Perhaps I ought to have mentioned it before."

Margaret was still gazing back uncomprehendingly, but a flicker of inspiration had certainly dawned on John's face. Mortified, Hannah tried to force another nonchalant bite of her meal.

"It is an excellent point, Margaret," he agreed. "If you like, I shall escort you to your room whenever you might wish to retire early."

Hannah swallowed. She had hoped that John would allow Margaret to retreat in peaceful solitude, freeing himself to spend a final quiet hour with her by the fire before his wife's demands consumed him. It was not to be so.

Margaret's cheeks brightened, and she stared, wide-eyed, at her plate. "Thank you for your consideration, madam."

Hannah only thinned her lips. It felt like the final blow to her long reign in his life, but in fact, those cords had begun to loosen over a year and a half ago. It was only strange, she consoled herself, because John had so long lived without any sort of feminine attention but her own. Perhaps she ought instead to be grateful that her son had chosen such a path when so many did not.

Six

Weston
17 October 1838

Fifteen-year-old John Thornton stopped before the door of the humble residence, jingling his week's earnings in his pocket. It was not his own door at which he stood, but one just a row down. It was a house near which one did not wish to be seen.

For a year now—exactly a year, in fact—he had assumed the role of a man, while yet a boy. He had borne the challenge stoically, refusing to cower under his feelings of shame. He was no longer a child… and he was no longer his father's son! That regret was long past, he had spent the year assuring himself.

The cares and labours of manhood were upon him, and with them, a new sense of himself. He had grown tall and broad of shoulder, and many mistook him for a young man of nine and ten. Nothing of his lost youth remained, and these days, he was feeling quite proud of that fact. New feelings and ideas had begun to occur to him in the past months, and in the consuming fire typical of burgeoning masculinity, he could think of little else.

It was his right, he consoled himself—his reward for this last year. He was a man now, and a man had needs. His observations informed him that he was far from the only one to bring them to this house.

His fingers twitched again in his pocket, sweating now. He was most certainly *not* nervous. A business transaction, that was all this was; one to alleviate his cravings and clear his head once more. He could conceive of no good reason for his throat to be suddenly parched.

Squaring his shoulders, he rapped on the door. It opened to him slowly, and, squinting, he entered. Rosemary—that was the only name anyone called her. She was in her late twenties, but the bloom had long since faded from her cheeks. She possessed other assets, however, which more than made up for her lack of innocence.

John stared at the ample flesh bared before him in the dark room. He was having some trouble swallowing. He had seen ladies' evening gowns that lavishly displayed the bounties of alluring young gentlewomen, eager to ensnare a husband, but this was more blatant, even, than that. Rosemary's low-scooped bodice left little to his active imagination. The blood pounded in his ears and in a number of other places as well.

Mumbling his request, he dipped his hand into his pocket and emptied it on her battered table. Rouge-tinted lips smiled, and his money disappeared. Uncertain what he was to do next, he stayed... waiting.

Rosemary turned away from him, and with practised fingers, began to free herself of her outer garments. His keen gaze caught a bare shoulder, and then a glimpse of her curved lower neck as her top slipped. His eager hands reached out, but just before he touched her, from somewhere in the back of the house, a babe started to cry. He stopped, his limbs quivering.

The fallen angel before him muttered a low curse and urged him to pay it no mind. Perhaps her bit of professional courtesy might have lent another man all the courage he required, but John's bravado shattered. Rather than the ravishing seductress he had seen a moment ago, the young lad now beheld a tired, care-worn mother, broken by other men. His forehead beaded in a sudden sweat.

He blinked, panting, and tried vainly to banish the righteous thoughts intruding upon his conscience. The rash moment of glory, however, was gone. Rosemary peered at him curiously, her bodice drooping provocatively, but John could not even bring himself to look on what he had so desired only seconds before. He twisted his head away, shielding his eyes with his hand. His breath heaved and his entire being flooded with regret and humiliation. Stammering a hasty excuse, he spun out of her door and slammed it behind himself.

John stood alone on the street, but this was not a place he could bear to linger. Not knowing quite what he was about, he began walking. He walked until he could breathe once more, and until the sweat had dried from his brow. He walked until he could hear the voices around him rather than the screaming of his own conscience in his ears. He walked until he almost forgot where he was—and then farther, until the passing humanity dissipated.

He hated himself. What a selfish, prideful little idiot he was! He had thought to call himself a man, but a man's honour was in the keeping of his own, not dissipation in idle pleasures. And what had he done with this week's wages? Lost!

How was he to confess this to his mother? She, who had so diligently taught him to work, to budget, to save—she, who had such faith in him! How was he to tell her he had intended to throw over his integrity for a few moments of boyish lust? He could not!

He looked around, at last recognising where nearly two hours of his aimless and frenetic strides had carried him. The Milton graveyard, on the farthest western outskirt of the city. There was no surer place to seek his solitude, to castigate himself without the trouble of witnesses. Well... if he could not confess the truth to his mother, he would take his anger out on his other parent. His steps coming in a frenzied rush, he descended upon that fresh stone—the one he and his mother had so painstakingly saved to purchase.

"You!" he snarled to the silent stone as he marched towards it. "*You* are to blame! For Mother's grief, for Fanny's illness, for the days I spend in the draper's shop—all of it! It was your selfishness which brought this shame to us!"

His fists beat upon that stone until his flesh was torn, then he slashed at the unyielding granite with a contemptuous and satisfyingly irreverent kick. Violent sobs racked him then, and he collapsed. He remained there, gasping through his inarticulate cries of fury, for many long moments.

Conviction was slow to dawn, but faithfully, it did so. He clenched his eyes against his own disgrace. How was he any better than his father? He had nearly succumbed to his own temporal desires, had he not? He had harmed his family by squandering his hard-earned pay. What were they even to eat for this next week? Burying his face in his grime-covered palms, he raged in anguish, his youthful body shaking in the throes of his disgust with himself.

After a few moments, an inspiration pricked him. It could all be forgotten. He need not return to his mother empty-handed! Furiously, he dug in his other pocket for the watch she had given him. His father's... as if he wanted *anything* belonging to that man! Snatching it up, he laughed in relief. He could sell it, fetch a handsome price, and perhaps even buy his mother that new dress she so badly needed!

As he wrung the chain, shaking the watch as if it were his own father's miserable neck, his eyes caught the time. Half-past three, on the nose.

It was wrong, of course. It was, in fact, much later now, as he had already worked his full shift at the draper's shop before his shameful errand. He shook the watch again, wondering why it had stopped with its hands in that precise position. What sadistic turn of events would cause it to pause at the exact moment when that gunshot rang out last year—and on this day, of all days?

His eyes flooded with emotion, but not a single tear did he shed. He was the only man left to his family, and a man did not do such a thing. He drew a long breath and restored the watch to its proper place in his pocket. A man did not weep, and a man did not lie. He rose, dusting the grass from his clothing, and made his long, sorrowful journey back to that little shack they called home.

He found his mother sitting in silence, her back to the door. She did not turn her face to him as he entered. He braced his lanky frame, not daring to allow himself to delay his confession even a moment, lest he forever lose the courage to do so. "Mother," rasped he, his voice hesitant and broken. "I have disgraced you!"

Hannah Thornton sat immovably. Her reply was faint, spoken in a shaken tone. "You could never disgrace me, John. You are my son."

He closed his eyes and swallowed. "You do not know what I have done!"

She turned to him at last, her ebony gaze tipping up to him. "I saw, John. I was on the street. I saw you go in, and I saw you leave."

He groaned and sank to the floor behind her, his face in his hands. "I have no right to even speak to you," he mumbled between his fingers. "What must you think of your son?"

"I think my son is a man."

"I am a fool! A selfish braggart who wished to please himself, to the detriment of his family!"

"A *boy* would not have come to such a conclusion."

He shuddered in another vexatious sob. "I have acted the coward this day! I thought to hide for a time from my own cares, and I have only increased your burden."

Hannah stood and rested a gentle hand on his shoulder as he hid his face from her. "John," she commanded his attention. Regretfully, he looked up. "It is not evidence of manhood to display your prowess before the world. A man's nobility is his own, independent of circumstances or prevailing opinions. Others may slink in shame and then try to cover their degradation, but that is not a path you need follow. You are free to choose a better way, but no other can determine your course for you."

He blinked, still uncomfortable holding her gaze. "Mother," he whispered, "I would have you know nothing happened."

"I know, John." She turned the flimsy chair round to him, then rested herself at his side and took his blood-streaked hand in hers. She squeezed it, looking down as if gathering her thoughts.

"One day, my son, some other woman will catch your eye. She will be fine and strong, and worthy of you, my John. Do not give your strength, your dignity, or your affections to one less deserving, for you would rob the woman you love of what ought rightfully to be hers."

His breath caught, his head sagged... and his blessed mother stroked his hair until his face leaned against her knee, as she had used to do when he was a child. She placed so much faith in him, but these glorious hopes of hers seemed so distant just now!

"Mother, I cannot at present see beyond our debts. What woman would ever have me?"

She caressed his roughened cheek with a tender hand. "A very fortunate one, John."

He stared at the hearth—dark as always, for coal was too costly—and his vision lost focus. "I went to Father's grave today," he murmured, as though the two subjects were somehow linked together.

His mother's hand stilled. "Oh?" she replied, a tremor in her voice.

"I think I understand something. What I want—what I expect... and what Father did not see."

She seemed to hold her breath. "And what is that?"

His jaw clenched. "Honour. I wish to be a man of honour, Mother, for my dignity is dearer to me than any other possession. And I shall begin by honouring the man who set me on this course. I shall no longer despise him. If not for him, I would not face my present difficulties, and I choose to be strengthened rather than broken. I will care for you and Fanny in every way, and I will look back with respect for the opportunity I have been granted."

Hannah released a tight breath. "Then, my John, you are indeed a man now."

He had been waiting for her.

Margaret smoothed her gown and stepped into her bedroom, her hair loosed, and her body flushed with innocent anticipation. John had been there some while already, seated by the fire in a simple dressing robe. He rose, walking towards her with his face awash in wonder, as if in a trance.

"Margaret, my own Margaret," he murmured dreamily, taking her into his arms. She closed her eyes and rested her cheek against him, secure and welcome at last. His chest rose in a long, steadying breath as he began to lovingly stroke the hidden contours of her body.

She slid her hands over his shoulders, down the fine muscles of his form. Her fingers caught and stiffened when they encountered his warm, bare flesh as his robe slipped under her touch. A tremor quaked through her—a final hesitation in this last moment before she gave him everything. He felt her pause and drew back, a question darkening his brow.

She allowed her gaze to wander his frame, so tall and powerful. Black, unfamiliar hairs curled where his clothing had pulled away… his shape, all the chiselled contours of his body were foreign to her experience. What was it, precisely, that he desired of her, and how could she begin to hold him?—he who was as a giant to her in both body and spirit? Again, came the sense that she barely knew him, could not understand his feelings, and some inner part of her shrank.

His fingers traced her chin, and he leaned close to brush a kiss over her forehead. "Love, are you as frightened as I?"

She shivered in a nervous acknowledgment, then her eyes grew wide and she looked to his face. "You?"

"I have… spent many years alone," he confessed. "Until you… it was impossible. I could not be so vulnerable with any other as with you—you, whom I worship above anything else under heaven, and you terrify me, my love. I can no longer conceal my darkest secrets, not from you. What will you think of me when you discover my frailties, my doubts, my inadequacies?"

"I will think… that you must understand something of my own insecurities, and that we are more alike than I had ever imagined. I will think perhaps… perhaps I have nothing to fear in you."

He smiled, those blue eyes kindling once more. "Will you come to me then, my Margaret?"

A thrill rose, heat building in her core as one of his hands dropped again to her waist and the other caressed the back of her neck. Her throat caught before she could speak, so she nodded faintly into his hand, blinking uncontrollably. "S-slowly?" she whispered.

He kissed the lobe of her ear, his breath hot on her bare skin. "If it takes the rest of my life."

Fire coursed through her flesh—prickling and searing. Her stomach fluttered wildly, and an ache welled up within her. More. She wanted… no, she *needed* more. *All* of him, this man who captivated her, and she would never be content until she had discovered his last secret, unveiled each passion and aroused every buried thirst so she might be the one to quench it.

It was as if his lips and his hands explored all her most intimate places. Every nerve snapped at his touch, his fervid, barely restrained caresses begetting violent quakes throughout her body. His kisses unravelled something deep within—an urgency and a boldness she had never experienced. If he did not satisfy this primal, desperate craving he had awakened, she would shatter!

"John," she panted, her teeth bared against his throat as she clutched his shoulders, "hold me!"

He cupped her face in trembling hands, stroking her cheeks with his thumbs, and trailed light kisses over her brows as his own tremors steadied. When he drew back, she looked up and answered the question she found in his eyes with breathless pleading. That moment of doubt was already a thing of distant memory, and her only wish to plunge fully into this rising swell of desire.

Her fingernails sank into the tender flesh at the back of his neck. Oh, how she loved the sense of him, the way his touch both ignited and soothed her! He bent to drop more kisses over her bared shoulders, and she shivered when the ghostly white cotton of her shift lifted, grazing over tender skin. She never felt, never saw, but she heard the filmy layers of his robe whisper to the ground. She pressed into him, trusting him to shield her and thrilling to the heat of his skin against hers.

Strong arms caught her up, and she left the cold floor for the soft warmth of her bed and *him*. She reached for him; his shadow fell over her, and there was nothing but his gentle hands, his finely muscled weight, and his deep loving voice in her ears. New sensations tingled and enflamed, piercing her core as they discovered the heavenly sanctuary made for lovers.

She tensed; a flash of pain, overcome by worshipful awe as they united in one flesh. His eyes, so eloquently declaring his astonished exhilaration, flashed brilliantly and then closed, engulfed in a wonder he could not express. She clasped him to herself, yearning for the same as he, and sobbed for joy as he cried out to her with a tender desperation she had never heard. They trembled together—a last, bated breath, and then a sheet of blinding ecstasy wrung his name from her lips before they fell as one in sated completion.

~

John, deliriously weary, cradled his arm beneath Margaret's body and pressed a reverent kiss to her neck, then pillowed his cheek on her soft shoulder. It was a long while before the heady rapture faded, so they lay, still shivering and astounded at the intimate miracle they had shared. Slowly, he came to himself, as her light fingers began drowsily to toy with his hair.

He rolled his head up and met her euphoric smile with one of his own. "Are you well?"

Her breast, on which his chin now rested, rose and fell in lethargic bliss. "Perfectly, John." Her fingers traced from his hair, up the back of his ear, and smoothed the lines of concern furrowing his brow.

He raised himself to kiss her, then resumed his comfortable posture gazing into her face. He sighed luxuriantly, and as fatigue began to take him, he nestled his cheek once more to her soft warmth. An entirely new vista awaited him there—rich, gentle curves and secret treasures he had never dared imagine. Perhaps, though, it was not right for him to stare so, when it left her vulnerable to any passing draught. Reluctantly, he tucked a corner of the rumpled sheets up over her prickled flesh and felt a minuscule drop under his chin as she relaxed still more.

"Better?" he mumbled into the one bit of bare skin he had claimed for himself.

"Mmmm." Her fingers found his hair once more, and his neck tingled with the pleasure of her touch.

In return, he slipped his hand beneath the sheet to trace out that curious little dimple in her stomach which testified to her mortality. But for that, he would have imagined himself to be dreaming, or perhaps even passed on to whatever eternal reward he might have merited.

A low chuckle rumbled in his throat at that thought. No, this could not be heaven, for he had earned no such paradise! It was all the work of her generous, gracious affection... and perhaps, more than her fair measure of loneliness.

"Why are you laughing?" she wondered, sounding far more alert than he felt.

He rocked upright again. "I was musing on my good fortune." His finger continued its lazy circles about her navel, and he dropped his eyes suggestively in that direction before smiling again at her.

"I thought you did not believe in fortune or luck—had no use at all for it."

"It never had much use for me, I will say that—until now."

Her eyes creased at the corners in gentle amusement. There was, however, that hint of sorrow behind them which he, of all people, could not fail to recognise.

His cheer faded instantly. "Oh, Margaret, forgive me! I did not mean—"

She hushed him with a finger to his lips and a slight shake of her head. "Please, John, not now. Let me think only of pleasant things tonight."

"Am I to be counted among these pleasant things?"

Her smile widened, and that flicker of sadness vanished. "The most pleasant of all."

He propped up on his elbow. "Margaret, you never told me why, and I was so eager to call you my own that I never dared to ask."

She straightened her neck to look at him more directly. "Why what, John?"

"What changed your mind about me? The things you told me this afternoon—am I justified in believing your feelings had altered before... well, some while ago?"

"I believe you had scarcely left me that first day—you remember—when I learned to think differently of you. Perhaps I realised then what I had refused to confess to myself—that I worked so hard to dislike you because there was some quality about you that I could not at all dislike."

"And you wished to? Too far beneath you, am I not?"

She hid her face in his chest in humiliated conviction. "John, I... oh, please, I was so wrong! I was proud and foolish, to have looked down on you as I did—but you did irritate me so! Why could you not simply have been what I expected you to be?"

"And what did you expect, love?"

"That you would prove safely and entirely disagreeable. How very contrary of you to make me love you! I tried to make you out as one I could ignore, but you simply would not permit me to do so."

"Fancy that! The most glorious woman I have ever known, and I should not wish for her to ignore me? Indeed, I was a recalcitrant beast."

"You have ruined my view of all men, I shall have you know," she informed him tartly. "It was most unfair, for now I am utterly incapable of admiring an ordinary gentleman."

"First you confess to wishing you did not love me, now you would call me—what was it—not ordinary? You may as well say I am peculiar! I wonder, love, to which of my attributes you object. Perhaps you find me too tall, or my voice too deep. My height I might ameliorate by a stooped posture, but I cannot alter the other."

"If you insist on teasing me, I shall refuse to pay you the compliments you so obviously wish to hear."

He adopted a perfectly sober expression, but his composed innocence was betrayed by the tormenting finger that continued to threaten her bare stomach and ticklish ribs. She arched a brow and he surrendered with a laugh. "I shall behave, love, but pray, be generous."

She captured his face between her hands. "The truth—the unvarnished, bothersome truth—is that I have grown to admire you excessively, perhaps to the point of absurdity. You did not make it easy, but there it is. I expect I was no better, so I must now beg your forgiveness for being so blind and stubborn at the beginning. Please, may we not put it behind us?"

"If it troubles you, I shall tease you no more about the past. I am most ardently content with our present understanding."

She raised a hand to his cheek, her thumb brushing over the creases near his eyes and her fingers threading into the hair along his jaw. "You pardon me too easily."

"Oh, I shall seek payment," he rasped, turning into her softness to spread tempting endearments over her skin. She trembled in shy laughter, squirming just a little when his attentions tickled. He smiled and made good use of the stubble at his chin until her hands slid over his face, compelling him to stop. She pulled him up to her smiling mouth, and he found something else to kiss.

Nothing in his previous experience had offered any true understanding of this moment. The warm sense of her, the tender, honest brush of her lips and the feel of her moving beneath him after their shared passion soothed into his being. *This* was the belonging and the communion for which his heart had always thirsted. Everything before this withered and could have ceased to exist, so pale was it by comparison.

He lifted from her to admire the play of emotions mirrored in her eyes. They needed no words to convey their promises and secrets. A touch, a breath, the slightest flicker—each detail of expression communicated what a thousand spoken vows would have failed to evoke. How could any man take a woman to himself without this love? The physical pleasure of holding her was beyond mortal comprehension, but this… this transcendent unity, this near perfect empathy, was the rightful province of lovers matched in spirit as well as in the flesh.

He swallowed, realising that his throat had begun to close and his eyes to moisten as his adoring gaze took in the face of his bride. She smiled up at him, her lips tightening in that queer way of one who struggles against joyous tears. He touched a chaste, pure kiss to her forehead, then, at long last, rolled his weight from her.

She turned and slid towards him, nestling on their shared pillow with her nose almost touching his. He groaned in sheer delight and tugged her body against his own. From here, many new possibilities presented themselves, and he meant at length to explore them all.

~

Margaret sighed, rolling more intimately against him, and thrilled to the tickling sensation of his chest hairs as his heart pulsed against her bare skin. She was toying with his hair again, flipping the dark ends over her fingers and teasing it into thick waves at his temple.

"What is it you find so fascinating about my hair?"

"I have never seen it so long. It curls just at the end here."

His cheek flinched. "Would you be good enough not to tell anyone?"

"Why ever not? I rather like it. The perfectly masterful and fastidious John Thornton, needing a haircut just as any other man. I find it most comforting."

"I am glad you do, but do not become too fond of it. I am afraid all my usual routines have been… disrupted of late."

Margaret released a slow breath as her fingers slid down to his chin. He need not clarify that *she* had been the cause of that disruption, for she understood well enough. She was only relieved now, confident that he had no complaints with the sudden alterations to his life. That made one person who was glad she had come to this house.

"Margaret," he whispered into her forehead, perhaps sensing where her thoughts had turned, "is there anything I can do to make you feel more at home here?"

She twirled her fingers into the hair curling just near the base of his throat, more discomfited by the prospect of answering his question than by her newfound access to his informally attired person. He seized her fingers, and that steady, serious expression, which was entirely his own, arrested her wandering eyes.

"I know my mother can be trying," he confessed, with a pained twinge about his face. "I hope she does not trouble you overmuch."

Margaret blinked away, shrugging. "When I first met her—met you—I gave her every reason to believe as she still does. I was vain and ignorant, I suppose. I do not think she has ever forgiven me for laughing, so long ago, at her suggestion that I might have some interest in you."

"She would not have minded that so much, had other events not followed."

Margaret pressed her lips and drew in a short, refreshing breath. She did not wish to think of her mother-in-law just now! She placed her palm flat over his heart. "I can excuse her, for I imagine that if situations were reversed, I would guard my own son with quite as much jealousy as she."

His brows lifted in profound interest. "Son, did you say?" He fell silent, introspective for a moment as his eyes darted from side to side.

"What did I say?"

A brilliant smile blossomed. Margaret was beginning to look more often for that expression, for she had seen it more frequently in the last day than the entire year and a half previous. He shifted his posture until he leaned over her somewhat, pressing her far shoulder down against the bed to nuzzle her in her most sensitive places.

"John," she chuckled, and pulled his face up. "What are you on about?"

"I realised what a splendid mother you will make for some lucky boy." He descended upon her neck while his hands began a pursuit of their own. "I thought perhaps I should do my part," he rasped into the base of her hair.

"Your part?" she asked vaguely, shivering as his breath swirled over her skin.

"Indeed, and I might have more success if you put your arms around my neck... like so... now, kiss me, Margaret."

Her eyebrow quirked, and she hesitated for a few seconds, as though she might defy him. Relent she did, however, and no more words were spoken for some while.

~

The warmth roused him first. The compact body lying next to his own radiated it as though she were her very own source of heat. His lids drowsily slitted and lifted, taking in the ivory laced sheets—decidedly not his—and the rose-papered room—also not his! A lazy grin tugged at the side of his mouth. It was surely the greatest coup of his life to awaken in a woman's bed.

He glanced over the shapely figure beside him to evaluate the light from the window. It was just about the time he normally awoke for his work day... but not today. No less than a force of nature could pry him from that bed so soon. Consoling himself that it was not so very selfish to take a late morning—after all, he and his bride had been denied the pleasure of a wedding trip—he settled once more into the pillow.

She was breathing gently, her face turned towards him, and little tendrils of dark hair fluttered near her mouth. Thick lashes twitched upon her cheeks in dreams, and the counterpane dipped over her bared shoulder with each breath. If she were to sigh deeply, it would shift altogether....

A more cynical observer might have claimed it was all the novelty of the thing, and a generous quantity of pent-up masculine need which held him spellbound, but he would have argued differently. He would never cease in his fascination with her delicate form. He could gaze on endlessly, admiring each new facet of the miracle that was woman—and not just any woman, but *his* Margaret. Even those small deviations in symmetry, to which a sculptor might object, only made her more perfect and more real in his eyes. His agonised imagination, tortured with longing for so many months, never could have dreamt those details!

Within a scant few moments, the ache to hold her overcame his reverent adoration. Perhaps he need not wake her fully, only take her in his arms.... As soon as he had touched her, however, her body filled with a fresh breath and her eyes startled open. She blinked a few times as if trying to determine whether she was still dreaming. "John?" she asked blearily.

Abandoning all efforts at not rousing her, he wrapped his arms about her waist to draw her close. "Good morning, Love," he murmured into her forehead.

He felt her sigh in contentment as she burrowed her face into the cavity of his chest. Her greeting was not distinct, but warm, nonetheless. He stroked up her bare back, quite enthralled to be so privileged. "Did you sleep well?"

"Once I was permitted to do so," she retorted, and he could feel her smiling against his skin.

"One can survive on very little sleep. I shall only need about two hours from now on."

"And what will you do with all that extra time, John?"

"I thought I would take up needlework. Perhaps I can fashion you a more attractive nightgown. What prig decreed that women's nightwear must be as shapeless as a cotton bale?"

"What need have I for a nightgown?" She arched back from him just enough to display a most appetising prospect.

His eyes dipped appreciatively. "Well, when you put it quite like that, I suppose my time might be better employed in keeping you warm. As a matter of fact, I believe this bit just here is a little chilled...."

It was well after seven, and the mill had already been operating for a full hour and a half, when the master at last descended the stairs, dressed and ready for his work. Never had he felt more refreshed and able to address himself to the tasks of his day, and yet never had his bed called to him more insistently! How grateful he was that the morrow would bring his weekly day of rest, and that he would have no cause to rouse his sleeping wife early for any reasons but those purely his own.

Seven

It was a somewhat less frigid atmosphere in the sitting room shared by the two Thornton ladies on this morning. Margaret brought with her a bit of point lace that she had begun months ago, and in a gallant gesture of goodwill, chose a seat opposite her mother-in-law to join in a kindred pursuit with her. Hannah lifted a brow and largely ignored her companion, but at least she offered no criticisms.

Margaret might have been more at ease if she had known Hannah was silent less out of disapproval than from complete loss for words. What was there to be said? John's glowing countenance and unusually late arrival to breakfast had spoken everything, and Hannah had been a young married woman herself once, after all.

She tried not to think… but she was trapped in the same house with them! With *her!* She shook herself, trying to block the indecent thoughts from her mind. She had expected that one morning she would see him thus but had not anticipated that it would come so soon.

She ripped out an unfortunate stitch, reflecting that there was a very good reason for young couples to take some manner of wedding tour… *away* from their homes. There was no more frightfully awkward company than that of besotted newlyweds. It was all dreadfully uncomfortable!

As a consequence of the rumpled sentiments of both females, total quiet suffocated that little room for over an hour before some disturbance occurred. "'Scuse me, ma'am," Jane entered and bobbed a curtsey. She addressed

Margaret, as the proper mistress of the home, but it was Hannah who responded.

"Yes, Jane?" she answered, casting a quick, guilty glance to Margaret.

"There's a gen'l'man, says 'e wants Miss Hale."

Margaret set her needlework to the side, her eyes narrowed curiously. How could anyone know to look for her here and still ask for her as Miss Hale? "Did he say what he wants, Nancy?"

"No, Mum. Henry Lennox, 'e said 'is name was."

Margaret froze, her eyes flown wide. Her gaze shifted to her mother-in-law, and found that familiar, stern expression hardening. She swallowed. In a trembling voice, she made answer, and prayed she sounded more assured than she felt. "Show him in, Nancy..." she glanced again at the older woman, "... and will you please send for Mr Thornton?"

Margaret hoped that the twitch upon the matron's cheek meant that her last request for John's presence during this interview had somewhat mollified the other's concerns. She rose to greet her caller, draping her hands nervously across her black skirts. She had not seen Henry since that day in Helstone... oh, what a distressing memory!

A moment later, a moderately tall and respectably dressed gentleman was shown into the room. Hannah kept a suspicious eye on her daughter-in-law, and it was not unfelt, causing Margaret's greeting to seem even more subdued than it might normally have. Henry came forward to offer eager felicitations, but she sombrely stood her ground.

"Good morning, Mr Lennox—" she dipped her head, speaking softly.

His brows, brown and somewhat coarse, jumped in disappointment at her cool detachment. "Margaret! Good heavens, I've been all over this god-forsaken city! I've only just heard the news about your father. I am so sorry! Are you well?"

"I am bearing up, thank you. Mr Henry Lennox, may I present Mrs Hannah Thornton."

Henry Lennox turned to extend a cursory greeting. "My pleasure, Mrs Thornton. It was good of you to take in Miss Hale at such a time."

Hannah twitched her mouth, neither a smile nor a frown upon her face. The next few moments would demonstrate the former Miss Hale's loyalties once and for all. Either she would find all her suspicions validated, or she would enjoy watching this brash young man and his assumptions all set on his ear. Margaret had proved rather adept at first luring then disappointing men, and it might be entertaining to watch the enchantress at work. She lifted her chin, waiting.

Mr Lennox spared her a brief look of confusion at her silent greeting, then turned back to Margaret. "Forgive my abruptness, Miss Hale." He cast another glance to the black cloud in the corner. Between Margaret's diminished attitude and her scowling chaperon, apparently, he could not bring himself to use her Christian name again.

"I heard about your father yesterday—ran into one of his old Oxford fellows at the club. I thought to look in on you, but the last address Maxwell and Edith left had you at another end of town. By heaven, what a mercy you were not there! Such a dreary, squalid place. A porter there told me I might find you here, and… well, I am glad to see you have some friends here in this frightful city!"

Margaret was gazing at the floor with glassy, unseeing eyes and hot cheeks, in the attitude of one trying to block out an unwelcome lecture. "I am sorry you were given such trouble," she murmured distantly. It was like hearing her own first impressions of Milton come back to taunt her, and the cavalier air in which the slights were given jarred in her ears and made her cringe in compassion for the loyal Milton woman beside her.

"Oh, think nothing of the trouble, Miss Hale. I am only glad to find you well. I've written to Maxwell—but surely you have written to your cousin? I expected you would wish to leave this place at once and go to them. It seemed better than going to Cadiz, I thought. I could escort you and your woman… Dickens, was that her name? There is a steamer leaving for Greece in two days—"

"Mr Lennox!" Margaret at last interrupted, her cheeks on fire. "I thank you for your consideration, but I am recently married."

He jerked forward in a faint stumble as if trying to retract his earlier assumptions. His eyes darted, bulged, and he gaped in absolute consternation. "E-excuse me? Married?" He whirled to verify her statement but found only a smug glitter in Hannah Thornton's dark eyes.

"I beg your pardon, but did I hear correctly? Just recently? Whom could you have married?" He turned back and started afresh when he finally noted the fine gold ring adorning her hand.

No classical playwright could have timed John's arrival more precisely, for he had been just on his way back to the house to enjoy an early luncheon with Margaret when Jane alerted him to the presence of a guest. He strode confidently into the room, looking every inch the master of the house and holding a clear distinction in height over the other man. He came forward, his hand extended.

"John Thornton, sir. It is a pleasure to meet any friend of my wife's."

"Henry Lennox," that fellow gulped, his eyes shifting to Margaret once more as he tentatively shook John's hand.

John released the man, then searched Margaret's expression. Her receptiveness to her caller would determine how he was to manage. Outright displeasure would eject Mr Lennox from the house immediately, and overt warmth would set him on his guard—not that he had any cause to be jealous, of course! Not after… well, not after the sort of morning he had enjoyed so far. She appeared unsettled, and perhaps even glad for his intervention, which meant that he was free to be as friendly as he wished with this brazen chap.

"You come from London, Mr Lennox?" Margaret drew a few steps closer to John and he placed a hand on the small of her back.

"I... yes, as a matter of fact, I am a barrister." Lennox straightened in an attempt to preserve his dignity.

Margaret touched her husband's arm. "John, Henry is Edith's brother-in-law. It was he who helped investigate the charges against Frederick last year." This simple clarification, emphasising to both men the depth of her confidences in them, caused John to stiffen and Henry to relax—but only a little.

"I see," John replied, his voice dropping to a deeper timbre. "I understand, Mr Lennox, that we owe you a debt of gratitude, though I was sorry to learn that you were unable to assist my brother-in-law."

"Yes... yes, that was unfortunate." Henry's fingers began to twitch at his sides. The trusting, quiet looks Margaret was exchanging with... with that man... he could not quit the house readily enough! It was demoralising already to have made such a grievous blunder, assuming she was waiting helplessly here for him. It was utterly mortifying that this tradesman had succeeded where he, a friend of her family, had failed!

He wondered briefly if it had been the work of a moment, a marriage born out of despondency and need. If only he had heard of Mr Hale's death right away! Perhaps it might have been he who now rested his hand possessively over hers, and he whose protection she sought. His gaze fell.

"Well, I... I only came to see that Miss... that everything was well," he stammered. "If you will excuse me, I believe the next train departs in half an hour."

"Lennox," John stopped him as he began to retreat, casting a glance down to his wife. "It was good of you to come. I am grateful to you, for your concern for Margaret. I am glad she has such friends."

Lennox did not quite know how to take this little speech. The tone was open enough, but there was the very faintest tightening around Thornton's eyes when he spoke. Was the man insinuating that Margaret's family—and by extension he himself—had abandoned her for all this time? He swallowed.

Well, had they not done just that? Had Mrs Shaw even sent more than a letter from her travels in Italy when her own sister had passed away? It all seemed unfair that he, who had no right to maintain contact with an unmarried girl—and one who had refused him, at that—should be lumped in with that lot. He sighed, his shoulders drooping in defeat.

"Of course," he answered, his eyes searching out Margaret once more. "Will you let me know if any assistance is required settling Mr Hale's affairs? I should be honoured to be of service."

"The matter is well in hand, but I thank you. Would you like any refreshment before catching your train, Mr Lennox?" Margaret glanced up in surprise, but John maintained a cool expression. He could afford to be gracious, for it was not he who had to leave this house without her!

"I... er, no, Mr Thornton. Thank you."

As the guest made his polite farewells to Mrs Thornton—whose face still blanched in shock at these new revelations—John caught his wife's eye. With a little tip of his head and a raised brow, they held a silent conversation. She blinked and nodded faintly.

Lennox shook hands with John once more, bowed briefly to Margaret, and left the room. Scarcely had he reached the corridor, however, when her voice halted him.

"Henry?" Margaret hurried to him, her eyes dark with some remorse.

He turned, barely able to meet her gaze. "Mrs Thornton?"

She hesitated, then drew herself up. "I wanted to thank you, for taking the trouble to come all this way. It was the gesture of a friend, and I shall never forget it."

"It was little enough. I would have done much more, madam."

"I know. Henry, I... I know what you must think. I want you to know you needn't fear for me."

He clenched his teeth, then blurted out what had troubled him since Thornton first walked into the room. "Can you be happy, Margaret? Truly, in this city, with... with *him*?"

She lifted that proud chin of hers, but her eyes flashed with compassion rather than hauteur. "I am, Henry. I married for love, not necessity."

The last spiteful hope, that she might regret her marriage, withered in his heart and left him deflated. He nodded, vanquished. "Then I wish you every joy, Margaret." He turned and let himself out, leaving her standing there with her fingers laced together and her brow furrowed in sympathy.

A respectable moment later, a pair of warm arms slid round her waist from behind, and a deliciously deep voice tickled her ear. "Are you well, love?"

She leaned back into him. "I am, John. Thank you for that."

"You were able to convince him of your happiness?" His lips teased the base of her hairline, his breath sending little thrills through her.

"More or less, I think." She turned about in his embrace to twine her arms up his shoulders and around his neck.

He bent to kiss her, then low tones swirled against her cheek, "Do you know, Margaret, you have always driven me a little mad when you do that."

She glanced to her arms in surprise. "This? But when else would I have done so before yesterday? Oh!" she flushed in sudden memory. "The riot? I did not suspect you would have felt so! I only thought to protect you."

"You thought I turned up on your doorstep the next day out of duty? Not so, my love! I never slept at all that night, and it had less to do with the riots than I would have cared to admit."

"I can see now why you believed my motives were personal. Perhaps they were, and I was deceiving myself."

"Not entirely. You acted out of nobility as well; it was my own vanity which saw only that brief second when you held me. I scarcely noticed at the moment, so angry was I, but later it was as if your arms were still about me, shielding me." He shook his head, offering his most disarming smile as he tried to express the vagaries of feeling connected with that event. "I only wished for the dream not to end," he whispered, tipping his forehead close to touch hers.

That look! Margaret could not resist caressing his face. That half-teasing, half-serious expression which was his alone—the one she used to struggle to ignore—warmed her in ways she never could have understood before last night.

Now she knew. She was meant to belong to him—wholly and without reserve—and to no other. All those youthful fantasies about her future life, where calm rationality displaced this deluge of passion, were thoroughly overturned.

He took her by the hand, tugging lightly, his eyes pleading her to seek some privacy with him—for a few minutes at least. Margaret yielded, her steps light and her head spinning like a schoolgirl. By some miracle, she had found the one soul in whom she could delight.

London
July 1847

"Edith? Edith, are you still awake?"

The blonde head twitched away, but Margaret was not satisfied with her cousin's groggy response. She tugged at the blanket. "Edith?"

Edith groaned and rolled over. "Can you not sleep again, Margaret? Oh, please, let us talk in the morning!"

Margaret squatted back to her knees in disappointment. "Forgive me." She rose to return to her own room, but with an exasperated sigh, Edith flipped the counterpane."You may as well stay here a while. Oh, you are cold as ice! You have been up pacing, again."

Shivering and realising how cold she truly was, Margaret climbed into the bed. The two girls bundled together as sisters, pulling the thick blankets up to their ears and giggling a little.

"What is the matter, Margaret?" Edith demanded through a yawn. "Is it that letter you had from your father today?"

Margaret hunched lower under the counterpane. "No. Oh, it is just so miserably hot here in London in the summer! How do you bear it?"

"Is that why you are shivering?"

"I…" she heaved a sigh and confessed the truth. "I was so hoping Papa would take me home this summer. I thought he and Mamma would wish me to be there."

Edith shrugged under the blankets. "Mamma says that surely Uncle will be here next week. Some of the sailors are to be brought back for trial, I heard her say."

"Oh, how dreadful!" Margaret shuddered. "No, Papa will not wish to come for that. I think I know how it is, Edith. He has locked himself in his study, and Mamma remains in her sitting room, and they are seeing no one at all when they can help it. I only wished that I could… could…." A choking little sob, quickly swallowed, cut off any further expressions of sorrow.

"Dearest Margaret! Surely, they only think to allow you to stay here and be happy with us this summer. What more could you do in Helstone?"

"I do not know!" sniffled the heartbroken girl. "Papa has told me nothing more of Fred's circumstances. I do not suppose he ever will. Mamma does not write at all, but at least she has Dixon."

This last was spoken in barely concealed resentment as another shuddering sob made her tremble. If only her own mother wished for her to come to her! Instead, it was almost as though she were pushed farther away, as an unsuitable replacement for the child her mother had lost.

"Margaret," Edith yawned again, "you must stop troubling yourself so. There is nothing you can do. Is there not something more cheerful we may think on?"

Margaret lapsed in to glum silence.

"Perhaps you ought to take up dancing again. I did have *such* fun today during my lesson, and do you know, I think the exercise might do you good."

"I went walking," Margaret mumbled defensively.

"With Mrs Drummond! Why, Mamma's old pug walks faster than she! That must have been insufferably dull."

"We went to the fountain. You know how I have always loved it."

"Since we were very small. The lovers sitting on the benches there are always so charming. I adore watching them."

Margaret's face crumpled in distaste. "Do you? I never pay them any mind."

"Do you not think it romantic? Oh, there was one tall officer when we went last, so handsome he was! His lady was so lucky, I thought. She was lovely, too, wearing such a soft blue walking dress. I simply could not cease gawking at them until Mrs Drummond caught me."

"Surely," Margaret objected rationally, "there is much more to consider than an officer's looks. I do not understand why you like a uniform so well."

Edith sputtered in a great gasp of derision. "How can you not? There is nothing to a sharp blue or red coat, with those bright buttons. Oh! Someday, I hope I shall catch some officer's eye. Would you not adore the adventure of travelling to posts with an officer husband?"

"I would prefer a sensible, grounded gentleman," Margaret answered flatly. "Perhaps his looks matter little enough, but I should like for him to be someone I could talk to. Every time I listen to Uncle's guests in the drawing-room, I hear only ceaseless prattle about betting at the races and the sporting season."

"Oh, of course they must speak of other things," Edith assured her comfortably. "Mamma says that she had the finest suitor once who admired gardening immensely, and he taught her all manner of flowers, and—"

Margaret groaned. "I meant a gentleman who can discuss books and ideas, who is able to express himself clearly. I think I should prefer a man something like Papa—educated and gentle… but perhaps a little more candid and sociable." Her forehead pinched in thought.

Her parents had once adored one another, that she knew, but it seemed that at least of late, her father was not a good companion for her mother—nor for anyone else since the word about Frederick. Intelligent and sympathetic company would satisfy her notions of an equal marriage—someone whom she could respect, who held a genuine affection for her and possessed the fortitude to stand beside her through tragedy. Margaret Hale, young though she was, had no desire to swoon over a man, only to find such frivolous emotions cooled within a few years.

"Oh, Margaret," Edith twisted her head about sleepily, "Mamma says such a man does not exist. Men do not look to their wives for conversation of that kind, nor do I think I would at all care for it. How dull! You speak as if you would marry a parson yourself, or some university fellow."

Margaret rolled to her back. "Perhaps. I shall not trouble myself about what is years in the future. In any case, I do not intend to make the pursuit of a husband my only occupation."

Edith scoffed. "What else would you do? You cannot consider spinsterhood!"

She shifted uncomfortably. "There are worse things, surely. I would not marry simply because it is expected, Edith. I do not think I could submit easily to a man such as any I have known."

"Mamma says you are too fond of your own way, Margaret," Edith warned with a yawn. "Too much like Fre—" She cut herself off with a gasp, but it was too late, for Margaret had heard well enough.

Margaret stiffened, her eyes wide in the darkness with renewed anguish.

"Oh, forgive me, Margaret!" Edith implored. She sniffed uncomfortably, gushing excuses to palliate the horror she had unwittingly inflicted. Predictably, she sought to distract her cousin by turning back to the question of romance.

"Surely you shall find a gentleman someday whom you can admire. Perhaps we shall marry brothers! Oh, come, Dearest, you are only tired. May we please sleep now?"

Margaret tugged the counterpane up under her chin and muttered a good night as Edith rolled away. She ought to have known better than to think Edith could understand her feelings, but it comforted her to at least have her cousin near. She closed her eyes, pretending to sleep, and wondering if anywhere in this world there existed the sort of companion with whom she could truly share her heart.

"Love, are you well?" John tugged at Margaret's hand as they moved to abandon the dining room. Hannah had already left them behind, and they lingered for a few stolen moments in privacy before he returned to the mill for the afternoon.

She hesitated, then turned back to him. The empty quality her eyes had taken on in the few seconds she had looked away terrified him. Grief was a fickle tormentor; raising its hideous aspect whenever it pleased, crushing any budding hopes of happiness beneath waves of guilt and remorse for aspiring to such.

Well did he know the conflict that bound her within its grasp. Her entire future—*their future*—hung on what measure of courage and faith she possessed to face her sorrows. She had begun to confide in him, but it was not yet with the strong force of habit which could break through the darkest melancholy.

"Margaret? What is it?"

She lifted her shoulders and her mouth worked helplessly. "It is nothing of any consequence, John. You mustn't be troubled… Dixon is to arrive this afternoon. I will be grateful for her company. I shall be well."

He narrowed his eyes. "Am I to understand that you have not found my mother's company very satisfying?"

She swallowed, and her gaze dropped to his waistcoat again.

"Margaret," he touched her chin, and those clear eyes braved his once more. "You are the only woman who never looked down to me, and I beg you not to start now. It is not your way."

She blinked, then drew a slow, steadying breath as her shoulders squared again. "*You* may not be put off by my manner, but it is not with you that I shall spend most of my days. I do not wish to be at odds with your mother, but...."

"I know how she can be. You frighten her, you know."

Astonishment swept over her face. "I? Frighten *her*? How is that possible?"

"Because you are yourself—my strong Margaret."

She shook her head, brushing off his words with a dismissive laugh. "I feel that I am neither myself, nor strong of late, John."

He pulled her close to press a loving kiss to her forehead. Had he perceived the unbearable frissons his breath sent through her hair and down her back, it is likely that he would not have returned to the mill at all that day. From him, at least, the gesture was one of innocent comfort.

"You will grow strong again, Margaret. It is your nature, and she knows it as well as I."

She sniffed and turned her face into his shoulder. "I do not understand why that should trouble her. She could not respect me otherwise, could she?"

"No, but neither would she be threatened by you. She likes her own ways and has been left untroubled by contradiction for too long. I never questioned her domestic arrangements, and in late years she has had every resource and influence her heart could desire. All that has changed, for everything that was hers is now yours."

"And I am undeserving! You need not say it, for I know that is how she feels. I never meant to displace her, either in her home or in your affections."

"And you have not done so," he insisted, tugging at her waist. "You have only brought to this home what has long been missing. It will take time for her to learn to trust in you as I do."

She drew a long breath and shone a grateful smile. "Perhaps I will sit with her this afternoon, instead of...."

"Instead of going to the mill kitchen to visit Mary Higgins?"

She blinked a few times, then her old boldness made a little gasp of reappearance. She straightened and met his eye. "I had intended to do so, yes. I regret if you are displeased."

"Not in the least. I was about to offer to escort you, but of course if you prefer to remain here with my mother...."

She studied him for a moment in puzzlement. "You would not feel it immodest of me, or a defiance of your authority, if I desire to pay social calls on one of the workers?"

"You would not be my Margaret if you did not defy me whenever the fancy struck you! I think I can withstand the shock. To be quite truthful, I have lately missed locking horns with you."

"John!" she protested. "I beg you would not speak of me in such a vulgar way."

"Vulgar! I suppose it was, but apt, nonetheless. I did not marry you expecting we would never disagree. Provoke me, challenge me, I beg you, for I will only love you the more for it."

She frowned, but it was more playful than chagrined. With a hitch of her chin and a flash of her old poise, she surveyed him through lowered lids. "I ought to have expected you, of all people, to thrill in such a challenge. You have ever carried your way against those who wish to come against you."

"Not always. I suspect you will have the better of me yet, but I plan to enjoy the battle. And, since we are speaking of differing opinions, there is one contrary old fellow who has been asking after you for days. What would you say to a brief tour of the mill before I walk you to the kitchen?"

Her eyes lit expressively, and it was the only answer he required. He leaned down to kiss her once more—a soft brush, a secret pledge of later delights. "I will wait for you to make yourself ready," he whispered against her lips.

As she turned away, her steps once more sparkling with energy, he gazed after her with the rapt admiration of a man hopelessly infatuated. She disappeared, and he laughed at himself. John Thornton, at last cowed and brought low by a proud look from a woman, and revelling in his own meekness!

He tapped a pensive finger against the leg of his trousers. Here was an opportune moment to speak with his mother, to salve her fears that he was lost to her, and to explain to her in detail that cryptic conversation with Henry Lennox. He found her not in her sitting room as he had expected, but in a small alcove of the stairwell, the window of which looked out to the mill beyond.

"Mother?"

She did not seem to hear his approach. When she did turn at last, he detected a redness about her eyes and a pallor to her complexion. Her thinned lips quivered, and her arms crossed defensively. "How long have you known about Margaret's brother?" she demanded in a fragile voice.

"She told me yesterday," he confessed, tugging his fingers through his unruly hair as he often did when he was troubled. "You may well have guessed that it was he who was walking out with Margaret at the station after Mrs Hale's death."

She turned her face back to the window, acknowledging his words with only a slight lift of her chin. "And what are these heinous charges she spoke of?"

"The Navy considers him a mutineer. Margaret tells me that his captain, a man named Reid, had gone mad—had antagonised and persecuted his men to the point of exhaustion and the limits of physical impossibility. The mutiny itself was instigated by the senseless death of a crew mate falling from the yard arm when he feared punishment by the captain. Lieutenant Hale is said to have restrained the men from hanging Reid there next.

"The captain and his officers were instead set in a boat which was found some days later by the *Amica*. They all survived, but the mutineers took the ship to South America, where most of them scattered in fear of their lives. Some poor devils were caught and hung regardless, and mad Captain Reid given his old command back."

He sighed in sympathetic exasperation. "I cannot condone the mutiny, but there seems little justice in the matter. I may as well tell you, Mother, I have promised to do what I can for him, if I ever find a way."

Hannah had tilted her head back over her shoulder as he spoke, the infamy of it all registering as shock over her stark features. She did not answer when he had finished—instead, her eyes drifted slowly to the floor.

"Mr Lennox spoke of a cousin," she at last ventured in a subdued voice.

"Margaret grew up with her in London. She married Lennox's brother, an army captain, just before the Hales moved to Milton. She has gone with her husband to Greece. They have a child by now and are expected to return to London sometime later this year. When they do, Mrs Hale's sister—a Mrs Shaw—will likely return as well. She had been travelling in Italy, but the last word Margaret had placed her in Paris."

She rounded on him at last. "She has family to aid her, and yet she stayed here… with you. John, she… she loves you!"

He smiled tightly. "Does that trouble you?"

She blinked in wonder, turning again to the window. "I hardly know! I had prayed for this, John, but I could not have believed it!"

"I scarcely can either—my arm will soon go black and blue from pinching myself! Nevertheless, it is true. Mother, will you not be happy for me?" He placed a hand on her shoulder, inviting her to turn into his embrace.

She held strong and defiant for a few doubtful seconds, then surrendered to his beckoning. He drew his arms tightly about her, sensing the extraordinary new shiver present in her bearing. She sniffled—very quietly, it must be confessed—and allowed her son to hold her.

After a moment, her shoulders shook in a weepy chuckle, and she brushed a stray tear from her eye. "And to think of the airs she once gave herself! My son, my good John, you have won her over at last, fine lady though she thought herself!"

He gave a short, heavy laugh of his own and looked down to her dewy eyes. "Do not claim she is the only one who has changed, Mother, for you would fail to credit the good work that her grace has done in me. I am not the same man I was a year ago."

"You have ever been the same man, John. You may be less reticent than formerly, and I have certainly questioned some of these new practices you have enacted at the mill, but your heart is as true as it ever was. She cannot take the credit for that."

"No, I owe that to you. You always had faith in me, Mother, even in the darkest days when disgrace was my only other companion. I never thought to find such pride and honour in life, or such glad joy in all my duties, as I do now, and I must pay homage to you both for that. I have been blessed with two fine, strong women to love, and who are not afraid to chastise me properly when I deserve it!"

Her deep-set brow crumpled in a sudden ripple of laughter, and she patted his cheek. The tears stood in her eyes, but a reluctant smile fought for expression.

"She may be a penniless girl, John, but never was there such a discriminating lass. If you have overcome her pride and won her affections, you have done more than I thought possible. I'd like to hear all of those who once doubted and scorned you see you now!"

Weston
October 1839

"Why, it *is* you, Thornton! By Jove, I never thought to see you. How have you been keeping, old fellow?"

John's back was turned, and he eased the heavy textile bolt from his shoulder. He had no need to round on the voice addressing him to identify the speaker, for he recognised it well enough. He squared his shoulders and looked back, his face a mask. "Good afternoon, Harold."

Harold Wright, the nineteen-year-old son of the egregious Daniel Wright—and three years John's senior—offered his former companion a flippant grin. "What are you doing in a dry little purlieu like this, Thornton? I thought you were a Milton chap, through and through!"

John, his cheek flinching somewhat, faced down the other. He had grown taller in the two years since they had last seen one another and now stood half a head above his old school comrade. "Not all are fortunate enough to live in Milton."

Harold permitted a flash of discomfort in his eyes but quenched it almost immediately with an easy shrug. "No, I suppose not. Devilish shame, all of that. Still, I had not thought to find you here. You must forgive me, I had no word of you these last two years."

"I do not doubt that." John's shoulders tightened with the urge to return to his work. He took some measure of satisfaction in his duties, while there was no pleasure at all to be found in discussing his misfortunes with one who, happy and blessed in life's circumstances, was far too apt to make light of another's trials. He was too well-brought up, however, to simply turn his back.

"What are you doing in Weston, Harold?" he growled.

"Oh!" Harold's cheerful grin returned, and he beckoned to a statuesque blonde who yet persisted in examining the window dressings of the shop. She came, taking Harold's arm, and raised crystal blue eyes to John. "How clumsy of me. John Thornton, may I present my wife Mildred—formerly Miss Harris. Surely you two must remember each other."

John did, in fact, remember the lady. His very shoes felt too tight as memories of his awkwardness in her presence returned to taunt him.

"We are just returning from our wedding trip at the seaside. My dear Mildred wished to step off the train for a respite and look about some of the shops here in this quaint old town."

The lady dipped a demure curtsey, then cast her gaze properly low. John inclined his head. "Madam," he greeted her respectfully.

So! Daniel Wright had at last contrived to wed his son to Abram Harris's daughter! That was surely a match to please the old tycoon's heart. Harris was one of the cleverest rail financiers in London, and even years ago John had seen the direction of Wright's desires for that association. Harold had certainly got the fine end of the bargain, but he wondered if the young lady fancied her own lot.

He had met Mildred Harris frequently during his time living with the Wrights. Most of those occasions had been family dinner parties when he was still a gawky adolescent and she wore her hair down like a girl. She was a fair little thing then, and he had often been forced to dance with her in the family's music room. He still shuddered at the memories.

John schooled his features into a neutral expression, reflecting on the tender age of the bride. It seemed that the two eager fathers had hardly wasted a moment in arranging the match, for Mildred could not be much more than eighteen, and Harold barely a man himself. *If* John thought sourly to himself, *Harold indeed qualified for the distinction of such a title.* Well, it was certainly none of *his* business.

"Congratulations to you both," he offered evenly, and with only a little sincerity. "If you will excuse me...."

"Thornton!" His employer, Mr Davis, drew to his side, halting his retreat. "Bring out the new emerald chiffon from the store room for the lady, and the matching velvet as well." This he spoke to John, but he turned next to the Wright couple. "My boy will have those brought up directly for you, ma'am."

Boy! John cringed, sensing his mortification complete. He did not need to glance back to sense the triumphant smirk in Harold's eyes. Instead, he obeyed, allowing the scorn to heap upon his shoulders until such time as he might vindicate himself. The samples were procured and brought for the lady's admiration, and John would have liked to withdraw, but found his continued assistance required with the couple's purchases.

As he waited, wishing he were invisible, he could not help but notice how the young Mrs Wright's gaze continually drifted in his direction. He drew back slightly, his ears burning with shame at the ignominious circumstance, but she only looked his way the more noticeably as he presented the various samples for her. Conscious, as he was, only of his own fall from grace, he attributed her attention to little more than amused derision.

This was, in fact, far from the truth of the matter. Younger though he was, work had hardened his physique and care had aged his features so that the no longer innocent eyes of the new wife found much to appreciate in the figure before her. If John was oblivious of her admiration, however, her husband was not. Harold interjected himself neatly, dismissing each of the samples John had brought as of inferior quality and requiring him to cart as many more back for the lady to inspect.

Only after a miserable half an hour was he able to pass off some of those duties to a much younger stock boy, whose usual job it was to sweep the floors and tidy shelving. Before they were satisfied, and to his very great chagrin, John's strength and height were again required to procure two final samples the lady wished to inspect.

At last the affluent young couple had settled their purchases, and John sighed in relief. He tried to disappear back into the store room, but Harold sought him out deliberately before they departed. "Well, old chap," he stood aloof, not offering his hand, "it was jolly good to see you again. I am certain my father wishes you his best."

John straightened, his shoulders stiff, his chin jutting in that dogged way that his mother employed so well. "Indeed," he agreed icily. He crossed his arms, but abruptly uncrossed them again to perform a cold bow to the lady. Blushing, she received his unwilling compliment and quickly turned her back, a mannerism he deliberately misinterpreted as contempt.

It was in a sour mood that he made his way home that night. He hunched within his thin coat, his hands shoved crudely into his pockets. He cared little for proper appearances at the moment—it was only the chill of the evening and his own bruised pride which concerned him. How dare Harold Wright waltz before him like that, parading his little heiress and patronising about his father—as though a man's suicide and the subsequent ruin of his family were merely a trifling affair!

"Had no word these two years…" John nearly bit a hole through his cheek. *I should think not!* What recognition or assumption of responsibility had ever troubled Daniel Wright? He had his own interests well protected after that shameful speculation, though plenty of others had lost the shirts from their

backs. Wright had broken no law of man, and that was the best that could be said for the aftermath of that debacle. What financial tragedies had befallen those who had trusted in him were quite another matter!

So bitter and brooding was he, that all his usual reserve was entirely worn down. When, only a street away from his home, the typical group of young boys came out to taunt him, he did not shrug them off as he did every other night. To catcalls of "Foundling!" and "Ragamuffin!" and several coarser descriptions of his heritage, he snapped up his fiery gaze.

His height made two of any of them, but he had always found it beneath his dignity to acknowledge their harassment. He had taught them early that it was utter folly to throw rocks or mud, but just as readily they had learned that he would not punish them for words alone. Tonight was different.

Gritting his teeth, he lashed after the nearest boy, snatching a flat stick they had been using for their sport. "Go home!" he snarled, slicing his makeshift weapon harmlessly—albeit with threatening accuracy—close upon their heels.

"Go, all of you worthless scoundrels, and do something useful for once!" He ran a short way after them, his long strides proving that he could catch them easily, should he desire, until he felt them sufficiently in awe of his wrath. Nearly spitting with disgust and rage, he flung the stick after them and spun on his heel to sulk the remaining distance to his door.

He found it open, with his mother standing before it. Hannah Thornton observed his sullen manner and tilted her head curiously in the direction from which he had just come. "What was that about, John?"

He sucked in a long, fresh draught of the autumn air, purposefully shedding his brittle thoughts at will. He had become supremely adept at that, and never more so than when he wished to project confidence to his mother. "Nothing to trouble yourself about, Mother. I only set them about a more constructive amusement."

Her dark brow edged upward. "Strange that you should suddenly go about it with such vehemence, when you have never troubled yourself before."

He forced a brave smile. "*Quod dignum sit facere, dignum est facere bene*," he pronounced, pleased and not a little surprised that the Latin slipped so easily from his tongue after so long. *Anything worth doing is worth doing well.*

He had taken that idea to his heart, and it was a refreshing perspective after his humiliating encounter. John Thornton need grovel in shame before no man! Work was his passport to independence and honour, and he would continue to set about it with a single-minded obsession.

Hannah Thornton cast her eyes to the heavens with a supplicating look, then sternly cocked her finger at him. "Do not spout that heathen gibberish at me, as if nothing is the matter! What troubles you, John?"

He pressed his mouth closed. She shook her head and sighed in exasperation. "Well, go on then, if you will not tell me about it. Only do not frighten your sister!"

"It is only a little matter of wounded pride, Mother, and nothing more. How is Fanny this evening?"

She gestured helplessly towards their abode, blinking in some sudden percolation of feeling. "She is better than yesterday. It comes and goes, John, but she has been up looking for you this last hour."

He pasted a cheerful smile to his face as the realities of his own existence settled comfortably around him once more. This was home, such as it was, and all Harold Wright's airs could not rob him of the dignity he had found in sheltering his little family.

"Come, Mother, let us set in on that excellent porridge I know you must have ready by now." He wrapped a long arm about her shoulders to steer her inside, but she looked up to him with some pleased defiance.

"It is potatoes and carrots tonight, saucy young man!"

"My, we *are* living high, are we not?" He held the door for her as she tartly elbowed him in the ribs, but his eyes searched for the sleeping pallet in the corner. "Fanny, dearest, how are you this evening?" he crooned, walking gently closer.

A restive little face greeted him—the streaked face of a child no longer a toddler, but not yet a young girl who dwelt most of her days in uncomfortable health and even worse humour. She rubbed her dark eyes, as if in indecision, then at last extended her arms to him. He lifted her, then settled them both into one of the two chairs by the wobbly table.

"Why, my princess, you have grown this week! Let me see, were you not just to my shoulder last week when you sat on my lap? I think you are nearly an inch taller now."

She stretched proudly, a smug grin easing the surly expression away. "Mamma says I may have a new frock when you are paid, John."

"Did she, now? That is excellent news! You will have to eat well tonight, and no complaining, I should say."

"John—" his mother interrupted, her face pale—"I had meant to talk to you about that before Fanny said anything. Have we enough saved that I might buy a little of Mr Davis' leftover bolt ends?"

"We've just over sixteen pounds put by. A healthy sum, is it not?"

She shook her head vigourously. "Not by half, John, not if you intend to pay back all those debts. I will ask among the neighbours; I think I shall have no trouble procuring scraps to make Fanny's dress decently long enough for her."

"I may be able to obtain some little material tomorrow. Allens are expected to make a large order, and there are always bits and ends rejected. Mother, you bring to mind something else that I intended to speak to you about. I have thought of taking porter work by nights at the rail station. Would you feel safe to be alone here at night?"

"John!" she protested. "Do not even consider it. It is not myself I would fear for, but you! You cannot work all day for Mr Davis, then all night at the station. You will kill yourself!"

"I am strong, Mother, and I could nearly double the amount we are able to put by every week. Think how much sooner we will have paid everything back and can live free from this shadow over us!"

"It is out of the question! I will not sacrifice my son for a few extra shillings. You already work better than thirteen hours out of the day as it is, and sometimes longer!"

"Which leaves five or six, at least, when I might work a little more. And you know, Mr Davis intends to hire a new stock boy as his shop is prospering so well of late. If he is quick enough, it might be an hour or two less that I will have to work each evening."

She snorted expressively. "His shop is prospering because he finally has an able clerk to keep his inventory and ordering records straight, to say nothing of the better floor plan you devised for his warehouse. A year ago, he sold only bargain drapery goods, but now he is attracting such a clientele that his shop is finer than most in Milton. He ought to pay *you* the extra shilling rather than hiring another useless boy."

John shrugged. "It is his business. He may bring on a dozen lads, or close up his shop tomorrow, and it would not be for me to judge what is best by his account books. Were I an employer, I would not feel obliged to share or explain such decisions with my workers. Let us not change the subject, Mother.

"I am well able to bring in a little more each week with additional work. I could go to the station directly after the draper shop, work through eleven or twelve, and return in time to rest for the next day. You need a new dress as badly as Fanny, and she cannot grow strong on water-porridge every day. If I brought home an extra six or eight shillings per week, you would both be better off. And think, within a couple of years we might even be able to move back to Milton! I know I could find good work there, once my name is cleared, and do we not owe as prompt a repayment as possible to Father's creditors?"

Hannah Thornton, every bit as determined as her son, crossed her arms with finality. "No, John. If it is our duty to act in good faith, I should say putting by a fifth of your weekly earnings is sufficient. If you do this thing, Fanny and I shall never see you, and you will grow to be nothing more than a ghost of yourself—and where would it end? I'll not have it, John Thornton! We shall get by."

He huffed in exasperation, frowning and turning his attention back to Fanny. The child gazed in some unease between them, sensing that their conversation both did, and yet did not, involve her. He chucked her pointed little chin, trying to startle a smile from her, but was only marginally successful.

"Fanny," her mother directed, "go make ready for supper." Fanny slid down from her brother's lap, leaving him to face his mother alone.

"John," she sighed, sinking into the other chair, "I know what you wish. You have every right to your pride as a man, and to see us restored from disgrace, but I will not have you ruin yourself in the attempt."

"Mother—" he tilted her a gentle but determined look. "A little hard work will not ruin me, and it would only be for a time. If you do not wish it, I will not do it, but I will continue to seek odd jobs where I can get them. It may not come to a regular thing, but I cannot rest, knowing I can do more than I do presently." There was such gravity and resolve glinting in his eyes as Hannah gazed at her boy that she could do little but yield.

That day marked the beginning of a shift in their relationship. No longer was he merely the dutiful son, obedient to her desires alone. His own will and motivation spurred him. Week by week, three shillings continued to drop into their savings box, but an occasional windfall would see one or two more joining them.

Earning back the family name became his alone as he steadily took more of the burden upon himself. By and by, she came to look to him as the authority and head of their little household; more than merely the boy she had raised, he became a help-meet and a partner, and eventually a figure of admiration. John had come into his own as a young man, and he gave every promise of becoming yet a far greater one than his father had been.

Eight

Marlborough Mills
October 1855

"G'mornin, Missus!" Nicholas Higgins tipped his worn grey cap in respect to the young woman crossing the yard.

She turned at his voice, a ready smile gracing her features. "Good morning, Nicholas!" she answered cheerfully. She glanced to her left, dodging a drayage cart, and wove her way towards him through the yard's foot traffic.

"Goin' to see the master?" he teased.

"Mr Thornton?" she scoffed. "You know I do not like him."

"No more do I," he winked. "Come on, Missus, I were goin' there m'self." He offered his elbow, and she hooked her arm through his.

"Is it the same loom again?"

"No, th' cotton i'self. 'Tis a ragged lot we've got in now. Master said we'd some orders wha' didn'a need th' finer weave, so I'm to ask where to send it a'."

Margaret nodded uncomprehendingly. The mill was still largely a mystery to her—after all, it was not fitting for her to traipse about the factory itself. Her mother-in-law, seasoned mistress though she was, had only occasionally wandered through the mill, and never did she stoop to meddle directly in any of its affairs. Even John, eager as he seemed to be for her to appreciate all aspects of his position, did not encourage her to explore the factory floor unless he escorted her. There was only so much she could understand from a distance.

"Nicholas, will you tell me what you mean by that? What is wrong with the cotton?"

"'Tis th' longer, cleaner fibres it wan's, Missus. This lot's a' fussed. A ri' waste o' good loom space."

"I see." She cast an encompassing glance about her and paused in some dismay as her gaze encountered a boy and a girl just leaving their duties for the day. They were at least fourteen—John would not employ them much younger—but the worn looks of care already etched into their youthful faces squeezed her heart.

Nicholas slowed his steps beside her, and she left him to speak with the children. The boy snapped smartly to attention while the girl looked bashfully to the ground.

"Are you both off to school now?"

"Aye, Missus Thornton," answered the lad. "Master Stevens won' like it if we're late, ma'am."

"Indeed, you must hurry. You are going to the building on Dorset Street, are you not? That is a long way to walk."

The lad blinked up to her and the girl scuffled her feet in silent acknowledgment.

Margaret frowned. It was a pity that no school room had ever been built at Marlborough Mills as some other mills had. It would have required a substantial effort, and though John was not unwilling, he had not yet found the resources to do so. Other matters were always more pressing. "I hope your walk is pleasant. Do you enjoy your studies?"

The boy shrugged doubtfully, but the girl—his sister, Margaret presumed—raised her eyes. "'Tis be'er than th' mill, Missus Thornton," she whispered.

Margaret swallowed, then dipped her head and wished them a good day. She was still grave and thoughtful when she turned back to Nicholas.

"'Tis the devil's own folly," he muttered in sympathy.

"They are so young! Why must it be so, Nicholas? I am glad the law protects them better than it used to, but it is still unfair!"

He shrugged. "If yo're looking for some'at to blame, Missus, yo'll be castin' 'bout a long while."

"I know," she sighed. "It is not so simple as I once thought, but those poor children! It is not right that they should have to work so."

His face crinkled in a sad smile and he offered his arm again. "They're be'er off workin' for Thornton than anywhere else. He pays be'er than other bosses, an' they go to their school wi' bellies full o' food, no' fluff. Tha's a deal more than most can say, an' their families eat from their wages."

She paused to smile up at him. "Thank you for that, Nicholas. It means a great deal, coming from you."

He chuckled and patted her hand. They had come to the outer door of the building now, and conversation became impossible. Smiling and offering a chivalrous bow, Nicholas held the door for her to pass. He allowed her to precede him through the staggering array of machinery and the downy snowfall of fresh cotton fluff.

John was standing up on the scaffolding with Mr Williams, his arm outstretched as he pointed and shouted directions to his overseer. He had not noted them yet—she was concealed still and could only see him through gaps in the towering equipment scattered over the floor. She paused, in some awe.

It had been a long while since she contemplated him as the Master of Marlborough Mills. He had simply become John to her—a kind, thoughtful, gentle man; tender lover, engaging companion and a man worthy of confidence, who took seriously all the cares entrusted to him. Though their wills were not always united, their opinions not always in harmony, she now blessed the day their hearts had entwined, and found all her hope in a new life well lived at his side.

Gazing up at him as he surveyed his domain, she remembered those first impressions he had made upon her and took a moment to re-examine them. There was a power and an authority about him, unmatched by any other she had known. They were not assumed unjustly but earned. The respect he commanded was no more than his due, and she, who now knew him so intimately, finally understood the depth of humanity veiled beneath the masterful exterior.

Nicholas nudged her unobtrusively with his elbow, indicating that she was blocking the work underway. She started from her brief daze, somewhat abashed, and made her way towards the steps of the scaffolding. She was watching for the moment when his sweeping gaze would discover her, and she was not disappointed. The iron slid from his expression and his eyes came alive as they only did when they lit on her. If Higgins also noted the change and chuckled some to himself, the sound was kept from her by the clamour of the looms.

John scampered down the steps to offer her his hand. He glanced curiously over her shoulder, as if only just then noting the presence of Higgins, but with a jerk of his head he beckoned them both to retire to his office. They followed him up, through the door above, and down a narrow corridor into the quiet of his private lair.

"What is it, Higgins?" John closed the door, then drew his desk chair out and held it for Margaret before he turned his attention back to his employee.

Nicholas explained his mission, John listening intently until he had finished. They spoke respectfully and at length, man and master, until a course was set upon to make the best use of the nearly worthless raw cotton. Higgins departed with a wink, and it was likely that he chuckled again to himself when the door was promptly closed and bolted behind him as he left.

John shed his stifling coat and turned eagerly back to her, drawing her to her feet and into his arms. "What brings you to the mill, love?" He then proceeded as if he did not really care what excuse had summoned her hence—he was delighted that she had come, and he expressed himself most eloquently on the subject.

Once he allowed her to catch her breath, she eased back to the floor once more. "Your sister called this morning with an invitation to a private family dinner next week."

His eyes rolled, and a low groan escaped him. "I am planning to be ill. Likely at death's door. Send for Donaldson, will you?"

"It is too late for you to contract such an ailment, for I have already accepted. I cannot attend regular parties yet, and I should like to know Fanny a little better."

"You do insist on tormenting me! Watson will spend the evening plaguing me to join in that speculation of his. I have refused him three times already."

She tipped a smile which was only partially sympathetic up to him. "I imagine that it is not you who shall be called upon to admire the Indian wallpaper or the new French draperies. I have not seen them yet, you know, and the proper initiations must be observed."

"She has new draperies?"

"She has had them for three months, I understand."

He shook his head in vague dismissal. "I had not noticed. When am I to be led to the gallows?"

She prodded his chest, provoking that maddening smile from him again. "Tuesday next. Your mother has informed me that your best dinner jacket has a large tear in it, which you somehow managed to keep hidden until this very morning when we sent to have it cleaned."

He frowned and cast his eyes upward for a moment. "Oh…" he chuckled after some deliberation. "I remember that."

She lifted teasing brows. "And?"

"I think the tale might reflect poorly on me. The last time I wore it was the dinner party we had here a year ago, and one particular guest was wearing this white evening gown…."

"You are blaming *me* for the rip under your sleeve?" she laughed incredulously.

"No—only for the way my hands trembled for the rest of the night, even long after you had gone home. The confounded thing was devilishly tight, and… well, let it suffice to say, I had factory business to attend afterward, and I was in a hurry to change. I never did regain full command of my faculties that night."

"I see." She folded her arms over his, letting the "business" he referred to slip into the ether of former days—days they both would have given a great deal to alter or forget.

John, too, was eager to put the past aside. He moved his hands to receive hers and kissed each by turn. "How did you find my sister today when she called?"

"The same as I usually do, I suppose," she frowned. "She seems well."

He lifted a brow. "She is not the companion and sister you might have hoped for, but all is not lost. Perhaps motherhood may improve her somewhat."

She jerked bac and regarded him with scandalised but inquiring eyes. "Have you some reason to suspect...?"

He shifted uncomfortably. "Well, no! How could I? I only assumed... oh, forget I said anything! We will have Mother all atwitter for nothing if she hears such talk."

"I think you needn't concern yourself there," Margaret retorted drily.

"No, I suppose not. She will save that for when it is our turn." He graced her with a provocative wink. She blushed furiously and scowled in censure, causing him to laugh all the more.

"Oh, come, love, I shall stop teasing!" he cried when she feigned even greater displeasure. "Stay with me a bit, will you? Perhaps you can help me sort through this mass of invoices before the noon meal."

Her eyes widened, and she glanced guiltily towards the door as if afraid his words had been overheard. "I would be happy to be of service, John, but... what will people say if I start working here at the mill? And while still in mourning, no less!"

"I doubt they will believe you are helping me with invoices," he replied with a saucy tilt to his mouth. "But I suppose you are right. I only wished for an excuse to keep you here. Perhaps if I bring them home in the evenings, you and I may retire to the study together. It seems a much pleasanter way to accomplish the task."

Margaret considered only briefly, then brightened. She found the idea most agreeable, for she had ever relished the notion of making herself useful. In addition, the long evenings spent as a threesome in the drawing-room were only marginally more comfortable than they had been that first week. Hannah had thawed towards her rather notably, but genuine affection between Margaret and her mother-in-law had yet to develop. Present relations between the Thornton women could best be described as an uneasy truce, with John as the disputed turf.

As quickly as it had risen, Margaret's enthusiasm faded. "Your mother would miss you...."

"It is not she whom I have married, now is it? Is it not written that *a man should leave his mother and cleave to his wife*? I cannot precisely cast my mother out in the street, but I do rather enjoy that cleaving bit."

She blushed again and rolled her eyes. "I see no point in deliberately creating *more* distance. She has only begun to believe I do not intend to monopolise you entirely. I fear such an alteration to the evening routine would unsettle her in the extreme."

"Not if your help means I may return home a little earlier and put my duties to rest a little sooner each evening. However, I fear it may cause me to linger over the accounts for an inordinate amount of time," he added with a mischievous little leer.

As it happened, Margaret proved a valuable asset in the daily battle waged against the accounts. Both learned to eagerly anticipate that hour set aside just after the evening meal when they would retreat together to the study—no longer exclusively John's domain—and pore over the tedious record of his day.

John developed a new appreciation for his wife's clever mind and sweet company to lighten even such a dreary task, but it was Margaret who reaped the greater reward. She at last began to understand the challenges of his business and to feel herself included as never before. The vagaries of the cotton trade, with its fluctuations and demands, became clear to her, and her mind, thus informed, became a valuable ally to her husband.

With two instead of one applying themselves to the chore, the numbers were transcribed and tallied with brisk efficiency, and even the suspicious Hannah Thornton could find little to complain of in the shifted order of the family's scripted evenings. Indeed, if forced to confess it, she would have observed that her beloved son's expression lost somewhat of its anxiety, its introspective tension and the tendency to drift into a preoccupied daze which had formerly characterised it.

Such was John's new sense of leisure that he resumed reading by evenings, with Margaret seated near enough to twine their hands together, and one of Mr Hale's old books cradled against his knee. The worries plaguing the mill had not lessened, yet he was better able to shrug them off and leave his work behind for a few hours each evening. For such a gift, everyone could be grateful.

Weston
17 October 1840

"Thank you, Mr Allen, that will be three and six," John touched his worn cap respectfully as he passed the wrapped parcel over the counter.

"Three and six!" Mr Allen objected. "Why, only a year ago, this same order would have been…." The greying fellow paused, his brow furrowed in good-natured frustration.

"Three exactly, sir," John furnished. "Cotton prices have gone up again, Mr Allen."

The man lifted his hands and eyes to the ceiling in a brief supplication, then shook his head in defeat as he drew out his pocketbook. "Every year of late! Never have I seen such a thing before. I tell my wife," he leaned confidentially close to the boy behind the counter, "that if cotton continues to rise, we shall be forced to buy linen by next year. She swears she will not pay so much, but you wait and see if she will prance out to church in naught but her stockings!"

John nearly choked on an abnormally large breath of air at Mr Allen's irreverent discussion of his wife's wardrobe. His face quite red, he turned away and sputtered into his shoulder. "I am sure," he coughed, "that Mrs Allen will find that cotton prices shall even out within the next year."

"Oh? Have you some particular source for your information? Tell me, young Thornton, shall my wife be able to afford the proper widow's weeds by then? I do hope so, for the current economic climate will surely drive me to an early grave."

"I have no such source as you speculate, Mr Allen. Common sense dictates that the weaver's unions will soon yield to the desires of their masters—it is always so in winter. Moreover, the industry is becoming more stable every year. Naturally, the demand is continuing to increase as cotton becomes a more fashionable product, but the supply will soon keep pace with the demand."

"Is that a fact! How so?"

"Well, sir, the new loom designs are far more efficient. Have you read of them?"

Allen dipped a quizzical brow as he studied the lad. "I confess, the manufacture of cloth is not the most riveting of topics."

"Sir, may I respectfully disagree!" John would never have taken such liberties with a customer's time if the shop were busy, or if he did not know the man well. Allen was, however, a favourite customer, and there was none other about. His cheeks flamed with youthful passion as he warmed to his subject.

"I speak not only of the manufacture of cloth, or paper or wool, but the progress of our nation! The machinery we have now is nothing short of a marvel, and a testament to man's ingenuity and determination. We chose to build an economy stable enough to power the empire, and by the strength of steel and steam, we have done so. These products our factories create clothe and feed the Empire at a much lesser cost than has ever before been possible."

"And what of the anti-slavery convention or the Factory Acts? You think my wife's clothing will not put me in the work-house when all the plantations lose their labourers and factory labour becomes more costly? Both must be only a matter of time."

"I do not deny that prices will necessarily increase, but that, too, should settle out in a few short years. As a rule, I object to the crown mandating conditions for an industry, but we must exert ourselves to some manner of conscience. And can it be so bad for the economy? Men shall be earning a wage, holding their heads high, and such persons will have leisure and resources to purchase more finished goods. The more affordable products of our new factories are the only logical choice, sir. It will need a few years, perhaps a generation or more, but I think we will be the stronger for it."

Allen shook his head, clucking in amusement. "You speak with the naivety of youth, Thornton, but I shall hope, for my sake, at least, that you are not wrong. I'd no idea you were such a capitalist!"

John reddened again. He had let his tongue run away with him before a customer, a thing he had cautioned himself against. His time in the draper's shop was not his own, and he must take care to remember that. "Pardon me, Mr Allen. It is a particular interest of mine. Would you like me have one of the boys bring your purchases to your door?"

"Eh? Oh, yes, that will do." Allen nodded. He moved to depart, but abruptly turned back. "Thornton, would you fancy a few engineering books?"

John's eyes widened before he could catch himself, but he gulped silently instead of blurting out his heart's desire. His trembling interest, however, spoke more than words.

"Aha. Have I ever told you of my son, Thornton?"

"The one who went to sea, sir?"

"The only son I had," Allen agreed, his face pinched somewhat. "He left a great stack of the things—technical manuals, engineering and political treatises—always reading, he was. His widow had no interest in such books, so I kept them—to honour his memory, I suppose, though I've done naught but let them collect dust. Would you like to read one or two?"

"Mr Allen," John breathed in awe, "I would be honoured beyond expression, but… your son's books! I cannot possibly accept."

"Nonsense," Allen waved, and his tones were gruff as he turned away again. "Charles knew I never cared for the musty things. I'll send a few of them back with your stock boy when he comes by." The door jingled, and the old man ambled up the street.

John's every nerve tingled to life. He remained fixed to his spot, but his thoughts began to soar, as they had not dared to do in three years. Engineering books, freely offered! His pulse thrummed jubilantly. The only scraps of information he had laid his hands upon in all that time had been from discarded newspapers, scavenged from here and there, for he would not permit the luxury of purchasing the newspaper, let alone books for himself. At last, his searching mind might once more satisfy its longing!

He glanced anxiously about the shop. No customers were present, and both the boys under him worked about their tasks with the brisk efficiency he had taught them. *Perhaps…* with quick decision, he strode to the rear of the shop to seek his employer. Obtaining permission to make Mr Allen's delivery himself was no challenge, for it was a large order and Allen a good customer. Mr Davis was only too happy that his most reliable employee should take on the task. It was the next request, to not return until the morrow, which was dearest to John's heart.

Davis looked up from his desk in some amazement, for only twice before in almost three years had John begged leave to depart early for the day… on the same day each year. Davis glanced at his calendar, narrowed his eyes, and silently assented. He knew something of John Thornton's history and permitting one afternoon per year was not a great hardship when such a valuable employee desired it.

John's heart skipped as he hefted the parcel on his shoulders. His feet, it must be confessed, nearly danced the entire way to his destination. Allen came to the door himself at his knock, and within a few minutes, John held the treasure of knowledge in his shaking hands. "Thank you, sir! I shall return them by Monday!"

Allen grunted. "Keep them, Thornton, and may they do you some good." Then, he closed the door without another word, nor even a nod of farewell.

John hesitated on the step a moment, torn between guilt over accepting such a sentimental and precious gift, and hope that the grieving father might now find peace in passing on his son's legacy. He lifted his hand to knock once more but stilled it. This had been Allen's wish, and he would honour it.

He clasped the books to his chest and began walking, not even examining their titles. What mattered their names? He would treasure them as a father's memory. His eyes stung, and he lengthened his strides. There was only one place in all the world where he needed to be just now, and the long walk would be necessary to regulate his mind and heart.

An hour later that familiar stone gazed back at him. John studied it, through eyes now a year older and wiser than on his last visit. *George Thornton.*

A bit of moss was starting at the bottom of the "G". John stepped close and gently carved it out with his finger, but small grooves were starting where the spores had worked into the stone. By next year, each letter would be similarly embellished. The earth was taking back its own.

His brow furrowed as he traced through each painful letter, cleaning and restoring, but his efforts would avail little. Man, in his natural state, lay defenceless against the ravages of time. He would be no different when his own turn came to pass into eternity. What remnant was Man's to leave? A moss-covered stone? A sunken place in the ground, testifying to what mouldered beneath? His jaw tightened. *A mountain of debt and shame?*

Instantly, he regretted that last thought. He clenched his teeth, hissing out a purposeful breath. *I promised myself not to hate him any longer!* Nothing good could come of such malicious sentiments.

John's shoulders dropped, and he remembered the slim volumes in his left hand. In them, he hoped to seek the key to his own future. Industry, that would be his legacy and his epitaph—*and may it be a more lasting one than a neglected stone!* At last, he turned the books over to inspect them.

There were four of them. The top volume, curiously, was an officer's copy of maritime law. What value he would ever find there he could not guess, but he resolved to devour it, all the same. The law had always fascinated him, and this was his first taste of the real thing.

Two technical manuals of nondescript subjects followed, their titles worn bare by countless hands. The last, simply entitled "Steam," by William Ripper, was covered in faded red binding and looked to have been the subject of many a long evening of study. To this volume he turned his passionate attention as he reverently fondled the cover.

"Father," he murmured, speaking to that stone for the first time since his humiliating encounter two years ago, when he had screamed in impotent rage. "I was given some books today. I thought you would like to know. I am studying again, Father! It is not Latin or Greek, I am sorry to say." He permitted himself a light chuckle, for surely his father would have laughed just then.

"Do you remember how I was always trying to take things apart and rebuild them? Oh, what trouble I must have given you! I never did properly repair your Barlow's Wheel, but never again did you rebuke me about it. Why did you not? I know you lost the investor on my account, but by then I had gone to London…." John's voice failed, his throat tightening around his words.

He blinked several times before he could find it within his power to continue. "Oh, Father, how I missed you those years! What I would give to have them back, to return home for holidays to you and to Mother, and to sit by the fire in the evening to tell you everything I had done!"

He had given up on blinking to control the flood from his eyes. "Do you remember that first time I came home? I thought Mother would never let me go. I knew then how her heart was breaking at my absence, and I could feel the sacrifice she made in each breath... oh, but Father, then you came, and you took my hand like a man. I think it was the first time anyone had ever done so, and I felt at last I was *someone*... a son you could be proud of...."

He halted as an uncontrollable shudder racked through his tall frame. His face was streaming—even his nose was running miserably by now, but he did not care. He fought valiantly against the lump in his throat and forged on. "Father, how I miss you!"

This last confession, words he had sworn would never leave his lips, tore through the final veil of his bitterness. He crumpled to his knees, heedless of the autumn damp through his thin and patched trousers and heaved a piteous sob. Three years now, his father had been gone; three years in which he had grown to full manhood while yet a boy. So much had changed! His mother was no longer the cheerful, tart, indomitable woman she had been; his sister no longer the innocently affectionate child of his father's years.

A scarce few moments passed in which he permitted himself the exorcism of all his grief. How much life his father had missed! In due course, however, the working fatigue which naturally accompanied a man's lot in life dulled and cut short the expressions of pain. His body's all-consuming will to thrive, more than his sense of reason, asserted itself once more. The tightness in his throat eased, and his eyes felt suddenly drier than they had done before.

He drew a slow breath, restoring himself, and glanced back to the book. Absently, he thumbed the cover open, and read the first line aloud. "*The object of the study of steam and its applications is to obtain from the steam engine the greatest possible amount of work for the least possible expenditure of fuel.*" He paused, smiled, then laughed. "I think you will enjoy this one, Father. Look here...."

And so, he read. Squatting there by that lonely stone, John read aloud until the light grew too dim for his eyes and his knees were stiff with cold. When at last he rose, he was shivering with the bone-chill of one who had fallen through the depths of his darkest feelings, but it was a warm welcome that awaited him at his door.

A few days later, John was greeted almost at the door by his wife as he entered for the evening. Her eyes were dilated unnaturally, and a slight flush stained her ivory cheeks. She held a slip of parchment to her heart and seemed full of something.

"Margaret? What has happened?"

"I have finally heard from Frederick," was her simple and pregnant response. She hesitated, then with slightly shaken fingers, pulled the letter from herself and extended it to him. "I wrote immediately when Papa died, and again just after we wed. The letters reached him almost at the same time, and it has taken until now to receive his answer."

He took her free hand, squeezing it in reassurance before he accepted the letter. "Are you well?"

She nodded, staring in foreboding at the pages. "His letter to me was… comforting. I have not read all, for he included one that was addressed strictly to you. I…" she drew breath, then her fingers twisted together. "I have no way of knowing what he will have to say."

"You fear he will speak harshly to me? Never mind that." He kissed her forehead. "I think I can manage a brother in another country, even if he disapproves of me so strongly that he would take the trouble to abuse me from a distance."

She drew a tight breath. "I do not think he will. His words to me sounded… surprised, I suppose, but I believe he took the time to master any feelings of astonishment before he wrote. It must be why he delayed in answering, for I expected to hear from him at least a fortnight ago."

"Come, love, you look far too nervous. Sit by me in the drawing-room while we read these. I confess to an insatiable curiosity about the man."

She complied, and a moment later they were seated on the sofa and he unfolded the first letter.

My dearest little sister,

I have grieved until I can scarcely draw breath. Father gone! And I never able to see him again, or to mourn with you. It is so monstrously unfair, it raises the bile in my gorge. My poor dear sister, to discover him yourself, with no one to help but old Dixon!

I ought to have been there, Margaret. I could have spared you! But perhaps it was better that I was not, for we both remember how it was when Mother died. It was you who sustained me though I wished to be of some good to you. I would have proved a burden, I know, but how I longed to board the first ship to see you!

Such was my wish when I received your letter, but then just after came the second. I cannot imagine my little sister wed! You must give me leave to think of you now and again as the girl you were when I left home. Yet, when I attempt it, the woman I saw last year returns to mind, and I can but think your husband the most fortunate man alive, whether he knows it or not.

Are you happy, Margaret? I know you well enough—for you are like myself—to believe you married Mr Thornton out of some measure of affection rather than the simple need for a protector. I must confess myself astonished, for I had not thought before that you were fond of the man, but the way you write of him now, and the way you defended him even then, set my mind at ease for you.

How I wish I could have seen you at your wedding, my dear! I have been denied the chance to kiss your cheek and walk with you on my arm. I shall never see your happiness, so you must take care to write often and well, so I may savour your words and form a picture in my mind of your life as it is to become.

My own dearest hopes for felicity have been answered. I have never known contentment as I have found with my Dolores. Margaret, I am to be a father! Can you believe it? I ought to have written when we first knew of it, but we were cautious, and did not want to raise false hope in you and our father until we could be certain.

Our joy shall be complete in the spring, and I am the veriest mooncalf of a husband as I wait with my Dolores. I hope this news brings you some happiness as well, for such news has been of short supply in our family of late. Be certain to tell Dixon, will you? How I miss the old dear!

The letter turned to more domestic matters, having set aside, after the beginning, the heaviness of grief. It was as if the author could no longer bear to think on his sorrows and was determined to seek some pleasure in the correspondence. He wrote minutely of his new family and home, then in more general terms of his flourishing business. He even reflected with some humour at one point that he, like Margaret, had married into the world of trade and commerce, and could yet hold his head high. John read with growing ease through two full sheets of paper, but Margaret's figure remained slightly tense beside him. It was at the last line that he understood some of her apprehension.

I am afraid I must close, Margaret. Do write to me soon to assure me again of your happiness, for I must confess, I still struggle somewhat to imagine it. I have included a note for your Mr Thornton. I hope he recognises the treasure he has been given, for I think no man could deserve you. Farewell for now, dear one.

Fred

John rested his hand over Margaret's, and her fingers squeezed his in answer. "He does not sound so very terrifying. He feels protective of you, and who can blame him? It was his place, now that your father is gone, and he was denied the right to catechise me properly. He knows nothing of me save that I saw my opportunity to marry the most dazzling woman of my acquaintance and snapped her up before any others could come about."

Margaret blushed. "John, you ought not speak so. People will overhear and think you serious."

"I am. Do you think I wanted to allow some other to 'help' you? Little would anyone else know just what they had bargained for, but I had a fair idea." He smiled as she nudged him with her elbow and turned his attention to the second letter to break the seal.

Dear Mr Thornton,

I congratulate you, sir, on your marriage to my sister. I will own that I wished when I visited Milton before to know you, but I never anticipated it to be in this manner that we would make an acquaintance. My impressions of you were not at all what I would have expected to feel for my future brother, and I had not the least prescience that it might be thus.

You must forgive me, the absent brother who scarcely knows his sister as she is now, but I wish to write to you very seriously about certain matters. My father spoke highly of you, and Margaret has done the same, so I am convinced that you are a respectable man who will treat her well. However, I wonder if her life to this point has adequately prepared her to become the wife of an industrialist.

I have no place to reproach or to doubt; no power of persuasion over my sister, nor present authority to dictate to you. I only beseech you as a gentleman—dare I presume a gentleman in love? For I know little of your motives for marriage, but I cannot fathom any man not holding my sister dear in his heart. I pray, sir, that you treat her with tenderness befitting her upbringing.

Think not that I admonish you because I believe you a boor—rather, as a man only married within the last year myself, I have come to understand the weaker sex in a manner I had never done before. I would see my sister happy and content in all things, and you are the only man now with the power to ensure that. I expect that Milton is all you have ever known as home, but I assure you, the lady you know as your wife keeps within her heart the memory of a far gentler place.

I share a similar misfortune to my sister, but when I think fondly of the home of my youth, it is with the practical sobriety of a man, untroubled by the sentiments which so often beset a woman. You would be a wise man to do all within your power to comfort and encourage your wife, so that in time, she comes to love the home you have given her quite as much as any other she has known.

I write in the hope that future years will see us as amicable acquaintances, perhaps even friends, if circumstances permit. I should like to meet you in person one day, but if I never do, know that my exile has been borne with bitterness. It has robbed me of both my beloved parents and left me with a sister I hardly know and have done nothing for. For her sake, I would not grieve her by returning to England now, but I shall hope that one day, a way might be found for you to come here, so I may see with my own eyes the contentment she professes.

I remain yours most respectfully,

Frederick Hale

John read the letter twice, then creased it thoughtfully again in its original folds. Margaret's brow was furrowed, for he had held it in such a way that she could read as well as he. She drew a slow breath, her thoughts seeming to turn inward as he put the letter aside.

"Do you know," he mused, "I had intended to take up my old naval regulations book and the clippings your father saved from the papers. Perhaps there is some defence left to his case that has been overlooked. It is worth investigating, after all."

"It is good of you to think of it, John, but I know there is nothing. Fred is safe where he is." Her hands were knotted in her lap, and her eyes fell to them as she seemed to exert some effort to steady her breathing.

"Margaret?" He reached for her hand, gratified at the easy way her fingers twined with his. "You seem troubled. Are you well?"

She released her breath as slowly as she had drawn it, then offered him a cheerful smile. "Perfectly, John. It was not so frightful as I expected."

He glanced to the bit of paper again. "Margaret, it would be no shame for you to confess some misgivings about…" he stopped, searching for the right words. "I know you never dreamed of marriage to a cotton manufacturer. A year ago, you were still horrified by this city and shocked by me, and now you have embraced both for the rest of your life. Have you never felt those moments of disquiet with how matters have settled?"

"No, John. That is not to say that I do not still remember Helstone, and even London with fondness, but I have no regrets. Regret and self-pity weakened my mother and father so, and I will make no place for them in my own heart."

"But as your brother has written, there may come a time… something unexpected, perhaps… a sorrow that overtakes your strength in the moment and renders your determination weaker than you had known it to be. You will not turn from me, will you, my Margaret? You will share your feelings and allow me to comfort you?"

She cupped both hands at his jaw, not speaking, but she tipped his face low until her forehead touched to his. Their noses brushed together as she nodded gently, then she pledged her agreement with a soft kiss. "Whatever comes, John, let us face this life as one."

His arms slipped around her, and she lowered her head to his chest to sigh in contentment. "Aye, love," he answered huskily. "I promise."

Helstone
June 1849

"Ah, Margaret! I was wondering where you had gone."

Margaret was just hanging her bonnet when her father greeted her, with genuine pleasure warming his dear voice. She turned round to him. "Good afternoon, Papa. I was out walking, and I encountered young Sammy Roberts. Did you know his mother has injured her leg? And Mr Roberts has a dreadful cough."

"Yes, I saw them a few days ago." Mr Hale smiled at her—that wistful, half-broken expression that had been his for two years now, each time he looked upon her—then, his eyes fell meaningfully to a letter in his hand.

Margaret drew near in interest. "Papa, is something wrong?"

"Wrong? No, my dear. It is from my old friend Mr Bell. You must remember him, I suppose."

"The one from Oxford?"

"He is in South America—or was, when he sent this a few weeks ago. He may be back in England by now. He often goes there for the winter, you remember. He prefers the warmer weather."

"It seems a long way to go! Is he well?"

"Other than the same complaint he has had for years." Mr Hale tapped the letter against his fingers and drew a hesitant breath. "Margaret, he has seen Frederick."

Margaret's limbs ran cold, and in the next moment she was touching his arm, pleading to know more. "Is Frederick well, Papa? Is he safe?"

Her father blinked several times, then passed her the letter. "Mr Bell writes that he has grown taller than I by now and has a great thick beard. He has been searching for better work. It sounds as if Bell was able to introduce him to someone who might have a position for him."

Margaret's eyes were flying over the letter as her father spoke. "In Spain! Why there?"

Mr Hale shrugged. "I suppose word must travel through ship hands and businessmen, around port cities, that sort of thing. It must be a very large trading house. Perhaps Frederick will find work as a clerk at their shipping yards or something. I understand he is already on his way there."

"I believe I shall be happier to think of him in Spain rather than in South America. It is not half so far away, but shall he be safe?"

Mr Hale's weariness had begun to show through his expression, and he merely shook his head. "I hope so." He turned away, then, as if he could not remember his purpose, sagged into his old chair and rubbed his brow.

Margaret hesitated, then softly claimed the seat beside him. "Papa?"

He lifted his face, once again blinking rapidly. "What is it, my dear?"

"Will you tell me how it happened? Did Fred ever write why he—"

Her father was shaking his head again. "Pray, do not ask me, Margaret. I cannot bear to think on it. Your mother has some letters from him. Perhaps she will show them to you, but I cannot speak of it." His face disappeared behind his hand once more, and he was silent.

Margaret sighed. No, her mother would not show her the letters. Someday, perhaps, but until then, she seemed doomed to ignorance. She frowned, and her gaze scanned the brooding walls, the musty books on the shelves, the old tapestries and rugs that were so familiar. It seemed to her that each summer when she came home, she should see Frederick there, ready to race her to the barn or count the stars with her. When she found that he was not there, she sought an escape from the house. Thus, she went walking every day.

"Papa," she ventured, nibbling her lip. "Would you like to go down to the stream with me this afternoon? It would be cheerful, would it not?"

He straightened—that fragile smile again—"Are you trying to save me from my own melancholy, Margaret? You may be easy, for I shall not remain so long. Let me be morose for a time, and then I shall be myself again. But stay—" he interjected as she began to rise—"will you take this letter to show your mother? I think... she would rather have it from you."

She glanced down at the paper in her hands but did not leave at once. "Papa, what do you do when you are grieved? Mama stays in her room on bad days, but I prefer to go out. Is it not that way for you? I cannot bear to leave you alone in your study if there is some way I might comfort you."

He raised his head in genuine surprise. "Why, Margaret! What a thing to hear you say. Forgive me, my dear, I occasionally forget that you are now sixteen, and no longer a child."

"But I am still your daughter, and it pains me to see you suffer. I know Frederick would not like to think of you despairing over him."

"Despairing? No, my dear, I do not despair… well, not entirely. That would be wrong, a grievous sin. Frederick is safe, he has been spared, and may even find himself happy someday. I pray for that! I pity myself, that is all, for the loss of his company, and I pity your mother that she has been robbed of her child, but there is nothing more I can do. And so, I keep myself busy. It does help stave off the gloom."

Margaret settled beside him again, eagerly leaning forward in attendance. "How so?"

"Well… of course it is my duty to counsel and offer solace to those in the parish. I often find that when my energies are directed to the cares of others, my own sorrows diminish—at least for a time. I cannot think that man was meant to languish in his own heartache, but to look about and serve his fellows, for he has some empathy in experience. Are not all thereby cheered and encouraged? For at least then…." He sighed, his brow pinched.

"Then, what?"

"Why, then… we see that there are others. We are curious creatures, Margaret. We can bear almost anything, so long as we understand that we are not alone." He pressed his mouth into a thin line, then smiled round at her again. "You had better take your mother that letter. She will wish to read it before her tea."

Reluctantly, she rose, her eyes on the letter. "Perhaps," she mused cautiously, "that is, if Mamma feels equal to it after her tea, I shall ask if she would like to come with me to take a basket to the Robertses."

Her father looked up, a curious light in his eye, then stood. He drew near, a hint of wonder in his manner, and nodded slowly. "If you can persuade her to it, Margaret. Indeed, you are no longer a child! Perhaps you will succeed where I have not."

***

John was not in his finest spirits when he entered his door. His work day had gone ill, but he could do nothing further to improve matters today. Thus, it was that he arrived home a full hour early, frustrated and useless and eager to salve his bruised dignity by a private interlude with his wife. The only trouble was that he did not see her.

He cast a bemused glance round the drawing-room, then looked to his mother in consternation. "Where is Margaret?"

Her brows raised, but she kept her eyes on her sewing. "Gone walking, as she does many an afternoon."

"Gone walking—alone? She does? But how did I not know of this?"

"It is not as if she did not do so before you wed. It ought not surprise you."

"Yes, but I thought she would have mentioned it to me. Where did she go?"

Silver scissors flashed in the fading light through the window, and she held her needlework up to evaluate the finished product. "She does not say. She goes, and then she returns in time to dress before you come home. That is all I know."

Annoyed, he turned round for his topcoat. "I will be back, Mother."

"Where do you go, John? You do not think to find her, do you? A pretty thing it would be, the master searching all over Milton for his wayward wife. You would do better to remain here and not make the buffoon of yourself. If you must upbraid her for her foolhardiness, do so in privacy so you do not lose face before others."

He grimaced. "I hardly think to lecture Margaret over walking out. She may have what freedoms she chooses, but I am concerned for her safety. Do you have no idea where she goes?"

"Like enough, she calls on the wives of workers. I heard her speak of a woman who takes in washing, and another who used to be in your employ but fell too ill for work. I told you, did I not, that lass would bring trouble?"

"Trouble! How do you mean?"

"If she is seen to act against your knowledge or wishes—"

"There are no strikes or uprisings at present. I do not think taking a basket, as was always her way, is any challenge to my position. Where is this washer woman she speaks of?"

His mother folded her needlework and tucked it away. "I only know that she usually returns in about half an hour from now. You may as well stay here, for you would not find her before that."

He hissed in vexation. If his only option was to wait, he would do so in his study, where he could be free to pace and chafe all he liked without scrutiny. When he entered it, however, weariness overcame him instead. He had looked for her to help ward off the draining fatigue of his day, and without her, he could only sink into his chair and scowl... or, perhaps he could read. At least it took his mind off her absence....

He frowned and rolled his eyes when the first book that came to hand was one of Mr Hale's old sermon notebooks, but he had not the energy to search for another. He flipped it open, scanning impatiently for a moment until his eyes slowed, captivated by the familiar script and recalling the mellifluous tones of his friend. Smiling in spite of himself, he forced his mind to do his bidding.

John did not hear her return to the house and started when his study door swung as if thrust by an agitated hand. He set the book aside and began to stand, prepared to make his demands about her whereabouts, but she preceded him.

"John! I have just heard that you intend to cut hours at the mill. Is it true?"

"I do not know where you might have heard that—nor do I know where you have been. What do you mean by leaving in the afternoons without giving word of your destination or taking someone with you?"

Her brow wrinkled, and she turned self-consciously round to close the door. "I have always walked out whenever I may, and never have I taken an attendant. I am not such a fine lady as that!"

"It is nothing to do with being a fine lady. You could have been insulted on the streets, or worse. No longer can you vanish in the crowds as an unknown; you are my wife, and there are those who would do me or mine harm."

"Really, John! I cannot walk down the street but half the people I pass offer me a kindly greeting, and not for your name but my own. Do you think anyone would suffer harm to come to me?"

He suppressed a frustrated grumble and paced round behind her, trying to form a rational argument without raising her ire. "You speak the truth, and I confess to some pride in what you say—you were honoured in this city before our marriage for your own merits, and you are more so now, for any would know you to be under my protection. But you have seen desperation and even wickedness. You know it can drive men beyond reason, and right or wrong, my name is anathema to some."

She raised a brow. "So, there is truth to the report that you might cut hours?"

"One subject at a time, I beg you. I cannot be satisfied with you walking out alone, and likely to the worst parts of town. Why would you not at least tell Mother where you had gone?"

"I told Dixon, who would have told you, if you had troubled yourself to ask her."

"I do not intend to run after your serving woman to learn of your whereabouts! Do I not do you the courtesy of sending a note when my duties take me from the mill? I think you owe me at least that much."

She turned, setting her hat aside on his desk. "You need to know all my affairs, is that it?" Her expression hardened, and he felt the hair raise on the back of his neck.

"All? Hardly, but we *are* married. Does that not indicate that I should know more than your maid? By heaven, Margaret, would you disrespect me so blatantly that all should know of my ignorance regarding your activities?"

"Is this how it is to be, then?" Her back was to him, but he could see her drawing breath, squaring her shoulders. Her voice trembled faintly. "To save face for you, I must defer to you in even the minutest of interests? Shall you provide me a list of the places and people whom I may visit?"

"Good Lord, Margaret, do not make me out to be a tyrant. You know I do not object to some liberties for you. I do not even protest that you call on the workers who would despise me—though common sense dictates I should."

"Indeed, you should!" she retorted in a mocking tone. "We cannot have Mrs Thornton defying the Master in public! Think how his pride would suffer for it."

He stopped before his bookcase, flexing his fists and pressing them into the wood until the shelves began to shake. His temper was sparking... he must control it! But it was too late, her provocation too painful. He whirled.

"I have no thought for my pride! I have told you before—I never expected that our interests would always be aligned, but I assumed we would speak to each other before acting, rather than doing battle behind closed doors afterwards. You take risks you do not, or worse, *will* not understand. Do you not know what offences have been done against women in the name of jealousy? Or do not consider that, if you please. You are a beautiful woman, Margaret. Think you that none would act on foolish impulse to satisfy their own base desires?"

She turned to face him, her lips curled back from flashing white teeth and her breast trembling in short, heated breaths. "None has ever dared to be impertinent to me, save for you! I believe it is *you* who are possessed of jealousy, John Thornton. I was under my father's protection before I was under yours, and never did he admonish me for my looks, or suggest that by simply walking on the street I presented a temptation. Shall I take to wearing sackcloth? Would that comfort you, knowing that I lure none to eternal perdition by looking upon me?"

"Dammit, Margaret, I meant nothing of the kind, and I am *not* your father!"

"No. You are a good deal more possessive." She lifted her chin. "And vulgar."

John yanked his fingers through his hair, quaking in rage. "Forgive my language." He paced again, trying to breathe, to see clearly, but it was no use.

He stepped quickly to her and grasped her upper arms in a fevered embrace, heedless of the way she tried to draw back. "What robbed your father of his will to live? Was it when he lost his son, or his wife?"

She blinked and ceased arching away from him. "I believe... Fred's exile weakened him, but it was Mamma's death that really killed him."

He shuddered and eased his grip on her arms but did not step back. Neither did she, and they stood so close that a passing draught blew a loosened strand of her hair before his eyes. "Margaret, do you think it would not kill me if something happened to you?"

She turned her face away, her mouth puckered in angry contemplation.

"Forgive me," he muttered, low and unsteadily as his hands fell. "I did not intend to frighten you."

"If you frightened me, it was not when you grabbed my arms." She faced him again, the rims of her eyes red and moist. "I fear losing myself. I feared—for years, I have feared—that marriage to any man would cause me to diminish in some way. I did not wish to be changed, so I avoided it, refused to consider it. You frightened me when you proposed that first time, and I found that the very sort of man who most had the power to bend a woman to his wishes was the one who would desire me... but the most terrifying moment of all was when I discovered I wanted none other."

"I do not understand."

"Have you never faced a prospect that daunted you, filled you with dread, and yet drew you so irresistibly that you would gladly see yourself destroyed rather than denied this thing you desired?"

His eyes narrowed. "Her name was Margaret Hale."

A crease appeared at the corner of her mouth. "And do you, John Thornton, have the least idea how intimidating you can be? Even without intending to be so, you are like living with a titan. Were I not determined to keep up something of my old self, I truly... honestly fear there would be nothing left of her." She looked away again, shuddering in some remnant of her wrath, and released a slow breath.

"Margaret—" he reached hesitantly for her hand, and she gave it. Her fingers were cold. "You know I do not wish to dominate you. How could I, when this very nature you fear losing is the one I worshipped from the moment we met? But you must also let me protect you."

"Perhaps it was foolish of me," she whispered guiltily. "I did not care to think on it, but you are right that I should at least leave you word of my intentions."

"That is all I ask. When we made our vows, I gave myself into your keeping, and you promised to do likewise. We no longer belong only to ourselves, but do not believe for a moment that I would bend or break you, my Margaret."

She crossed her arms; her look had softened, but a doubtful shiver remained. "Even when my wishes are contrary to yours? I still wish to go alone when I choose... shall you object to that?"

"Are you speaking from your good sense, or your old cursed defiance?"

She laughed, a teary, relenting sound, and shook her head. "In London, a lady would never dream of venturing out on her own. It was simply not done. But here... I have always had that freedom, simply because I had not the means to keep a maid everywhere I went. I suppose... that has changed. Perhaps I will not go alone to certain neighbourhoods."

"Promise me you will be more judicious, and I shall make no more protests."

"John—" her lips pinched, and she raised those glorious eyes, now flooded with emotion. "Perhaps it is a poor time to ask again...."

He sighed. "You are the most stubborn, maddening creature I have ever met."

"Do you not have a mirror?"

He shook his head and tugged her hand towards a sofa. "Sit with me, rather than squaring off as if we each held a pistol. Yes—" he eased her into the seat— "there is talk of cutting hours. I have not yet decided about it."

"But in the winter! The workers will go hungry!"

"Winter is always one of the leanest times for a cotton mill, and they all know it. Some other masters have talked of it—raw cotton remains the same because of some supply issues from America. Finished prices have dropped, though, and we'll not see them raise until spring. It makes little sense to continue buying and producing cotton as if we cannot keep it on the shelves."

"But the warehouse is hardly full. Are you not still trying to catch up with your orders from months ago?"

"So is everyone. One month out of work, and it takes us a year to recover! But we are nearly out of it, and if everyone slows production during a bad season, none could cast blame on us for doing likewise. It might be the very reprieve we need."

"Reprieve from what? How is everyone not harmed?"

"Why, Margaret, we cannot continue paying to produce something we cannot sell for a fair price. If we did, the price would drop even lower, and then I should never be able to pay back the bank."

She twisted her fingers in her lap, her brow knit thoughtfully. "The others have the same trouble?"

"Not precisely. Marlborough Mills is unique—three years ago I replaced all the looms with the newest designs. We are far more efficient than any others. At peak capacity, this mill dominates the market, but at low times, we are the most vulnerable. The debt is not yet repaid, and it weighs as an anchor about our necks."

"I have often wondered about that, since you are generally so averse to financial obligations."

"Where there is no prospect of recovery, yes. I will never involve myself in the sorts of schemes my father did, borrowing money with no means of repaying it other than vain hope. I considered this a necessary investment, and the debt is secured by the equipment itself. If we were ever to face ruin, only the business would suffer. I have no intention of spending another half of my life repaying such a debt."

"But the situation now, with the workers—"

He cut her off with a sigh. "I have made no decisions. I do not wish to send any home with shortened pay, but neither do I wish to tell them in six months that they must seek employment elsewhere. Where did you hear this rumour?"

She lifted her shoulders. "A few women I stopped and talked to, they said it was common knowledge."

"And you were as annoyed with me for not telling you as I was when I did not know your whereabouts?" She rewarded him with an abashed smile.

"Do me the justice of believing I would tell you before you were obliged to listen to hearsay. I suppose I might have told you that the subject had been raised, but I am not considering it seriously. Knowing, as I do, your sentiments on the matter, you may be assured that I will give them due consideration... but my decision will be for the good of the mill, not sentiment—yours or mine."

She pressed her hands on her knees, nodding jerkily. "I understand. Thank you, John."

"You needn't thank me. I owe you that much, just as I am also bound to see you content in your life here. Margaret, if you wish to retain some sense of your old ways, why do your family's things still darken the back room? I thought you would have brought them out to see the light of day and lend these austere rooms of ours a bit of Hampshire charm."

"Oh...." She nibbled her lip uncomfortably. "I did not intend to disrupt...."

"My mother expects you to make whatever changes to the house you see fit. It would be no surprise to her."

"Nor would such changes be precisely welcome. I shall not win her regard by sweeping away all she holds dear. If the price of harmony between myself and your mother is enduring a few furnishings that are not to my taste, then I will gladly pay it."

"What of the management of the house? Surely she could not object to your rights there."

"She does not. Some matters have become my concern, but there are others, such as the ordering of candles in the evening or the reading of devotions, which she guards as her own. I do not think she means offence. I suppose we all like to feel ourselves useful and necessary, and it would be unfair for me to demand all her privileges at once."

He brushed her cheek and leaned close to kiss her forehead. "Then I shall keep out of the matter. If any can earn her place in my mother's heart, it is you. And what of myself? Am I forgiven my brutish behaviour?"

"Not quite."

"Not quite! What further penance would you have of me?"

She smiled, a slightly wicked light in her eye. "A few hours of your unmitigated devotion should suffice to restore my spirits. Perhaps after dinner?"

He hooked his finger in his cravat and yanked at the knot. "Who needs dinner?"

Nine

Marlborough Mills, Milton
April 1842

George Kramer dropped his pen when a knock sounded at his door. "Come!" he called in irritation to his unseen visitor.

The door to his office swung open, the hinges complaining at such assertive treatment. A tall, well-built young man still held the latch. His hair was dark, nearly black, but his brilliant blue eyes flashed in contrast to the rest of his stern face.

Kramer evaluated his caller for half a second. He looked to be about twenty; full-grown at something impressively over six feet. There was nothing lanky or lean about him, as one often saw in a youth so tall, for his chest and shoulders were already filled out. By the firm set of his jaw and the agile way he carried himself, he looked as though he knew hard work. There was something strikingly familiar about the young man, but… Kramer furrowed his brow. Whatever memory the lad's appearance had jogged seemed lost to the rolling sands of time.

"Good afternoon, Mr Kramer." The young man's voice was already deep and sure for his years, and Kramer wondered fleetingly if he were not older than he looked. "Thank you for seeing me. My name is John Thornton."

Kramer felt his expression turn from puzzled to horrified. His gaze swept the lad's face over again, and he was assured of his conclusion. "Why, you... you're George Thornton's boy!"

Young Thornton's jaw tightened in acknowledgment. "I am, sir. I believe I have a debt to settle with you." He searched within the pocket of his meticulously clean, but threadbare coat, and produced an envelope. Without ceremony, he extended it. "If my records are correct, this should be ten percent of the total debt, including an allowance for interest."

Mystified, Kramer hesitantly accepted the envelope. "Young man, I never expected you and your mother to assume such an obligation. It has been at least three or four years now!"

"Five, sir," the youth corrected him.

"Five!" Kramer shook his head. "I am sorry, my good fellow. I applaud you for taking this duty on yourself, but you have a mother and sister to care for, if I am not mistaken. I cannot accept." He pressed the folded paper away from himself, but the boy would not lift his hand to touch it.

"Do you not wish to count it?"

Kramer drew back the envelope, offended. "I meant no slight, young man! I would not wish to take from a widow and her orphans."

George Thornton's son squared his already strong shoulders, and the youthful innocence of his face took on a hard, worldly look. "I am no orphan, sir, and I am well able to care for my family. I would live a free, honest man, and once I have repaid all my father's creditors, I shall do so."

"Do you mean, son, that you have held the record of this all these years? Why, it was only thirty pounds, as I recall. I had written it off ages ago!"

"Thirty-five, Mr Kramer, and I have calculated an additional five for interest. If you do not think that amount fair, name your figure and I shall recompense you adequately."

Mr Kramer lowered the envelope, and when he spoke, his voice was gentle. "Tell me, young man—if I may be so bold—how many others have you begun to repay?"

"All of them, sir, as I have said. My father had numerous creditors."

"Recently?"

"It has taken me three days to call upon everyone. You are the last. I regret that it is not yet the full amount you are due, but I intend to return next year with another instalment."

Kramer squinted, deciding to test the boy. "I saw Mr Hamper only this morning. He said nothing about any of this." He allowed the statement to hang, wondering how young Thornton might justify himself.

"I saw him yesterday," was the steady response. "As the matter concerned no other, I asked for his confidence."

Kramer's eyes widened so startlingly that his glasses slipped down his nose. This was a brassy youth indeed, to approach Miles Hamper with a five-year-old debt, and then to ask the man to keep the repayment of it to himself! The very thought of recovery was so wonderful that Kramer could scarce believe it.

How was the entire town not abuzz with word of this singular young man's actions? Why, the sheer novelty of the idea alone would be enough to amuse all his acquaintance for weeks—and Hamper! The man was not known to still his tongue at any man's pleasure, much less the request of a boy who was scarcely shaving!

"How is it that Hamper agreed to your conditions?"

"It was not a condition, sir. I had already paid him his due. Very likely he is content to remain silent because he does not wish to appear ungenerous, as you do not yourself. I have no fear of shame for myself, sir—my father's actions were his own, and they are in the past. I do not seek praise, only justice. It is mine to set right a wrong, and I am satisfied at last to begin to do so. I will thank you for your time, sir, and for your patience. I have not taken it lightly, I assure you. Good-day, Mr Kramer."

Young John Thornton replaced his tattered hat and turned to the corridor once more. Kramer stared after him in mute astonishment. Seldom—almost never—had he encountered one of such mildness and force all at once. He sensed that few would dare to defy the lad when he was grown to full manhood—and such a man as he might be!

Thornton must have laboured devotedly all these years, saving a substantial portion of what meagre earnings the family could survive without. To at last find satisfaction in the repayment of a debt which could not rightfully be called his own, and to do all without pomp or fanfare was too remarkable for him to take in. He stood frozen by his own desk, staring blankly at the envelope.

What might such a lad make of himself? The boy's character was fixed. He only wanted for opportunity, and with such an air of authority already, Kramer had no doubt it would seek him out. His fingers tightened on the bulging paper in his hand. He could use an honest man at his side just now.

The wizening old man cast the envelope towards his desk, for it was not the prize he sought. Hurriedly, he stumped out to the corridor outside his office. "Thornton!"

The tall figure had already rounded the corner and descended the steps, but at Kramer's voice, he retraced his path. "Yes, sir?"

Kramer panted as he jogged to meet him. "Do you need work, boy?"

The grim jaw thrust forward in a flash of pride. "I have work, sir. I thought that much was obvious."

"Aye, and what do you make? Eighteen shillings a week?" The smooth face flinched involuntarily, and Kramer guessed that he would not get a straight answer, but the boy's true pay was somewhat less than that.

The blue eyes sparked in defiance. "I do not need charity, Mr Kramer." He turned to go once more.

Kramer felt a sly smile growing. He was starting to like this boy! Proud in all the ways a man ought to be, yet unafraid of the humility of truth, he possessed the essential qualities that would help him go far. The broad back was already disappearing, and with a last hopeful summons, he beckoned once more. "Is it charity, lad, to recognise one who might be useful to me?" The figure did not turn, but he had stopped.

Encouraged, Kramer tried again. "How old are you, Thornton?"

The square profile moved to face him. "Nineteen, sir. In three months."

Kramer's brows jumped in surprise. "Not quite nineteen! Oh, that is young," he mused, stroking his jaw in apparent thought.

Thornton's eyes narrowed, taking up the challenge. "I have been performing a man's work for a long while now, Mr Kramer."

"Aye," Kramer shook his head in mock worry. "But you can have no experience, I think. Not in something like my business here. Where is it you have been working?"

"A draper's shop in Weston, about ten miles from here," was the unabashed response. "I know textiles, sir."

"Hmm, but it is the machinery that concerns me. I need a man who understands it. I imagine also that you have never had the management of others?"

"I have two lads who work under me, sir. As for the machinery, I can learn, and I would not burden anyone overmuch with the necessity of teaching me."

Kramer pursed his lips, pleased with the boy's staunch defence of himself. "Come with me, Thornton."

Choosing his destination with care, he deliberately led the youth to what was, admittedly, one of the worst work stations in his entire factory. He watched the fascination lighting in the dark eyes as he beheld for the first time the massive carding room where the cotton fibres were combed and aligned in preparation for the weaving process. The noise was deafening, the humidity stifling in the summer heat, and the sheer force of the machinery violent and fearsome.

Kramer observed in silence. It would have done him no good to speak, for even the sharp ears of youth would be overwhelmed in such an environ. John Thornton walked slowly among the various monstrosities dominating the room, needing no shepherd or guide to usher him about. It seemed to Kramer almost as though the lad grew yet taller as the power of the room energised his frame.

He paused at one point and stared at the workers, his quick eyes following every movement, every flick of cotton, every shuddering pulse of the carding machine. With swift intuition, the boy's gaze flitted to the long overhead belt running to the next room, where the next phase of the process was already underway.

Kramer allowed a triumphant smile. The lad was well and truly hooked. With a very little more exposure, it would be a steam engine that beat within that young body, and precision gears would drive that active mind. This was a man he could work with! When Thornton looked back to him at last, he waved him to his side.

Together, they moved to the relative cool and peace of the warehouse. Kramer wished to see a little more of how this fellow would conduct himself. He fairly abandoned the young man in the midst of the workers who hauled about cotton bales on their shoulders and on hand trucks. An honest heart and a clever mind were of little use if Thornton lacked common sense or the will to work.

His patience was soon rewarded, because as he looked on, the lad moved with unassuming grace about the warehouse, keeping out of the constantly changing path of the men with their burdens. At one point, he even had cause to jump into action, assisting with a broken cotton bale that threatened to block the flow of traffic. Kramer had seen enough.

"Come to my office, Thornton."

Once they had returned, he convinced his guest to take a seat, as he had not done before. "How much do you make, Thornton?" he asked kindly.

The young man's body was trembling with the excitement of all he had beheld. "Fifteen per week, sir," he confessed.

"I will pay you double that, lad. I've need of an able overseer who will not swindle me, and who can keep the hands in line."

Young Thornton's eyes widened. "Are you certain, Mr Kramer?"

"I've never been more certain of anything in my life. Tell me, how did you manage to save enough to begin paying back all those debts? I do not pretend to know the actual figure, but I know it must have been hefty."

His new employee pressed his lips. "Three shillings per week, we set aside, my mother and I. I could not have done without her, Mr Kramer. She has taught me self-denial, and I thank her for her diligent training."

Kramer grew still. He remembered Hannah Thornton as a veritable force—a stalwart lass she had been in former days. Hearing her son—a grown man in his own right—credit her with the dignity and restraint she had bestowed, raised this young man even further in his estimation. An honest chap, and a generous one.

"Thornton," he sighed, "I think I have changed my mind about hiring you as my overseer."

The blue eyes darkened, the firm young jaw set in regret. "I am sorry to hear that, Mr Kramer." He began to rise. "Forgive me for having taken so much of your time."

"You misunderstand me, Thornton. I prefer," Kramer put out his hand, "to have you as a partner. Welcome to Marlborough Mills."

"Welcome, John and my dear sister!" Fanny Watson's fair features warmed with dramatic flair. She spread her arms and embraced Margaret's neck before she could even enter the house, as if they had been old friends. "I have *so* longed for you to come to my house, and now here you are!"

John's elbow tightened in sympathy as Margaret pulled her hand from his arm. "Fanny—" she greeted her hostess with a tepid smile. "Thank you so much for having us." James Watson next took her attention as he paid his respects, while Fanny showered her brother with her felicitations.

Hannah Thornton enjoyed her momentary invisibility as she observed her children and their spouses. It did not surprise her that John and his wife conducted themselves with decorum, Fanny gushed exuberantly, and Watson—though gracious—puffed his chest and strutted like the penguin he was. Whether Fanny realised it or not, there were elements of her husband that were eerily reminiscent of her departed father.

Watson offered John a drink, but Fanny was bustling with eagerness to display her home. "There!" she led Margaret almost by force through a series of rooms, gesturing at each turn to her new décor. "Is it not simply splendid?"

Margaret nodded and smiled dutifully, flicking her eyes to her mother-in-law, who followed in silence. She looked to be holding her breath.

"I saw some like this in Bath when we took our wedding tour, and I admired them *so* excessively that I simply had to finish my own house in the same manner. It really is a pity that you and John could not take a wedding tour, Margaret, but surely once you are out of mourning, John can afford to take you *somewhere*, even if it is not a fine place such as Bath. Only do not let him take you to Manchester!" Fanny wrinkled her nose.

"I am not at all discontented."

"Oh, you poor thing, you must be so weary of black! Mother, you ought to take Margaret to Gentry's and have her fitted for something new, for she simply *must* have suitable gowns for when she comes out of mourning."

"I am sure that would be premature," Margaret interjected, "for I did intend to observe the full year for my father."

Fanny verily gaped. "Impossible! Mother, you must talk some sense into her. Why, you are a married woman now, Margaret, and mistress at the mill. Surely you will have far too many social obligations to carry on with mourning any longer than necessary."

Margaret's spine stiffened, and she draped her hands over her skirts as she so often did when she had set herself inflexibly upon a course. "Nevertheless, I shall make do. John is not troubled by it, and I think it only proper."

The other caught her implicit rebuke and replied defensively, "Well, I am sure I meant no offence. I suppose it is not likely that you would be hosting a dinner party anyway this year, with things the way they are at the mill. If only John would listen to my Watson!"

The fine curves of Margaret's nostrils flared as she visibly bristled. In ordinary conversation with reasonable people, she was sensible enough to separate the mill's struggles for capital from any incompetence on John's part—or even if there had been some professional failure of his, it was the private man she knew and loved, and could never again denigrate. Fanny, however, was not a terribly reasonable person, and in her economy, any slight against the enterprise naturally must attach itself personally to the man.

It was fortunate that Margaret was spared from making any provoking answer by her mother-in-law. "Mr Horsfall, as you remember, Fanny, does not come to Milton this year. With Mrs Hamper ill and Mr Slickson often travelling to his other mill in Leeds just now, the usual dinner party is of little import." Hannah slid her dark blue eyes in Margaret's direction with the faintest twitch of her cheek. Margaret drew a calming breath, recognising the gift for what it was—a chance for her to regather her wits and serenity. She would have need of both. Hannah Thornton really was a rather convenient ally when she chose to exert herself on another's behalf.

July 1843

Hannah Thornton glanced uneasily up and down the street. There was a curious absence of bodies milling about in the Princeton district; a silent, brooding restraint, as though some great beast was holding its breath. From a window, a child cried out as she passed, but another girl quickly silenced it. Solemn, hungry eyes looked to Hannah through the window, then the older child turned her back and disappeared.

John would be at work. Though all the hands had turned out, John was dutifully at the mill each day, waiting with the master, should any dare to break the lines. None had, for three long weeks, but today… today was different.

The mother's heart rose in her throat as a sense of foreboding made her shiver. This deadly calm, this violent silence in the streets, could only mean that somewhere else in the city, voices were raised in anger and fists were shaken against the masters and their men—against her son.

It was not Marlborough Mills which had incited the greater part of the wrath during this most recent labour strike. That would not preserve it from becoming a target, but Mr Hamper was more likely to be the mob's object of choice. It was his lowered wages and pressure on the other masters that had enraged the workers to begin with. It was he who had, after a fortnight of empty promises, declared that he would not raise pay again for at least a year. Further, he had announced the day before that his mill would operate on shortened hours when it did reopen.

John had been livid over the affair. He was ever respectful of his place and Mr Kramer's authority, but in the privacy of their own home, he had brooded and fumed over Hamper's deceitful practices. That he had once been in the man's employ only enraged him further—he had witnessed the calculated manipulation of workers' sentiments years ago, while still a powerless young clerk. Now a man, he was wise and mature enough to speak out against Hamper's schemes, but he had not yet the place to do so.

Hannah paused, listening carefully for any sound to discern its direction. The errand which had called her out that day lost all importance. John was her sole concern, and his safety dearer to her heart than her own life. Surely, he must be aware of the danger—he was no fool, though others might be. He could not be ignorant of the danger posed by the roiling crowd kept behind doors. She traced her steps back towards the mill, thinking perhaps that her son could do with at least some intelligence of matters on the street, so he might alert the master to take precautions.

As she passed Francis Street, a harsh voice called out to her. "Lady! Yo' best ge' yo'rself inside. My 'usband says there's to be trouble."

Hannah paused. The woman before her held a young girl in her arms—perhaps three years old, but thin and small for her age, and crying lustily. Another child, this one likely old enough to work, clung to her skirts, her figure gaunt from poor food. She turned her face from Hannah, whimpering and stifling a cough.

"Trouble? Where is it to be?" Hannah demanded of the woman.

"Ach, as if I cou' tell what th' mob'll do! Get yo'rself home. Fine lady like yo', yo'r safe enough off th' streets."

"They are not concerned with Marlborough Mills, are they?"

The woman stared at her as if she were stupid. "I've warned yo', lady, and tha's no' for my conscience. Me and mine'll face th' streets, and yo' can choose our lot if yo' will."

The elder girl beside her coughed, and the woman pulled her closer. "Aye, there's my poor Bess! Is it fair, tha' yo'r girl 'as a fine house, but my lass 'as taken ill from workin' in Hamper's? T'is she or myself who'll pay dear for our bread, an' who's to feed my own Mary? Curse Hamper and all the masters!" This last utterance was as vile spittle, the final oaths of a failing woman as she railed against the inevitable.

Hannah glanced at the girl, who now dared to gaze back at her. Like her own Fanny, she was a fair blonde with liquid blue eyes and a visibly frail constitution.

"Go, lady!" The woman bundled her children close to her breast and turned into the door of the tenement they must have called home. Not another word would she utter to the woman she had already disdained as a fine lady—neither capable of sympathy nor worthy of appeal.

Hannah Thornton would never confess to any other how this exchange shook her and made her heart faint. How very nearly this woman's circumstances could have been her own! *But for John.* Yes, but for her fine, strong son, who had learned to sacrifice and work and save to lift them from such poverty. But for John, who had risen above his circumstances!

Oh, yes, she knew hunger. She knew fear for her child's life, worry for a wayward husband, and she knew what it was to have no control over any of it. There was, however, that introspective part of her which sought to justify the differences between herself and this other woman. She could not put herself in such a way again, and would never be forced to, because of her noble son's fierce courage.

He had raised himself from the very depths, proving that the deed was not impossible, and that despair need not prevail—and what he had achieved, she determined, could have been done by any other who proved himself worthy. This woman had chosen her man poorly, and he had used his life's strength ill. Thus, she settled in her mind that if the family in question did not precisely deserve poverty, they had done too little to prevent it.

Setting her teeth into a grim line, she made her stately way towards Marlborough Street, where that very salvation of hers stood faithfully at his duties. She would tell him what she had seen, assure herself of his safety, and salve her guilt in her own life's comforts by looking on his stalwart young figure and counting the cost of his success.

Such had been her intention, at least. Only a few streets onward, she heard a distant rushing, a furious onslaught. The mob had at last been unleashed, and it sounded as if she lay in their path. No fear had she for herself. Despite the other woman's dire warnings, she was a lady, robed in the protection of feminine dignity. None would dare to molest her!

As they swept by her in a tide of anguish, her confidence proved well-founded. One or two spoke rough words in her direction but were quickly cuffed by their fellows. "Save it for Hamper," one of them cautioned his mate. "Don't hurt th' cause by roughin' up a lady!"

They rushed onwards, none touching and only a few more even looking at her. She proceeded in her stately way, her steps untroubled and her head held high. She listened to the shouts and discerned an amassment growing before her. The procession had stopped, some dispute having arisen among the ranks. Several voices were raised to a fever pitch, shrieking bloody revenge on the man, while others argued in favour of simple property vandalism. Whatever the damage espoused by the multiple factions, the cry on every lip was Hamper's name.

Hannah stopped. Fool though he was, it would be unjust to leave Hamper unprotected at the maddened hands of the mob. Doubtless he knew something was afoot, as all the masters had for days. But could he know that his blood was being cried for in the streets? Could he know the extent of the mob's ire? It would be impossible, unless he were present as she to hear them. Someone must warn him!

Two streets more brought her to the gates of Slickson's mill. Marlborough Street was another half mile, but help was before her, and Hannah marched in without hesitation. Slickson was, as John and Kramer likely were, standing at the gate with his overseer. He waved her within the building at once. "Come in where you will be safe, madam!"

"I am not concerned for myself," she replied crisply. "I have heard the intentions of the crowds, and they mean harm to Mr Hamper. You must send someone to warn him."

Slickson gave a short huff. "I've got troubles enough without bothering with him who started this business. Let Hamper look to his own, I say. Go to the house, madam. You will be safe enough with my wife until this is all over."

"Do you mean you will do nothing? You will cower within your own mill, perfectly safe, and leave one of your own exposed to violence?"

"Hamper is hardly 'one of my own.' It was his foolishness that made all the hands turn out. Do you expect me to walk among the mob, gentle as you please, and knock on his gates to tell him that I had brought two hundred guests to tea? Forgive me for speaking bluntly, madam, but you do not know of what you speak. I would just as quickly fall beneath their boots. Now please, do go into my house with the other women. You will be safe enough there."

"I will do no such thing. If you have not the courage to go, then I shall. Perhaps you are correct, after all. They would do you or your men harm. Who else can walk untouched among the masses but a woman?"

With steady grace, she ignored his protestations, turned her back, and paraded boldly once more through the throng in the streets. They seemed hesitant to act, paralysed by indecision and terrified by the force of their own wrath. Such pause offered only a few minutes more of reprieve, for even now, the press of humanity was beginning to take direction again. Her decision unalterable, she turned towards Hamper's mill instead of John's.

She discovered his residence to be curiously quiet. None of the usual servants milled about, and certainly no precautions had been taken for his safety. When at last a maid showed her into the drawing-room, she found him sitting quietly with his wife and reading his morning paper. He looked up at her entry and seemed puzzled as to her identity. The maid was obliged to speak her name again, when it appeared obvious that he had not recognised the initial introduction.

"Mrs Thornton?" His brow furrowed. "Oh, yes! Mother of... er, yes, let me see, George Thornton's boy. What was his name? Oh! I remember. John Thornton. A good lad, that. Old Kramer took him on, if I'm not mistaken. How has he weathered his first strike? Ready to pack up and leave Milton?"

"Mr Hamper—" Hannah bristled—"I came to make you aware of certain events in the street."

"The street? Oh, yes. They will stage their rallies and cry out their demands. Fear not, Mrs Thornton, they will settle soon enough. You will see—when they are hungry enough to return to work and all the fight has sapped from them, they will be back at my gates with hats in hand. It is always the way."

"Mr Hamper, they are indeed at your gates, however it is stones in their hands rather than hats. I am a Milton woman from birth and I know the city as well as you. This is no ordinary rally. They intend to do violence, and they intend it towards you."

"Towards me? Now Mrs Thornton, I understand that since your son is now an overseer, you are more cautious than usual. My wife suffered the same sort of anxiety for a time. You must not fear, for strikes such as this are quite normal."

"Mr Hamper!" she interrupted him. "The words I heard spoke of murder; of making your wife a widow and your children orphans so they would know hunger. Is that the usual sort of threat you are accustomed to?"

This appeared to shake him. "They spoke of killing me?"

"Some did. Others were more restrained, but the last words I heard before on the street mentioned throwing you down from the steps of your house to see if the change that fell from your pockets would feed their children. You would do well, sir, to make some preparations for your family's protection."

He was rubbing his lip with his forefinger and beginning to pace. "Yes, I would do very well," he mused distractedly. "Mrs Thornton, if this is indeed accurate, I think I must thank you. You have endangered yourself for my sake! You have my eternal gratitude, and my wife's, I am sure, for facing violence as you have done to come to us."

"I have done no such thing, for the mob would never touch me. I was placing myself in no danger by ensuring that their madness could do no harm. If you must thank me, let it be for soiling my walking skirts, but not for risking my safety."

"All the same, Mrs Thornton I am rather impressed by your courage. Would you stay here with us within the gates? I will order them locked and send straightaway for the regiment. I can only pray they will arrive before the mob does!"

"There is no need for me to stay," she calmly decided. "I have done what I came to do, and I will now go to my own house. Good day, Mr Hamper."

Margaret left her dressing room that night in a rumpled state. Had it not been for Hannah Thornton's timely intercessions, she might have thoroughly lost her temper. Certainly, Watson would have attempted to run roughshod over the entire gathering, but the elder woman—cunning and experienced among men of business—proved a salvation of sorts. Still, there had been Fanny and her insufferable banalities. Margaret had spent the evening in a constant state of vexation and was in no clearer frame of mind after her nightly ablutions.

She emerged to a room that was silent and brooding as she, and for a moment, she looked about herself in some disorientation. John's near constant presence in the evenings had grown to be the accustomed order, and she could not at first account for his absence. Even if he were not yet ready to join her, she could always hear him moving about in the next room… *oh*. She sighed, recognising her blunder just as a hesitant tap sounded on the door.

She hastened to open it and found her husband cringing on the other side. "Did the evening pass so badly as that?"

She released the bridled groan she had kept in check for the past several hours, but it came out as a rueful laugh. "I was distracted. I did not mean to bolt the door."

"I had hoped that it was not I you were put out with." He pulled her into his arms and pressed a kiss to her hairline. "My mother and sister proved too much for you?"

"How can you possibly be related? Your mother I am coming to understand and even appreciate, but Fanny… Can she have been a foundling? I ought not to go on so, I fear I will say something I shall later regret!"

A low laugh rumbled in his chest. "We spoiled her, I am afraid. We so wished for at least one person not to feel the pain and disrepute of our circumstances that we sheltered her, perhaps more than we ever would have if we had not been through such times."

Margaret gritted her teeth in exasperation. She would *not* permit herself to speak ill of her sister-in-law, but an entire evening listening to Fanny's empty chatter, her insulting presumptions, and her unwanted marital advice had shattered her reserves of emotional fortitude. To make matters worse, it was obvious within their first half hour in the house that the invitation had really only been a strategy for Watson to once again assail John with requests for support in his speculation.

She continued to simmer quietly, doing her best to bring her thoughts under regulation as she had her tongue. She had known it was fruitless to expect the sort of bond she had shared with Edith, but she had cherished the hope of building *some* manner of kinship with her new sister. She might have been less discouraged in her quest to make a companion of Fanny Watson if she had not cultivated such an admiration for her brother! John's long shadow had not fallen upon his sister—that powerful way he had of persuading and inspiring, had not found its irresistible way to her character, and Fanny seemed all the dryer and more flavourless by comparison.

John's hand slid up the back of her neck to cradle her head and cheek, and she found the task of turning her thoughts suddenly much lighter. She began to unwind, allowing him to kiss her while she wrapped her own arms up over his shoulders. Slowly, she sensed herself melting into his embrace as he worked to soothe away her frustration.

After a few productive moments, he pulled back in marked satisfaction to speak low words of reassurance. "It matters little to me whether you ever come to adore my sister. I love that you try, and I love that you and Mother seem to be getting on better."

Margaret drew a quick sniff. "She is not half so fearsome now. She almost smiled at me as we were leaving this evening."

"Why, you are favoured indeed! She gives those out sparingly. Margaret," he became serious, cupping her face in both hands. "I want you to know how blessed—how grateful I am."

"Grateful for what?"

"Grateful—" he nuzzled another kiss into her hair—"that you are such a woman as a man might be proud to call his own."

"Though I do test you at each turn?"

"I would be disappointed if you did not, for your iron continually sharpens my own. It is as the proverb says: such a woman's worth is above rubies. I know not what I have done to win your favour, but I am humbled whenever I see you in company, and think to myself that the most magnificent woman in the room is to come home with *me*—" here, he leaned close to whisper scandalously into her ear, "and that she has never yet barred her door."

She turned her blushing cheeks into his shoulder, laughing modestly. "You are far more generous than I deserve!"

"I think you underestimate the value of an open door," he grinned, ruffling the new silk night gown affectionately against her lower back. "*I do not take it lightly, I assure you.*"

Margaret, cool and dignified as she had always been, found herself giggling like a school girl into his chest. The greater her chagrin, the more devotedly he teased her, and the more difficult she found it to remain gloomy. None, not even Frederick or Edith, had ever found such unfaltering success in lifting her spirits. Even if the disagreement had been between themselves, something about him could always provoke her to cheer after all was settled.

John swept his fingers through the masses of her dark hair, cradling her head and kissing her with a fierce abandon she would have dreamt impossible only a few weeks ago. He held her close, seeming to drink her in as one takes up a fragrant rose, crushing it to the senses to devour its delicacy and languish in its intoxicating embrace.

An eternity later, it seemed, he had carried her to her bed, and Margaret lost herself to him. For these precious few moments of intimacy, she could take for herself his eager strength, could revel in his hammering pulse beating within her own breast. This power she held in his arms was heady, sweet communion; their hearts joining and overlapping until his pleasure was hers, and each piercing ecstasy spun them to dizzying heights together.

John shuddered and groaned his contentment, rolling them to their sides. He pulled her under his arm with a final kiss of surrender, pillowing her head on his shoulder. They lay tangled, delirious, and utterly vulnerable in the darkness, until enveloping bliss shrouded round them and they were as one being, slipping luxuriantly towards slumber.

At length, her growing fatigue startled away when she felt John draw a short breath of awareness. "I should go," he whispered into her hair.

She caught sleepily at the hand wrapping over her stomach. "Stay, John."

"I do not wish to disturb you in the morning." But he made no move to depart.

"You do not disturb me." She turned her head, allowing him to glimpse the ghost of a smile in the moonlight. "I have come to look for you. I do not sleep so well when you do not stay."

"Truly, or do you only say this to comfort me?"

She rolled over in his embrace to wrap an arm about him. "Stay, John. I have been alone often enough."

"Then I shall, and gladly." He drew a sigh of deepest gratification and tucked her body close to his. "Perhaps we ought to begin using my bed, for I think it is larger."

"Your room is too cold," she mumbled drowsily into his chest.

He laughed silently, tightening his arms as she shifted to sleep. "Do you not know, Love? No room of this house has ever seemed cold since you have come to it."

Ten

3 weeks later

"Margaret, there is a letter for you." Hannah Thornton strode into the drawing-room as Margaret was returning from another midday visit to John's office. She extended the envelope with a sly little twist to her mouth.

Margaret blushed at her inspection and fought the impulse to smooth her hair or brush down her skirts. There was no reason that the short walk to the mill should have taken her well over an hour. However, John's sweetly expressed gratitude to her for his luncheon had easily compensated her for any embarrassment incurred by her delay.

She took the letter Hannah offered with interest. "It is from Edith! At last, I wondered why she had not written sooner." She tore into it, glancing uncomfortably at Hannah. The matriarch of the Thornton household lingered for an imposing second too long before granting Margaret her privacy.

Margaret waited for her to retreat before turning to the missive in her trembling hands. She expected some tearful lamentation from her cousin; or at the very least, a treatise on Edith's disappointment that she had not chosen Henry over John. What she read, however, drew such a flood of tears to her eyes that the reading of the short note took far longer than it should have.

Dear Margaret,

I do not know how to write this to you. Maxwell and I were away on holiday to Igoumenitsa, so I did not receive either of your letters until we returned. Uncle gone! You must comprehend my shock when I read your first letter, but that is nothing to the second. I can scarcely credit it, and indeed could not do so, had Henry not also written to confirm the truth. To think you married under such circumstances! I would not have thought it of you.

How could you do this to us, Margaret? Did you truly not believe we would welcome you? Why, I know that you and Maxwell never came to know one another well, but I know you would come to like him for my sake. Could you not have placed your confidence in us, instead of some unknown tradesman?

You must know that I had scarcely read your first letter about Uncle when I thought instantly to write for you to come to us. I would have asked Henry to escort you—or better yet, Margaret, could you not have waited but a few days for Henry to make you an offer? I know how he adores you. You could have married him instead of Mr Thornton, and I would have even sent word for you both to live at Harley Street until we should come back from Greece! Old Hodges would have opened the house to you, and then we could have all remained together when Maxwell and I return. We wished very much to have you with us, yet you have turned your back on your family.

What could have caused you to marry such a man? Henry wrote that he is a perfect oaf, a rough-handed master; the worst sort of tradesman imaginable! You always called such people 'shoppy,' and I can hardly credit that you have married into such a situation. You would never have done so if you had truly believed you still had a home with us. I cannot think whether the failure is my own, or that your time in the North has quite corrupted you.

I know not how I shall visit you when I return. I do not wish to bring Sholto to such a city as I hear Milton is, and yet how shall I welcome you to London? Does your tradesman mingle well in polite society, Margaret? I do hope for your sake that he is an educated man, for if a wife cannot respect her husband, it is a sorry affair.

Do please write again and assure me you are well, for I shall fret incessantly, thinking how miserable you must be. I hope you can keep well in that odious city, for Henry tells me the air is positively dreadful, and that you looked very pale, Margaret. I do hope you do not contract the same illness which took my aunt.

If you are unhappy, you must know that many couples do live apart. Naturally, you could not marry another, but there can be no harm in asking your husband to permit you an extended holiday to visit your family. I shall await your reply.

Edith

Margaret's limbs had failed her. Numb and shaken, she dropped to a chair, unconsciously crumpling the missive against the arm of the furniture. How could Edith have misconstrued her letter so badly? Had she truly written so hopelessly of her imminent marriage that day after John had spoken? She ought to have written again, perhaps, assuring her cousin that all was well, but she had awaited some answer first.

Now it had come, and Margaret tasted bitter sorrow at her cousin's assumption of betrayal. Could not Edith have understood her letter?—how she had declared herself betrothed to an honourable man, her father's friend, and one she respected as she did no other? Surely, Edith would not cast such blame to her, if she comprehended her reasons for accepting John!

Perhaps her own grief at the time had blighted the hopeful phrases she might have penned as she looked forward to her abrupt marriage. Her lingering doubts regarding John's changing sentiments towards her might have caused her to write more guardedly than she intended. Fear and uncertainly had been her constant companions in those heart-breaking few days—fear of John's true opinions, terror of the expectations which would be placed upon her, and the nagging worry that she would be found wanting in the eyes of her new husband.

It was not likely that Edith would ever appreciate a man such as John. How could she, when she had not seen, as Margaret had, his integral dignity, his veiled compassion, or his thoughtful intellect? Still, Margaret ached for her cousin to admire her husband, to recognise at least some measure of his true worth. She would have Edith know that she had not wed John out of need, but in the hope of becoming worthy of that great love he had first professed to her so many months before.

She resolved to write to Edith again, and attempt to correct whatever misapprehensions she had created. Her cousin's anguish and stinging asperity over her actions lashed her heart most painfully, and she would wash it all away if possible. It would be no easy task to make amends with one she loved but could not make understand. She clenched her eyes, the dewy sorrow slipping down her cheeks.

Perhaps… Margaret blinked and gasped, seized with a new thought. No kinship was quite so binding as the knowledge of unity in circumstance, and no report on her well-being could be so convincing as the glad tidings she suspected were to be hers. Edith knew such happiness for her own already, and surely would not fail to rejoice with her, if Margaret were to share all her secret hopes. She whirled from the room, passing a very surprised Hannah in the hall, and sought John's writing desk.

~

Unable to bear even half a day's delay in setting right Edith's misapprehensions, Margaret had posted the letter herself. Her heart sang deliriously as she returned to the mill. For the first time since the earliest twinges of suspicion had come upon her, she had dared to confess her private little dream. Committed to paper and sent irretrievably afar, her secret was no longer a matter for herself alone. Had she written rashly?

Margaret's cheeks plumped softly, her eyes sparkling in hidden triumph. No, she had not; she was certain of it! Fierce had been her prior vigilance, but now, after once permitting herself to taste the thrill of acknowledgment, she was bursting to return to such delight. Even if she dared not confess the whole in words, surely there was another—at least one!—who might sense her buoyant spirits, and willingly indulge a young wife's unseemly gaiety.

She paused upon entering the mill yard, her heart skipping. No! She should not speak yet to John. It was too precious to bait him with hopes of which she could not be fully sure, not during his market day. Alone with him, in the hallowed stillness of the evening, a soft whisper might speak the words she could not yet proclaim from the rooftops.

She looked about, noting the quiet of the kitchen in the corner of the yard at this time of the day. Drawing in a deep breath and aching to squeal in joy, she bent her steps towards the little building and Mary Higgins.

The girl smiled in delighted surprise at Margaret's entry. "Missus Marg'et!" she bobbed happily, setting her water kettle on the stove. She was quick to seek out a chair for the young mistress of the mill, followed quickly by a bit of biscuit and tea she had undoubtedly set aside for her own meal.

"Please, Mary, you needn't trouble yourself. I only stopped by for a short visit."

"Nay, Missus, if yo' had a fine lady come to ca', yo'd ha' some'at for 'em," Mary insisted. She bustled about for another minute, clearly understanding that her guest would not partake of her hospitality unless she herself were likewise suited with some refreshment.

Margaret relented with a little inner shrug. There was some comforting quality about food and drink, even if the portions were small, which had a way of settling a guest and easing conversation. Mary had her pride, after all, and deserved the honour due a hostess though the venue happened to be only the mill kitchen.

Margaret cast her eyes about the dark, shoddy little room, and tried to imagine the reactions of one such as her aunt to taking tea in that building. Why, it was hardly fit to warehouse the potatoes, let alone serve as both kitchen and dining room! She resolved to speak to John about improving the building someday. She dared not place such a burden upon him just now, but perhaps when times were better, something might be done.

Mary joined her at last, dropping tiredly into a chair opposite Margaret. "How are you today, Mary?"

"Well 'nough, Missus," she sighed. "Me da's 'ad a cough, an' some o' the childer's got's it too."

"Has he?" Margaret sat up in concern. "This cough, Mary, it is not…."

"Nay, Missus," Mary was quick to assure her. "'Tisn't what Bess 'ad."

"That is well. How do the other children get on? It has been nearly a fortnight since I have seen them. Is Daniel still doing well in school?"

They carried on so, exchanging pleasant small talk and attempting to make each of their meagre portions extend through their visit. When Margaret at last rose to go, she found that she had stood too quickly, and experienced a brief wave of disorientation. She gasped, reaching for the back of her chair for support.

Mary started at once, alarmed by the sudden glassy look in Margaret's eye. "Missus? Were it the biscuit?"

Margaret shook herself, resting her left hand unconsciously upon her abdomen as her guard slipped. "No, Mary. I am only a little dizzy." She paused to collect herself when another strange twinge through her core caused her to flinch.

Mary, raw and young though she was, was no simpleton. Her gaze had fallen to Margaret's hand—the one adorned with John's ring—and she drew her own conclusion. She raised wide eyes. "Missus, coul' I walk wi' yo' to th' 'ouse? Yo' oughtn't be out, yo're no' well!"

"Nonsense, Mary!" Margaret laughed. "I have already been out for a long walk. I am just a little tired, but I thank you for your consideration."

Mary's eyes narrowed stubbornly. "Master Thornton won' like it. 'Ow's I t'answer when 'e finds out I let yo' go alone, unwell and a'?"

"It is only across the yard, Mary! I hardly embark upon a dangerous voyage. Mr Thornton would only be more alarmed, not the less, should I suddenly require an escort for such a short distance."

"Nay!" The girl crossed her arms, blocking Margaret's path. "Master's for yo' to bother wi', but I gots to answer to me da'. 'Look ou' for Lady Thornton,' 'e'd say, an' 'e'll be ri' chafed if I dunna do it."

Margaret lifted a brow. "'Lady Thornton?' You speak as if I were a duchess, Mary!"

"'Tis what a' th' workers ca' yo', Missus. Yo're a gen'le lady, an' it were be'er than to say th' same 'Missus Thornton' as is th' other's name."

"Plain Mrs Thornton is a name which suits me quite well, Mary, although I do suppose it might be confusing. Perhaps there might be some other way of distinguishing which you mean."

Mary's eyes shifted uncomfortably. "Some o' the pacer girls…. Nay, Missus, I canna' repeat it!" At a commanding frown, Mary forced herself to whisper a name into Margaret's ear.

"Oh!" Margaret objected in horror. "Oh, you mustn't call Mrs Thornton that. By all means, I should prefer being known by 'Lady Thornton' if you must make some distinction."

"Aye, Missus, tha's as me da' says too!" Mary agreed. With a firmness Margaret had not expected of her, Mary retrieved Margaret's shawl, then placed herself by her side to see her to her door.

~

John pressed his fingers into his eyes, attempting to massage away the fatigue of the last three hours. For the better part of the day, he had been dredging through correspondence—first from his suppliers, then from four of his buyers. His banker had brought up the bottom of the stack, with a revised statement of his obligations and an updated estimate of the collateral placed against them.

The mill was struggling still. Though he had tried to shield Margaret and his mother from the tension gnawing away at him, he would have been dishonest to conceal the whole of the matter. He needed capital, and badly, if he was to continue paying his hands.

Cutting hours might do something to see the mill through the winter. He could not deny the numbers, but neither could he face her, when she saw the hardship his economies would inflict upon his workers... upon the only friends she had. No, he would press on, fulfil the orders he had, and hope that business as usual would improve before he came to the bottom of his resources. He had dared to take a few new orders, but the fresh income had done little against the mountain of orders he must still honour.

He had nurtured some hope—but a small one, of course—that when word came at last from Mr Bell, it would carry some hint of aid. He hated himself for thinking of it, but Margaret was Bell's god-daughter. It would not have surprised him overmuch if the old gentleman had pledged some sort of gift upon their marriage.

No mention of any such gift had been made. When Bell's letter had arrived three days earlier, he had been understandably heartbroken over the news of Mr Hale, and rather terse as to John and Margaret's subsequent marriage. He had not expressed disapproval... exactly. He sounded doubtful of Margaret's eventual happiness, admonishing John most severely to take care of her delicacy, and to consider her gentle proclivities with the understanding that she had not been brought up to his own crude—he had stopped just short of calling it barbaric—northern culture.

Bell had then gone on to state that if his health was agreeable to the journey, he wished to come to his god-daughter by spring. Not once did he offer a congratulation, nor, under the circumstances, did it seem warranted. One does not rejoice, after all, that a suddenly orphaned young gentlewoman is forced to bind herself in marriage to a calloused tradesman.

He refused to acknowledge his own disappointment, for he felt it unjust that he should have even contemplated any sort of monetary advantages for marrying the woman he loved. He would have married her a dozen times over again though the marriage came with the certain promise of financial ruin! Bitterly chastising himself that such graceless—nay, *wicked*—hopes could have ever entered his heart, John had tucked the note away and shown it to her in privacy.

Margaret's deep regret that her dear godfather did not heartily wish her joy only caused him to upbraid himself the more. What right had he, even for a moment, to consider the prosperity of the mill when his beloved Margaret had altered the very course of her life for him?

Declaring himself finished for the evening, he rose from his chair and reclaimed his coat. Trials he had, for a certainty, but never had he felt more the victor in his life. His greatest desire had fallen into his hands, the work of his life was at its pinnacle, and nothing could dampen the pride and satisfaction growing in his bosom with each passing day.

~

"John—" Mrs Thornton stopped her son as he entered the house that evening. "Stay a moment."

His brow furrowed curiously at her unaccustomed greeting, he followed her to the drawing-room. "Is something amiss?"

She made no immediate response, other than to settle her sweeping skirts into a seat. He lowered himself to a chair opposite, his gaze still fixed upon her unyielding features. "Mother? Is there some trouble I ought to know of?"

Her cheek flickered, and she smoothed the rich material of her gown over her lap. "There is no trouble, John. Only that you must not go up to Margaret yet."

As she no doubt expected, his whole bearing shot up at such cryptic mention of his wife's name. His face pricked with awareness, his breath tight. "Is she unwell? Speak, I beg you, or I shall defy your instruction and go to her this instant!"

Mrs Thornton cast her face upward in a gesture of exasperated surrender. "Come, John, you must have thought to expect it at some point. It is quite the usual order of events."

His eyes narrowed, his brow now twitching in agitation and his teeth flashing. "Mother speak plainly!" he warned.

She sighed, apparently deciding that, male as he was, John was incapable of understanding her thinly veiled revelation, or of comporting himself with decorum until he knew all. "Margaret has been unwell in the mornings of late. I suppose she would not have told you so early, but Sarah and Dixon have been hovering about her as if she were made of glass. John! Stay in your seat!" she cried, for he had risen to bolt towards the door.

"Is she unwell now, then? Why such mystery?" he demanded as he cautiously took his seat once more.

"She experienced some marked discomfort this afternoon. Oh, do not be troubled overmuch, John, it is quite normal, and I daresay brought on more by her long walk than any physical distress. I do not know why one of the usual midwives would not have sufficed, but that woman of hers demanded to send for Dr Donaldson as soon as she had arrived home. He is with her even now."

"How long has he been here? It is nothing serious, surely!"

Mrs Thornton opened her mouth to reply, but a distant creak of the stair from the outer hall brought John's head sharply round. He never paused for an instant, bursting as he was in his need to know that his Margaret was well.

Robert Donaldson was no longer the strapping young doctor John had met all those years ago, on that one hideous day which had brought them so memorably into company. Years of grit and worry, waging a daily battle against death and disease in an industrial city, had told on his physique and in the set lines of his face. Had it not been for John's own determined search to recover and thank the man who had once attempted to shield his newly widowed mother from all that he himself had seen, he would scarcely have known Donaldson again when they had returned to Milton.

Older and less dapper he was now, but still the same kindness shone in his face, and it was one John could read as plainly as print. He was waiting for Donaldson at the bottom of the stair, even before the man had looked up from his careful steps to notice John's presence. In those few seconds, the nervous husband sifted the doctor's contented expression and found courage to breathe once more.

"Thornton!" Donaldson started when he had finally raised his head. "I did not fancy I would have the pleasure today. Is it so much later in the evening than I had thought?"

"I try to come in a little earlier these days," he smiled, but the smile did not reach his eyes. He remained, brooding and tense, waiting for the doctor's verdict.

"So I gathered." Donaldson shifted his satchel from one hand to the other. He must have known by now John's dogged disposition and understood what was expected of him. John Thornton held hundreds of livelihoods in his hand, but it was the doctor who held the one life—nay, two lives—that owned his heart.

"Mrs Thornton is quite well, sir," he promised, and John felt his fears sigh out of him at last. "You may go up to her now, if you wish."

John swallowed. "Would you join me in my study first, Doctor?"

"By all means."

John poured two glasses, his hand trembling only faintly.

Donaldson accepted the drink and lifted it in a cheerful salute. "Congratulations, Thornton. I expect your family will be a little larger, come late June."

"June?"

"Or perhaps early July," Donaldson confirmed.

John gripped his glass more tightly. Naming a date to such an ethereal event brought the reality home to him. He was to be a father! Those dreams of setting right all the wrongs of his own youth were to be given breath and life at last. Now his worth was to be weighed by the scales of the future, for it was not the mill which would testify one day to his legacy. It would be his children, and grandchildren—those precious heirs he had thought never to call his own, until bestowed with the miracle of a woman's love.

"Doctor," he spoke hoarsely—whether due to the burning in his throat or his tumultuous feelings, he did not know. "Is Margaret well? Is she strong? Is there anything I can do to ensure her comfort and health?"

The doctor chuckled indulgently. "So it is with every expectant father, from the poorest foundryman to the most powerful manufacturer in the city! Now, Thornton, you have nothing to fear. That young lady is made of as fine a steel as any in Milton. I saw it when poor Mrs Hale was dying; how it broke her heart, but she bore up in an instant, for that is her way. How she wrung my hand! I said then she was as stout a lass as any I'd known, thoroughbred or not. You are a lucky man, though I suppose you already know as much."

"I do!" he rasped. "But you do not answer my question. You have examined her, I presume. Has she a good chance for a smooth confinement? Has the… the child…." his words crumbled beneath the weight of his breath.

"Thornton, your wife is not one of your looms. Bearing a babe is not a mechanised process where the expected results always yield up in the ordered fashion. Every woman is different. However, you must not trouble yourself. As I have said, Mrs Thornton is perfectly strong, and she is a clever young lady. I've no doubt she will take diligent care for her babe—and even if she should not, she has a bevy of rather protective souls around her!"

"What am I to do to care for her? Shall I take her to the coast for the air? Ought she to cease going for her long walks?"

"Thornton, have you any idea how many of the women on your carding floor worked in factory smoke through nine months, only to rush home on foot when their travails were upon them? No, no, I am sure it is the fashion in London, but you needn't treat your wife as if she were about to break. I daresay she would become cross with you by week's end. She may do as she pleases, if she does not fatigue herself. See that she has fresh fruit, if you can get it, and try to procure whatever else she might crave.

"Above all, Thornton, you must guard her against melancholy. She has had a trying year, losing her family as she has done. She should be granted every consideration. I have seen women in far less sorrowful circumstances brought low by the vagaries of childbearing. No man understands, I suppose, the mysteries of a woman's sentiments at such a time. Why, the littlest thing can set them off! I've heard husbands declare they did not even know their wives until they were safely delivered and began to settle to themselves once more."

"I shall see that she is not over-troubled and is granted her privacy," John murmured vaguely. His heart sank as his gaze drifted to some unseen point. Was he to detach from her company so soon after at last coming together? Thoughts of enduring his cold room once more, only listening to Margaret and knowing that his presence might overwhelm her newly sharpened sensibilities, squeezed his chest. If it were for her good, and that of their child, he would grant her every peace, but, *oh!* the sacrifice of all his earthly consolations, however temporary, seemed unbearable.

"You misunderstand my meaning, Thornton," the doctor chortled in his friendly way, readily disabusing John of his fears. "Your wife will require *more*... succour... not less. The only constraints I suggest should be moderated by her well-being and wishes. So long as Mrs Thornton remains healthy and comfortable, I see no reason for you to... er... withdraw from your wife's company. I do not think she would desire it."

Life trembled once more into his limbs. Had he really come to depend upon her passionate affection and gentle companionship so much that he considered a closed door akin to starvation? "Thank you, Donaldson. I will go speak to her now."

"An excellent plan," Donaldson winked. "I will thank you for the scotch."

"It is I who am grateful," he replied, his mind already racing up the stairs.

"Oh, Thornton, there is one question I wished to ask of you." Donaldson stared hard into his empty glass as though hoping it might provide the answer he sought.

Impatient now to be off, John checked himself. "Yes, Donaldson, what is it?"

The doctor cleared his throat. "I wonder if I might bid Mrs Thornton a good evening before I go."

John cocked his head quizzically. "You were just with her."

"No, I… I meant the *elder* Mrs Thornton. I… well, you know, Thornton, I thought I might leave with her some directives concerning your wife's care and preparation for her confinement… you know how attentive the lady is to such details."

Comprehension dawned slowly, but when it did so, the mother's son stood aghast. In seventeen years, no man had ever spoken to his mother as anything but a figure to be held in awe and reverence. Certainly, none had dared! Perhaps Donaldson hoped that John's marriage might have done some little to soften the widow's notions for her own future.

He found himself nodding, unblinking eyes fastened on the last man to show them kindness before his family's public ruin had driven his mother from her home. "I am certain she would welcome your advice, Doctor. Perhaps you might stop by now and again… to look in on Margaret?"

Donaldson drew a breath, his rounded cheeks shining with pleasure. "Naturally, Thornton."

Eleven

Margaret smiled to herself when she heard the tightly rapid, yet politely soft knock. "Come in, John."

He peered round the door as it opened. "You know me by the sound of my knuckles now?"

"Only you could manage to sound both commanding and hesitant, John."

"In other words, you were expecting me to rush up."

"I was not surprised." She turned to Dixon, who was just then exiting the dressing room. The woman was in the middle of sorting a variety of Margaret's undergarments, and she stammered and flushed at the entrance of a man to her mistress' chambers while she was so occupied—even though he had, at one time or another, assisted with the removal of each of those articles.

John, impatient to speak to his wife and not desiring to force Dixon to abandon her task, clasped Margaret by the hand. He led her through the door to his own room, then closed it behind her. Before she could draw breath to speak, he had lovingly pressed her up against the wall and claimed those sweet lips as if it had been weeks, rather than mere hours, since he had last tasted them.

"Margaret, is it true?"

A cheeky lilt touched her eyes, one she reserved only for him. "You will have to be more specific, John."

"You know what I speak of," he insisted, capturing her once more. He twined his arms about her waist as she soothed and tempted, annihilating the last reserves of the daily defences he wore before the world and restoring him to the man he could only be when in her arms.

"Forgive me, John," she whispered, drifting her mouth up his cheek to hover beneath his ear. "You do not seem to be *speaking* much at all. How am I to understand what you ask?"

He rumbled a soft laugh, so low and deep she felt the shivers through her throat, where his lips touched her. "I will give you a good long while to think it through. Meanwhile, I shall bide my time, for I am in no hurry."

She tilted her head back, her spirits dancing with the unbridled joy of her news, but her body and heart responding to John with the same ardent welcome his touch always inspired. She rippled a small laugh as he traced down her throat with apparent intent to seduce, but the fevered tightening of his hands upon her waist belied his outward calm.

"You are truly in no hurry?" she taunted. "That is well, for I find myself most contented with the present activity."

He growled, drawing back only enough to glare at her with those twinkling blue eyes. "Saucy wench!"

In the next moment, Margaret found herself swiftly caught up and tenderly deposited upon his bed. John's body followed, but instead of rolling up to kiss her, as she expected, he paused at her middle. Strong hands, unfathomably gentle, caressed her stomach in wonder—the fingers reverently brushing the lowest point of her bodice, as though sketching in his mind a portrait of the babe within. He looked up to her then, his eyes glittering brightly with unshed tears. "Do you have something to tell me, my love?"

She reached for his face, his hair, and he came. "I am with child, John."

Confessing her great treasure aloud to him broke free the final clasps of her long-battled reserve. Her throat constricted, her eyes burned, a choking, laughing cry trembled within her bosom. "Oh, John! Tell me I am not dreaming, that this can be true! Bring me back to the earth, I pray, for I feel I shall dance into the heavens! I do not deserve such joy—can this all truly be for me?"

He was laughing, in that same halting, broken manner. "I would never dream of bringing you down, my lady! Is there room in this paradise of yours for me?"

She sniffled, realising that they were both weeping. Wishing only to drink him in, to reach for the assurance of his solid body when the world was spinning so incoherently, she snaked her arms about his neck and drew him close until his cheek rested against hers, their tears mingling. There were no words, only expressive sighs and awe-struck gazes. Margaret's heart was too full, her emotions too overpowering and exhausting to further spend herself in speech.

John hovered his weight carefully over her, wishing to press her ever closer, but fearful of harming her. Only this morning, she had simply been his Margaret, his beloved. He had been perfectly free with her, but now, the certain knowledge of all that was to come and of the blessing she carried within her caused him to quail. Confronted with this evidence of his strength, he felt at once powerless.

How was it possible that pure, simple love had conceived his greatest work? Did not an achievement of such magnitude require blood and sacrifice? Miraculous! There was no other description for the new life that had flourished out of the tiny seed of love he shared with his Margaret.

He kissed her for several long, cherished moments, then helped her to sit up. His hand stroked comfortingly down the small of her back as she settled herself at his side, and his gaze fixed with paternal obsession on that spot at her centre, where he imagined their child to rest.

"Are you well? Mother said you had experienced some discomfort."

She shook her head, resting her fingers upon his lips. "It was nothing to alarm. I suppose some… accommodation was in order." She blushed, suddenly shy about the details of her changing physique.

"You must not hesitate to send again for the doctor, though," he demanded. "I will not have you brushing off concerns which might be of great import. You must be careful—oh, love, I could not bear if something were to happen to you!"

"I will be well, John. Dr Donaldson has given his assurances."

"He has told me the same, but I shall not be easy until you are delivered, and I may see you holding our child with my own eyes."

Her cheeks dimpled in joy, she lifted her mouth to touch his. "John," she whispered, a hint of mischief in her tones, "do you fancy a boy or a girl?"

"From what I understand, that has already been decided, and it only remains for us to be patient."

"If it is to be my torment to wait in suspense all these months, why should you not share it?" she laughingly goaded, apparently unwilling to allow him any peace whatsoever on the subject. "Surely you must have some opinion."

"I do."

"Well? Son or daughter, which would you prefer?"

"Yes."

"*Yes*? Oh, you are impossible, John. I only meant to have a little sport with you. Is it not assumed that I should now begin writing long lists of name choices?"

"The matter is simple enough. Your parents are both passed on, so I think it right to honour their memories. There, we have a choice for either sex."

She lifted a brow. "You did not mention your own father. George is a fine name." She spoke gently, lightly, but there was a seriousness to her tone he wished he could ignore.

"No."

She levelled her sweet, prying gaze at him as her fingers traced his cravat. Margaret needed no words—she had ever wielded such power over him, that he felt the sure weight of her silence when she desired him to speak.

His sigh came out as something of a groan. "Do not assume I still bear a grudge against my father because I would not name a son for him. We both knew and loved your father. Please let that be enough."

"For now, John. Should we have a second son...."

"One at a time, I beg you!" he laughed. "And I am not at all certain how I shall like sharing you with so many males."

"If they have your captivating eyes and dastardly smile, your competition shall be stiff, indeed. Oh!" Her hand darted involuntarily to her side and her eyes glazed in shock at the novel sensations within her womb.

"Margaret! What was that?"

She gasped and shook herself, relaxing once more. "It is nothing. Dr Donaldson said some shifting was quite normal for a first child."

He was still eying her with deep suspicion. It rattled him more than he liked that his strong, almost stoic Margaret would already express discomfort. "How long have you been feeling thus? Have you been keeping this hidden from me?"

"Several days, but it is infrequent. It is the surprise of the pain which caught me off my guard, not the severity. Please, John, you must not worry so! You will only make me fear upsetting you."

He thinned his lips, clamping down his concerns. "Aye, love, I shall worry. It is my own life you carry as well. Give me the honour that is my due; I have been the cause of such discomfort for you, therefore the right to care for you is entirely mine."

"Then help me to my feet, John." She held up her hand for him to take, washing away the pointless argument with an arch smile. He complied, shaking his head and allowing his imagination to spin an image several months hence, when she would require such assistance out of her physical encumbrance rather than merely requesting it of his gentlemanly courtesy.

When she stood once more before him, he could not stop himself from grazing his fingertips again over her abdomen. Impulsively, he dropped to his knees and pressed his mouth to her stomach, kissing the black satin as if his child could already sense his presence. Margaret's fingers threaded through his hair, and he tipped his shining face up to her. In that moment, he made a silent vow to God in heaven, that he would strive with every fibre, every sinew, to stand strong and faithful, as his own father had failed to do.

What that meant... the inspired man on his knees could not say. The future was not his to determine, and he had already been heavy with cares when he had left the mill that day. The weight of his new obligations, what he owed to his growing family, could no more grant him the ability to achieve the impossible than had the comparative freedom he had known only an hour ago. His determination might be renewed, but much was beyond his grasp.

He clenched his eyes, sensing the fresh prickle of emotion brimming to the fore. His treasure was in his hands, and come what may, he would not relinquish it. All he need do was prove worthy of everything laid before him.

Milton-Northern
October 1847

"You are proving the consummate manager, Thornton," Mr Kramer pronounced. "Not only sharp with the accounts but a mechanic as well! Excellent work."

"Thank you, sir." John straightened and rested an easy hand on the loom. "It was a design flaw, sir. The shuttles were wearing out too quickly because of the blend of metal on the tip. A harder alloy, and they have been functioning without a mishap."

Kramer nodded vaguely, his eyes still on the machinery. "Thornton, there is something I wished to talk over with you. Come over to dinner this evening, will you?"

"Sir? Of course."

"Good lad. I shall see you again in a few hours."

John watched as Kramer shuffled away—a little more slowly these days than five and a half years prior, when they had first met. He turned his attention to the worker at the loom and gave the nod to continue his duties, then moved on himself. Within half an hour, he had canvassed the main room on the first floor, the spinners at their web, and then the snowfall of the carding room. Each sight and sound were now so familiar to him that he need not pause long to identify some dissonance to the perfect order. Everything was operating smoothly.

In the last hour before the steam whistle declared an end to the work day, he moved through the upper floors. More looms, whole cavernous rooms of them, dominated the next two levels. The top floor was reserved for the finished cloth. Wringers spat out entire bolts at a time from the bath, then tenterhooks stretched yards of freshly washed material for the trimmers to inspect. All was as it should be, and when he had scarcely warmed to his task, the whistle blew, and the day was over.

"Mother," announced he upon returning home, "Mr Kramer has invited us to dine this evening."

Hannah Thornton looked up from the crate of new silver her maids were unpacking—a recent gift from him. "This evening? That is rather unexpected."

"Come, Mother, have you not a fine new gown to wear? I should like to see you in it. We ought to leave in an hour, can you be ready?"

She admitted that yes, she could, and he eagerly bounded up the stair to his own room. It was something, to have a house with stairs again! This was their third dwelling since returning to Milton. The first had been little better than the dark flat they had occupied in Weston. After a year, a raise in pay had permitted another hefty wave of instalments to his father's creditors. He had felt justified in seeking a modest apartment, with room enough for his mother to keep two maids to lighten her burden. This Crampton house had been their home now for just over a year, and it had been his special surprise to his mother when the remainder of the debts had been paid. At last, they had left their past behind, and were poised to relish the future.

They presented themselves at the great stone house on Marlborough Street at the appointed time and were shown to the drawing-room. John offered his hand when his host arrived, and then shook hands with Kramer's daughter, a young sailor's widow who now kept house for her father. "Mrs Brockett, thank you for inviting us."

Kramer approached and offered Mrs Thornton his arm. "Deborah and I have been wishing to have you for some weeks. Come, dinner is ready. Mrs Thornton, delighted to see you."

As his employer led his mother away, John fell behind, escorting Mrs Brockett. "You are looking well this evening."

She laughed. "John Thornton, you shameless tease."

"I was quite serious," he protested. "You are looking stronger after your mishap last spring."

She inclined her head. "Thank you. My back no longer pains me, and Dr Donaldson says I should be able to tolerate a little more walking soon."

"That is well," he commented neutrally.

She glanced up at him as they entered the dining room, with a strange expression he could not read. He had not the chance to ask about it, however, for the small party were settling into their places. As Mrs Brockett's escort, John helped the lady into her seat.

The conversation flowed comfortably. There was no political debate between the parties at this table, and no reservations on discussing trade with the two women present, therefore the mill dominated the evening. Coal prices had gone up, but cotton demand had not, so there was talk among the mills of cutting hours to preserve fuel costs and drive up the cotton price.

"It is a sound notion," Kramer advised, but with that look of surrender already about his features.

"I do not expect the coal prices will drop again for some while," John argued—respectfully, of course. "What then will we have gained? The winter promises to be light, giving us cause to hope for a warm spring. Would we not do better to operate at our usual capacity and put by whatever we cannot sell for a fair price? The numbers bear it out—we would not be harmed by warehousing some product, and it is decidedly preferable to falling behind with orders and paying more to hire on inexperienced hands at such a time."

"Are you certain you do not merely wish to avoid more union conflict?" chuckled Kramer.

"We ought not allow prevailing sentiments to dictate sound business decisions. Other mills may resent our intention to carry forward, but that would be their trouble, not ours. Also, I believe with the damper we spoke of, our coal costs might not be so heavily impacted.

"Perhaps I have not told you yet, Mother—" John interrupted himself— "but there is a new damper design for the coal stacks, which captures the coal ash from the engines and returns it to be burned a second time. Some mills in Manchester are already operating with this design, and they report notable fuel savings. I understand the smoke is less thick now than it was as well."

"It will never work, Thornton. You choke the furnace and it cannot exhaust properly. How then will you keep your heat high enough to power the engine?"

"The ventilation must be more strategic, but it is being done. I would like to go to Manchester soon to see the design in operation, unless you object, sir."

Kramer paused, looking steadily back at John, then glanced towards his daughter. He shook his head and drained his glass. "No. I do not object, Thornton."

"Thank you, sir."

"And have you other schemes while you are in Manchester?"

"I would also like to see the wheel in use, sir. I understand it wonderfully reduces the fluff in the air for the workers."

"I thought that would be your intent. It will be a lavish outlay for little to no return."

"It will be expensive, but if it keeps our workers healthier and they may remain longer rather than having the constant influx of untrained new hires, is that expense not recaptured in time? And with the new regulations on industry, it is likely that the crown will one day impose both the damper and the wheel by law. Would we not do better to make that decision for ourselves? There is also the consideration that if we wait until everyone is required to install them, the cost may rise."

Kramer shook his head, glanced towards his daughter again, and dropped his napkin on his plate. "Well, do as you will, Thornton. I'll not hinder you. Come, I have a fresh box of cigars, and you must help me open them."

With that, the dinner was informally concluded. Mrs Brockett and his mother adjourned to the sitting room while John followed Mr Kramer to the study. The master of the house closed the door and poured them each a glass of very fine Scotch. He then turned, giving John one of the glasses, and raised his own.

"Are we celebrating something, sir?"

"To the master of Marlborough Mills."

John's brow furrowed. "Sir?"

"I am retiring, Thornton. The mill is to be yours. Congratulations." Kramer raised his glass again but paused. "Will you not drink with me?"

John felt his chest swell and his head spun slightly. "So soon! We have spoken of this, of course, but I do not yet have the funds—"

"You will." Kramer gave up on trying to toast his associate and simply drank. He turned to the desk then for a sheet of paper. "I have worked it out. A portion of your income has been going towards the eventual purchase of the business since you first started here, as you know. You are already a fifteen percent owner, and I suspect you have enough put by for another ten."

John examined the numbers. "I do," he agreed. "But twenty-five percent is hardly a majority holding."

"No, but it is enough to set me up comfortably elsewhere. My health is not what it once was, Thornton. This cough of mine has been coming on since before I knew you, and I do not feel equal to another winter in Milton."

"Where will you go, sir?"

"Oh! I know not. A little country hamlet in the South would suit my health well enough, but I doubt I could suffer the people."

John laughed. "I imagine not. They cannot comprehend our sort of livelihood. Do they not while away their days in the drawing-rooms and strolling about their rose gardens? What then would those southern gentry make of a Milton man come to settle among them!"

"They do work some little, Thornton, or at least the labouring class do, but do not trouble yourself over me. You shall be paying me well enough to find comforts wherever I go."

John sobered and looked back to the paper.

"You were bringing in thirty-five percent of the mill's profits. As sole proprietor, all of it will be yours. You will easily be able to purchase at least ten, perhaps fifteen percent of the mill each year, with still enough to put by for whatever other purpose you might have."

"Once I have a bit saved for my mother's comforts, I would sooner put it all, every penny, towards the purchase of the mill."

"Then you may own it outright in four years, and perhaps less if the market continues as you anticipate."

John's fingers trembled, very faintly, as he gripped the paper. *Full owner of the mill!* And he just shy of four and twenty now... what other opportunities might come?

"Sir," his throat tightened, but he manfully controlled his voice. "I... I am honoured, sir."

"You deserve it, Thornton. I have never met a man worthier of a chance, and I have thought that since I first met you."

"Thank you, sir." This time his voice was slightly hoarse, but if Kramer noticed, he chose to overlook it.

"I ought to be thanking you. You have made my retirement a possibility. The mill has been more profitable every single year since you have been with me, and not once was I troubled by some emergency or oversight while you were managing things. Nor—" he refilled his glass and dandled it proudly in the firelight—"did I ever have cause to lose faith in you. That is a deal to say about any man, particularly one so young when he is entrusted with the payroll for so many, but I knew from the beginning that I need never concern myself about your character."

John made no response. What could he say? He merely lifted his eyes to the crabbed old fellow who had given him an opportunity, held his gaze with a firmness born of full manhood, and nodded his gratitude.

Kramer cleared his throat. "There will be no trouble about transferring the lease on the property. I spoke to Bell when he was here this summer, and I wrote to him again last month to inform him of my plans. I told him I expected you would wish to lease the house as well as the mill property, but of course, you may need to speak with Mrs Thornton on the matter."

"The house!" John flicked his eyes about the study. "It is far larger than we need, sir."

"There are only Deborah and myself here now. I expect Mrs Thornton could manage it well enough. Master of the mill, you must look the part, and I presume you will be thinking of taking a wife soon and filling this house."

John looked down to his glass and drew another thoughtful swallow. "I doubt I will have the leisure to devote to a wife."

Kramer seemed to pause, and when John looked back to him, he was gazing with an expression John could not read. "Naturally. Well…" he finished his own glass and changed the subject, glancing nostalgically about the room. "I shall miss my study here. Deborah, too, I think, will fret in the beginning, but we will manage."

"She is not pleased to be leaving Milton?"

"Deborah? Oh, she could be content nearly anywhere. I had thought she might marry again, but you know, she cannot settle for just any man. He must be one of wisdom and character for my Deborah."

"I am certain that once away from Milton and less concerned for you, she might be induced to look to her own happiness."

Kramer's mouth puckered. "Perhaps you are right. Well, shall we not join the ladies? I imagine your mother will be pleased to hear our little announcement."

Mrs Thornton was, indeed, pleased. Her eyes sparkled, and her face reflected a glow of radiant satisfaction—as if she had known all along how it ought to be, and her work had now come to an end. She looked to have shed those ten years she had lost in poverty and sacrifice at the very moment of her son's elevation to the elite of Milton's industry.

As the mother and son made their parting farewells for the night, Kramer stood with his daughter on his arm and watched the man he had taken as his heir. Straight and powerful, in the early prime of his strength, none could ever again hold his youth against him, yet he simmered with unspent energy and willpower.

He sighed as the door closed behind the one he had trained up and set on his path to fortune, then looked down to his daughter. "Well. It is done. You are content, my dear?"

"Should I not be, Papa?"

Kramer patted her hand. "Do you know, I had hoped… well, the thought occurred to me once or twice…."

She tilted her head. "Yes, Papa?"

"It only seemed to me a capital notion that… perhaps… you might remain in Milton when I go."

She glanced at the door. "What, and marry John Thornton?"

"He would have made you a splendid husband, would he not?"

She stared incredulously at her father, then began to laugh. "I am two years older than he, Papa. Why should he be looking to a widow when he will now have his choice among all the women of Milton?"

"He was always rather chivalrous with you, and I see how he enjoys speaking with you about the mill. He respects you, and I thought you would have done him much good."

"John Thornton has a wife already. It is his work, and his ambition is his mistress. No, Papa, he will not take a wife from the shelf as if she were some furnishing to his happiness. I never saw a man more oblivious to women than he. Oh, he is gentlemanly and considerate, but you wait and see. Half the ladies in Milton will set their cap for him, and he will fail to notice them all."

"His blood is as red as the next man's. Surely, once he is settled—"

"No," she shook her head firmly. "If any lady manages to secure him, it will not be for her fine figure or even connections. She will have to startle him from his complacency somehow… and then she must be willing to live with Mrs Thornton for a mother-in-law."

Kramer laughed. "You would find this feat a little too trying for your tastes?"

"Any woman wishing to become the first in John Thornton's life must be more commanding than the mill, more jealous than Mrs Thornton, and more determined than I."

"I should have thought he might be taken in by a lady of intelligence and good character. A soft-spoken lady who did not dispute his authority might do very well for him."

"I think the sort of intelligence he would admire would be precisely the opposite. He would thrive on a woman who would challenge him. I am not that sort."

"Well—" her father put an arm around her and drew her back to the fire— "I suppose it is useless to debate it now. John Thornton is now the master at Marlborough Mills, and I daresay he will direct his own destiny well enough."

December 1855

"Margaret?"

Hannah Thornton waited outside Margaret's bedroom, her hands clasped lightly before her and her dark eyes shifting discreetly about the interior. In the way of one who once held authority and has since lost certain rights, she was cataloguing all the minor changes brought to that room by its new mistress. She did not lower herself so far as to crane her head about as she awaited an invitation to enter, but her gaze dwelt for two or three seconds upon the worn little settee by the hearth; a relic from the Hale house which would never have suited Hannah's more formal taste.

Margaret had been within her dressing room when Hannah called, and had not at first heard her voice. The sense of company—that queer prescience Margaret seemed to command—brought her to the door.

"Please do come in." Margaret stepped back invitingly, but Hannah followed only a few steps.

Hannah had, by now, reined in her curiosity about the chamber, and set to her business without preamble. "I came to speak with you about arranging a nursery for the child."

Margaret blinked, her jaw relaxing somewhat in astonishment. It was still quite early for such considerations, but Hannah suspected—correctly—that Margaret would never dream of discouraging such an olive branch.

"That is most thoughtful of you!" Margaret warmed prettily, that old charm of hers surging into her tones and softening her countenance.

Hannah stiffened. This lass and her handsome ways had taken from her what she held as precious, and it was only with a valiant effort she reminded herself that it had not been done with malice or pretence. It was simply the girl's natural manner when she desired to please, but it grated when compared to her own rigidity.

What other young woman of her acquaintance was so unaffectedly enchanting, casting her spell over all in her path? Charm, and the appearance of such, had always seemed to Hannah deceitful, but four months in the same house as Margaret had made her question her own judgement—and indeed, her own sense of worth.

She forced herself to draw an inconspicuous breath, and continued. "I presume you have not yet had an opportunity to explore the garret, but there is a deal of furniture you may wish to consider for your purposes."

"I did not know." Margaret's expression lit with inspiration. "Oh, how lovely it would be—do you still have John's or Fanny's cradles? I would treasure such an heirloom!"

"No." Hannah shifted. "I am not one given to sentiment in such matters. It was more practical for those items to be sold."

Margaret closed her eyes in some self-chastisement. "Naturally. Of course, I had not considered."

"However," Hannah continued as if Margaret had not spoken, "the prior resident of this house, Mr Kramer, left a number of items that may be useful. He found it convenient to sell whatever remained to John rather than remove it all. If you are presently at leisure, I may show you."

Margaret agreed, and the two figures in black ascended to the darkness of the upper floors. Hannah carried the lantern herself and dismissed Jane before they went up the steps. Margaret paused near the top, her complexion strangely flushed.

Hannah looked back in curiosity. Margaret was a hardy young woman—one quality Hannah had grudgingly respected from the early days of their acquaintance—but she had seemed somewhat weakened of late. She tilted her lantern to examine the younger woman's face. "Are you well?"

Margaret blinked and released a shaken breath as she drew her hand away from her middle with visible effort. "Just a slight pain. It is normal, I understand, and I am becoming accustomed to it."

"Normal pains at this early juncture should not give you such pause. Perhaps we ought to return below."

"No, I am quite well," Margaret insisted. As evidence of the truth of her statement, she climbed the remaining steps and stood expectantly at Hannah's side. Hannah lifted a brow and turned to address the locked door.

The room was startlingly clean, by most standards of a garret, for Hannah had kept a practice of having the maids go over it four times each year. The furniture itself was all shrouded, but the cobwebs were minimal and even the film covering the floor was thin. She strode directly to the corner where the desired items were stored and suffered but a small moment of pride when she tugged the coverings away and scarcely a breath of dust rose. Her greater satisfaction was in the younger woman's gasp of appreciation.

"I did not expect it to be so fine!" Margaret touched her fingers hesitantly to the ornate old wood, exploring ridges caressed smooth by other loving hands.

"A Milton manufacturer's house is hardly a hermitage, and his furnishings should testify to his station," Mrs Thornton answered stiffly.

Margaret glanced up, her great eyes round with innocent regret. "Such was not my implication. I should perhaps have remarked that such a lovely piece seems far too grand for me. I am more the country parson's daughter than the London girl. Oh, how my mother would have admired something like this!"

There was a momentary silence, then the slightly flattered matron asked, "Will it suit your purposes?"

"Indeed, thank you. It was most considerate of you to think so early of answering this need."

"The child is to be a Thornton." Hannah sniffed, as if that were the only explanation required to account for her thoughtful provision. "I believe there are a few other articles which may serve a household with an infant." She indicated two ghostly shapes resting nearby.

The smaller was obviously a second cradle, perhaps intended to sit beside a mother's sewing chair. Margaret glanced at it in interest, but her curiosity was more piqued by the larger shape. She drew the shroud aside and allowed it to slip noiselessly to the ground. "Oh!" was her muted cry. Before them, bathed in the softly dusted light from the garret window, stood a graceful antique rocking chair.

"I presume you are aware that it has not been the fashion in Milton to hire a wet nurse."

Margaret turned to her with an amused smile. "Nor would I wish it. I have read much lately of the harms which may befall an infant without his mother… that is, harms to the nurse's *own* infant, when it is put aside for her to live with her employer's family," Margaret amended, for Hannah's eyes had flickered at the suggestion of her own flesh's flesh being sent to live in a nurse's untidy and disease-riddled house.

"Even if a nurse were to move into our own home, I think I should not be best pleased to share my child. It is of little consequence, for I believe the practice is beginning to fall out of favour even in the more fashionable circles, is it not?"

"As well it should. I always thought it vanity to bear a child, then continue on as if the only alteration to the mother's life was her period of confinement. That a mother should live in careless ease while another takes on what is rightfully hers—or worse, be at the beck and call of her social calendar, but a wilting flower when it comes to her own flesh and blood!"

"You may put your fears to rest on that point. Even if I could countenance handing my child to another, whom might I find to give up factory wages for such a position here?" Margaret's eyes flashed with a moment of laughter, waiting for her mild jest to be acknowledged in the spirit it was intended, then she turned her admiration back to the beautiful rocking chair.

Hannah found a warmth teasing her mouth. Aye, this enchantress had her way, she would grant her that. It had been far less difficult than she had imagined it might be, accepting the woman her son loved. She was not yet without her pangs of jealousy—and was it not perfectly natural? Had not that very young woman just confessed a similar feeling towards the child she had yet to bear? But there was a sympathy in possession, an insidiously growing companionship, which brought Margaret ever more frequently into her small circle of tender thoughts. It was never consciously done, but often of an early morning she would vex herself by worrying over the expectant mother's health that day, when such thoughts had never been her design.

Thus, it was with some surprise that she felt her own heart lurch when a sudden pallor washed over Margaret's features. The young woman gasped sharply, then a violent tremor shook her. One hand went to her side while the other grasped the back of the chair.

"Margaret!" Hannah heard herself cry out. Gentleness forgotten, she forcibly turned her daughter-in-law's face to hers with both hands. Her skin was cool, her complexion chalky even in the pale light. There was a dazed emptiness to her eyes, and Hannah could see her panting for steady breath. "Sit down, girl!"

Margaret shakily obeyed, seeking the shelter of the old rocking chair with uncertain strength. "'Tis but a moment of light-headedness," she was stammering. "Nothing to concern. I understand it is quite common."

"If you think to discourage me from reporting these incidents to my son, you may save your breath," Hannah retorted.

"Oh, surely that is unnecessary! You have experience in these matters, but John does not. You must remember that there are moments of discomfort, and there is little to do but wait for them to pass. I would not concern him needlessly; he has so many other concerns on his mind."

As she finished the last syllables of her plea, her eyes crossed in a sharp pain. She winced, gritting her teeth, then forced a smile. "There, do you see? It is all over."

Hannah fisted a hand at her waist. "You have been experiencing these sensations more frequently. Is it always on the same side?"

Margaret blanched for a moment. "Well, yes, I… I suppose. The babe must be resting more to that side."

Hannah narrowed her eyes. "And have you noted any other symptoms of distress? Speak plainly, girl, for I care little for your sensibilities at present."

Margaret's eyes widened. "I… once or twice…." She swallowed and cast her gaze to the floor. "I am certain it is nothing!"

"Nothing, indeed! You may be careless with your own health all you like, and it would not be my place to speak, but you've no right to brush off concerns regarding John's child. I'll not have it, Margaret *Thornton!* We are calling for Dr Donaldson at once."

"I suppose it could do no harm… oh, please, if you insist on sending for him, promise he shall be gone again when John returns from the mill!"

"That, my girl," Hannah answered in tones thick with worry, "will depend on what he finds."

~

"Doctor, is it serious?"

Hannah had not left Margaret's side during the doctor's examination, though her eyes had remained steadfastly on the window. The young woman was curled on her side and staring at the floor as the doctor made his mortifying survey, and Hannah would not increase her discomfort by looking on directly. Margaret would clutch no one's hand, though her maid had posted herself to Margaret's left during the entire procedure.

At last, the doctor had excused himself from the bedside, and Hannah followed close at his heels with her demand. He did not answer the question immediately but directed Sarah to pour a pitcher of water over his hands. That task done, he turned to Hannah with a significant expression. She dismissed the maid with a single look and led him to another room where they could not be overheard.

Donaldson removed his spectacles and kneaded his eyes. "I fear it could be a bad case, Mrs Thornton. There is no way to be certain, but she has nearly all the signs."

"Signs of what?"

"I fear the pregnancy is situated outside the womb. If so, it is only a matter of time…."

"Then you must act quickly! What is to be done?"

Donaldson sagged into a chair, invited or not, and met her glittering dark gaze with a weary one of his own. "There is an operation, but fewer women survive the surgery than the ordeal itself. Her chances are better if we leave her be."

"Do you mean you will do nothing? You will let that girl suffer and perhaps die, without lifting a finger?"

"Mrs Thornton, you may be assured that your daughter-in-law's well-being is dear to my heart. I have long thought highly of her, and of Mr Thornton. I will be in constant attendance, but I have seen too many young mothers die on the operating table—or later, of toxaemia. It is a risk I do not recommend."

"She could just as easily die of the agony and blood loss!"

Donaldson's head was low as he shook it in sorrow. "Some do survive."

"Some! How many?"

He lifted his hands in a helpless gesture. "Perhaps three out of nine or ten. If I were to operate, her chances would drop even further."

Hannah turned away, unseeing as she paced the familiar room. A morbid sheet of horror had fallen over her eyes, blurring all before her save the stark reality. "How long?" she whispered.

"I should think the matter will come to the point rather soon. By her symptoms, and what I know of her stage of pregnancy, I would be surprised if it wants a week yet. There are a few more signs, and then…. You must watch her carefully. If she experiences any pain through her shoulder, then we know for a certainty that the end is near."

"And there is no saving the child?" Hannah did not like the desperate quaver in her voice.

"No! Nothing is to be done there, if my suspicions are correct. All our efforts must centre on saving the mother."

She turned slowly, meeting Donaldson's gaze. Neither needed speak, for both knew what must be done next. "I will speak to him," she managed in a choked voice.

Donaldson dropped his head, still shaking it in pity. "I shall attend you."

Twelve

Margaret's agony came upon her with little warning. All through the evening meal, John and his mother had watched her with wan, hollow eyes, but when she pressed them for the cause, neither would make any confession. She was no simpleton—such an oppressive darkness over her husband could not be excused by his struggles at the mill. No one had told her the results of Dr Donaldson's findings, and the funereal silence spoke eloquently enough.

She wielded her fork with trembling fingers, sensing all the while that John's eyes hungrily drank in every motion, every flicker of health he could possibly discern to allay the doctor's nameless fears. She passed her attention from son to mother, and back again, as both attempted—unsuccessfully—to make a show of enjoying their meal. At last, she could tolerate their brooding no longer.

She laid her silverware aside, met each of their gazes with quiet insistence, and made her appeal. "Will one of you have the goodness to tell me what Dr Donaldson has said?"

John and his mother exchanged conscious glances, and Margaret noticed for the first time that evening the red rims about his eyes. "John?"

He drew a shallow breath, his fingers flexing upon the table. "He is needlessly concerned, Margaret. I told him how strong you are, that we need not fear for you. He is a doctor, and naturally sees only the worst situations, while he has less experience with someone perfectly healthy as you are."

She narrowed her eyes and glanced to her mother-in-law for her concurrence. Hannah Thornton was dabbing her mouth with her napkin and staring at her plate.

"Donaldson fears for the child," Margaret stated flatly, still attempting to force the lady to meet her eyes.

"No!" John interjected. "You and our child are both well, Margaret. Donaldson knows nothing for certain, and I will not have his baseless fears causing you any distress."

Hannah chose that moment to rise from the table, turning quickly away so Margaret could no longer see her face as she left the room. Little she might have done could have so effectively reinforced the terror twisting round Margaret's heart, and she sought her husband's expression again for reassurance. His head was bowed, his hand writhing upon the table, and his shoulders were quivering.

"John?" Margaret rose unsteadily to draw to his side. "John, you must not fear for me! I do not know what Dr Donaldson has told you, but I am certain my experiences have been nothing out of the common way. Carrying a babe is not intended to be an effortless process, but a baptism of sorts. I shall come out of the waters whole and new, and the most blessed creature alive. You shall see!"

His mouth trembling, he captured her hand to kiss it with a hungry fervency, then he rose to stand beside her and envelop her in his quaking arms. "I cannot bear the thought of you coming to harm," he rasped in her ear. "God could not be so unjust!"

"He is not. I shall be perfectly well, John."

He pressed fearful kisses over her cheeks and brows, then drew back to cup her face, slaking his obvious need to feel her confidence, her calm assertions. "Margaret, I have sent for another doctor. He cannot come until tomorrow, but I wished to see that you have the best care. Donaldson is growing old, and he could easily have mistaken…. Margaret?"

Margaret was stretching her neck and shoulder in discomfort, blinking as a low gasp hissed between her teeth. "It is nothing, John. Just a slight pain in my shoulder."

John's eyes flew wild with terror, and if he had been pale before, he appeared positively ghost-like now. He grasped her arms, gently but with a feverish intensity as he swept his panicked gaze over her face. "Love, you must retire now! I will carry you, but you must lie down at once!"

She shook her head. "John, you are behaving erratically! First you tell me I am perfectly well, then I must take to my bed at the littlest thing?"

"Margaret, do this for me." He gave her no option to do otherwise, as the next instant saw him sweep her, skirts and all, into his arms. Her protests went unheard by any in the house, for his voice thundered more loudly. "Mother! Send for Donaldson at once!"

By the time John had laid her out on her bed and summoned Dixon to assist her, Margaret had ceased her objections. Pain radiated through her body, stabbing through her breast and ripping her abdomen with unspeakable torment. Shock and fear had blinded her eyes to all save John's face, and she reached for his hand, then clung to it with a death-like grip.

"John! Oh, John, hold me! My baby, my baby!" she sobbed, over and over again, until she could speak no more, and others had pulled him away.

~

They forced him from her bed. John had collapsed just outside her door, on his own side of the wall dividing their rooms, his head sunken into his hands and great heaving moans defining each breath. Just a few feet away, every gasp of distress, every cry of anguish, and every strained directive given by the doctor informed him of the horror his Margaret endured. She was fighting for her very life on the other side of that door, and he powerless to even hold her hand. Would that she were a loom or boiler! Then he could confidently bend a new piece of metal or adjust a bolt to make things right again.

He had tried. Heaven knew his heart tore open afresh with each shock of grief and each ripping agony of pain he heard washing over her. How many times had he burst back through that door, snarling and raging at those who bent over her in her sufferings?

Each time, his mother, Dixon, or Donaldson himself would cajole, plead, or outright force him from the room. Even their efforts at shielding him would have failed, had Margaret but called for him. Instead, she had turned away, implored him to leave her.

His mind simply refused to understand. How could she not long for him to carry her away from them, from her torment? If only she would reach for him, he could soothe her brow and hold her when the pains came upon her. He could comfort her as she mourned their child, as he had been privileged to do when she had lost her father. He could share in her grief, could offer his strength and his warmth in exchange for that lonely, blood-covered bed. How he longed to *do* something—*anything* to save her!

The only resort left to him was prayer. He clung to it, preferring it to despair. Would not her father have joined him? Hale would have bowed his head, his preacher's heart breaking for his flock, as he wept tears of intercession.

John was not so eloquent. By turns he swore epithets and then wordlessly begged heaven above for a miracle, for deliverance. He pleaded for her life, repeatedly offering his own in exchange, if only God would spare his Margaret. Heaven, however, seemed silent and barred to him as he railed against its gates.

His fingers tore into his hair when another sob from Margaret shook him. This was not a cry of physical torment, as had been others, but of heart-wrenching sorrow, and he echoed it through his own soul. For the first time in his adult life, tears were flooding down his face with no sign of abatement. Only once had he approached this sort of despair since his father's death—the day Margaret had sworn she would never have him. That grief, haunting as it was, could not compare, for this new sense of mourning was not for his own bereavement, but for hers.

John could bear it no longer. He lurched unsteadily to his feet, prepared to break down the door if Dixon had locked it again. It yielded easily and swung wide, unguarded by any glowering sentry. John hesitated, his heart pulsing in his throat.

Donaldson was at the basin, his shoulders stooped as he rinsed his hands. Dixon had retired to a corner chair, shaking her old head and covering her eyes with a handkerchief as she wept quietly. His mother stood off to one side, holding a doctor's lantern equipped with a shining reflector in one hand and a blood-soaked towel in the other. It was her empty look, and the stillness of the white-shrouded form on the bed, which sent a spear through his being.

"Margaret?" he cried, stumbling forward, and caring nothing for anyone's scrutiny. "Margaret, my Margaret!"

There was a faint stirring on the pillow, a pale face lifted at the sound of his voice, and in the next instant he had gathered her into his arms. She curled instinctively in his embrace but did not clasp him to her heart; she passively allowed him to cradle her. She felt so weak and lifeless! His anguished gaze swept over the lips he loved to kiss—now grey and cool; the dull eyes which no longer sparkled with her usual passion, and he felt a bit of his heart die.

"Margaret," he whispered—gently. "You are strong. So strong! Margaret, my precious Margaret, do not leave me. I cannot live without you. I will not! Speak to me, love."

He felt her shoulders tremble as a silent sob passed through her, and she laid her cold cheek upon his shoulder. "The baby, John," she whispered.

He caught the tear sliding from her lashes and kissed her hair. "I know, love. I know. I care about you now."

She made no answer, save another shiver, another choked lament, and then she lay like death in his arms. He tightened his embrace as though he could imbue her nearly lifeless form with his will for her to thrive. There was a soft intake of breath and her eyes fluttered closed once more. Panic struck his heart, and he pinned Donaldson with a heated gaze.

"Are you going to do something? Look at her!"

Donaldson cleared his throat. "Mr Thornton, a word, please."

John looked back to his wife. How could he leave her, even for an instant? Each breath might be her last. "Margaret?"

She drew in a low sigh, gave a feeble nod, and agreed with the doctor. "Go, John. I will be well."

Well! Empty promises from a woman too brave or too stubborn to confess that she lay helpless at death's door. He shook his head and clasped her hand.

"Mr Thornton," Donaldson urged. "Please, we must speak. It is in Mrs Thornton's best interests."

He raised his head to stare defiantly back at the doctor, then his mother added her voice. "John, he speaks the truth. You must allow her to rest."

He narrowed his eyes at the woman he had trusted all his life, and at last heeded her words. "Very well."

Gently, he eased Margaret back to the pillows, and Dixon was there in an instant, coddling and clucking over her. He did not permit himself a backwards glance as Donaldson led him from the room, for he knew, as surely as he knew his own name, that his feet would carry him back to her if he looked again upon her face. Brisk efficiency ruled now, and he took the fore as their small procession entered his study.

"Donaldson, is she out of danger?"

The doctor wiped his forehead, tucked away his spectacles, and glanced up to Hannah Thornton with a significant look in his eye. "No," he confessed at length. "Her condition at present is due more to pain and grief than true affliction. The worst may be yet to come."

"The worst! How can there be more?"

"The bleeding has only just begun. I am afraid Mrs Thornton may have a deal yet to endure."

"And what are you doing about it? There must be a surgery you can perform, or a cure you can prescribe! I care nothing for the pregnancy. You must save her, Donaldson!"

"Mr Thornton, the surgery would kill her in her present state. It is too late to stop the haemorrhaging."

"Too late! What more shall your delays cost her? There must be a surgeon somewhere who can save her!"

"We are doing all that can be done, sir."

"*It is not enough!*" he thundered.

"John," his mother drew near and rested a hand on his arm. "No one could do more than Dr Donaldson is doing. You must leave this in wiser hands."

He glared and, for the first time in his life, shook off her loving touch. She flinched, her eyes wide at the defection of his faith, and fell back. He spared her only another instant, a heartbeat of regret made imperceptible by fear. He turned away, unable to bear her sorrow along with his own.

"What do I pay you for," he roared now at the helpless Donaldson, "but for wisdom! How dare you call yourself a doctor—you, who do nothing while my wife suffers! Let her be seen by someone who knows how to help her!"

"John!" His mother's horror was inscribed plainly across her features. "It is the way of the world. Margaret is hardly the first to experience this. How could you dare blame Dr Donaldson? You are no boy that you could be so foolish!"

"Indeed, Mother, I am no boy. I am a husband, and I was to be a father. My wife shall live if I must bargain with Death itself for her life!"

"Mr Thornton—" Donaldson's face was red with discomfort at John's uncontrolled outbursts. "There is yet hope for Mrs Thornton. As I have said before, she is a remarkably strong young lady, and if any has a chance, it is she."

"What chance has she? You will do nothing, and your previous incompetence and carelessness have cost her weeks, perhaps, when another could have seen and prevented such suffering."

"There is no prevention! We can scarcely diagnose her condition with accuracy, even moments before the crisis comes upon her, and the surgery is far too dangerous. I would not risk it. I have explained as much to your mother—"

"My mother!" John cut his broken glare to that lady. "I should be disappointed to think, Mother, that you would not do all that could be done for Margaret."

Hannah Thornton paled, and her son, grieved beyond reason, refused to acknowledge the tear of betrayal sliding down her weathered cheek.

"Now just one minute, Thornton!" Donaldson positioned himself between them. "You are perfectly within your rights to be distraught, but there is no call to abuse your mother!"

He rounded on the doctor. "Get out of my house, Donaldson. I am sending for someone who knows how to care for my wife." Upon these words, he stormed from the room, banging doors in his impotent rage as he hurried to return to the woman who owned his heart.

~

Hannah Thornton sat erect in her sewing chair, her back stiff and her jaw clenched. She was the only one in the room, and she preferred it so. It would never do for Jane or Sarah to observe the faint tremble to her mouth or the strange sheen in her eyes. No, she would be entirely undisturbed here… everyone else was attending to Margaret.

It was unjust. Her motherly heart bled, but did her son take note? Did he ascribe any faith, any sentiment to her as she suffered with him? And Margaret! A choking sob welled up in her bosom. Too late had she confessed to herself her true esteem for that girl, and now there was none who could credit her own grief at beholding Margaret's pain and anguish. She, who knew better than any a mother's sorrows, was not welcomed at her daughter-in-law's bedside.

Hannah released a shaken breath and tried to address herself to the scripture in her lap. Her eyes would not focus, but she had more success in reading that one sentence four times over than she had in holding a sewing needle in her trembling fingers. If only the house were not so still!

Her wish was soon granted, but not perhaps, in the way she might have liked, for her daughter burst through the door. "Oh! Mamma, there you are. I have heard the most dreadful thing, and I came to see if it is true! Is Margaret really dead?"

"Dead!" Hannah scoffed, but her voice was unsteady. "Fanny do not be ridiculous."

"Well, she must be very near it. I saw Dr Donaldson today, and I declare, the poor man was nearly speechless. He would say nothing, but that Margaret was in a bad way, and my maid told me the rest."

"Your maid takes liberties with the truth. Margaret has lost the child and is very ill, but she is not dead."

"Oh! Well, I am sorry for her. Surely, every wife must sympathise with her plight." Fanny dropped into a seat opposite her mother, her hands clasped within the frills of her skirts as she frowned. She seemed to be waiting for her mother to make some response, but none was forthcoming.

"I say," Fanny continued, less subtly than before, "it must have come as quite a disappointment for her, and for John. It is only natural that they were anticipating a son, as most couples do."

Mrs Thornton had cast her gaze back to her reading, two weak fingers shading her eyes.

"Of course," Fanny suggested comfortingly, "a woman who has lost a child can always have another. That is a mercy, for the next is just as good, they say, for it is not as if she ever saw this one. Provided, naturally, that she recovers, and is not too far damaged from the ordeal."

Hannah's grip slipped, and the Bible fell unheeded into her lap. "What... I can assure you, no one is thinking of another child just now! How can you speak so callously, Fanny?"

"Callously? I came to comfort everyone, and most particularly Margaret, since happily she survives. I found that a rather hopeful thought, and I cannot see why you do not. Besides, as you will not heed my little hints, I may as well tell you outright that you shall still be a grandmother. There, does that not please you? John might have suffered a misfortune, but we must not all mourn. I expect it shall be in late June. Had you not noticed?" Fanny rubbed a hand over her corseted middle, which looked no different to her mother's eyes than it ever had.

Mrs Thornton looked back down to her lap, wetting her lips. "Now is hardly the time to be airing your news, Fanny."

"Why ever not? Must I be denied congratulations because of Margaret's circumstances? That is hardly fair, Mother," Fanny sniffed. "Am I to be sent away without even seeing her, then? Surely, she would appreciate a visitor, and that is what I came for, after all."

"At the moment, the last thing she wishes for is a visitor. She remains in mortal danger, Fanny."

The younger woman looked about. "Why, where is John? He has usually returned from the mill by this time of the day, has he not?"

Hannah set her teeth and bent to commence a silent examination of her sewing basket.

"Oh! Of course, he is with Margaret. Well, he must come down some time or other, so I shall wait to speak with him. Perhaps he will carry my condolences to her."

"He has scarcely left her side for two days, even to eat or sleep. I expect you will have a rather long wait."

"What? Is he not even working? Mother, you do know what they are saying about the mill. I should think it the stupidest sort of nonsense for him to turn his attention from his duties just now."

"It is not my place to trouble him with such matters. John has never been the man to neglect his duty, and I shall not accuse him of it now."

"It should concern you, nevertheless. If he spends a fortnight with a sick wife and returns to work later—whether she survives or not—to find the mill bankrupted during his time away, where shall you all go? But perhaps I may speak with Watson again. I think it is not yet too late for John to invest with him."

Mrs Thornton dropped the little articles she had been fingering back into her sewing basket and rose. "Go home, Fanny."

Fanny's mouth dropped open. "Mother! I only meant to help. I know no one here is thinking of such things, so—"

"Your help and your advice and your condolences are not required at present."

Fanny stood to face off against her mother, then snatched a small item from the sewing basket that rested between them. "You were making these little bonnets for Margaret's child, were you not? Will you do the same for me, Mother? I will spare you an answer, for John was always your favourite. I shall not look for congratulations from you, I suppose."

She dropped the white bonnet with contempt, then deliberately stomped it with the heel of her shoe as she walked away from her mother. "Do send someone to tell me if Margaret dies," she cast over her shoulder. "I expect I shall have to have my black gown let out."

~

Margaret was not asleep... not precisely. She lingered in that dreamlike netherworld where conscious thought mingled with nightmares; where one was lured by the promise of escape from reality but devoured by tormenting fear of being overtaken by it regardless, until it could no longer be determined which was real and which an illusion.

She would stir herself occasionally, desiring to rally her strength—usually at the sound of John's voice—but more often than not, her courage and her flesh failed her. It was easier to sleep. In sleep, her arms were not always empty, and her body not always racked with pain.

She felt herself blink and offer a groan of recognition when John's hand brushed her forehead. "Love? Can you sit up to drink?"

From some distant place in the recesses of her mind, she longed to answer him. One breath... she could manage that... a long, slow one, much different from the shallow breaths of a moment ago.

"Margaret, my heart," he pleaded. "You must take something."

She felt her face pinch. Did he mean for her to respond? He could not possibly... but how sweet it would be to look upon him, to please him... and then be left in peace again. She forced her eyes to twitch, and then to blink open. His face was blurred, his expression unintelligible to her, and she squeezed her lashes once more.

"No! Margaret, you must wake. Come, darling. Dixon has brought you your favourite."

Margaret's head rolled to the side, her cheek flinching in both refusal and mocking. Who was this deep voice who called her his darling, and how could Dixon know what her favourite was? She had no favourites and would reject any efforts to make her like whatever it was. Where was her mother? Mamma would know how best to comfort her.

"Margaret! Please, look at me again. Let me lift you, love. Come, do not fight me."

The wave of delirium passed more quickly this time. How could she have forgotten that voice? She moaned and tried to lift a hand to rub her crusted eyes, but it would not move. She swallowed and tried speech instead, but somehow in the attempt, her eyes fluttered open of their own accord.

She squinted, the better to obtain some measure of focus, and stared at him as if seeing him for the first time. His eyes were red and swollen, his complexion uneven and pale. He was thinner, too, as though age had stolen his vigour... and were those silver shards marking the days-old stubble at his chin?

"Margaret—" he leaned towards her eagerly, and she discovered why her hand would not move before. He lifted it to his lips, his eyes brimming with tears. "You are looking stronger today!"

She opened her mouth to speak, to deny his claim. She felt a part of herself slipping farther beyond her grasp, a spectre of the Margaret she had always been who could nevermore exist. Stronger? The comforts of her eternal reward seemed to call her incessantly, and she would reach for them… if she could move her hand.

"Do not try to speak, love. Here, let me raise you."

Passively, she allowed him to brace her up, to support her with more pillows than she had ever supposed could exist. She lay limp for a moment, her head spinning at the change in posture, but she did not care enough to complain. He brought her warmest shawl then, tucking it round her shoulders so she might not feel the draught, and before he drew back, he kissed her brow as he used to do… in the days *before*.

Margaret's gaze shifted from his face to a figure that moved now behind him. Dixon, her apron stained and her eyes likewise swollen, braved a quivering smile of encouragement. "It's my good bone broth, miss, like I used to make your mother. It's got a bit of sage and cranesbill—the master's idea. I brought you a pot full of chamomile too, for after your broth."

Margaret watched in dull fascination as John took the steaming bowl from Dixon's hands. When had Dixon ever yielded willingly to him? But the proof was before her own eyes if she could believe them. He turned back, and she understood that she was to watch the trembling spoon as it approached her mouth, then to submit to it.

John ladled the half-spoonfuls with aching slowness, giving her more time, even than she required, to swallow. "I had a note from Higgins a bit ago," he informed her with a valiant effort at cheer. "He and Mary and the children send their regards. Higgins says—" here, he almost smiled—"you have at last turned him into a praying man, Margaret. I've put the note there by your lamp, if you wish to read it."

She feigned what she supposed to be a proper response.

"They sent you a gift as well." John gestured to the bed, and Margaret at last noticed the blanket covering her lower body. "Mary said it used to belong to Bess, and the children mended it for you."

"But it's not very warm, miss," Dixon complained from beyond him. "I've put your mother's good quilt beneath it. And I had it laundered! I won't have you taking another fever."

"Fever? Have I had a fever?"

John's colour seemed to drain even more than it had already done. "You have been feverish for four days now. It has still not broken, not in the usual way. Feel." He pressed his cool fingers to her forehead, and the stark contrast in temperature caused her to blink. He seemed to hesitate, then returned his attention to the spoon.

"What day is it?" Her lips felt thick, and she was not even certain they had formed the words properly.

His head was bowed, but she could see his lashes blinking furiously. "The first. It is the year eighteen hundred fifty-six today, love."

She allowed her eyes to roll up to the ceiling. She had lived to see the new year… at least the first day of it. Whether there would be more, she could not even bring herself to care.

"Dr Bailey says you are making improvement each day, and indeed, you do look a great deal better."

She strained to lower her chin, to focus on him again. "Dr Bailey? Where is Dr Donaldson?"

Dixon seemed to turn abruptly away, and John's eyes fell to the bowl. "Dr Bailey is from London. He has been seeing to you during your recovery." He filled the spoon again and offered it, but she shook her head and resolutely closed her mouth.

"Margaret, please, you must take some nourishment."

"My stomach hurts. The broth… I think it is making it worse."

Alarm widened his eyes. "Dixon! What did you put in the broth?"

"John, it is not that," she protested. "I only mean I feel too much… pressure. Please, no more just now."

His eyes flashed defiantly as he lowered the bowl. "I do not wish for you to be uncomfortable, Margaret, but you have scarcely taken even a sip of water since—"

"Do not speak of it!" Her lip quivered, and she felt her eyes beginning to burn. "I cannot think of it now, John."

His gaze fell, and his broad shoulders sagged. "I know, love."

"Let me sleep," she begged.

John sighed reluctantly and passed the bowl back to Dixon. He rose to bend over her and had just lowered her back to the bed when a knock sounded at the door. At a look from him, Dixon answered it.

Margaret could not see the face, but the voice belonged to no one she knew. "Dr Bailey." John sounded relieved. "I am glad you have come just now. She is awake."

Margaret's view of the ceiling was presently blocked by a sandy-haired man, perhaps slightly younger than John. He leaned low and nodded briskly. "Mrs Thornton, a pleasure to make your acquaintance. I see you are looking well today. If you please, madam, I must examine your progress."

Margaret shivered and decided that she did not at all like being touched. John's hands had been familiar, almost as her own flesh, but her skin crawled even at the brush of the blankets over her shoulders as the doctor made ready.

"It is all right, Margaret," John spoke lowly from her side and took her hand.

With Dixon's help he rolled her into the proper position and offered her a cloth to shield her face... as if that bit of modesty would ease her discomfort with the whole situation. Apparently, he had decided that he would no longer leave the room when a doctor examined her, and she wished she could draw the pillow and all the blankets over her head. This was the man with whom she had shared every intimacy, but even in the best of times, a medical examination was hideously mortifying. She was not at all herself, and she knew, by the sticky feeling of her clothing, that what John would behold when the doctor lifted the last blankets would be nothing short of horrifying to him. How much of her disgrace had he already witnessed?

She closed her eyes against the ignominy but could not help wincing and crying out when the doctor began prodding her tender stomach. The remainder of his inspection was even worse. She felt John's hand lock, saw the tightening of his cheek, and sensed that he was close to pushing the doctor from her. She clenched her eyes even tighter and turned away.

The doctor rose a moment later, and she felt John covering her, tucking the warm blankets lovingly round her chin and ears. A quiet conference ensued in the corner of her room, and the unnaturally sharpened senses of fever caught every syllable. Whether her mind had understood them properly was less certain.

"I must bleed her again, Mr Thornton. She still carries an ascendancy of blood to the head, and it is the best way to lower her fever."

"She weakens every time you do so!" sputtered John. "She nearly died last time."

"It is only the appearance of faintness as the blood is redistributed through the body," the doctor reasoned. "There is still the matter of the confluence around her womb. I begin to think a more direct approach will lessen the pressure and promote recovery."

"Explain yourself," John snapped.

"I propose to open her stomach and draw out the haemorrhaging."

There was no answer from John for a long moment. Margaret groaned in protest, but her response was seemingly perceived only as a shiver, for in the next moment, Dixon brought her another quilt.

"When?"

"The sooner the better, Mr Thornton. Every day increases her risk of septicaemia. I can send for my surgical supplies and begin this afternoon."

Margaret could feel the weight of her husband's deliberating gaze settling over her. He was silent, and she heard no more save for the clicking of the door latch before delirium claimed her once more.

Thirteen

Hannah's limbs turned to ice. "What did you say, Dixon?"

"The master! He's going to let that young fellow cut Miss Margaret. He says he can drain away the bleeding!"

"By causing more bleeding? That is the most ridiculous notion I have ever heard."

"Missus Thornton," Dixon shifted her ponderous weight, fumbling with the lukewarm pot of tea she had carried down, "will you not speak to the master? I'd not have said so before, but he's a good man, he is. I've never seen anyone at such ends over a sickbed, but he's not thinking clearly, ma'am. I'm no doctor, ma'am, but I've nursed my fair share, and what Miss Margaret needs is rest and a bit of healing. That doctor is going to kill my girl!" Dixon's face crumpled at this last pronouncement, her body shaking with tears.

Hannah drew a long breath. "Go to the kitchen, Dixon. Cook has set aside a plate for you. You need rest as well."

Dixon sniffled, nodded morosely, and turned away. "You'll stop him, won't you, Missus?"

"I…" Hannah blinked, swallowed, then simply nodded towards Margaret's maid. "You must eat, Dixon."

Hannah stared after her. Never in her life had she quailed from speaking the truth as she saw it. Occasionally, it had pained her to do so, and once or twice it had even brought her the sweet vindication of justice. Always before, however, it had been in the collective defence of herself and her children—more specifically, her son—for they had been one and the same entity. Was she to confront him now, after already arguing with him over how best to care for the woman he loved? He was blinded by his passions, ready to grasp any remedy that made him feel as if *something* was being done. Had it now fallen to her to save Margaret from John's desperate love?

She stood, clasping the back of her chair for support, as if it were a ship captain's wheel and she the one who determined the direction it should spin. A dozen scenes flitted through her mind—days gone by. A youthful John collapsing in his chair when they lived in Weston after sixteen hours of work, and rousing only long enough to assure her that he was not tired. The light in his face the day he had told her he meant to journey to Milton with the first of the debts to repay; and the pride in his eyes when he returned and announced that he had been offered a future. The steady calm of the young man of twenty, facing down his first mill riot and seeking her face to be certain she was not afraid as she sheltered behind him.

These and more taunted her as she tried to summon her courage. How could she defy him, who had become as her protector, and accuse him of failing in that duty to his own wife? She set her jaw when one more image nearly brought her to her knees—John, in blackest mourning, standing by yet another gravestone. This time, she feared, he would not have the strength to walk away. She bore herself up, dashing the tears from her cheeks, and set out to find him.

She had turned to the stairs, but a faint sound called her back. From where she stood in the passage, she could see that John's study door had been closed. That was as it should be, but it had stood ajar for three days. He had tried to go there and work for a distraction when first evicted from Margaret's bedroom, but had failed miserably and left it in a rush. Since none in the house would touch even the door handle without the master's leave, it had remained half-opened with papers scattered about.

Curiously, she approached, and from beyond the door, she could hear his breath. It was ragged and hoarse, racked with just the sort of pain she would have expected. She longed to cradle the boy she had once known, to sweep him into her embrace and make his cares disappear with her motherly affection. If only she could! She rested her fingers on the handle, whispering a plea for understanding, and pushed it open.

His head was buried in his arms and cast over his desk. His meticulous stack of invoices and order sheets had been shoved off, and with great force, for some had sailed as far as the bookshelf. She closed the door behind herself and crossed the room, but he seemed deaf to her footsteps. Her hand, lifted now to rest upon his shoulder, trembled. Perhaps he was deliberately ignoring her and wishing her away! But she would not... could not go. Her resolve thus fixed, she touched him.

He started, lifting his head. "Mother!"

"John... oh, John!" She shook her head when she beheld his worn face. When had her son's strength failed him so? She would scarcely have known him, this haggard wretch with the sunken features and haunted expression.

He pressed his face into his hand now, rubbing his eyes. "She still lives, Mother."

"I have just spoken to Dixon."

He dropped his hand and gazed up at her, as if only then rousing himself from a nightmare, and drew a second chair up for her. Hannah glanced at it with some trepidation. It was Margaret's chair, the one she always occupied when she helped John with the invoices. Counting it the honour it was, she gingerly seated herself.

His elbows had returned to the desk, his head clasped in his hands. "I am losing her, Mother! What shall I do? What has been left undone, what I have not seen? There must be something!"

"We cannot always *do* anything about our circumstances, John."

"But I must! Do you not understand? I cannot lose her, for it would be all my own doing!"

"Your doing? You hold the keys to death and life, do you?"

"She trusted me with her life, Mother—she, who was so far above me that even her favour was a blessing I never deserved. I promised I would take care of her, and what has my love brought her? It was I who… oh, dear God!" He fell to the desk, his shoulders heaving as great sobs shook him.

She watched him in mournful silence. What was she to say? He was insensible to reason and cared nothing for condolences. She rested her hand on his shoulder and bowed her head for a moment as he wept.

John had never been one to yield to tears, and he struggled valiantly against them even now. The agonising cries became choked gasps as he fought to continue on *doing*. He raised up his head again with a jerk, wiping his eyes. "We are going to save her. The doctor, he has a remedy—"

"That doctor is a quack and a butcher!"

"Mother! He is one of the best, and he knows all the latest medical procedures. He came from London almost exclusively to treat Margaret!"

"I don't care if he came from Hippocrates' temple. Why in the world would he propose operating on her now?"

"He intends to drain away the haemorrhaging. Mother, we are not doctors. Who are we to question one who has studied extensively—"

"We are her family!" She blinked at that pronouncement, stunned at how naturally it had flowed from her lips. "Or as good as family, since the rest seem to care little enough. Who else is to advocate for her, but we?"

"And I, her husband, have decided that she is to have the best possible care!"

"By draining her when she is already weak, or cutting her when she is already bleeding?"

"By seeking means of lowering her fever and reducing the pressure. You must not advise on matters you do not understand."

"Aye, my lad," she almost snarled, the hair standing on the back of her neck, "I may not understand medicine, but I know one who does, and I know whom to trust. I know more than that—that you have lost all reason. You cannot save her with your bare hands, John."

"My hands are hardly bare! I would give her all I have and bankrupt myself on the doctor who can save her!"

"You have chosen the wrong one. How often have you said Margaret is strong? Why allow that doctor to weaken her? The swelling may diminish with time, but if she loses more blood or infection sets in from the surgery, she will have not a prayer."

He shook his head, still unwilling to listen, as his forehead fell into his hand. "You do not understand, Mother, you—"

"I! I who bore and then nursed three children through their ailments? Who watched one of them weaken and die, and grieved that no means could be found to save her?"

He drew an unsteady breath, still not willing to look at her or even lower his hand.

"John, let me go up to her."

"I have never forbidden you from seeing her."

"Yet you accused me of not wishing to help her. Was I to go after that?"

Tears were sliding under his hand now, unheeded but by Hannah. "I should never have... forgive me, Mother. I would never speak such to you—"

"Unless you had lost your head, which you have done. Let us go up to her now, John. Come, we will bow our heads over her and seek wisdom and healing."

He did not stir for a long moment, but his irregular breaths, the trembling of his jaw, gave evidence to the battle waging within him. At last, his determined mother drew his hand away from his face and clasped it in her own.

"Have I ever advised you ill, John? Have I ever sought any but your good? Come."

He was blinking rapidly and rose, if somewhat reluctantly. He followed, his steps dragging, as she ushered him out of the room and into the hall. They approached the stair but halted when a figure emerged from the drawing-room.

"Donaldson." John's voice would have been a growl, had he not been so exhausted.

"Mr Thornton." Donaldson dipped his head, then his gaze shifted to the lady in the fore.

"I thought I asked you to stay away."

"John—" Hannah turned to her son—"he has been calling every day... to ask after Margaret."

John glanced back to the doctor to verify these words. "It is true, sir," he sheepishly admitted. "I feared for the young lady... and I wished to comfort Mrs Thornton, if need be."

John stared at the floor, then set his jaw. "You may as well come up, Donaldson."

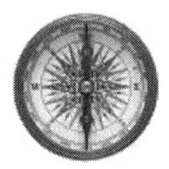

Milton-Northern
March 1834

"There is nothing you can do?" Hannah Thornton, heavy with her third child, clasped the fevered hand of her daughter as imploring eyes sought the apothecary. "No medicine can help?"

The man shook his head as he buttoned his leather case. "No, ma'am, and if I had something that would help, it would be very dear."

"What is to be done? Surely, there must be something!"

"In cases such as these, I usually recommend some time at the coast. There is no cure for the disease, but the fresh air may make her more comfortable."

She blinked, her breath short and helpless. "We could not afford such a trip, not now. Mr Thornton says in a year or two, perhaps…."

"With all due respect, ma'am, the lass does not have that long, but I doubt it shall matter. Even if you had a place to go tomorrow, it is not likely she could withstand the journey."

Hannah brushed the damp locks from Elizabeth's forehead. Even at four years old, her hair was rich and dark, just as her father's. The child fluttered her eyes—blue, like her brother's—and tried to gaze up at her mother, but the cough racked her again. Hannah was quick to cover the girl's little cherub lips with a cloth, lest the bloodied sputum spread to the blankets.

"Ma'am—" the apothecary stopped on his way to the door—"if I might say so, it is not wise for you to tend her. Could not the kitchen maid watch over her?"

Hannah shook her head, gritting her teeth in determination. "My child will have her mother."

"I understand your feelings, ma'am, but it would not do to endanger the younger babe. It could be born sickly and weak. Perhaps your son could assist the maid, to reassure her?"

"I will not put John at risk! He must be kept safe. What more can be done?"

"Well, ma'am, as you know, it is this neighbourhood. The houses are all built on drained marshland. It is a wonder I do not see more cases such as these, but there, it would not be Milton without its mills, and mills must have water. If you could remove to somewhere with gravel soil, like Crampton—the houses may not be so fine and new, but the ground is healthier. Perhaps the coming babe would fare better in such a place."

"My husband would never hear of it."

"I am afraid that is the best advice I have to offer, ma'am. Good day." He collected his hat and left, tipping it respectfully as he closed the door behind himself.

All that afternoon, the weary mother cradled her child alone; soothing her whimpers, cooling her forehead, and cleansing away the blood. She had seated herself in Elizabeth's bed, her back against the wall with her girl curled in her lap. Late in the night, the door creaked.

Hannah opened her eyes, realising belatedly that her vigilance had faltered, and somewhere between dusk and darkness, she had fallen asleep. She blinked, and her first instinct was to be certain that Elizabeth still breathed. Her hands swept in terror over her child, and she sighed in relief when she found that she had not yet failed her. Only then did she look to the door.

"John! You should not be here. Go below, this instant."

He stood reluctantly in the doorway, his boyish figure silhouetted by the candle in the hall. "I wanted to see if you were well, Mother. Is Elizabeth…?"

"She lives. You must go to bed, John."

He looked down at his toes. "Father has just come home. I wanted to tell him."

She closed her eyes and could barely keep the growl of her breath from her son's hearing. *George….*

"You may ask him to come up. He ought to see."

Yes, let him see! See what this house had cost them, diseased and ill-designed as it had been. Would that at last satisfy his craving for prestige and appearances? Let him see his daughter one last time, let that memory of his failings torment him as her own helplessness would afflict her the rest of her days!

She watched as John turned from the door, listened to his steps retreating down the hall, and waited. It was an eternity before heavier steps returned and a darker shadow filled that doorway. He paused, staring wordlessly for a moment.

"You may as well come in," she muttered.

He did, shuffling, until the light of her own small lantern bathed his face in a haggard glow. "How is she?"

Hannah turned her face away, her throat too tight for words.

She heard the slow release of his breath as he slumped into a chair at the bedside. "Nothing? Nothing can be done?"

She turned back to him, her eyes hard. "It is too late for that."

The defeat seemed to line his mouth as he opened it, searching for words. "I am sorry, Hannah."

"Sorry! Will that buy back her life? Will that erase the sickness from her room, or the debt that keeps us from taking her to better air?"

His head was hanging, and his shoulders trembled. "Have I failed you entirely, then?"

She closed her eyes and rested her head back against the wall. "I spoke too harshly."

"You spoke your true feelings."

"It does not matter," she snapped impatiently. "Nothing can change now, and we should not speak so loudly."

He turned his face to the side, biting his upper lip, and Hannah felt her heart split. That profile, that manner, it was the very image of her John—older, harder, but still her own flesh. And the thick curl that fell at his brow, the tender heartbreak in his eyes, that was her sweet Elizabeth. The love and care she had lavished on him these ten years were not so easily forgotten, sharp as was her disappointment in him.

The child writhed in her lap. "Mamma?" Elizabeth murmured, but her eyes did not open. Hannah bent to croon soft reassurances, to pray once more over her fevered little cheeks, but the rasping breath had changed to a futile rattle. She did not cough—there was no longer breath enough to do so. A mother's sorrow blinded her as she cried out in mournful denial.

Her husband's hand searched out her own. "Hannah, you should not weary yourself so."

She bowed her face, her lips quivering as the tears ran down the bridge of her nose, then she sniffed abruptly and shook her head. "I cannot leave. What if she calls for me, and I am not here? What if she…?" She dashed the saltwater from her eyes, gasping as she tried to pronounce the hideous word. She covered her mouth with a stifled shriek of grief, but the tears would not cease.

"My darling," soothed the broken voice of her husband. She felt his arms come about her, permitted him to slide her over so he might share in cradling their child, and allowed him to pull her head against his shoulder. He smelled of cigar smoke and brandy, of business meetings and too many oil lanterns burnt in the dark hours.

She would never forgive him these many nights of late, when he had stayed out at dinner meetings—were they only business matters that kept him away from her?—while she battled alone against death. Would that he had been there, even if he could do little more than hold her hand as she prayed! She was losing the battle, but she would have given her very heart's blood if he would but stand by her side.

He had buried his face in her hair now, and she could feel the moisture from his own tears. His large hands were stroking Elizabeth's chin, massaging her tiny arms, and cupping possessively over her heart, as if he could will the air back into her lungs.

"Hannah," he whispered into her ear, "it is too late, I know that well. But I pray you, my darling, do not give up on me yet! I will see you all well and secure. We will take that tour to the coast and watch our children play in the sand. John will go to school, and our girl will break hearts. I need just a little more time... soon, my darling! Have faith, I beg you."

She closed her eyes, feeling the damp lashes pooling together. How lovely his words! But it would all be too late for Elizabeth. No miracle on earth could save her now, and all that could have been done for her was yet to come, a gift to be bestowed on the child still unborn.

"Hannah, I have done all in my power," he groaned, the ache of his heart trembling in his voice. "Would you have the impossible of me?"

She sniffed again, shaking her head. Shattered she might be, but never foolish. "I know, George," she replied, her voice devoid of feeling.

"Would that I had the power of life!" he returned bitterly. "I fear the only power given to mankind is that of death."

Hannah did not answer. Her eyes were on his hand, still covering Elizabeth's little chest. It had grown still. "No," she breathed, snatching his hand away. "No!"

He raised the child at once, pressing his head to her heart and holding the back of his hand to her lips, in case any breath should tickle his skin.

"*Elizabeth!*" Hannah groaned, the name ripping from her throat as she clutched the emptiness before her.

George carefully lay the child back on her pillow, his features stricken as he turned to his wife. "Hannah... Hannah!" he shook her shoulders, trying to force her to look into his eyes.

She could not. Her face covered in her hands, she could only cry out, "My baby! Oh, George, my baby girl!"

He wrapped her in a tight embrace, both to buffer her violent cries and to keep her from clasping the child who was beyond all hope. She allowed him to hold her, for she was too weak to lean upon her own strength. She was deaf to his words, lost to all comfort, and cared not whether death should claim her next.

One reason alone stood before her; one staying hand raised before she allowed herself to plunge to the depths of hopelessness. Hearing a small creak in the floorboards, she lifted her head from her husband's embrace. He brushed the tears from her cheeks, with a tenderness he had not shown since the earliest days of their marriage, then both turned their faces to the door.

John stood there, his great blue eyes already rounded in sorrow. There was no need for him to speak to his mother, for he could read her feelings. His gaze shifted instead to his father, as if waiting for the man to answer this tragedy from the depths of his true nature.

George Thornton did not disappoint his son. "Come, John," he spoke in a low rasp, extending one arm. "It is only we three now."

The family debate was heated, loud, and unevenly matched. Two voices raised staunchly against the third, and there was nothing more to be done. John's wavering resolve and fears eventually yielded to his wife's own misgivings and the united wills of Dixon and his mother, and they sent the young doctor back to London in a huff.

Margaret roused somewhat at Donaldson's re-examination, making a show of bravery for John's sake, and pleading with him not to fear for her. She trusted Dr Donaldson, she vowed, and in truth, he wished to do likewise, though his faith had been shaken. Never had he doubted his own wisdom more than when he was forced to throw his support behind one or the other's medical opinions, and stake Margaret's very life on the outcome.

He continued to sit by her bed morning and night, only troubling himself to look in at the mill on those days when she drank enough broth to satisfy him. Dr Donaldson visited twice daily, his face grey as he surveyed her progress until the one, blessed day when he announced that Margaret's fever had fully abated on its own. The bleeding had slowed, and the pain in her stomach had lessened. She would live.

This news was as air to a drowning man, and for the first time in well over a fortnight, John was seen to eat more than two bites together. He was still unsuccessful at sleep—he would not lie beside her and thus disturb her, but he would not leave her alone in her chamber, defenceless against the ravages of her grief.

God and Dr Donaldson may have healed her body, but there was precious little balm he could offer to ease the pain in her heart. A careless word, a fragrance which struck her differently, or even the whisper of a breeze against the drapes—all served to remind her of the life which was never to be lived. So often during these days, either John or Hannah would discover her quietly weeping and unwilling to confess it.

John set up a pallet for himself near her bed, but even his proximity in the nights did not stop her from crying out in her dreams, desolate from fear and loneliness. Nevermore could she be innocent of heartbreak. Margaret was no stranger to loss, but this emptiness seemed to pierce her with a devastation unmatched by prior griefs.

After her father's death she seemed to gradually lay aside her sorrow in favour of the new hope set before her, but now, with that desired future blighted, her shattered dreams seemed to loom over all, defining both future and past. No memory was sacred from the withering touch of dread; no pleasant remembrance of better days was to be borne at such a time. She would think only on memories befitting her grieving heart, and those dark times lurking firmly in the past only stretched their cold fingers, whispering their mournful souvenirs of all that was never meant for mortal souls to bear.

Try as he might, John could scarcely engage her in so small a thing as what she wished to eat. She was simply... empty. Her body grew again in strength, but her heart failed to do the same—it seemed that she had lost a piece of herself. She did speak to him, but only because he insisted upon it. She did not look anxiously for his return after each parting, but when he was with her, she did not appear to wish for him to leave, and so he persisted—agonising over each sigh, each dropped eye contact, each blank stare. She was there, and yet not.

A week passed in this way, and then another. John looked for even a wavering sense of equilibrium, some indication that she had come to the bottom of her grief. Perhaps, after some days, it could be said that her emotions had regulated, if only for the simple reason that she had slipped into a constant state of numbness. From this, she did not appear to improve.

John, if it was possible, was more lost during these days than when her life was in danger. Her heartbreak pained him, it was true, but the injustice done to her, and the recognition that he was still powerless to ease her pain, filled him with such fury and such grief that he could barely speak. How could the heavens have permitted such a wrong and nearly cost her life in the process? And how could she, the woman who soothed the weary and set down the powerful, have so little to say on the matter?

On one such an afternoon, he had agonised in silence for longer than he could bear. He had tried, and largely failed, to tempt her with some sweet berries, and now they both stared at the same wall—she on the bed, he on the chair at her side. "What are you thinking of?" he asked abruptly.

She turned limpid, innocent eyes to him—eyes wide in astonishment that he would break her precious reverie. She fingered the lace at the edge of her sleeve. "Nothing in particular," she murmured vaguely. She must have thought she had answered him adequately, for she looked away, but there was nothing she could do to disguise the far-off quality to her expression or the choking noise in her throat.

"Margaret, will you not speak to me as you used to do? What can I do to bring you back to me?"

She fluttered her lashes in a vain attempt to blink away the tears that threatened. "I am here, and I *was* speaking to you, John. I have not ceased. Do you believe I am vexed with you?"

"No...." He looked down to his hands. "It seems that you have withdrawn, lost all interest in anything of life. I can think of nothing more hopeless. I would rather have you vexed with me, even arguing with me. Come, Margaret, I have been hardly perfect throughout this affair; you must have your grievances against me."

"But I do not—" she lifted her shoulders softly. "I... I feel the same as I always have. You have done nothing wrong. How could I be angry?"

"How can you not be? Was it not my own doing that caused you such pain? I wish you would, Margaret. I wish your eyes would come alive again, even if it was I who provoked you to indignation. I wish you would find the strength of feeling once more, to give you some definition. Some direction! You are not yourself."

"Myself?" Her gaze wandered to the window. "Who is that? I cannot be myself, for I do not know... everything is different now, John. I do not know how to be, or how to act, where to go next."

"It will take time. You have been ill and grieved. But you—" he growled, clasping his hands in his hair and jerked to his feet. "Forgive me. Forget I said anything. I asked too much of you."

"Where do you go, John?"

He paused at the door, gazing back at the pale face he loved so dearly. "To my office. I have some papers to begin sorting."

"Will you not bring your work home, so we may go over it together as we used to do?"

He hesitated, allowing a soft look of adoration to linger on her. She seemed so intent upon his answer, so desirous of hearing he wished to include her, that he could not disappoint her. "When you are strong enough, Margaret. I would not have you trouble yourself yet."

Her gaze fell. "How long shall you be?"

His head was down, his hand on the latch. "Some hours. I have much to do." He opened the door and missed the quiet look of sorrow in her eyes.

~

The numbers looked bad. John had scanned and parsed and recalculated until his eyes burned, but there was no help for it. The mill was simply falling farther behind on its obligations. Orders were shipping out, some of them paid for, but there was too much ground to recover.

There must be something he had overlooked! Some buyer he could pressure for faster payment, some investor who might be more patient... he felt as though he were a tug at sea, trying to push apart two behemoths, but the larger ships were rolling over him.

A part of his mind scolded him for the days spent at Margaret's bedside. So much time he had lost in tracking orders and staying abreast of each detail... but even could he have torn himself from her for an hour, it would have mattered little, and he knew it. Williams had done a remarkable job in his place, but no one could have performed a feat of alchemy. Cotton simply was not bank notes, and even if it were, there was not enough of it.

"Master?"

John turned from his pacing. "What is it, Higgins?"

Higgins stepped softly into the mill office, treading as one who wishes not to cause the floor to squeak, and rumpled his hat in his hands. "Mr Williams said to ask wha's to be done wi' th' order for Bakers? Yo' said to hold it, bu' tis up next."

John sighed. Bakers had not paid for their last two orders, and he had pushed this one back ten days already. However, their last letter had promised full payment next month, if only they could meet the demands of their own buyers. "You may as well run it, Higgins. We shall test our luck and see if it holds."

"Sir," Higgins nodded. He looked at the floor.

John permitted the ghost of a smile. "Margaret's strength is improving today."

Higgins looked up in glad relief. "Thank yo', Master. Hoo's a fine lass. Me an' th' childer's been frettin' o'er hoo."

"She is... not quite herself yet." His hand fell to the back of his office chair and tightened, his face turned away as his jaw worked. "I..." he shook his head. "Miss Mary's visits have done a deal to brighten her spirits."

Higgins looked pleased. "Thank yo', Master. The mistress, hoo's made o' flint an' steel."

John tried to smile, and almost succeeded. "See to that order, Higgins."

"Ta, Master." He shuffled out.

John fell into his desk chair. How was he to help his Margaret recover her spirits if he could barely promise her a home for the next year? Before, he had found comfort in sharing each of the mill's struggles with her. Perhaps there had been little she could do to resolve his troubles, but she was brilliantly capable of showing him new perspectives.

Now... no, he could not risk disclosing his fears to her. Her way had been dark enough already. She ought to have only tender words, the gentlest of care. Every consideration was due her, for had it not been his own selfishness and coarseness which had brought her such pain? Would that he could have borne some of it for her!

His elbows pinned the ledgers to his desk as he cradled his head in his hands. She must not be troubled by this. Surely there was something...

A quick rap sounded on his door and he abandoned the thought. Assuming it to be Williams, come to ascertain that Higgins had spoken the truth, he beckoned entry. To his surprise, it was not Williams but Watson. He rose... and then nearly fell back to his seat when another entered behind him.

"Thornton," Watson grinned, "I hope I'm not interrupting anything. I have just learned that we've a mutual acquaintance, and—"

"Harold Wright." A shiver pierced John's spine and shot through his forearms. "What are you doing in Milton?"

"Not a very cordial greeting, Thornton." The other drew near and offered his hand. "What has it been, ten years? Twelve since I saw you in Weston?"

"Sixteen," John replied through clenched teeth. "What brings you to my door?"

"The very best of things," Wright answered smoothly. "Business and friendships, eh, Watson?"

"That's right, Thornton," the other agreed. "Wright here has just offered me a chance at a most promising rail speculation. We met in London last month, introduced by my banker, of course, and I do say our prospects are marvellous."

"Ah, yes, the possibilities are endless, as they say. Why, Thornton, you do not look at all pleased to see me. Were we not old friends?"

"Aye, we were friends." John turned his back as he walked around his desk, then drew near, unblinking. "As were our fathers, if such is your definition of friendship."

"Oh, come, Thornton, you cannot still be soured about that nonsense. It was seventeen years ago!"

"Eighteen, last October."

"Yes, yes," Wright waved impatiently. "But we are men of business, not boys playing at boxing and what-not. It is we who settle affairs now, is that not right, Watson?"

"Indeed! That is why we came to speak with you, Thornton. We are wishing to broaden our partnership. With one enterprise so handily underway and promising such an excellent profit within the year, we are seeking out other opportunities. None can be quite so large, you understand, but we had thought to invest in some local ventures—four hundred pounds here, three there, that sort of thing."

Three or four hundred pounds! What such a figure could purchase him just then. John swallowed, but his face remained a mask. "Are you seeking recommendations?"

Watson cleared his throat, and a look which might have been described as amusement passed between them. "No, Thornton, not precisely."

"We would like to invest in Marlborough Mills," Wright announced. "You must be in some straits after all the strikes. Come, Thornton, it is no secret. Your sheds are practically bare, and have been so for months, from what I understand. My own advisers have heard talk among your men that you may have to cut hours. Now, I know you for a practical fellow. Surely you would consider any honest offer of the kind we are prepared to make."

"Honest?" John turned away to pace back around his desk. "I am not sure you know the meaning of the word."

"Come, now Thornton, there is no cause for insult," Watson objected. "He makes a fair point, and you and I are brothers, after all. Would I see harm come to my wife's brother? No, indeed! That is why we thought of you first, as we have both some connection with you."

"I have no connection with *you*." John retorted, glaring at Wright.

The men exchanged a glance. "Thornton, be reasonable. Surely you can see the advantages!" protested Watson.

"And what are your terms? First lienholder? I am afraid you are too late, as the bank holds that honour."

Wright stepped nearer. "What if we were to pay off your loan? That is your largest debt, is it not? I've an arrangement with the bank myself, and I am certain they will accept some of my other accounts as security. Then with the additional loan of… oh, perhaps a hundred? If I am to work with the bank on your behalf, of course I could not offer as much liquid cash."

"What benefit would it be to me if you took over my loan? You offer what I have no interest in accepting."

"Well, perhaps we could ease your terms. What do you think, would that be of interest to you?"

"I cannot think why you would bother."

"Thornton, we are family now," interjected Watson. "Surely you cannot think your welfare might not be of interest to me."

"It has never been so with your partner." John abruptly turned his back on the affronted stares, the gaping mouths, and crossed his arms to sulk out of his window.

"Now, Thornton, is that any way to repay me for my family's kindness to you? My father put you in school, got you advantageous introductions—"

"And squeezed my father for every farthing he could leverage! Do you think I did not see it then? How he forced favours, manipulated his partners, bled men dry until they had naught but debt and disgrace to call their own? And what happened to Daniel Wright after that affair?"

Wright's face had flushed, but Watson was looking rather pale. "Thornton, do you dare accuse—"

"Watson, you are a damned fool for listening to this swindler. It will be you back at my door in a year's time begging a roof over your head, mark my words!"

Wright's veneer of calm snapped. He stormed near, his countenance red and finger jabbing towards John's chest. "How dare you, Thornton! You accuse my father when your own was the one who over-extended himself. And then you assume that I would intentionally ruin my own partner!"

"I have heard enough, Wright." John's voice had lowered to a snarl. "There is the door. Take it, or I shall show you the window."

Wright had already shoved his hat back on his head, and now Watson was reaching for the door. "You'll wish you had listened, Thornton."

John slammed the door behind them.

Fourteen

29 January 1856

Another hot tear slid down her cheek as she stared towards the window. She was not yet permitted to walk to it, and the view was far from scenic even if she did so, but she knew what was on the other side. If she leaned far enough to the right of the sash and peered to her left, the light of John's desk lantern would wink across the mill yard on those evenings when he worked late.

Such nights had become more frequent—naturally so, since he had spent weeks watching over her. Somehow, he thought to make up for that neglect by working when he thought her to be asleep. Now, however, it was the middle of the day, and he had been obliged to resume something of his former routine.

That stinging sensation had returned to her eyes, the familiar burn to her throat, and with them, that new notion of resentment. His comment the previous week, that he wished for her to be angry with him rather than to remain quiet, had festered in her heart from a mere mystery to a distraction. How dare he ask her to feel? How could he imply that she was exerting herself too little? Did he not know that every sense, every stirring of her heart was anguish she could not explain? Could he not see what it cost her to check those feelings, so she did not spend all her energies in unruly displays of grief?

Margaret closed her eyes and counted... five seconds for the unbidden wave of anger to subside... ten seconds for the uneven thrum of her heart to still... twenty before reason claimed her thinking once more.

John was a man, after all. What could he know of the torrent of emotion that held her in its thrall, crashing her helplessly against the shoals of physical weakness and despondency? He only wished for her to be well, and she knew not the way to make him understand how very far she was from that happy estate, without causing him to worry anew. He had other concerns, and at least at the mill he could be more productive than in her bedroom... watching over her every breath and word.

Now that John had gone back to the mill, it was not uncommon that Hannah would spend her entire day sitting at Margaret's side. This had rather the reverse effect of what the lady probably intended, for instead of finding peace in her mother-in-law's sensible companionship, she grew restive, feeling that she somehow missed the mark—that her recovery was yet unsatisfactory in Hannah Thornton's eyes. The woman never spoke so much, but Margaret felt the gravity of her expression pressing upon her.

To be fair, Hannah Thornton was not so stern and forbidding as she had once been. She was never so solicitous as Dixon, but mysterious kindnesses often found their way to Margaret which had not come from John—a particular shawl, a special blend of tea, the best serving ware. There were even those few blessed occasions when she had somehow secured for Margaret the company of Mary Higgins.

Welcome as these visits were, they also tended to fatigue rather than to strengthen her. Such had been the case once again today, and though Margaret strove to converse cheerfully for the benefit of her guest, she now nursed a pulsing headache. Nevertheless, it had been John's wish that she should not be permitted to sit too long alone, and as though some invisible timing bell had sounded after Mary's departure, Dixon appeared with the tea tray.

"I thought you might like something, Miss. There were oranges in town."

Margaret attempted to smile. It was not Dixon who would have procured the fresh fruit, but John himself. It would have been selected by his hand, just as the cluster of grapes he had presented to her that very morning and the exotic bananas he had brought to tempt her last week. She scolded herself as a wicked woman to have, for even a moment, chafed under his care for her. "Thank you, Dixon, an orange would be welcome."

"And Miss... I didn't want to say as much, but that Watson woman is here again. She's come every day this week, but Mrs Thornton wouldn't let her up to you."

Margaret straightened on the pillows. "Fanny is here to see me? Of course, she must be shown in. Why would she not be permitted to come before?"

"I don't know. Mrs Thornton is out just now so that Watson lady insisted that I speak to you for her."

Margaret plucked at the quilt resting over her lap. She could not imagine Fanny having much of interest to say, but it would be pleasant to speak with someone new for a change. The aching behind her eyes would remain whether she sat in solitude or not. "Please, Dixon, show her in."

A dark frown lined Dixon's face, but she could do no more than she was bidden. In a very few moments, Fanny Watson breezed into the room, and another teacup was brought.

"My dear Margaret, at last! I was beginning to think I would never see you. John has been ever so particular, to say nothing of Mamma. You are looking so much stronger than they claimed!"

"I am well, Fanny," Margaret smiled—almost convincingly. "It is wonderful to see you." Margaret tried to straighten enough to perform a hostess' duty, but Fanny waved her off and served herself.

"Well, now, was it not a splendid Christmas? Oh, I suppose it was a bad time for you. But the weather is not so very cold, is it? John must be pleased as it should be a good year for cotton."

Margaret attempted a pleasant, neutral expression. "I have heard it is fine, but I have not… that is, I am looking forward to a fine spring. How are you, Fanny? I hope you have some news other than that directly related to the house, for I am in great need of something different to think upon."

"Well—" Fanny smiled proudly and fussed with her skirts, "Perhaps mother has not told you, but my Watson has made an old acquaintance again. I suppose John has never mentioned a Mr Harold Wright?"

Margaret's eyes misted in thought. "The name is familiar… I know he has, but I do not recall at present."

"His father was my father's business partner, years ago. John even lived at their house for two years, though he probably made little of it. You know John! London is nothing to Milton for him."

Margaret blinked. "Oh! *That* Harold Wright."

"None other! My Watson was looking for one last supporter for his speculation, and as John proved so disobliging, he was forced to look to London and beyond. Fancy our pleasure when we came across Mr Wright! Mr Daniel Wright, the father, has retired, but his son Harold has taken his place. Such a clever gentleman he is!"

"You have met him?"

"Naturally! The Wrights had us to London while they were sorting the details. Oh, my dear sister, you simply *must* meet Mildred Wright—she is Harold's wife, of course. I declare, she is the most fashionable lady I have ever met and has the most *ex*quisite taste! I am certain you will adore her, for she speaks so very fondly of John from long ago, and she asked ever so many questions about you! If I did not know better, I should have thought she was sorry she missed a chance with John herself, but of course, that is silly, for she and Mr Wright were sweethearts as children.

"Oh, but I have quite lost what I was thinking to say. Ah! The partnership! You will never believe how it all came out. My dear Watson thought to offer an opportunity to Mr Wright but found instead that the man had his own schemes, and it was in our better interest to join *his* venture."

"I would have thought you would not do business with him at all, after everything that happened."

"Oh, stuff and nonsense. Certainly, Father was ruined long years ago, but it was no more Mr Wright's fault than his own. No one made my father invest more than he could afford, and you know none put that gun to his head but himself. It would be foolish to blame the Wrights over that sorry business. At any rate, it is the most promising partnership, and Watson is terribly pleased how well it has come out."

"What is their purpose?"

"I believe they had something to do with building rail lines in Australia, or some such thing. No... perhaps they were sending them to Canada's western territories. Oh, I cannot recall. But you know, such an enterprise cannot hope to fail. Only think of the advantages to a properly functioning rail network in such a backwards place, and the profits to be gained!"

Margaret could well imagine the advantages, but she doubted very seriously that Fanny had paused long enough to ponder such an undertaking. Money would always be wanted and building railroads over open country was no easy task, but Watson was likely correct—if they could afford to buy in and had the additional capital to cover any unforeseen setbacks, the rewards would be monumental and nearly secure.

"That is wonderful news, Fanny," she murmured.

"Oh—" the other shook her head—"I know what you are thinking. You are worried about what John will say. He is not always right, you know. He is inclined to cling to old grudges over that affair, but it will be his loss."

"From what I understand, such a feeling would not be without some foundation, but I would not expect such of John. He would speak reasonably to anyone, regardless of past injuries, I am sure."

Fanny gave a short laugh and then poured herself another cup. "That was not how he responded when my Watson and Mr Wright spoke to him. Why, my husband could not even repeat John's words in my hearing, so foul was his language! I pity you, Margaret, truly I do, for he can have *such* a fearful temper when provoked."

Margaret's head was pounding, and her weary gaze had drifted to the floor, but at this accusation, her eyes sharpened again. "John knows of this? He has spoken to Mr Wright in person?"

"Well, of course! It is all over town, how he fairly threw two respectable men from his office, but perhaps you have not heard. Naturally not, for you have been sequestered away here. You poor thing! Mamma can be ever so dull, I know. Of course, you aren't to be walking about town, I did not mean to imply that, but you could at least have been given the news. I suppose Mamma and John did not trust you to remain calm, but I declare, you are the very picture of composure. They are often overbearing, are they not? I feared you would not have been told a thing, so I am glad I came today."

Margaret smiled weakly.

"I suppose Mamma has told you little else?" Fanny was lifting her cup with a suggestive lilt to her voice.

Margaret examined her suspiciously, wondering what further gossip Fanny wished to inform her of. "Only that Dr Donaldson stays to tea every afternoon, after he has looked in on me."

"Dr Donaldson! Yes, I think he must come to you after he has seen me. For, you know, he comes rather often to our house as well of late."

"Has Mr Watson been unwell?" Margaret asked, with only feigned interest.

"Unwell! Do not be silly, he has never been better. Nor have *I*." Fanny stirred her tea with a smug pleasure.

Margaret's brow furrowed in confusion. "If he is not coming for professional purposes...."

"Oh, but he is! I have asked Watson to delay the tour we had planned to India next spring, for I shall not be fit to travel. There—" she smiled at the spark of understanding in Margaret's eyes—"I knew you would be pleased for me. Mamma did not think so, but I know you are a generous sort, after all. I thought it would cheer you to hear you will be an aunt."

Margaret's face washed to a chalky hue, and her breath grew raspy. She could find no words, so she set aside her cup and looked towards the window, blinking rapidly and trying to swallow.

"I am certain that Mamma has already told John, but I wonder why they would have kept it from you? Is it not a wonderful thing that we are sisters now and you can share in my happiness?" Fanny buttered her bread as she spoke in comforting tones. "You have pulled through miraculously well, Margaret. Why, poor Harriet Andrews died two years ago of the very same, but now that you are better, certainly there is nothing more to fear. I declare, within the year you should have a child of your own, I am sure of it, and the cousins shall grow close as two peas. Oh! I know you must be frightened to try again, but this can be no more than an accidental happenstance. Dr Donaldson says that so long as—"

"Please leave me," Margaret whispered.

Fanny glanced up from her bread in surprise. "I beg your pardon?"

"I am not feeling well. Please... I must lie down."

Fanny looked somewhat affronted, but she set aside her bread, uneaten, and rose. "Well, I hope you have been stronger than you are today. I would have thought you could bear a little longer visit, but perhaps your condition must be more delicate than I had expected. It must be rather trying, cooped up in this dark room with nothing to do."

Margaret pressed her throbbing eyes into her hand, trembling with a chill that went deeper than her bones. She made no answer, and Fanny turned to go, muttering to herself. Margaret heard her sister-in-law proclaiming her wounded dignity as she opened the door for herself.

"Never in my life! She always did give herself airs...."

The door had scarcely closed before Margaret crumpled in her chair and gave way to shrieking, gasping tremors of anguish.

~

A month had fallen from his calendar since Margaret's ordeal, and it had been a full week since the insult of Wright's visit. Marlborough Mills had plunged into the coldest depths of winter, and everything seemed as frozen as the water lines in the mornings.

John was staring at the paper on his desk as though he had forgotten how to read. He knew quite well what it said, for it was written in his hand, but his head was failing to comprehend. How had matters come to this? He dropped the pen from numb fingers and scrubbed his face until his eyes were blurry. There was nothing else for it tonight but to crawl into his bed and hope that in the morning, his mind would have cleared, and he might think and plan.

He found his mother sewing in her usual place. She rose to meet him, likely only waiting for his return before she went to her own bed. "John, have you eaten?"

He shook his head. "No, and I've not the appetite. How is Margaret this evening?"

His mother looked troubled. "She has been quiet. She spoke almost nothing when I was with her before."

"That is often her way of late."

"Fanny was here this afternoon. I had forbidden her from visiting, but she took it upon herself to do so while I was out."

John felt his fingers curl and his neck prickle. "What did she tell her?"

His mother's only answer was silence.

John released a tight breath, forcing himself to civility. "It is done. Go to bed, Mother." He laid a hand on her shoulder and left her, steeling himself to face... he knew not what.

Margaret's door was closed. A hesitant tap yielded no answer, but surely, she was merely asleep, and Dixon had wished to shield her from the draught from his own room. He turned the knob and gently pushed the door open.

She was not asleep, nor was she even lying down. She was out of bed and on her feet, against all the doctor's injunctions. It appeared she had been so some while, for her steps had that aching, hesitant quality of one who wearies and yet will not cease.

"Margaret! What is this?"

She did not check her pacing until she had reached the end of the room, and then she stopped, rather than turning back. Her arms were crossed defensively over her breast, and her head bowed low.

"Love! You must not be out of bed." He was by her side in an instant, his arms circling around her, but she did not submit to his embrace as she always had. She stood stiff, trembling, and refusing to look at him.

"Margaret? Speak to me, what is troubling you?" She still did not answer—in fact, tried to hide her face from him—so he turned her against her will. She covered her face with her hands.

"Love," he insisted again, but she vehemently shook her head.

"It is no good, John! I am the most wretched being alive," she mumbled between her fingers.

"How can you speak so? Tell me what happened. Fanny was here?"

She hesitated, then nodded into her hands.

"I am sorry for it. We had asked her not to see you until you were stronger. I shall speak with her—"

"For what, John? For telling me about Watson's new investment partner, and how they are lording it over you?"

He felt his ears growing hot. "It is nothing of any concern to us. Watson may do as he pleases."

"Then it was her other news. You knew—" here, her words became unintelligible. She still refused to look at him, hiding her face more deeply in her hands, until at last he pulled them away and beheld her tears.

"I knew… yes, I did," he rumbled hoarsely. "Pay her no mind, Margaret! It was unfeeling of her to come to you as she did."

"How can I ignore it?" A sob shook her, and robbed of the use of her hands, she hid her face against his shoulder. "I am miserably wicked, John! I could not even wish her well. I only looked on with envy—*oh!* yes, I will tell you all, and you will know the truth. I could think only of how I loved our child, and how she seems incapable of such a feeling. If the same were to happen to her, she could find some other diversion to please her equally well, but J-j—" her body racked and heaved into another helpless sob, followed by such mournful cries as would break her husband's heart.

"Margaret, you must listen to me." He pulled her close. "What you are feeling is natural. You must not be so harsh on yourself!"

"And what of the commandment to rejoice with those who rejoice? I am incapable of bearing any such feeling!"

"You forget the other half, which is to weep with those who weep. Fanny had no business speaking as she did."

"I can do nothing for her, but my own feelings are wicked, John. I only wished her far away, and wished… oh, but you will truly know me for the vile creature I am!"

"You wished Fanny to know grief? For her to taste some measure of suffering? Aye, I have felt the same before."

"But such a feeling is unjust! How could I ever have conceived of it?"

"Margaret, come," he soothed into her ear. He gave her no opportunity to protest, for he gathered her into his arms and removed her forcibly to her bed, then curled himself at her side, still fully clothed. She shivered, and he drew the blankets over her and pulled her near.

"I think none could demand that you deny such feelings. I would far rather see you angry than numb, as you have been. Grief such as yours is a long path and strewn with many a rocky blunder."

"But I have no right…" she sniffed.

"You have every right, Margaret. I will not have you labouring under some false sense of righteousness or conviction. Perhaps your feelings might become twisted into genuine envy were you to permit them to linger beyond what is natural, but I think such a thing impossible for you."

She lay silent, and he had no means of knowing if she considered his words or had grown deaf to him. There was little he could do but to cease speaking, so he tightened his arms around her. Though she did not precisely object, she made no attempt to yield to his embrace.

They remained so for nearly twenty minutes, until he believed she had fallen asleep. He shifted his feet, thinking to kick off his shoes and undress, and debating about returning to his own bed, when she stirred at last.

"John, how does the mill?" she asked sleepily.

He stilled. "I do not know what I ought to tell you just now. You should rest—"

"What did Watson want from you? Surely you had already given your answer, and it is too late to join his venture. He would have known you to be determined on that point. Why would he come to provoke you?"

"Provoke me? You sound as though you believe Watson delighted in frustrating me. It was nothing of the kind."

"Will you not tell me, as you used to do?"

He sighed, helpless against her ploy of repeating his own words back to him. "Watson is no fool—neither is Wright, for that matter. They know the general trend of the market, and it is no secret that Marlborough Mills is leveraged. They assumed the reason I would not purchase into their rail speculation was that I had not the capital—which is not precisely true, although it is money I cannot rightfully call my own. They came to enquire about purchasing an interest in the mill."

She stiffened in his arms. "You are not considering it?"

"Of course not. If I were to take on a partner, it would not be they. Do not trouble yourself now, Margaret. I will tell you all once you have rested."

She quieted again, and this time he waited longer to stir himself. He could not bear disturbing her as she slept, and he would not permit himself to stay, achingly as he longed to do so. When a light rasping in her throat announced fitful slumber, he at last dared to slip from her warm body and return to his own cold bedroom.

~

12 February 1856

My Dearest Margaret,

By the time you receive this letter, I imagine we shall be in London. I am afraid I had quite forgotten to write sooner. Motherhood and the bother of packing up our house here has made me a neglectful correspondent, and I confess, it was hard to think of you in that dark and dreary city when I had my darling Sholto occupying most of my time. At any rate, dear Margaret, we are coming home. Maxwell's tour is complete, and I do so wish to bring Sholto back to London.

Mamma is to follow, of course, for she has not yet seen my boy. She has been so long in Venice and Paris, I shouldn't wonder if she has forgotten how to speak English! She has promised that my sweet boy will begin speaking French to his grandmother even as he speaks English to the rest of us.

Oh, Margaret, you must persuade your husband to permit you to come to us! I have ever so many things to tell you, and I know that you will love our dear Sholto as I do, the moment you set eyes upon him. I fancy you will learn much in the ways of managing an infant that will profit you in the months to come.

Never fear about travelling back as the time advances, for there are better accoucheurs to be found in London, I am certain. There would be no cause for you to rush to Milton for your confinement, for we can help you in so many ways! A good nursemaid is indispensable, of course, and we can begin interviewing candidates directly. The nurse may direct his daily routines while you must take a hand in properly spoiling the child. I wonder if your husband will permit you to spoil a child as he ought to be? If he is difficult to persuade to your ways of thinking, Margaret, there are always means for a wife to manage a husband. I trust you have discovered that by now.

I cannot think of the winter you must have had to endure there! Is it really grey all year round, with hardly any sun? I understand that the curtains do not even stay clean a week for all the coal ash in the air. Why, I should be nervous to have a fire in the grate, lest the air in my drawing-room itself ignite! Margaret, dear, when your child is born, you simply must remain with us in London for a time, for the better air. Perhaps you may be able to introduce the child to some culture that way, for I understand that a tradesman's son will be expected to work straightaway, as soon as the law allows. How perfectly shocking!

Maxwell had another letter from Henry two days ago. He is well, of course. He had begun to court a Miss Parkins of Chelsea, a lady whose father is a manager at the Exchange. I think perhaps nothing came of it, for he has not mentioned her again in the last three letters. He asked after you, and Maxwell told him we supposed you would be eager for a holiday from Milton as soon as we are home in London.

I must close now, for the last of my trunks are nearly packed and my wax and pens are next to go. I shall depend upon hearing from you as soon as you can possibly write.

Yours,
Edith

Margaret winced as she read the first part of the letter. In truth, the entirety of the missive was condescending and petulant. Had she once sounded that way herself? She prayed not. Every line dripped disdain and superiority... but the first half, with its assumptions of her impending motherhood, burned and ached in her heart. Oh, how she wished she had said nothing at all to Edith!

Yet for all the pain of such expectations, at least she could be assured of sympathy when Edith knew the whole truth. She had not written—could not bring herself to do so, particularly when Edith had never before replied to her announcement—but the mere fact that Edith had known about the babe meant that she might also share in Margaret's mourning. Such agony as had been hers, yet she could not wish that fleeting life unlived and unacknowledged.

Her eyes clouded, and that familiar cry shrilled helplessly in her throat; the herald of more shameful tears. The bitter anguish would follow next, the rage and denial, then the pointless questioning, until she was fully engulfed in trembling, irrational hysterics... no, she had not the strength for such again today.

She deliberately folded the top of the page down, so those paragraphs were covered, and she could force her mind elsewhere. She read the remaining lines... and decided that she had no interest in hearing about Henry or his doings. The top fold drew down a little farther until all that could be read was Edith's last line and the adieu.

Those words committed to memory, she dropped the letter to the pillow at her side and stared up at her ceiling. She hated this bedroom.

There was nothing so terribly offensive about the room itself. She was simply tired of looking at it, and breathing its stifling, grief-laden air. She closed her eyes and instead imagined what Corfu must have been like—white sands, blue sky, as Edith had described. Sea birds chattering in the breeze, bustling marketplaces where people of all sorts gathered to buy and sell.

Margaret opened her eyes. *People.*

She sat up in the bed, her decision made before she realised she had done so. Five minutes later, Dixon entered the room carrying her tea tray.

"Miss Margaret! You aren't supposed to be out of bed!"

"I shall not remain in it a day longer, Dixon. I am better, and I wish to be downstairs."

"Better! You look as if you'd faint where you stand. Nay, Miss, you cannot stand there half-dressed. What are you about, without your dressing robe?"

"Help me with my garments, Dixon. The corset may have to be loosened for comfort, but I think—"

Dixon stuffed her fists into her ample hips. "Nay, Miss. There's not a pick of flesh on your bones."

"I have flesh enough Dixon, and I daresay more than I ought, from lying about so long and trying to eat everything you and John have demanded."

"'Tis none of it strength. You're pale as one of them little white mushrooms, and you're like to catch your death from the chill."

"A mushroom! Yes, I feel like that. Help me with my chemise, Dixon."

Dixon crossed her arms, her cheeks mottled with consternation. "I'll get Mr Thornton, I will, if you don't go back to bed."

"I intend to go below, and whether I do so properly attired is up to you. Now, will you help me with my stays, or shall I do it myself?"

"I'll get *Mrs* Thornton!" Dixon threatened.

Margaret ignored her and searched out a pair of stockings. Her throat was still tight, her eyes still damp, but she had committed herself to leaving this room. It was the first time she had felt a breath of air in her lungs in weeks. Dixon's threats might fall on other ears, for so deaf was she to them that Dixon herself at last relented—provided that she bundle herself beyond the limits of reason.

Half an hour later, dressed and coiffed and looking, if not feeling, respectable and well, Margaret laid a shaking hand on the bannister. Her head swirled as she looked down, a wave of dizzy nausea reminding her of how little she had eaten. Perhaps the stairs were more than she should have engaged for... but if she returned to her room, she would re-read Edith's letter. She tightened her grip on the railing and forced one trembling step at a time.

"Margaret!" Hannah Thornton rose from her seat, a scolding tone on her lips, as Margaret entered the sitting room. "You cannot be well enough, girl."

Margaret did not, in fact, feel well enough. The stairs had left her with a cold sheen on her brow and a twisted feeling in her stomach, and she wanted nothing more than to lie down again. Her chair would suffice, and she stubbornly declared the same to her mother-in-law.

Hannah was staring dubiously as Margaret's uncertain hand trailed the back of her chair. Her vision was growing dim around the periphery, and if she did not seat herself quickly, she was at a very real risk of fainting. Moving as swiftly as she dared, and not caring that she suffered some measure of clumsiness, she settled herself.

It was a full minute before the sick feeling passed. A maid, perhaps responding to some gesture from the elder Mrs Thornton that Margaret had not seen, arrived at once with a tray of fruit. "I'll bring your tea, ma'am."

Margaret drew an unsteady breath. "Yes, thank you, Jane."

"Well—" Hannah picked up her needlework again—"shall I send for Dr Donaldson?"

"No, thank you. I am well enough, as you see."

"You will need to convince John of that. The word of a wilfull lass, particularly one who looks as green as you do, will be insufficient to persuade him."

"I am not used to moving about so much, and I cannot regain my strength without doing so. Dr Donaldson has said, has he not, that I am out of danger?"

A small crease appeared beside Hannah Thornton's mouth, and her eyes twinkled for a moment. "Do as you like, then. I refuse to encourage your folly."

Margaret rested her head back, closing her eyes for the briefest moment before Jane returned with her tea. "Has John already taken his luncheon?"

"I doubt he will today. The hour has come and gone, and he has hardly slowed a moment of late."

Margaret frowned. A fortnight ago, John was still taking all his meals with her in her room. He had even come home for his luncheon every day, whether or not he desired the meal. When had he ceased? Perhaps it was the day that she had informed him the odour of the food he liked troubled her. Or perhaps it was just after Fanny's visit. He had seemed so desirous of shielding her from anything that might distress her. Had he, perhaps, withdrawn so his business affairs might not trouble her? Perhaps it would have been a noble sentiment, but she could hardly appreciate the gesture. She would far rather know, than not.

"Your Miss Higgins has apparently taken ill."

Margaret's eyes flashed up. "I beg your pardon? Mary? How do you know?"

"She had intended to call this afternoon, after the men's dinner hour, but her father brought a note expressing their regrets. She went home with a fever."

"A fever! Has she been seen by a doctor?"

The elder Mrs Thornton raised a brow. "I believe that might be beyond the family's means."

"But surely, she must be seen. Can we not do something for her ourselves? Perhaps Dr Donaldson could—"

"Mr Higgins would not hear of it. Like all his kind, he refuses anything that might be called charity, even if it's to save one of his own," she snorted.

"Is she really so bad?"

"Well—" Hannah frowned down to her needlework—"he will say she is not, but I heard another had to finish the dinner shift for her."

Margaret felt the blood drain from her face. "Are others ill, or is it only she?"

"I have heard of no other, but it is not usual that any should report their illnesses to me."

"But perhaps it is diphtheria, or cholera! She must be seen if she is so ill she could not work. It may be something very serious!"

"Do calm yourself, Margaret. Like as not it is a simple fever, and she will be back to work in a day or two."

Margaret could not help drumming her fingers on the chair. Hannah Thornton was correct, she must confess, but her heart pounded in fearful anxiety.

Hannah had lowered her gaze again and was picking out a thread to make a fancy knot. "I did happen to send a note of my own to the doctor. I am certain John will wish to ensure that the girl handling the workers' food could not have infected any others."

Margaret narrowed her eyes, observing her mother-in-law carefully. "That… was most prudent."

Hannah met her look with one of silent assurance. "Doctor Donaldson will do all he can for the lass, unless I must call him back here instead to tend a foolish girl who insists on over-exerting herself."

Margaret bowed her head, a warmth spreading through her heart for the first time in a long while. She almost caught herself smiling, but not quite. "I shall take care that no such measures are necessary."

Hannah raised a brow, then returned her attention to her needlework. "If you insist on sitting with me—" she flicked a finger to her basket without looking up—"you might take up the darning."

Margaret moved eagerly towards it, relieved that the spell of dizziness seemed to have passed… and grateful to have something to do.

Fifteen

26 February 1856

John's prospects had not improved. He was now facing the very real danger of being unable to purchase more cotton by the end of April, and the payroll would soon follow. Too few orders were coming in, and too few of those were paid. He struggled to keep up the appearance of solvency, for that had been his only remaining hope against ruin. A mill in good standing attracted orders. One tottering on the brink… did not.

To make matters yet worse, influenza was running rampant through the sheds. Mary Higgins had been the first, but now, two weeks later, production at the mill had nearly ground to a halt. Perhaps because everyone had encountered Mary during their mealtimes, or perhaps because it was bound to happen some way or another, nearly half his work force was struggling with the fever.

They came back to work every day all the same, because none could afford to stay home, but the sickness rendered them slow, miserable, and prone to dangerous mistakes. Only that afternoon, one young woman who desired to warm her chilled hands had been cast out of the carding rooms by her fellow workers when she carried a hot little lantern to set on the floor by her feet. John still shuddered at the horrific thought. Aye, she would have been warm enough, had she tipped that lantern over with her foot! All their problems would then be at an end.

So far, none had died of the fever, but the children, and the older workers… it was only a matter of time before the weakest would fall. He had done all he could, even supplementing the wholesale meat and vegetables purchased for the kitchen with resources from his own pocket to make sure that even the poorest might be sustained, but his pockets were not deep enough, his hands not strong enough to save them all. He would do better to ensure that they might still have work after the fever had ravaged their numbers… but he could not even guarantee that.

He must make the decision—now, while he could yet repay his creditors, and his workers might still find employment elsewhere. He must speak with his wife and his mother. Those words sounded again and again in his mind, like the knells of doom, as he strode slowly back to his house late that night.

What he would have given if Margaret had seen fit to comfort him with a bit of supper and a few moments of her company as he finished his work! But he would not have wished her to walk so far, even had she been inclined to do so. Cold, tired, and hungry, he looked to the task before him with dread and a sense of hopelessness.

Margaret rose when he entered the drawing-room, and for half a moment, he drew courage from the smile she offered, the hand she extended to him. She, at least, had begun to regain her strength, just as his own was failing.

"Good evening, John," she murmured. He kissed her on the cheek and wondered at the way she stiffened at the intimacy. It was not as though he had not done so in his mother's presence before… but when he turned to greet his mother, he found that she had a guest.

"Dr Donaldson! I did not know we had the pleasure."

"Ah, good evening, Thornton. I was sorry to hear you were detained this evening. I was hoping for the chance to speak with you."

John shifted to his mother. She stood, serene and poised as ever, not yielding any indication of the doctor's intended request or her feelings on the matter.

"Something of import, Donaldson?" he asked cautiously.

"Very much so, but you must be weary. I'll not trouble you the moment you walk in your door. In fact, I was just about to take my leave."

John nodded and realised only much later that his farewell to Donaldson was rather brusque. Once the privacy of his home was restored, he fell into the chair, and Margaret directed a tray to be brought for him. He looked it over, picked off a bite or two of bread and cheese, and then ignored it.

"You are not ill?" Margaret touched his arm in concern.

"No. Only tired."

A look passed from Margaret to his mother—that knowing, feminine look of dismay—but neither replied.

Margaret sent the tray back and sat beside him on the sofa. She raised frequent glances his way, as though hoping to ask something or to peer into his thoughts, but she did not speak for long moments.

At last, she brightened somewhat. "I had another letter today from my cousin Edith. She is home again in London. My aunt also arrived last week."

"That is well," he answered neutrally.

A faint shadow passed over Margaret's features, but smoothed at will as she spoke again. "Edith has been home a fortnight already. She has been very busy with callers and setting up house again, I suppose that is why she was so long in writing."

"Of course." He kneaded his forehead, wishing the pounding behind his eyes would cease. How could he find the words he must speak if he could not think clearly?

"John, you do look rather pale," his mother informed him. "Ought we to have someone call Dr Donaldson back?"

"Mother, I am never ill."

She did not appear convinced. He straightened somewhat and attempted to rally his thoughts, but then he saw his mother's hand falling to her Bible. He glanced at the clock—ten, already.

"John, are you certain you are well?" whispered Margaret from his side.

"Just a headache. Mother, I beg you, not tonight. I do not have it in me. Please, excuse me."

He ran. Perhaps his feet carried him at a sedate pace, but he was running, and he knew it. The truth would be there, waiting for him again in the morning, but just for a few hours, he consoled himself, he could rest. He need not lay it all before them now.

~

Margaret watched him go, stunned and disheartened. She longed to race after him, for it was not like John to answer news in monosyllables, then abruptly quit the room like that. She was already out of her seat and nearly to the door when she met some of the household staff gathered for Hannah's evening ritual. She sent a swift glance of apology to her mother-in-law, which was received with understanding, and followed him.

"John?" she tapped on the door between their rooms. "Are you well?"

He opened it; cravat hanging, waistcoat gone. "Just a little weary, Margaret. You should rest, too."

"I am perfectly strong. Dr Donaldson has pronounced me fit. I only want more exercise to return to my old self."

"I am glad to hear it." A tender smile lit his face, and for a moment, his loving eyes swept over her.

"John, I was thinking…" she lowered her gaze, nibbling her lip. "Would you consider sharing my room tonight? You look cold, and it is warmer in here."

"I am not certain…."

"John," she whispered, and boldly threw her arms about his neck. "Will you let me ease your cares?"

He stiffened. "Margaret, we should not. You cannot possibly be recovered."

"But I am, as I have said. It is two months now since… John, I have missed you."

She felt his shoulders relax as his hands slid around her waist. In another breath, he had drawn her close and was nuzzling her hair. "I have missed you as well, love."

She began inching slowly backward, easing him over the threshold. "Then stay with me, John."

He was too weary, too frayed to resist her, and she knew it. Her lips grazed the lower line of his jaw, and she felt a shiver pass through him. "Margaret," he protested softly.

She had his buttons now, and then her hands were sliding over his well-remembered form. "Let me help you," she pleaded. Oh, how she longed for him to turn to her, to share his heart again! Civil words and light touches on her hand were too little to satisfy her yearning. She wanted *him* once more—all of him, as he had given himself to her once before in her sorrows.

She slipped the braces from his shoulders and felt his arms tighten about her in the first stirrings of longing—far preferable to the porcelain doll treatment she had known of late. Encouraged, she brushed tender kisses over that little hollow at the base of his throat, where his flesh was warm and soft.

He was shaking his head and lifting his hands to press down her arms. "It is good of you to wish to comfort me, but it is too soon for you. You must regain your strength."

"Strength is as much a matter of feeling as it is physical well-being. Please, John, I will not break. I have wished to feel close to you again."

"We could sit by your fire together. I could brush out your hair, and we could talk."

She cupped his shadowed face in her hands and tipped it down to her. "I have nothing of interest to say," she whispered, then began to express herself by other means. She caught his lips, rewarding his hesitant responses with increasing warmth. Slowly, reluctantly, his mouth opened to her, and she was kissing him with an urgency which he would only match by half.

Her hands now preyed upon the rest of his body—his lean waist, his taut shoulders, his tender stomach. His pulse drummed against her cheek, and his hands tightened to cradle her more closely. When she slipped her fingers beneath his loosened clothing and began to caress his bare skin, she felt his breath catch.

"Margaret, are you certain?"

She drew back to look steadily into his face, then with deliberate intent, reached to pluck the comb from her hair. His eyes widened as she shook loose the careful ringlets and coils, then lit as she turned to present her back. "Will you help me with my gown?"

Light fingers worked against her lower neck; hesitant at first, then growing in boldness. Inch by inch, she felt her bodice loosen and begin to fall away. A throaty groan rose, just behind her ear, and then his hands were pushing the sleeves down her arms, caressing her back, nipping at the ribbons of her corset. She rested her head back against his shoulder, revelling once more in the feel of him reaching for her, desiring her.

"Margaret," his hot breath was now upon her neck, his voice quivering with awakened hunger. "We needn't… rush. We could—"

She spun and captured his mouth with a searing caress that would not be denied, trailing her fingers over his cheeks. All protests, all reluctance—indeed, all sense of reason—seemed to leave him. He renewed his efforts at unwinding her from her remaining clothing while his lips began a prescribed assault on her earlobe, her neck, and her exposed bosom.

He spoke not a word and seemed to care little for the occasional sounds of seams ripping. The fear and emptiness in his eyes had been replaced by a feral gleam as he turned her against the wall, pinning her with his weight and lifting her upon his thighs. His movements were all hasty need; power, long restrained so savagely, unleashed in a moment of wanton indulgence.

It was exhilarating, the swift change that had swept over him; their cares of the day thrown to the ashes… for a moment. Margaret tipped her head, trying to catch his eye to offer a tempting smile, but he would not look at her. His hands and eyes raked liberally over her body, seeming to find it as he had known it before, and his breath started coming in short little pants. She felt less like he was loving her and more as though he was slaking a need long denied him.

Margaret had never before feared her husband, but a gnawing uncertainty began to nibble at her heart. This was not John as she had known him. He was a strong man, as she had grown to appreciate on many a previous night. His passion and vigour had so often kindled her own spark, as if she could glory in his strength, letting him carry her to places she could not reach, and bestowing on him a grace he could attain nowhere else. But John, at his most ardent and eager, had always been still *hers*. His energies would be softened by tenderness, by that silver thread of communion and intimacy. Now… perhaps she should have accepted his offer merely to talk by the fire.

He was not satisfied with the wall, and she felt his arms capture her from below. A moment later he was above her on her bed. She smiled, even laughed a little, seeking his face. He kissed her, but not lingeringly, for his mouth was again grazing over her skin, taking and claiming once more all he had nearly lost.

Margaret's eyes drifted from his dark head, bent low over her, to his bared shoulders... the blanket he had cast aside... her knee, tucked close to his waist as his hand slipped down her thigh... the clock ticking on the wall. A shift in the air brought a cool draught from the window over her skin, and she longed for nothing more than to retrieve the blanket on the floor and cover herself with it.

He was heavy. She was already beginning to struggle uncomfortably for breath when a rasping pain, both familiar and novel, caused her to gasp and tense. She closed her eyes, gritting her teeth as his weight rocked, but she could not relax as she had always done. Too many memories flashed—of blood and tears, of the doctor washing his hands, of humiliation and loss and exposure. And this, this secret vulnerability she had offered the man she loved, had slipped into something else entirely.

John froze, his head turned away from her. He began to lift his body, to pull back, but she caught at his shoulders. "Is something wrong?" Had he now found her less than what he remembered?

"I have hurt you," he rasped, and raised to a sitting posture.

"You have not hurt me, precisely."

"Is that why you were flinching and pushing me away?"

"I did not intend... it was only a... a little too fast, I suppose."

He backed away, disentangling their limbs, and turned to sit sideways on the bed. "You wished for this," he reminded her, a hint of accusation in his tones. "I told you it was too soon, but you begged me... insisted, rather."

"That is not what I meant. I—I know how trying your days are lately. I wished to comfort you, and I could think of no better way."

"Am I such a beast, then, that I can only be satisfied in bed? Is there truly no other way for you, of all people, to comfort me? Then I am the monster you once thought me to be."

"John! I said nothing of the kind. I wanted to love you and hold you as we used to do. I wished to feel close to you, as I have not done since before...." She swallowed and cast her eyes to the floor.

"I thought we were."

"But it was not the same. I felt as if I barely knew you."

He turned, his eyes wide in astonishment and hurt. In the candlelight, she could catch the glimmer of moisture in them. He was blinking, and his mouth opened once or twice to speak, but he could not. He looked away once more, then pushed off the bed and wrapped a sheet around himself.

"John?"

"Was it another babe you wished for? Another chance to win back what you lost? Another risk? I ought never to have allowed myself."

"How can you say such a thing?" She rose to stand beside him, trying to wrap her arms about him, but his remained firmly twisted into the sheet. "Of course, I long for another, but it was not in my thoughts tonight. I do not even know if it is possible—very likely it is not. I only wanted you, John, but you have seemed so… distant."

"No more than you have."

"I?"

"You share nothing with me, Margaret. I find you weeping, and you will not tell me why. I try to cheer you, and nothing works. Have I failed you so miserably that you have lost all hope of my redemption?"

"Failed me? John, my feelings have nothing to do with you. How can I tell you why I weep when I do not understand myself? I wish I did!"

"Not half so much as I. Margaret—" he stepped away from her hands on his shoulders and looked seriously down into her face. "Do you still love me at all?"

She stared, struck mute for a moment. *Love him?* She could not live without him, that much she knew, but love?

"I… I love you with all my heart." After she had said the words, however, she wondered what they could have meant. She did not even know where her heart was—shattered in a thousand pieces, and swept into the coal ashes, no doubt. And what was love to her? It was giving and pain, comforting and loss. What was that feeling she had once called love?

He waited for another moment, perhaps expecting her to recant her hesitant words. He made no answer, but the moisture pooling in his eyes before was now threatening to spill at the corners. She reached to brush it away, but found she was blinded by tears of her own. He pulled back.

"It is late, Margaret. You should rest."

"I have wounded you. Please, John, let us talk on it."

"We are both weary. I think it best if we do not, just now. I fear we may speak something we would regret."

"But, John—" she was shaking her head, disbelief stinging her eyes as she watched him take another step back. "I want you. Please, will you not at least stay?"

He paused, the longing in his look crying out for her to soothe away his pain, but she did not dare pursue him lest he flee. "Not tonight," he decided, his voice cracking. He stepped near to kiss her on the cheek, then removed his sheet to wrap it around her. "Good night, Margaret."

She fell back to the bed, bitter tears streaming down her face as she watched him go, and heard the door click between them.

~

It was the most brutal night he had spent yet. John had gone back to his room, defeated and feeling like a beast. He had trespassed against the sacred, driven his love out of his own arms, because the truth—the ugly, horrible truth—had been waiting for him all along, hungry jaws open and ready for him to slip. And that truth was that he never did, and never could, truly belong in her life.

He stared into the vacuous cavern of his empty fire grate, stained in coal ash and grown cold from disuse. Half a glass of brandy later, he could no longer see it—or he tried not to. His own dirty hands pressed into his eyes as silent moans shook him.

How could he have dared? His horror at his own desires and actions this night was merely symptomatic of the unholy lust that had always accompanied his thoughts about her. She was a guilty pleasure to look upon, the glorious crystal vase on the top shelf that was not meant for touching—or at least not by hands such as his own.

He poured another glass of brandy, from the very same bottle he had drunk in celebration with Dr Donaldson only a few months before. Now it seemed to be a wake of sorts, this harsh reality toasted with bitter recognition. She, gentle perfection, had tumbled into his clutches, and he had proved at last that he was no better than the vilest sort of man.

But it was worse, by far, than that! For even a wicked man, when he discovered himself to be such, might withdraw utterly and leave his wife in blessed peace the rest of her days. What had he to offer her? Failure! Financial ruin, a life of distress and worry as he sought other work. A smaller house where she would be forced more often into his path. He could not even grant her the solitude she seemed to crave!

The brandy was gone. John lifted the bottle and peered through it towards his lantern. The truth must be told, and soon. By his best estimate, he had enough of his own money to continue six more weeks—possibly longer if enough of his workers remained home with their sickness—using up whatever cotton was left in his sheds. The hands could be paid, his debts settled, and that would be the end for John Thornton, Master of Marlborough Mills.

He snorted. A fine master! He was as wretched a creature as Margaret had once accused him of being. Unfeeling, yes, that suited him. Unjust could certainly be applied. Cruel… he closed his eyes before that particular tear could drop. Was it not each of those depictions of his character that had driven his offenses against her this night?

The worst of it was that he was still uncertain where he had fallen. The heady thrill of being desired once again, of feeling her arms about his neck and hearing her whispered pleas panted into his ear… was that when he had abandoned his reason? Was it when she had bared her back to him, trusting and vulnerable, that he had snatched her up like a predator? Or was it the culmination, when he had taken her heavenly embrace as a balm for his own wounded pride, caring nothing if he scarred her in the moment of his pleasure? Whenever the treacherous slip had occurred, he had done nothing to prevent it. Indeed, had welcomed it—this chance to forget his woes, to take and devour, stealing love from the one who was precious to him.

Love… could she truly love him? The empty brandy bottle declared that she could not. Oh, perhaps he had done one or two nice things for her, and her gratitude was of such a faithful nature that she would not now deny him, but love? Could a rose love a lump of coal? It was inconceivable to even ask such a thing.

Fool that he was, he had thought to share in her life, to find his true home at her side, even to—most blasphemous of all notions—join with her in the most sacred of unions and then to cherish the fruit of their love. A family… good God! He dropped the bottle and his fingers tore through his hair as he confessed to heaven and earth how foolish he had been in thinking it possible. Nothing could be more unnatural!

No answer from the skies thundered through his darkened chamber. No help poured forth from the bottle rolling at his feet. He was alone, a man on a raft with a broken oar, and a map in his hands to a paradise he could never reach. He curled his long legs into his tight seat, bowed his head against the wing of the chair, and wept.

~

Margaret's eyes were swollen, and she knew it. Dixon had done her best with cool cloths and a tea compress, but nothing could do away with the redness or the haggard look of her features. She had passed off her appearance as the symptoms of a slight malaise, nothing more.

Hannah Thornton was not convinced, as her silence testified. She looked Margaret over once, suggested that she might have rested better by remaining in her room, and then flung her attention into arranging a new vase of flowers to be displayed under one of her many glass cloches. She took great pains with it; pruning a stray leaf here, bending a wayward petal there, until at last she was satisfied. The vase she then carried to be displayed in a place of prominence. The glass was lowered to protect it from soot and dust, and she stood back to appraise her work.

"It is lovely," Margaret offered, by way of promoting some conversation for a diversion.

Hannah narrowed her eyes, still looking over the arrangement. "It will do."

"Where did the flowers come from? I do not recall seeing them before."

Hannah turned back, then moved to a seat. "Doctor Donaldson. He has been very attentive."

Margaret was quiet for a moment. "Does John know?" she asked in a small voice.

Hannah sighed. "I am certain he suspects. I intended to speak with him this morning, but he was gone to the mill by four." She slid a significant glance towards her daughter-in-law, then looked away. "Doctor Donaldson has not spoken to me, but his intentions are clear."

"Would you accept? I had not thought your feelings so engaged. Forgive me, if I ask more than I ought."

"A woman does not agree to receive flowers or other offerings from a man if she intends to refuse." Here, she spared Margaret another long look.

Margaret swallowed and looked down, her cheeks flaming. "Of course. Please, excuse me."

"I had never thought to marry again," Hannah volunteered, surprising Margaret. "Even now, I am not certain I have the temperament for it."

"Yet you are willing to proceed?"

"I am willing…" she still gazed at the flowers, as if their dusky petals could describe the remaining years of her life if she chose this path. "I am willing to pursue the wisest course. Doctor Donaldson is a respectable man, a bachelor these many years with a comfortable home. His company is agreeable, and I have long held him in my esteem."

"You would not consider it a… reduction in your circumstances?"

One of the lady's expressive snorts, then; "Did you, when you married a manufacturer?"

Margaret's cheeks burned again, and the puffy feeling of her face seemed to throb with a nervous pulse. "I married for affection. I believe John the worthiest man alive, and I was deeply honoured that he would have asked again."

"Indeed. And you do not regret that decision?"

"I never shall," she answered swiftly, but her voice trembled. "And I hope that his feelings on the matter are the same."

Hannah frowned thoughtfully, staring again at the expensive hot-house flowers which were so rare in Milton at this time of year. "I thought your illness would be the death of him, either in body or spirit."

Margaret wetted her lips. "I know."

"Then you must never doubt my son's affections!"

"That… was not my intention," Margaret winced. "I only meant that… that he is not without cause for disappointment."

"Your marriage is hardly the first to suffer loss. Others have done so, and managed."

"Yes," Margaret agreed in a whisper.

"And it is far from the first time John has seen such trial."

Margaret was blinking and turned away to rest her chin on her hand and stare at the far wall. "He told me about his father."

"There was more, before that."

Margaret lifted her head. "You…?"

Hannah returned her questioning look with a grave, steady expression. "John had another sister. Elizabeth… she died of consumption, when she was only four."

Margaret stirred uncomfortably. "I did not know. I am sorry."

"Many children are buried in Milton's graveyard."

"And many more have not even that honour," Margaret mumbled, though Hannah did not seem to hear.

The older woman paced round the room again, her arms crossing restlessly as her weathered face set and re-formed into lines of agitation, long repressed. "It is not a thing one speaks of. We make a virtue of mourning, all the proper appearances and the pride of the bereaved. We braid hair into our jewellery and drape ourselves in black—everywhere black!—but to speak of the dead as people we once loved… it might inspire genuine feeling, perhaps even passionate behaviour, and that is not to be borne."

Margaret, by this time, was covering her mouth with the tips of her fingers as her eyes filled. "Will…" she ventured in a quavering voice… "will you tell me about her, then?"

Hannah did not face her, but her tones, when she spoke, were soft. "She was like her father. She laughed as he did, even possessed his dark turn of countenance at times. Her eyes were like John's, and she had the same iron will. But she was beautiful! You would not have known her for my own flesh, Margaret, for her spirit was a thing of another world. She loved to sing in her nursery. She used to—"

Here, Hannah's voice seemed to dry up, and her shoulders bunched together within her dark gown. She shivered, drew a long, visible breath, then appeared to be pausing long enough to collect herself. When she turned back to Margaret, her eyes still glittered but her expression was sober and calm once more.

"I blamed myself. So did George—and we blamed each other. I believe he bore that guilt to his grave."

"As does John—blame himself, I mean. I am sure of it. I wonder why everyone is so determined to find fault in something or someone? So often there was nothing to be done!"

"Do you not know? Where there can be fault and responsibility, there may be control. Where we can blame—even ourselves—we can assert our will that it cannot, it *will* not, happen again. And yet, it always does, somewhere. It is the way of the world."

Margaret drew a shaky breath. Hannah's words, her unwonted revelations, her vulnerable manner, had drawn back a thick tapestry, that sacred veil shrouding the close sanctuary of her innermost feeling. It seemed a permission of sorts, for the cascades of sorrow to blind her once more with their salty baptism, and for the ache deep in her breast to take shape and form in a single, strangling cry.

Other women *must* know such grief. They must! Hannah Thornton must… and yet in this moment, the distinction was entirely hers, the right to passion selfishly claimed as her own. She felt herself crumble, there in the centre of the drawing-room—knew herself to be beyond sense or reason even in the presence of one whose claim was no less than her own.

Yes, it was also for that other lost child she wept—and it was for her own brokenness and weak spirits, for the unheard-of tremble in a strong woman's voice, for the fracture between herself and for the only person she longed to hold for comfort, and for all the wrongs she had ever witnessed and had no power over. Yet more than that; it was for all the months and all the years she had remained steady and true, faithful to something greater—believing, in her simple naivety, that the pure ought to be spared such suffering. What now to do with the evidence of her own delusions?

She turned her face into the heel of her hand, her shoulders heaving and her breath gasping in a throat long gone raw and swollen. And then, a gentle touch…. Hannah Thornton was at her side then, an arm about her and her jaw set in grim solidarity.

Margaret lifted her head, only enough to lay it across the other's shoulder, and sobbed.

Sixteen

"Mother? Why are you up so late?"

His mother lifted her lantern in the darkened hallway, and John looked anxiously behind her to be certain that there was not some emergency.

"I have not spoken more than two words with you since Sunday," she reasoned calmly.

He turned to drop his gloves on a side table. "Is there something important you wished to discuss?"

"There is, but must that be my only reason for wishing to speak with my son?"

He remained turned away, still staring down at the gloves for a moment. "I did not realise I was so difficult to engage."

"A natural result of never entering your own house, save when others are asleep."

He winced, then dared to look back at her. "Perhaps we ought to speak in the study, so we disturb no one."

She led the way with her lantern, and he closed the door and drew two chairs together. "Mother," he began apologetically, "I understand that my time and sentiments have been more divided than in the past—"

"I am planning to marry."

"You… to-to marry? Dr Donaldson, I presume?"

"He has been waiting to speak with you for several days, but you have been returning late all week. I intend to accept him. Have you any objections?"

"I… well, no. He is an honourable man, and I know no harm of him. But marriage! Why now? Is it because I have married? Have you been made to feel unwelcome in your own home? I never intended for you to—"

"On the contrary—" she folded her hands slowly—"I have developed something of an attachment to Margaret."

"Then why? Can you hold deeper feelings for Donaldson?"

"I am fond of him, and I believe he esteems me equally. I see no impediments to my happiness in his household."

"Hardly the language of one desperately in love," he retorted. "Mother, I beg you, do not do this thing. There can be no cause for you to leave your home and begin anew at your stage of life."

"Do you object to the notion of me marrying another man after your father, or the idea of me leaving your house at last?"

"I have no cause to object to you marrying again. If I thought you loved the man, I would carry you on my shoulders to the altar, but I fear that you find this a less uncomfortable option than remaining in a home with another mistress. Is that it?"

She drew a long breath, studying him. "Perhaps, but not in the way you suppose."

"I do not understand. Do you feel that your support has become a burden for me? Mother! Remember the old days when it was you who sustained me in my struggles? I need you!"

"No, you do not. Perhaps that realisation has been the most mortifying of my life. What you need, John, is to *not* need me."

"Has Margaret ever indicated that she is resentful of your place? Have I passed you over unfairly?"

"Stop it, John," she scolded.

He subsided, still regarding her with baffled hurt. She pressed her lips, her fingers toying with her skirt, then spoke again.

"Have you told her?"

He narrowed his eyes. "Margaret? Told her what?"

"That the mill is failing. I see it in your eyes, and along with it, another fear."

He sighed, rubbed his brow, and bit his upper lip. "Not in so many words. She knows matters have not improved, and she is no fool. However, I think it is unfair to accuse me of fear."

"Is it not fear which keeps you at the mill until your wife has retired for the night?"

"I have work. It is not intentional."

"Indeed."

"Mother, I am tired. Have you some point you are attempting to prove?"

She smiled, a little sadly. "Do you remember how dear we became to each other when we had no one else?"

"You are still so to me. Nothing has changed."

"In that, you are wrong. I can no longer claim first place in your heart."

"You cannot assume that there is room for only one woman in my life. Am I a well that I should run dry? No! I depend upon your strength and affection, just as surely as I live for Margaret's."

"You do not need me any longer. I daresay my presence prevents you from finding something which has so far eluded you."

"And what is that?"

"Your own wife."

He pressed his fingers into his eyes, then pinched the bridge of his nose. "Mother, what are you speaking of? Margaret is not jealous of you—in fact she holds you in high regard. What is more, she has not been strong enough of late to manage the household. I would imagine she looks to you with gratitude."

"Perhaps."

"Then why do you wish to leave?"

She sighed, then rose to pace the room. "I wish to be needed."

"But I have told you, you are needed here!"

"As an accessory? No, John. If anything, I have stifled what could be. It is wiser that I go."

"Stifled... what can you possibly mean by that?"

"I mean that as we clung to each other before, now you must turn to your wife, and I will seek the same with another. I am no longer young, John. There is a certain charm in spending my energies with one like myself in tastes and pursuits."

"But why Donaldson? Is he merely a convenient choice, the first man who dared approach you?"

"And what is wrong with that? I could not count worthy the man who would *not* dare."

"Mother, I need none of your salt. It makes no sense—why now? Why him? I would not see you settle and find yourself dissatisfied."

"John...." She frowned, glanced down, then raised her eyes to his. "It is not the same as choosing the husband of my youth. I do not know how to make you understand that. I am not the fool I was then. What I thought I had with your father... what you and Margaret could have—"

"*Could* have? Are you implying that my own marriage is a disappointment?"

"Not yet. Stop interrupting and hear me out."

He clamped his jaw.

"That sort of... affection—" she rolled her eyes, seemingly embarrassed to voice the word—"it is the province of the young. Few there are who find what they thought they had, and great the number who are disappointed in their choice. I have no patience for that at this stage of life. I am content to seek companionship, for I would greatly prefer a steady and sensible partner to an ardent romance."

"But why marry at all? What is so uncomfortable for you here that you think it better to go?"

"Do not be so pig-headed, John! I have told you, my place is no longer here."

He stilled, leaning forward on his weary elbows and gazing into the fire grate for long minutes. "Is it decided, then? Have you accepted?"

"I intend to."

He met her eyes again, a strange new feeling dawning upon him. "We have never been apart, you and I."

She reached to take his hand. "No, son John, not since you were in school. As it was then, it will be more bitter for me than for you!"

A film had crept over his vision, and he blinked it away. "I cannot change your mind, can I?"

She shook her head resolutely. "You have your own life to pursue. If I am not mistaken, it awaits you upstairs."

A long breath left him, and he felt his shoulders sag. "I fear I am only proving myself unworthy of that life."

"And why would you think this? You believe these temporal griefs too much?" She snorted softly. "I had not thought you capable of surrender."

"Surrender! Sometimes there is no alternative. The mill cannot sustain itself much longer, and Margaret has never seen failure of that kind. She has already too much to bear. I cannot know how to tell her."

"The truth is one place to begin."

"The truth… it is an ugly thing. I have discovered a dark side to my own character—a failure, of all that I should have been as her husband. How now to ask her to trust me with the turbulent times that lie ahead?"

"You have not been unfaithful, John!"

He jerked. "Mother, I would die before touching another woman! I have never even wanted any other… only her. Therein lies my weakness. She would be justified in desiring some distance from me. My failings—"

"Nay, do not tell me more than I ought to know. What is spoken between a husband and his wife must remain there, but I think you do the lass a disservice in thinking she does not wish for your confidences."

He fisted his hands over one another and pressed them to his lips, staring back to the fire with hazy eyes. What he would give—his soul, his strength, his very life!—if he thought his mother's words were true. But how could they be? Fear, such as he had never known, had begun its dreaded spiral about his heart, and it seized his every waking thought until there was no escape even in sleep, for that rest was denied him.

He felt his mother's hand patting his arm and turned to watch her rise. It had been several minutes since another word had passed, while he stumbled in his nightmarish musings. Apparently, his mother sensed her continued presence an intrusion upon his private thoughts and had determined to go without speaking more. She bent once to caress his cheek, with a soft, "Goodnight, John," and left him alone.

He could not tell how long he remained there—too weak to stir, too doubtful to go up to his own room. His mind could see the door to hers already, and it was surely closed to him. Somehow, it seemed less painful to imagine the worst than to face it in truth and risk being correct.

At length, the shame of being discovered by one of the maids, sleeping in the study in his clothing, drove him to that place. He undressed, in the exhausted way of one who is too tired to prepare for bed and looked to every other matter before he could force himself to acknowledge her door. He drew near, his heart sinking when he found that indeed, it was not open, but as his longing fingertips brushed the latch, it gave way.

Neither closed nor open... could she have meant something by that? Or had a passing draught merely blown it farther closed than she had intended? Or... he swallowed... had she meant to close it, and the latch simply did not click?

Unable to abide not knowing, he peered inside. She was asleep, of course. He could hear her steady breathing, and there was neither break nor pause when the door creaked wider and he hesitated in the shadows. He dared a few more steps, hovering near the back wall where he could see her, and she might recognise him in the light from his own room if she should startle awake. She did not.

He sighed in bitter disappointment. He would not dream of waking her and could not know what to say to her even if she roused herself. His hand fell to the chair at the nearby escritoire, but something on the surface drew his attention. He narrowed his eyes in the dusky light and found a note lying on the desk.

Warmth returned to his fingertips, and he reached eagerly for it. She cared enough, at least, to leave him something of her thoughts as she slept! Even as he caught up the folded paper, an ache of foreboding shot through his hands, but he could not ignore it. He must know, even if the words were a scathing admonishment for all his failings. He clasped it to his heart, backing out of the room as he gazed lovingly at her sleeping form.

Once returned to his own desk and lantern, he could not unfold it quickly enough. Perhaps she had left him permission to wake her, hoping to speak to him! Hope died almost immediately in his chest when the light bathed her elegant script, and he discovered that he was not the intended recipient.

Dear Edith,

I am glad to hear of your safe return to London. How I long to see everyone! Please give my aunt my love and tell her I will write to her within the next day or two. I am pleased that Maxwell found his assignment satisfactory, and that little Sholto is growing well. I wish I could see him and discover whether I still have any artistic talent, for I could attempt a modest portrait.

You asked of the winters; I will not embellish the truth. Winter here in Milton is darker than you can imagine, for you are correct that the smoke makes everything dreary. We are farther north, you understand, so it is remarkably colder here than in London, and certainly more so than my dear old Helstone. I have seen little of this winter, as I have been much confined these last months, but I believe this to be the hardest I have known here.

I am surprised at what you tell me of Henry. I have always wished him happiness, and I feel badly that he has yet to find it. Please convey my sentiments on the matter, for I have missed his friendship.

Edith, I must now set my pen to a grim task. I beg you would not ask me again to speak of the joy I had anticipated. It is too bitter for me to think on now, but my disappointment cannot be measured in words. There has been precious little comfort

John blinked, dashing away the flood of disbelief from his eyes, and stared at the page again. The writing had simply stopped, left to be continued at another time. He might have expected a melodramatic blotting of tears, blurring the lines and staining the paper, but it was clean, crisp, and cold.

He turned the page over, half expecting to find the recipient's original letter folded behind it, but there was nothing. He read it again, dwelling painfully upon each despondent word written in his wife's hand. Guilt there was, in reading that which was not meant for his eyes, but so starved was he for any indication of her sentiments he gladly claimed that disgrace, bared his flesh to the lash of her words, simply to hear her express herself.

The truth was too plain, even for one such as he, to miss. She hated Milton. She missed her family, longed to return to the gentle ways of the South… regretted not waiting for Henry Lennox.

The fatal stab to his heart, however, was her unfinished last line—*precious little comfort.* That was what he had offered her! Her words could only refer to himself, could they not? Somehow, he had not understood, not been sufficient, and all his woeful efforts had fallen short of expectations and need. Surely, he could not be found wanting in motive, for securing her happiness was the sublime purpose of his life. He was simply not good enough.

His hands trembled, his fingers scarcely daring to touch the edges of the paper as he read the list of indictments again. He *would* force himself to know all, to stare into the depth of the disappointment that was his own doing. He wished to burn it into his forehead, so that all who saw him might know the shame that was his, but it was not his own possession.

Her door looked more forbidding than ever, hanging half-opened as he had left it in his haste. With breathless care, he eased into her room and replaced the letter on the desk. This time, he would not permit himself to look at her. He bowed his head low as he withdrew, a whispered apology on his lips as he hid his eyes, and then silently closed the door.

~

Margaret rose early the next morning in hopes of seeing John, but it was not early enough. She pushed the door to his room, but found that it had been latched somehow, and puzzled over it. Slowly, she made her preparations, and some while later she was below stairs.

The morning passed unremarkably enough. Margaret busied herself with the kitchen accounts, making revisions here and there to minimise the family's expenditures. John had mentioned nothing of finances to her, but she could only assume that matters with the mill were not improving. She offered the ledgers to Hannah for her approval but was politely refused.

Not long before the dinner hour, she was engaged with one of her father's old books while her mother-in-law sewed industriously. Jane came to the door, announcing that Mrs Watson had arrived with a guest.

Margaret tensed like a frightened hare. She had not seen Fanny for more than a few moments since that day she had called on her in her room, and still could not rid herself of the sting. It wanted every muscle and sinew at attention and required the last drop of willpower she possessed to remain in the room to receive her sister-in-law, whose figure now openly declared everything Margaret did not wish to think on.

"Well, Mamma!" Fanny breezed prettily into the room, swathed in a new gown expensively tailored for her changing shape. "How very cold it is out there! We thought at first to remain at my house, but it is so insufferably dull, with none but ourselves to speak to. I came to introduce someone to you who has been longing to meet you both. Ah, good morning, Margaret," she added as an afterthought. "This is Mildred Wright. She and her husband, Mr Harold Wright, are staying with us a few days. Mildred, my mother and John's wife Margaret."

Margaret studied the woman. Mrs Wright was older than herself by several years, but age had not diminished her beauty. Rather, she was one of those rare specimens who becomes only more graceful and imposing as the freshness of youth fades. Her hair was a perfect shade of flaxen, with crystal blue eyes and flawless skin. She was slender through her shoulders down to her ivory fingertips, and her figure gave no evidence that the passing of children had ever marred it. Margaret's hand touched unconsciously over her own softened middle, where her long lying-in had left some remembrance of her recent trials.

Hannah was dipping her head in a tight, controlled greeting, her heavy jowls clenched so that only her lips moved as she performed the required civility. "How do you do, Mrs Wright?"

The lady answered more generously than her hostess. "Very well, Mrs Thornton. I am delighted to make your acquaintance at last, for I have heard much of you for many years."

Hannah's nostrils were distending, and she lifted her chin when the other woman's words struck her as a slight against her age.

Clearly sensing the older lady less amenable to conversation, Mrs Wright turned then to Margaret. "And Margaret Thornton, I am delighted to know you at last! It is a very great pleasure to meet the woman who finally captured the finest prize in Milton."

Margaret felt her cheek flicker. "I am sure I do not know what you mean by 'capture,' madam."

"Do forgive me, Mrs Thornton!" Mrs Wright laughed. "I am afraid I can be dreadfully impertinent. But you must know, I meant my words as a compliment. Mr Thornton could have had his choosing of many for years, and so I must conclude that only the most remarkable woman in Milton would have at last caught his eye."

Margaret returned an uncomfortable smile. "I am obliged to you. Will you be seated?"

"Yes, thank you." Mrs Wright gathered her ample skirts, which rivalled Fanny's for flounces and detail, and settled herself. "I beg you will forgive my little tease, Mrs Thornton. I have known John Thornton since I was very young, practically a girl still, and I must confess to some degree of fascination that he remained a bachelor for so many years. It must have been a particular affection which decided him to take the yoke; I am looking forward to knowing you better."

"I see, Mrs Wright." Margaret gestured to Jane that a tray should be brought for their guests, then fell silent.

"I declare, Mamma—" Fanny was gazing about the room—"not a stitch in this house has changed! I would have thought that you would all redecorate, particularly after Margaret came here. Margaret, was not your mother's taste very different? I should have expected you to add some of that Herefordshire charm to our dreary old Milton house."

"I am from Hampshire, Mrs Watson. I am content with this house as it is and have not felt the need to make any changes."

"Fanny," her mother interjected, a testy note in her voice, "where is your husband?"

Margaret met Hannah's eyes in mild alarm. Oh, dear, Mr Watson and Mr Wright had not set upon John at his office again, had they?

"Oh! I am sure the men are at the bank this morning. They had another day or two of business before these latest dealings are settled. I am certainly glad that lot falls to them, and not to me!"

"But how fortunate that their affairs required a few days visit," Mrs Wright soothed, "for I was able to convince Mr Wright that I ought to accompany him on this trip. I am pleased to meet new friends, for I have hardly set foot in Milton before now. I am from London, Mrs Thornton, but my father was a man of business, as is my husband. Consequently, much of my life has been influenced by matters here in Milton."

"I hope the city pleases you, Mrs Wright," Margaret acknowledged. "In what part of London do you live?"

"Paddington, not far from Marylebone. I understand you have family in Harley Street?"

"My aunt and cousin live there. I spent much of my childhood in their home."

"You were fortunate, indeed! And I have heard that your father was a rector?"

"He was, until he retired to Milton to teach."

"How curious! I have never heard of anyone coming to Milton to retire. It must have been a most peculiar circumstance that inspired that move. And that is how you met Mr Thornton, of course."

"Yes." Margaret took an uncomfortable sip of her tea. "He was my father's friend and read the classics with him."

"Ah! Yes, I remember John Thornton was always fond of his books as a youth. Why, I could hardly draw more than two words together out of him, even when we were dancing. And when he had to turn pages for me when I played the piano!" She rolled her eyes in delicate mirth. "A hopeless case!"

Margaret's brow furrowed. "You must have known my husband rather well, Mrs Wright."

"Oh, yes! When he was living with my husband's family, my father was a business partner of the elder Mr Wright, and our families were intimate. I saw him frequently, those two years. Oh, the tales I could tell of your Mr Thornton! I am certain he would not thank me for sharing them, but you know, someday I shall do so simply to delight his wife and mother. You must imagine what a great pleasure it gives me to know that the acquaintance has been renewed. Mrs Thornton—" here, Mrs Wright turned her attention to Hannah—"may I compliment you on your fine needlework? I have not seen such excellent point work since my own mother's."

Hannah made a very decent reply, if somewhat terse, and Margaret was left free for a moment to gaze at the woman. Though shockingly forward, she was still as poised and elegant as anyone Margaret had ever seen. If her manner was studied, it was done with such finesse that one would never suspect. She could easily imagine such a woman holding court in the salons of London; the envy of dozens of other women and the intrigue of as many men.

A door closed from the outer passage, and every feminine voice in the drawing-room stilled. Margaret's eyes went to the clock first, and a flutter of joy beat in her heart, for it would be John come home for his luncheon. She had not spoken to him in a full day and a half, and jealously wished their company long gone so she might have him for herself.

It was obvious by his expression that he had not expected to find his wife and mother entertaining guests, but he recovered quickly when he recognised his sister. "Fanny. You are looking well."

"Never better, John!" Fanny's hand stroked her stomach with a look of perfect unconsciousness. "Here, you must remember my friend, Mildred Wright."

The barest flicker passed over his eyes, but then Margaret could not see his full face, for he turned to the newcomer. "Mrs Wright. It has been a long time. I trust you are well?"

"Perfectly so, John Thornton. The years have been exceedingly kind to you, sir." The lady's voice tinkled with delight, and Margaret's skin started to crawl.

"As they have been to you, madam." He began to turn towards Margaret, but Mrs Wright was speaking again.

"I am so pleased to know the new Mrs Thornton! You are a fortunate man, sir."

"I am, indeed." He glanced to Margaret with a shadow of a smile, then looked down to the floor.

"Mrs Thornton," Mrs Wright continued, "you must call while I am staying with Fanny, so we may further our acquaintance. Better yet, let us have a dinner party—you do not mind, do you, dear Fanny? We shall make it a small affair, but only think how gay we might all be! Do you play, Mrs Thornton? We must have music, of course. As you were educated in London, you may have even had the same masters as I. Perhaps we might attempt a duet. What do you think of that, Mr Thornton?"

Margaret was quailing slightly in her seat, her cheeks flinching with the effort of sustaining the false smile she wore. A dinner party! And she would be asked to exhibit her woeful skills beside this London goddess? She shuddered, then drew a breath of reassurance when reason crept back in. Even if she could endure another dinner party at Fanny's so soon after her illness, surely John would never accept!

"That sounds most agreeable," he replied.

Margaret blinked, then tilted her head. Had he just…? She stared at him but could read neither his expression nor his voice.

"Wonderful!" Mrs Wright enthused. "Dear Fanny, do you suppose we might have a bit of dancing as well? You have that charming drawing-room just adjacent to the music room, and certainly we could push about the furniture. Mr Thornton, do you recall how we used to have such parties at the Wrights' house?"

"Fondly." He shot a swift, indecipherable glance to Margaret, then looked at the floor once more. "I beg your pardon, madam, but I only had a few moments to spare now. If you ladies will excuse me, I must return to the mill soon."

Fanny made some exasperated noise. "Oh, John, you never have a minute to call your own!"

"It is quite all right, Fanny." Mrs Wright smiled—an expression which lingered long enough on John to make Margaret's stomach flip. "We have staid a little over a quarter of an hour, Mrs Thornton, and Mrs Thornton—" she rose and nodded to each—"I thank you for your hospitality." She came then to John, offering her hand with a knowing smile. "It has been delightful to see you again, sir."

John took her hand, murmured something Margaret could not quite hear, and smiled back. Was that a peculiar warmth in his expression? There was certainly that in Mrs Wright's manner which bespoke invitation, familiarity, and regret at leave-taking. Margaret could not help but to narrow her eyes in suspicion as Mrs Wright recalled some former episode in their mutual experiences, as if attempting to delay her departure.

Once the guests had finally gone, Hannah excused herself. Margaret drew hesitantly close to her husband, but he seemed preoccupied in looking down at one of his mother's flower vases.

"John?" She touched his arm.

He flinched.

Margaret drew back her hand, surprised and hurt by his response. "Are you well?"

"I am not unwell."

"I... that is not quite what I meant."

"I have no fear of influenza, if that is your concern. Most of its victims have been the young...." His mouth worked, and he released a weary sigh. "The very young... and the old."

"Influenza! Strange that you should assume I asked about that. Have there been more deaths?"

"One child I heard of today, and at least one old woman very near it. I expect there may be more."

"But the healthy adults, most of your workers, are safe?"

"I did not say they were safe, only that most of them will not die. It is their children who will suffer the worst."

"Is there nothing that can be done?"

"Apart from sending them all home to remain in their own houses until the fever has finished with the city? No."

"That would do little good, for their houses are so close together. Even then, everyone must eat."

He blew out a long sigh. "Indeed." He stared down at the dried flowers again.

"John—" she raised her hand to touch him again, hesitated, then drew back. "Is something else troubling you?"

He glanced quickly to her. "Why do you ask?"

"We have not spoken since two nights ago. I had wished to apologise—"

"You do not need to apologise, Margaret."

"But I do! I fear we misunderstood one another. It was never my wish that you would feel I did not desire… did not want…."

"I was to blame. I ought never to have permitted myself. I am not quite certain what possessed me to think it possible. The risk to your health is too great to consider any… intimacy. We should not speak of this here."

Margaret drew an unsteady breath, wetting her lips as her eyes fell to the floor. The subject was as uncomfortable for her as for him, but if she did not urge him to speak now, she feared she would not have another opportunity for days—that the prospect would fester as an old, untended wound.

"You look weary."

She raised her face. "I am only a little tired."

"You should not be up so much. I fear your strength is not recovered. Think nothing of that dinner party, I do not know what came over me. We shall not accept if they truly do issue an invitation—which I doubt they will."

She released a long, tense sigh. "I did not wish to go."

"Of course, it is impossible. Wright aside, we could not think of it. You should be resting… in fact, I do not like you exerting yourself so much, even, as you have been."

"On the contrary, John, I wished to resume walking out. I believe it would help me—"

"No," he was shaking his head forcefully. "It is out of the question."

She tilted her head. "Why? I have always found that walking improves my constitution. I may not be strong enough to walk for long, but—"

"Did you hear nothing I said before? The fever is ravaging the city. I have little fear for myself, but you must not risk it."

"Surely that fear is unwarranted. I am not a child, nor am I elderly. I am not even malnourished or overworked. I should—"

"No. I will hear not another word on the matter, Margaret."

Margaret felt an iron annoyance slipping into her shoulders and squaring her chin. "Mary Higgins has been ill. Am I not to be permitted the privilege of calling on my friend as she recovers? As she did for me? May I not even carry them a basket and try to comfort them?"

"We will have something sent, if you insist, but you must not go yourself. The chances of infection are too great."

"What of them? Why should I be protected under a glass vase while others are still struggling to come to work?"

"You are not a factory worker!"

She narrowed her eyes, her heart twisting. Had he truly said that? "And what is that but an accident of birth? Why must they face a risk I am spared?"

"Margaret—" he shook his head and pulled away from her to pace the room—"your argument makes no sense. Had I the means to protect every one of them, I would do so. You are my wife, and I *will* protect you, whether you cooperate or fight me over the matter!"

She stilled, her heart pounding and spurring her on to the battle, while her mind attempted to reason with him. "I do not care to be dictated to," she managed coolly.

He spun back, his face a confusion of irritation and disbelief. "And I do not understand why you would choose to argue about this! The matter is settled, Margaret. Heavens above, you nearly died! Would you fling yourself at death's doorstep again?"

"That was over two months ago! I am recovered as well as I can be in this house. I must go out, take the air, and perhaps see my friends."

"And you will, as soon as the fever is finished. Until then… Good lord, two months and you think yourself whole and healed! It is only in this last week you are not white as a sheet. I cannot believe I must dictate to you in this manner! You are an intelligent woman, Margaret, and I would see you behave as one."

At the shock in her face, his fury seemed to wane. He put up a hand in apology, but she spoke first, her voice low and tight.

"You think me a child, prone to foolishness? You must become like my father now?"

"Margaret, please, do not make more of it than what it is. I had not intended to speak so harshly."

"Yes—" she was nodding slowly—"that is it." She gave a bitter laugh. "And it always has been so, despite whatever pretty words you use. John Thornton: Master of the mill, master of his wife."

He had begun to approach her, but stopped at her accusation, all the colour drained from his face. "That is unfair!"

"Were your words any less so?"

He turned away again, his hands falling to his sides as he walked to face the wall. "I apologised. What more shall I say?"

Margaret crossed her arms over her breast, tears pricking her eyes as she struggled for words.

He turned back at her silence, presuming it for defiance, and began to stalk towards her again. "Aye, you may well castigate and deride me, for you were right! I am a despot in my own home, where the life of one I love is at stake."

She shook her head and extended a pleading hand. "John, I should not have—"

"What would please you, Margaret? I will not permit you to walk out so soon, but even a tyrant must keep the peace. Thus far I have tried and failed to cheer you."

The stinging in her eyes intensified, and she feared if she did speak, her voice would betray her. He was too cruel! Nothing she could say would erase that self-loathing in his expression, nor the reproach he so justly cast at her feet.

She shook her head and covered her lips with her hands while she steadied her breath. At last, she risked a few quavering words. "I have no friends, John."

He drew a few steps closer, his head cocked to hear her better. "What was that?"

"I have no one!"

"No one! What of my mother, and Dixon and Jane and Sarah… what of me? Have we not all been by your side?"

"All pushing me back to my bed, save your mother, and she is leaving. I miss having someone to talk to…." She crumbled then, her face collapsing back to her hands and her body shaking as if her heart within had already shattered.

He did not speak, but a hesitant hand touched her shoulder. She was not yet mistress of herself to respond, so she continued to fight for breath through her tears.

"I know it has been hard for you, since your… since—"

"Since I first came to Milton!" she supplied in a broken voice.

His hand stiffened. "Even since then?"

"I miss my family! I miss my father and my mother, and Fred… I miss Edith, and my aunt!"

His hand slipped from her shoulder. "I see." There was a long pause, and then; "Perhaps… perhaps you… you should go to London for a visit. After… after Mother is married." He turned away, so she could not see his face, but his voice cracked. "Write to your cousin."

~

John paced his study, his fingers tearing through his hair and his stomach in knots. It was true—all his nameless dread and all the doubt inspired by broken communion. The light of day had tempted him to deny it all, to pass it off as the natural product of fear and distress, but he could do so no longer. She wanted to leave.

He could not—no, he *would* not—stop her. What better way to make her despise him irrevocably? For now, perhaps she had seen too much of him, of this house. A short respite; a holiday from Milton, from the smoke and disease—from *him*—perhaps it would be enough to restore her strength and allow her to again face the life she had chosen.

He had to hope. John prowled to the window, then restlessly to the desk and again to the bookshelves. He *must* hope... for if he could not... an almost animal groan shuddered in his chest. If he could not, then everything he was, all he had ever desired, was a sham.

There must be some way to mend her spirits, to reassure her that all she once loved was not lost to her. The queen of his life would be no deceived and ensnared Persephone, forced to divide her loyalties! Would that she could belong entirely to him... but why would she? What good had he ever brought her?

He rounded the study again, growling under his breath with every step. One thing he knew, of a certainty—she was his strength, even at her weakest, and he could not endure all he must, could not devote his energies anywhere else, while she was miserable. And if even his mother intended to leave him... why, what then!

He dropped to his chair, drumming his fingers over the dark wood of his desk. Something, there must be *something* to bring her even the least measure of happiness! He hissed and lurched from his chair again.

Her brother! She said she missed her family. He could take her to Spain—his heart sank. No, it was impossible. And bringing Hale here was even more so... was it not?

Perhaps he ought to write to Hale, to learn more of his case. He was pacing again, his mind an agitated tangle, but he halted before the bookcase. Where was it?

Ah. His fingers reached to extract the slim, nearly forgotten volume of maritime regulations from between two others. If nothing else, he could learn more about the magnitude of the problem before he endangered a man by trying to defend him. Of all the directions his churning thoughts could take, at least this one did not scorch his own conscience.

27 March 1856

The marriage of the widow Hannah Thornton to Doctor Robert Donaldson of Milton was a quiet affair, little attended. Donaldson had no family of his own, save a brother who lived too far away to justify the journey, so only the bride's children and their spouses, along with a handful of others from Milton's better families, were in attendance. The most notable feature of the ceremony was that it marked the first time in over seventeen years that the bride had appeared in public wearing a colour other than black.

They held a modest breakfast at the stone house on Marlborough Street, with provisions enough for the handful of neighbours and the servants of the house. Only a few neighbours could be troubled to pay their respects, for most were keeping to their homes. Over a month had passed, and the sickness plaguing the city was no less potent than it had been—indeed, Donaldson would be called out on his very wedding afternoon to tend a young girl whose parents feared for her life. Upon his arrival, he found her writhing with fever and her three younger siblings all displaying the early symptoms of illness.

This much he would confide upon his return to his new bride, who would receive the intelligence with due gravity. She would employ herself during his absence in settling a few more of her belongings and learning to wait, as all doctor's wives must, for the next call, the next word.

Most of the items she desired to bring to her new home had been sent over the previous week, but there remained a few curios, clothing trunks, and her tea service. Margaret had her own mother's china, and after the wedding breakfast, Hannah's would no longer be needed in this house.

Jane was to accompany Hannah to her new home, and her leave-taking of the house was far more verbose and tearful than that of its former mistress. She was outside on the box of the waiting carriage now while the new Dr and Mrs Donaldson bade their parting greetings at the door. Any tender sentiments between mother and son had already been shared in privacy, and now both couples stood facing one another on the step. The groom beamed, the bride's countenance reflected calm satisfaction, and the host and hostess seemed at a loss.

"Thornton," Donaldson put out his hand, "I must thank you again, for… for everything."

John took the doctor's hand, his voice stirring in his throat, but he could not seem to find the proper words for his mother's new husband.

Margaret caught Hannah's gaze, covering smoothly for John's discomfort. "Congratulations to you both. We wish you every joy."

"Thank you, Margaret. John." The mother covered her son's hand with her own, her dark blue eyes dwelling lovingly upon his face for one moment more, then she turned. This was to be her home no longer, and as its remaining residents entered once again through the door, the house seemed sterner and more forbidding even than when she had dominated its centre rooms.

Margaret followed her husband's leading for a few steps, then halted as his arm fell from her and he began to walk away. "You do not go back to the mill, John?"

He stopped, meeting her eyes for a faint second before his gaze dropped to the floor. "It cannot be helped. If we are to leave for London tomorrow, I must look to certain matters."

"But you will not work late?"

She watched the knot at his throat bobbing as he swallowed. "It is likely. Do not wait up for me."

Margaret searched for something—anything—to say that would keep him with her. She would have offered to help, or at least take him some supper, but he had expressly forbidden her to enter the mill just now. It had been a long while since he had brought his account books home with him, as he used to do… but certainly if his business could be done at home, he would have already said as much.

She raised her hand to catch him, to embrace him for just a moment, but he was already turning to go. "Do not stay too late," she murmured to his retreating back.

Seventeen

"Margaret! Oh, my dear, look at you, how pale you are!" John stood at his wife's shoulder, a little behind her as her cousin rushed to greet her. Mrs Lennox reminded him a great deal of Fanny upon first impression, with her prim curls and excessive flounces. She was embracing Margaret now, somewhat possessively, if he were forced to give his opinion, and whispering something into Margaret's ear. He thought he caught the word "brute," but surely, he was mistaken.

Margaret stiffened, then pulled back a step to gesture to him. "Edith, this is my husband, John Thornton. John, my cousin Edith Lennox."

He had already removed his hat at the door, and now he stepped forward to offer his hand. "I am pleased to meet you, Mrs Lennox."

She glanced down as if he were offering her a snake and shrank somewhat. Chastened, he dropped it as she offered a short bob of her head. "Delighted to make your acquaintance, Mr Thornton."

"The honour is mine, Mrs Lennox. Thank you for receiving us."

She smiled—a patent, tight expression—and then turned her attention back to Margaret. "Oh, darling, I simply cannot wait until you see my little Sholto! He is napping just now, and one must never interrupt a child's nap, you know. Maxwell has been eager to see you as well, and I am certain he will be back from his club within the hour. Oh! Mamma, there you are. Look, our dear Margaret has come back to us!"

John felt himself the object of the woman's scrutiny as she entered. Margaret had told him of her aunt Shaw, her mother's sister, but he could not for the life of him trace a resemblance to Maria Hale. Rather, she was of a kind with her daughter; a confectioner's vision of tucks and bows, round cheeks and dimpled arms. She stopped a couple of paces away, her hands linked over her skirts, and scanned him in a manner which was hardly discreet or optimistic.

This time, he caught himself before offering his hand. He dipped his head graciously and allowed Margaret to perform the introductions. "I am very pleased to meet you, Mrs Shaw," he answered when prompted.

"Mr Thornton—" she lowered her lashes in reply. "How kind of you to bring my dear niece all the way from Milton. It must have been difficult for you to leave your mill."

"Not at all, Mrs Shaw." *A miserable lie.* He could scarcely afford half a day from the mill, and for this trip he proposed to take three or four—if he was welcome for so long. He smiled, or made some approximation thereof. "I have been eager to meet Margaret's family, and it was most considerate of you to extend the invitation."

Mrs Shaw simpered, a mirror of her daughter's cold brush-off, and took her niece by the hand. "Margaret, dear, how thin you have grown! I think it is this dark gown—I always did fancy lighter colours for your complexion. But there, I suppose that such fabrics would not be suited for the streets in Milton, would they?"

"Papa always liked this gown," Margaret objected. John was watching her cheeks, and how the colour rose from her neck. Why would she not simply tell her aunt that she was still wearing half-mourning for that dear old gentleman?

"You always did favour him in your looks and taste," Mrs Shaw smiled warmly. "Well, come my dear, for you must be weary to the bone after coming so far!"

"Milton is but three and a half hours, Aunt," Margaret protested. She then cast him a glance—was it embarrassment or pleading he read there? "We were quite comfortable."

Another lie. It had been the most uncomfortable train ride of his life. Oh, perhaps they had sat side by side, sharing the lap rug because she had desired his warmth in the cold car, but scarcely a word had passed the entire journey. Margaret had read a book while he stared blankly out the window, consumed by all the troubles he left behind in Milton.

"Mr Thornton—" Mrs Lennox drew his gaze from Margaret's back as they moved to the drawing-room—"perhaps you would like to be shown to your room? I fancy Mamma has all manner of gossip for Margaret. Surely, French fashions and talk of her darling grandson will seem rather tedious to you."

As a matter of fact, he would have greatly preferred to remain at Margaret's side, but he was not fool enough to wedge himself into a conversation where he was not welcome. His mouth tightened. "Of course, Mrs Lennox. You are most kind."

~

"Mr Thornton, I had not the opportunity to ask you about your business." Maxwell Lennox flicked out the twist of paper he had used to light his cigar, then lifted his Havana in a rich cloud of decadent smoke. His lips formed a faint puff as he raised his eyebrows to his guest. "I had heard that cotton is quite the thing; a sure means of prosperity, they say."

John straightened his waistcoat as he shifted in his chair. They were alone in the dining room now, the ladies having deserted them in favour of the drawing-room fire. "There is no sure path to prosperity. There is great potential, but as in such cases, equal risk."

"Risk? Oh, I had heard very little of that. I suppose you must refer to strikes and whatnot. Surely there is much a clever master can do to prevent them."

"Not so much as I would wish. I think we will never see the end of strikes, but a careful manager can do somewhat to alleviate the general complaints. Fair wages, better conditions to encourage long-term employment—these are essential to the honest and efficient working of a mill."

"That sounds rather expensive!" Maxwell laughed. "Are you a bluestocking or a master?"

"I am not a charity. Many say I am the hardest master in Milton, but I treat my men in a manner that is fair to both them and to myself. I have not the time to squander on either petty worker's complaints or philanthropic notions that do not produce cotton."

"I suppose it is why you lot are always at work, eh? That is the reputation of you Milton men."

"It is well-earned, I assure you." John could not keep the note of pride from his voice. "The proper management of a mill comes at a cost."

"I'd no idea! My brother Henry and I—have you met Henry? Yes, well, we had once talked of dabbling a bit in cotton. No harm, eh? I heard of a smaller mill out to let in Manchester. Had a trained overseer and everything, only wanted about a hundred fifty a month to begin operations. What do you think, Thornton, how much profit could a man turn on such an operation? We had estimated over eighty per month for each of us after expenses were covered."

John could barely conceal the condescension in his voice. "Only a hundred fifty per month? It must have had but a handful of looms. With such a small operation, it is little wonder the place was to let. The former master must have struggled even to feed himself, to say nothing for paying the fifty or so hands it would take to keep the place running."

"Fifty! I thought the mills were more modernised than that. How can a man possibly turn a profit, with fifty holding out their hands for ten shillings each week?"

"My men start at fourteen a week. Most earn closer to eighteen, and a handful earn almost twenty."

"Why that makes…" Maxwell rolled his eyes backwards as his fingers twitched on his cigar. "Good heavens, man, what are you to purchase your cotton with? Is the hire of labour always so costly?"

"Always, but it is less of an impact with greater volume. For instance, a mill of any size requires two men to operate the boiler. My mill, large as it is, still only requires one full-time mechanic and one overseer. Yard operations, warehousing, dye baths—all these can be performed more efficiently than a small mill can possibly achieve. That is why the larger mills are more successful. The expenses are naturally higher, but with more machines, better equipment, and bulk price on the cotton, profits are improved. I have three hundred working for me, but forty-five looms against your handful. For an operation such as you describe, I imagine raw cotton alone would have consumed nearly seventy percent of the profits, which is far too high a figure to sustain."

"So much! Well—" Maxwell stubbed out his cigar and uncrossed his legs, an indication that he had tired of the conversation and wished to remove. "I suppose it is as well we never took on that venture, would you not agree?"

"That would not be for me to say. I would never discourage a man from an honest effort at business, but not all are suited for it."

Maxwell Lennox paused to stare at him with a curious, almost shocked expression, as if trying to decide if John meant his words as an insult. His eyes narrowed faintly, then his face smoothed into a smile and he stood. "Well, I expect our wives are wondering what has become of us. By the by, I have never seen anyone so altered as Margaret since I last saw her! It must have been a dreadful illness, the poor girl."

John rose from his own chair but could not meet his host's eyes. "It was."

"You have brought her to the right place. Never fear, for my wife and her mother will fête her with tea parties and dinner parties and evenings out until her feet tire of it all. She will eat so much cake and glazed ham that in a month's time, her cheeks will be bright pink and will dimple when she smiles. You won't even know her!"

John followed, his eyes on the carpet as they walked. *A month's time.* Indeed, he might not know her at all.

~

"Have you not missed our dear old rector, Margaret? I know how you always used to love listening to him."

Margaret, walking beside her cousin the short distance from the church, made some soft noise of agreement. John, following closely behind, heard the hesitation in her voice, but Edith did not.

"I thought you would wish to stop and speak to him as we were dismissed," Edith continued reproachfully. "I remember you always used to do so, making observations about the sermon and asking after his family. How I used to dread your long discussions at the church door!"

"I am tired today."

Indeed, it had been Margaret's first real outing since… he shuddered. He had spent the entire service watching her in anxiety, nearly expecting her to faint from the exertions of walking and remaining attentive in public. She did not, but her cheeks were a little paler, her eyes glittered a little more, and she had spoken hardly a word.

"I imagine it must have been strange, coming back to a proper service again," Edith observed. "Was not Uncle attending a Unitarian church in Milton? You do not still do so, do you?"

"Oh—" Margaret directed her gaze across the street, gesturing for her cousin to do likewise—"there is Mrs Hewitt. Do you remember how she always used to give us sugar mice?"

Edith was easily diverted, and she spent the remaining street until their own door reminiscing with Margaret about some of their neighbours.

Once within, John offered Margaret his arm and leaned near her ear. "Did you wish to retire upstairs? You are not looking well."

She straightened self-consciously. "I feel well enough. I shall go up to change, but I would like to come back down for luncheon. Perhaps you could walk me up?"

He obliged, happily, since in two days at the Harley Street house he had been permitted scarcely ten minutes alone with her. Their rooms were even on different floors, with hers just below his and close to the mistress' chambers. He had refused to make complaint but could not help observing that the door in his own room adjoined another vacant and perfectly well-appointed guest chamber.

He assisted her on the stairs and to her room, settling her gently on the bed so she could catch her breath. He sat beside her, caressing her hand. "Are you certain you are well?"

She nodded, still breathing more deeply than he would have liked. "Yes. I only need to accustom myself to going out. I have walked so little of late."

John glanced at the floor. "I know you have missed going out, but you know why it has not been possible."

She smiled tightly, that expression which told plainly that she did not agree but did not wish to argue at present.

He smoothed his hand over her shoulder. "Would you like me to help you with your gown?"

Her eyes fell. "Edith's maid will do that. I expect her in a few moments, as soon as Edith no longer needs her."

John allowed his hand to drop and sighed, looking about the spacious chamber. "Was this your room when you used to live here?"

"It was Edith's, before she married. Mine was a few doors down, but that room has become a nursery again." Her tones were wooden, her eyes glazed faintly as she stared straight ahead.

"Margaret?" He touched her elbow in concern when she did not reply at first.

She started and drew a quick breath, pasting a brave smile on her face. "I am well, John."

"You are lying, Margaret—not to me, but to yourself. It still troubles you."

Her eyes fluttered, her lips parted, but the expression of doubt cleared swiftly, to be replaced by cheerful bravado. "Somewhat, perhaps. I am happy for Edith. I am not sorry we came. It is… it is good for me, to be around one who is so happy, and to see her little boy growing. H-he is…." Her breath seemed to catch, and she heaved three or four ragged breaths before she could continue. "Any m-mother would be p-proud."

He could not know how to answer this. He looked away, out the window, while his hand still curled around her elbow. A moment later, she rose, pulling away from him.

"She was telling me how clever he is, and how he teaches his nurse what he wants," Margaret continued with a false smile. "He even has a few words, though none but Edith and his nurse understand them. And such a beautiful child! Have you held him? How sweet he smells!"

"You are finding it… comforting?"

"Of course. I love Edith like a sister, and her boy… well, I shall never see F-Frederick's children, at—at least not while they are small. Perhaps s-someday…."

"We will see them, Margaret. I will take you to Spain as soon as we can possibly go."

She sniffled, with another one of those artificial smiles, and lifted her shoulders. "Naturally."

He rose to join her, but hesitated before he touched her. "Margaret, I am sorry."

Her brow clouded. "Sorry for what?"

"That I could not have taken you to see him before now. That I cannot even give you the freedom to recover your strength without fearing more harm to you. And I am sorry that you…." He swallowed, his fingers reaching to trace the lower buttons on her bodice. "You deserve the same joy as your cousin."

He hoped, as one often does after such a confession, for swift absolution, but it did not come. She looked away, blinking afresh, and was forced to press her lips to still their quivering.

"Margaret, this house—" he glanced about the room—"it is comforting to you, is it not?"

She swallowed and looked down, nodding. "I have many happy memories here."

"You can move about, more so than you can do in Milton just now. Your strength will return. And you are among those who love you."

She raised her eyes to his, a question beginning to brim over her dark lashes. He cupped his hand to her cheek. "Margaret, I cannot stay, but you can."

She shook her head faintly. "I do not understand."

"I have to work, love. I cannot afford to stay. I intended to take the train back tonight, but we had not spoken of it yet."

"So soon! But we have been here only two days. Did we not speak of a week?"

"Unfortunately, we hardly spoke at all. I believe you wished for a week, and I am happy to arrange that—or longer, if you wish. I cannot stay with you."

"But John," she began to protest, a tear slipping over the edge of her cheek.

He put a finger to her lips. "It is best, love. I will send Dixon on tomorrow's train. She will be only too glad to come. As for me, you would scarcely see me at home, as I have so much work to do just now. You no longer have even my mother for company, and I would protect you from the fever in Milton while you are still recovering. Would you not enjoy some time here, with your relations?"

Her shoulders were trembling, and she stared down at the buttons of his waistcoat. She made no answer for several excruciating seconds, then at last in a whisper, "If you think it is best, John."

Helstone
June 1850

"Maria, my dear, good morning. And Margaret—" Mr Hale added, almost in surprise at finding her there—"good morning to you."

Margaret smiled at her father as he entered the dining room. She was seated beside her mother at the table, pouring her tea and trying to learn all she could of what had gone on in Helstone since last autumn. It was difficult not to mention Frederick, for she ached to hear of him. His name seemed still on the lips of each of the neighbours, but it pained her parents too greatly to ask what she longed to know.

"Mamma," she reminded her gently, "you were speaking of Farmer Grady suffering some misfortune. Has he been ill?"

Maria Hale's watery eyes were on her husband as he settled into his chair and bowed his head in a humble—and belated—blessing over the family breakfast. She seemed not to hear her daughter, but neither did she attempt to speak to her husband. She appeared rather to be waiting on him to offer her some further notice, but none such was forthcoming.

Margaret suffocated a small sigh of dismay. Nine months she had spent in London, as she had done each of the last seven years. Her return this spring had been delayed by nearly a tenth month before her father had at last arrived to take her home. She had been alive with eagerness to see her mother, and Dixon, and all her childhood friends. On this, however, her second day at home, her return seemed to generate as little interest from her parents as a new hen in the coop.

"Papa—" she attempted a new strategy—"what will you preach on this morning?"

Mr Hale glanced up in surprise from his plate. "What? Oh, I speak on… on Titus."

"*'That the aged men be sober, grave, temperate, sound in faith, in charity, in patience. The aged women likewise, that they be in behaviour as becometh holiness, not false accusers, not given to much wine, teachers of good things; That they may teach the young women to be sober, to love their husbands, to love their children,'*" quoted Margaret.[1]

---

[1] Titus 2:2-4 KJV

If she hoped to please her father by her quick recitation, she was mistaken. He seemed to have hardly noticed, but her mother's mood darkened even further. Margaret drew back in her chair and toyed with the handle of her cup.

In short order, the family had all set out for the church. It was, however, with some dismay that Margaret noted her mother leaning heavily on Dixon as they walked. Mr Hale had offered his arm, but it had been declined. When he submitted to walk ahead, Margaret drew to her mother's left and took her other arm, invited or not.

The usual faces greeted her that morning—welcoming, kindly folk, who all seemed glad to see her. Several bowed or curtsied, a few expressed their delight at her return, and one or two made some passing comment that she would bring great comfort to her parents just now. Margaret's only response was a tight smile and a murmured agreement that she, too, was happy to be home. It was a relief when she could take her seat and lose herself in the service, and her dear father's beloved voice from the pulpit.

> *"'Put them in mind to be subject to principalities and powers, to obey magistrates, to be ready to every good work, To speak evil of no man, to be no brawlers, but gentle, shewing all meekness unto all men.*²"

Her father looked up from his lectern, his grey eyes sober as he surveyed his flock. "Is that not our highest mortal calling, to be submissive and gentle towards one another? How, then, shall we render ourselves unto authority? Shall even an unjust administrator be obeyed without question? Indeed, it is written so. Yet we are not slaves bound to our earthly masters, for freedom and prerogative await us all, succeeding the laying aside of our worldly trappings. I refer you to the writings of Seneca;

> *'The story of the Spartan lad has been preserved: taken captive while still a stripling, he kept crying in his Doric dialect, 'I will not be a slave!' and he made good his word; for the very first time he was ordered to perform a menial and degrading service,—and the command was to fetch a chamber-pot,—he dashed out his brains against the wall. So near at hand is freedom, and is anyone still a slave?*³"

"Now, my brethren, Seneca had not, as we, the hope which surpasses all understanding, yet even he understood that our present earthly lives are merely squandered when spent serving injustice. Let him be humble before righteous authority, and willing to lay himself on the altar for the sake of justice."

---

² Titus 3:1-2 KJV

³ Seneca #77, 14-15

Margaret, as always, was listening raptly to her father's words, parsing them and taking them to her heart. It was some minutes before she perceived the faint murmuring passing through the church. A few pews squeaked, heads tipped towards one another, and eyes began seeking any object but the man in the pulpit. Margaret watched curiously, uncertain what could be the cause. Perhaps such esoteric comparisons made little sense to them, unlearned as most were. Margaret determined to pay them no mind, and to devote her thoughts instead to discovering her father's meaning.

The Hale family were always the last to leave the church on Sundays. The parishioners paid their brief respects to Mr Hale, several greeted Margaret again, but most passed by Maria Hale as she stood, silent and withdrawn behind her husband. Margaret laced her arm through her mother's as the last family lingered to speak a moment with her father.

"It was a wonderful sermon," she suggested hopefully.

Her mother only shifted her eyes back to her husband.

"I particularly loved the references to Seneca. Is not Papa brilliant to have discovered such an insight to share? I do hope his intent was understood properly."

Maria Hale's lips puckered unhappily, but she would not speak a word. Margaret sighed and gave it up until her father turned back and offered them his arm. "Come, Mamma," Margaret insisted, leaving Mrs Hale with no alternative but to accept her husband's escort.

Once returned to the privacy of their own drawing-room, Maria Hale let her woes be known. Margaret had again complimented her father on his plundering of the old Latin texts, but her mother rose up.

"And what are we all to think? You uphold that pagan mystic as though he possessed some great spiritual wisdom, but not a single person even knew who he was! One moment you spoke of submission, the next of defiance and mortal sin! It is little wonder the bishop sent you that letter of remonstrance."

Hale's face softened, vulnerable as he was to his wife's criticism. He turned gently away, his head down, to shelve the book he held in his hand.

"You did not think it fine, Mamma? He was not proclaiming Seneca as the fount of all wisdom, but merely observing that even—"

"He spoke of choosing defiance and death rather than to compromise and be left in peace," Mrs Hale interrupted, her eyes limpid now with tears. "What honour is that? It is nothing of the kind, but a wicked heresy. Do you think it right to advise the people that death is preferable to seeking some workable accord?"

"I do not believe that is what he meant, Mamma. I think only that Papa meant to demonstrate that there is something greater than this life, and that spending it in some noble way is no loss, when compared to the great hope beyond." She looked to her father, to see what he would have to say in response to her summary, but apart from a brief glance, he would not engage the conversation.

"And what are these words about living as a slave? We have no slaves in our country. How are any of us to make sense of such words?"

"I think he refers to spiritual bondage, Mamma. Were we not all slaves before our deliverance? Or perhaps we could apply it to our social dignity, for everyone has their betters in society, I suppose, save the queen. Is there not something noble and fine in a man who rejects the unlawful expectations of his superiors in favour of what is good and right?"

"That is what I spoke of," Mr Hale put in quietly. "And the sacrifice one must expect to render, if such a determination is made. It is better to keep a clean conscience than to live a slave to what is wrong."

"You speak of such high-minded things," Mrs Hale protested, "but what has that brought to you? You are still here in miserable little Helstone, preaching meaningless words to those who will not understand them, and all because you would not pay proper respects to the bishop when last he was here."

"I did not, it is true," Mr Hale sighed. Margaret watched his shoulders droop as he turned away from them. A moment later, he had disappeared into his little study, just missing Nancy as she brought the tea tray. Margaret watched him go with some regret but turned to help her mother situate herself for their midday repast. Dixon, however, was already there.

"Don't know what the master was thinking of," mumbled the lady's maid as she assisted her mistress. "Rambling on about some slave boy and all that. If he'd only stay with the right topics, folks wouldn't wonder so about him."

"What does she mean, Mamma?" Margaret had, at least, secured a tea cup for her mother before Dixon could. She drew near with it and dropped three sugar cubes in, just as her mother liked it. "Are people speaking ill of Papa?"

"Oh, Margaret!" Mrs Hale's tears flowed freely. "Do not we all wonder what he is about? I cannot bear the whispers of the neighbours. He could have had a better position last winter, but he refused to please the bishop. He simply *will* preach these meaningless sermons that do us no good. Of what use is it to preach about slave boys—I dare not even repeat the words! He should have spoken on the Eucharist or the Beatitudes or some other safe topic. I fear he will offend so many that the bishop will send us off to somewhere even smaller and more miserable than Helstone."

"Helstone miserable! Dear Mamma, I think you are weary. Come, you must take your luncheon, and then perhaps this afternoon we may walk about the rose garden together."

"My roses are scarcely fit to be seen," Mrs Hale nearly sobbed. "I had not the strength to touch them this spring as I used to do. If only your father had not let Freddy go!"

"Fred?" Margaret brightened. "Oh, have you heard from him? How has he settled in Spain?"

Mrs Hale shook her head, now pressing a handkerchief to her mouth. Dixon took the teacup Margaret had filled from her other hand, and, with a poorly concealed glare towards the daughter, proceeded to comfort her mistress. "Now, Missus, there's no sense making your eyes puffy again," she observed practically. "I'll fetch you some nice salts. Here, drink this cup, the other has grown cold."

Margaret did not miss the resentful glance Dixon cast her way as she rose but chose not to address it. "Mamma, I do not understand," she persisted as soon as Dixon had gone. "What has Fred to do with Papa's standing in the church?"

"Oh! We are disgraced, Margaret. Everyone knows it all and they have still not forgotten. And your father, with his dusty old books, stands there in his church and preaches that Frederick was right to mutiny. How can he dare? What would have been right is having my boy back again. Oh, I am not ashamed of my Freddy—I am proud that he did what he felt was right, but if only he had not listened to your father! It would be all right then, if only—"

"Mamma, what happened? Why was Fred counted among the mutineers? What did he do? Will you not tell me some day?"

Mrs Hale fell silent, deaf to her daughter's pleas, and merely dabbed her eyes until Dixon's return. The maid bestowed on her another dark look, and Margaret understood that she was occupying the coveted seat which Dixon had claimed as her own. Meekly she shifted to the other and watched as Dixon ministered to her mother.

No one walked with Margaret that afternoon in the rose garden. Undeterred, she took her watercolours and attempted a close study of one of the season's lushest roses, but the colours would not mix properly. Try as she might, every mixture was contaminated with hints of green and grey. In the end, she set the easel and paints aside, never touching them again all that summer.

Margaret watched through blurred eyes as her husband bade farewell to his host and hostesses. She flinched at each cool expression of regret, at each insensitive remark cloaked in sympathy about his work calling him away. They could not have meant to be callous, but such they were, and John's tight responses did nothing to encourage warmth. He looked slighted—offended, even—and his pride had long ago scorched a thick callous of disdain for any who would attempt to lord their ancestral gentility over his hard-earned respectability. He seemed glad to be making his escape from London.

At last it fell to her to make the proper farewell expressions, those naturally expected of a gently bred wife parting from her husband for a short few days. Maxwell Lennox had the goodness to withdraw—whether he intended to offer privacy for the couple or sought a fresh cigar, Margaret could not be certain. Her aunt and cousin remained. She felt their gazes on her, casting restraint and possibly censure as she slipped her small hand into John's familiar, calloused fingers. His eyes flashed over her shoulder for an instant, then met hers with one last look of regret tinged with annoyance.

If only they had a moment of privacy! She had tried to secure that moment upstairs as he made his preparations, but she had been detained by Edith's demand to give audience to Sholto's antics before his mother sent him up for his nap. She had gone then, only to encounter John on the stairs with his bag in hand.

She bowed her head over their hands, the tears beginning to threaten in earnest. Oh, how she longed to pull herself into his arms, to bury her griefs into his strong shoulders as she had done before! How was she to manage without him? Even in the depth of her illness or on his busiest nights, he had been near. She had never yet parted from him since those first delirious days of their marriage. How was she to do so now, when it seemed an ever-growing wall was building between them?

For an instant, she considered clasping the front of his coat, pulling his shoulders down to her, and sobbing into his ear—pleading for him to stay, or to take her with him, but a sigh from Mrs Shaw stilled her. She could not embarrass him, not in front of her aunt who already looked dubiously upon her choice of husband. She besought his face one last time, praying he would understand the longing and heartache she tried to pour into that single glance.

His jaw tightened in resolve, even as those dark blue eyes she loved softened with tender adieu. "I will come Friday night," he whispered, too low for the others to hear.

She nodded, and a tear slipped down her nose. She felt his finger twitch to capture it, but he stopped himself, ever mindful of their witnesses. His hand pulled away then, and a footman gave him his hat. He made a final parting gesture of gratitude to her relations, one last faint smile for her, and then he was gone.

Margaret stood empty, staring at the closed door as if she expected him to change his mind. He would not, she knew. For good or ill, John was never indecisive. She drew a quaking breath to steady herself and felt her cousin's hand on her shoulder.

"Come, dear Margaret, you are looking faint again. I am sure that long walk to church today was very bad for you. You must sit by the fire and have a little wine to strengthen you."

Margaret turned away from Edith, and her eyes encountered her aunt. Mrs Shaw pursed her lips. "A pity about his work. Ah, well, that is what comes of marrying such a man. Come, dear, I suppose you must accustom yourself to it. There is no need for you to languish, is there?"

Margaret moved her feet obediently towards the drawing-room. Soon, and quite without any participation of her own, she was seated by the fire and presented with the wine her cousin had determined she must have. She tasted it only for a moment, then left the remainder of the glass untouched. Edith seemed not to notice, content as she was to be settled at a game of checkers with her husband. Margaret watched them with a distant sort of awareness, the greater part of her thoughts centred not in that room, but several miles to the north.

It was nearly the time for the evening tea, and Margaret now nursed a headache—no doubt brought on by brooding and fatigue. She had just determined to excuse herself for the night when a caller was heard at the door. The family turned expectant eyes in that direction, and a moment later, Henry Lennox appeared.

His gaze went immediately to Margaret, with the hint of a question in his expression when he saw her seated alone. Nevertheless, he greeted the rest of the family and came to her last. "Mrs Thornton, delighted to see you again. I had heard you were visiting. I hope your stay has been pleasant?"

"Yes, thank you, Mr Lennox."

"Henry, I am so glad you came! How wonderful!" Edith enthused. "Now the whole family are here. Oh, Henry, you must help us make a fourth for Hearts, for Mamma hates playing cards."

"I am at your service, as always." He smiled, then glanced to Margaret. "Is Mr Thornton not joining us this evening?"

Margaret's gaze faltered. "His presence was required in Milton. He expects to return in a few days."

"Ah," he replied, his tones gravid with meaning. "Then, as we are both without a partner, I suggest we ally ourselves against my brother and his bride. They are a formidable pair at the game, as I am sure you recall."

"I must beg to be excused." She held up a hand as he gestured towards the table. "I am a little weary this evening and I was about to retire."

"Oh, Margaret," Edith pouted, "you must not leave us. I was so looking forward to one of our old evenings in, and we would all be terribly sad if you did not join us. Come, sit beside me, and we will be merry as we used to do!"

Margaret felt her cheeks burning, for Henry's gaze had not left her. She glanced back at him now, offering a pitiful excuse for a smile, and submitted herself to be led to the card table.

Eighteen

Milton-Northern
1 April 1856

The house on Marlborough Street had never, since its first construction, been so empty.

John had turned his back to the window in his office, refusing to look at or even think about the vacant house… but his resolve was weak. All the women in his life were gone, as were their women—Jane and Dixon, and even Ruth, who had left at Fanny's marriage—only Sarah, Mrs Adams the cook and her scullery girl, and one grizzled man of all work remained. They would be communing with one another this evening in the kitchen, leaving the master to himself.

Not that he could have gone home in any case. John's head drooped to his hand as he surveyed the wreckage of his desk. The dreaded day had finally arrived when he could not honour all his obligations. The hands were paid, his private investors compensated, but his loan with the bank would receive only a partial payment this month. Had only another of his buyers come through with their own portion….

He could yet hope that next month would be better. For that matter, even next week could be better, but only marginally so. The devil of it was that he knew… he *knew* how he could have avoided it! It would have meant hard tactics, conflict with the union, and displeasing his wife, but he could have bought at least two more months. It might have been enough… but not now.

He could still sell. He would see almost nothing of the profits after his debts were covered, but he could walk away a free man, before the ruin was devastating. He was still young enough, could turn his hand to a new task. It would not be his preference, but there could be worse things to befall a man than retrenching.

But Margaret… how was he to face her and tell her the tenuous sense of belonging she had found in her latest home must be forgotten? That they would have to take a lesser house, perhaps even something humbler than her old Crampton residence? What shame would she then feel in telling her haughty relations of their circumstances!

His head fell to his desk, for he wanted to see nothing before him. How he missed her, already! Even in the depths of her grief and the darkest days of fear, her light had warmed his life. He tried telling himself that he was being foolish. How was she any less his inspiration from London than she had been on those late nights when he had not even seen her after his work?

Yet, some scales had fallen from his eyes during those two days in London. He was a fool, a damned, miserable blockhead, if he had ever expected one such as she to be content with him. Her relations were not bad people, but their position was clear: he had reached above his head to pluck the forbidden fruit, and both were now disgraced for it. There was no recourse, no annulment possible for her—that very word speared anguish through his heart!

How could she not regret it… all of it? But they were bound to one another, by law, if no longer by the heartfelt love so briefly glimpsed. She had hazarded a chance on him, likely blinded by grief and dulled by her time in Milton, and the price of such risk had been higher than he could have imagined. She could not be other than disappointed, and yet she was bound still.

His doom was not yet complete, he tried to convince himself. She need not hang her head on his account—no more than she might already have had cause to do. He owed her every effort to cling to his purchased gentility. Perhaps on the morrow, he would pay a visit to his bank. Surely, his could not be the only business seeking creative means of repayment.

~

That was a bloody waste of time.

John snatched his coat from the porter as he neared the door of the bank, a scowl he could feel deepening over his face. Two hours! All that wasted hope, spent energy, for a flat refusal. Nay, it was not even so much as that. New policies, they said. New board, new directives. They could not possibly consider any alterations at present. That left John Thornton, with his hat in his hand, turning back out on the street in search of another who might hear him.

His foot had scarcely touched the cobblestones when he heard his name spoken in a familiar voice. "John Thornton! What a surprise!"

He looked up from the pavement to identify the woman. Why, it was old Kramer's daughter! Despite his frustrations, John could not help a smile of greeting. "Mrs Brockett. A surprise, yes, but a pleasant one. What brings you back to Milton?"

The lady had aged rather comfortably—one might say she had settled into her middle years with ease. She was walking with a man John had never seen, one with thick shoulders, a ramrod straight spine, and a wary frown upon his bearded face. The couple drew near, and the lady gestured. "Mr Thornton, you have not met my husband, Captain Fortin. My dear, this is the Mr Thornton who is presently the master of Marlborough Mills."

The man's broad face softened at once, and he extended his hand. "A pleasure, sir."

"Likewise," John agreed. "Forgive me, Mrs Fortin, I did not know you had married again. Congratulations. I am afraid it has been two or three years since I last wrote to your father."

Her face pinched. "Papa was never one to keep up a correspondence."

"Nonetheless, I ought to have continued to write, even when a reply did not come. I must beg forgiveness for being so negligent."

"It matters no more, for Papa died two months ago. That is why Captain Fortin and I have come to Milton, to move the last of his accounts from the Milton bank."

"Mr Kramer gone!" John felt as if the air had been punched from his chest. He swayed—a momentary instinct to seek out some stable object to rest his hand upon, to stop the reeling in his head. "My condolences, Mrs Fortin."

She smiled a little sadly. "He did not expect to have so many years after he left Milton, so I shall not lament the time he did have."

"I knew his health troubled him, but...." His eyebrows jerked in feeling. "I assumed he would enjoy a long retirement."

"He had seven years, thanks to you—so he always said. He spoke of you often, for he was terribly fond of you, sir. Mr Thornton, I hope you will not consider us too bold, but Captain Fortin and I had hoped to encounter you in Milton. Would you find it a very great imposition on your time to take tea with us before we leave?"

"Not at all, the pleasure would be mine. Would you like to tour the mill, Captain? Or perhaps see the house again, madam?"

The couple exchanged a look, then Captain Fortin seemed to understand his wife's desires. "I thank you, sir, but that will not be necessary. We have taken a room in the hotel on New Street. Would you dine with us there this evening?"

"Your offer is more enticing than you can know, for my alternative is an empty house. My mother has also recently married, and my... my wife is visiting her relations in London."

Mrs Fortin's eyes widened, and a knowing smile grew upon her face. "I see we have some catching up to do, John Thornton. Will seven be too early for you?"

"Not a bit. I look forward to it, madam."

~

"Were you a captain in the Navy, sir, or the merchant fleet?" John asked his host as they were seated.

"Both. I joined the Navy as a wee lad and got out when I could afford a stake of me own. I spent my last ten years on the Indian routes. Ye may imagine that I have seen my fair share of cotton," he added with a twinkle in his eye.

"I do not doubt it. I must confess that were I at sea, I would prefer cotton bales to guns in the lower decks."

The captain laughed. "Just so!"

Mrs Fortin shook her head in exasperation. "Now, we are not to speak of ships and such nonsense all night. Come now, Mr Thornton, you have put me off long enough. You have been here ten full minutes, and I have not heard another word about your marriage. How long ago did this take place?"

"Last autumn, madam."

"And what is the lady's name? How did you come to know her?"

Fortin poured John a drink, shaking his head. "It is no good trying short answers with Mrs Fortin. She will have the whole of the story, so you may as well share it all and have done with it."

John steepled his fingers, releasing a slow, unsteady breath. "Margaret Hale was her name before we wed. Her father was a retired rector from Hampshire, and he was in search of some other situation. Mr Bell—you remember him, I suppose? He was an old friend of Mr Hale, and it was upon his recommendation that the family came to Milton. Mr Hale found work as a tutor. He became as much a friend and counsellor to me as your own father was."

"You speak fondly of the man," observed the lady.

John shifted in his chair. "I did think very highly of him."

The couple opposite him seemed to lift their brows in unison. "Oh," Mrs Fortin replied in a whisper. "So, condolences are again in order?"

"Father and mother are both gone now."

"And Mrs Thornton? It must have been a dreadful blow for her, losing both parents."

"I see what you are about, madam, and I will correct your assumption before it is spoken. I did wed Miss Hale after the loss of her father, but it was not done out of pity on my part. It was I who was honoured by her hand."

A smile quirked upon her lips. "Then I hope I shall have the pleasure of meeting her one day. She must be a remarkable lady."

He bit the inside of his cheek as his gaze fell. Why were his eyes misting over in company? "She is, Mrs Fortin," he answered huskily.

The couple fell silent for a moment, sharing another glance, and at last Mrs Fortin spoke again. "Well, Mr Thornton, you have obliged me on one point. You gentlemen may now continue on with talk of ships and cotton mills, and I shall content myself with listening."

Captain Fortin wanted no further encouragement. He was a jovial man, and like most men who had spent a lifetime at sea, seemed inclined to spin tales which might have been at least half true. Deborah Fortin's responses, which ranged from serious attendance to merry dismissal, gave subtle cues as to which stories might be credited and which were more fanciful.

"I saw it, Mr Thornton, the Leviathan. I tell ye, it be no mere fable! It came below the gun ship, must have been eighty feet if it were twenty. It rolled over and I saw its eye—red like the devil! I swear, it stared right through me. I thought it were going to capsize the ship, but it swam to the starboard and then slipped below the inky waters." Fortin huffed in amazement at his own tale—as did his wife—and drew another draught from his glass.

John was rolling his eyes towards Mrs Fortin but acknowledged the tale in the seriousness with which it had been told. "You must have seen a great deal, Captain."

"Aye, I have. Men throwing themselves overboard for madness, the craze that comes upon them when ale runs low, the absolute hedonism of shore leave on the wilder coasts… have ye ever seen—"

"My dear, I am certain Mr Thornton does not wish to hear some of your more sordid tales," Deborah Fortin interrupted.

The captain settled back into submission. "Of course."

"I do not doubt your experiences have been something most would consider fantastical," John returned with a hint of amusement. "What of your time in the Navy? Were you ever on any of the older sailing ships, or only the steamers?"

"Aye, lad, the sheet blew much of the fleet about in my day. So many ships we had then, for it were so blasted slow! Why, I remember many a worthless captain promoted to rank, simply because it was a month back to port and he was the only man at hand without a bullet in his chest or his own ship already to command."

John tilted his head. "I would have thought after the immediate crisis was over, such emergency appointments would be passed over in favour of more qualified replacement officers."

"Ye'd think, lad, but more often, there were none better. Some of the worst never stepped down again, and the crew are what suffered for it. I once knew a ship, the *Russell*, where the men were so bloody fired up by their captain—mad he was—that they set him to sea. Good riddance, I should say, but it were called a mutiny, worthless captain or no."

John narrowed his eyes, his neck prickling. "I know of that ship."

Fortin lowered his glass and pierced John with a long, pensive stare. "What did ye say yer lady wife's name was? Hale?"

John looked down at his empty glass. "Captain and Mrs Fortin, it has been a pleasure, but I am afraid I must go."

"Nay, my good fellow," the captain put out a large hand to capture John's sleeve. "Lieutenant Hale. Ye know the lad, do ye not?"

John's breath froze in his chest. He slid his gaze towards Mrs Fortin, a woman he had long considered respectable, and saw only concern written upon her features. He tugged his arm free of Fortin's grip and attempted to steady himself. "I am familiar with his name."

"There is a reward out for that young man's head. Quite a fine one, too, if a man knew where he might be found."

John gestured nonchalantly with his right hand. "A pity I do not."

"Hold, sir, ye mistake my meaning. I were on the Amica, the ship that picked up the survivors when the Reid and his men were set adrift. There were testimony what never saw the light of day."

John furrowed his brow. "What, do you mean the military courts did not give the case a proper hearing?"

Fortin scoffed. "Worse than that. We were all threatened if we talked, we'd hang beside the *Russell's* crew."

"Captain, perhaps we should not speak of this, if there is any danger to yourself or others." John cast a doubtful eye to Mrs Fortin, assuming this was yet another fabrication, but her face had gone grey.

"That were Admiral Trenton. Broke regulation, he did, but he died two years ago. I had wondered, now that he's gone, if there be any hope of justice for the crew, but most of the poor devils were hanged."

"How can there be justice? Whatever the cause, mutiny is mutiny. No exoneration is possible."

The captain smiled. "Aye, but there is. Reid were the mutineer."

Mrs Fortin gasped aloud. Fortin glanced at each of them and then continued. "This is how it were. Ye heard about the mate what fell from the yard arm? That were only the beginning. Ship's doctor said Reid were mad for it and ordered him locked away, but he shot the man in cold blood. His officers sided with him, save for Hale. Five of us were there when the bos'n told the tale, but the admiral had it hushed up. It were easier—less embarrassing for the Navy—to punish the crew."

John stared hard at the captain. Fortin's face reflected none of the mischievous twinkle from his earlier fish tales. He was all earnest gravity, and beside him, Mrs Fortin's eyes were rounded in her pale face.

He thinned his lips. "If it is direction to Lieutenant Hale you desire, I am afraid I cannot help you, sir."

"Nay, Thornton! I thought the whole crew dead. If there be a poor soul or two still alive, after all this time, then perhaps it be worth seeking a fair judgement. I am not the only man who would testify to this, but there seemed that no good could come of it. Tell me, sir, is Hale still alive?"

John drummed his fingers, looking away.

The captain leaned back in satisfaction. "Ye've said enough. Fear not that I will harm the man, but if ye know him, perhaps ye know how to write to him."

"I will not."

"I do not mean for ye to lure him back to England for a trial, but it's considerable fuss to open the case, if the man is not 'alive'."

John shook his head. "If the Navy believed a convicted man still alive, they would redouble their efforts at seeking him."

"Not if that revelation exonerated him."

John pulled the napkin from his lap. "I am afraid I cannot help you, sir."

"Mr Thornton, please—" Mrs Fortin rose from her seat, extending a hand. "I am sorry if the captain has troubled you! He means no harm, I can assure you."

John stopped, his jaw working. She saw his hesitation and sent an imploring look to her husband.

"'Tis true, sir," Fortin agreed. "Mr Kramer and my dear Deborah have spoken well of ye these years I have known them. I'd not bring harm upon any man, but even less would I grieve my wife."

John slowly sank into his chair. "Nor would I wish to grieve mine."

"Then it's settled." Fortin put out his thick palm. "I'll write to an old friend at once."

~

"Margaret, are you coming down? The morning is half gone, silly!" Edith leaned impatiently against the door frame of Margaret's room, stopping there only because Dixon's generous form blocked her path to the dressing table where Margaret was seated. "Mamma is entertaining callers, and Mrs White and Mrs Phillips were just asking after you."

Margaret's movements were all languor and reluctance as she dabbed a little cosmetic powder beneath her eyes to conceal the dark circles. Dixon had finished her hair and hovered now only because Margaret did not appear satisfied with something. With a sigh, she blinked, made a gesture of resignation towards the mirror, and rose.

Edith tsked, shaking her head. "I wish you would go to Mrs Pritchard's and get measured for some new gowns, Margaret. Or at least you could wear one of those you left here before—you remember, you left a few gowns you thought would not be suitable for Helstone. What about that lovely green one? This one is hardly fit to be seen! It is at least two years out of fashion, and though you claim not to see it, I declare those hems are stained. It may be dark brown, but it does not hide everything."

"It will serve until I have finished mourning for Papa."

"Come, you cannot expect me to think that even Milton ladies do not notice. And surely, Mr Thornton can afford to attire you in a few new gowns. Why, I have heard the tradesmen's wives dress more lavishly than the queen's ladies! How they contrive to do so in that dirty place, I shall never know, but that there must be a deal of money to be had in trade. Is it true, Margaret?"

Margaret had drawn near now, her hands draped low over her thick skirts. "It is true that many of the ladies dress very finely indeed."

"And must constantly be wanting new petticoats! Are the hems generally higher there?"

Margaret did not answer, staring as she was at the floor.

"Come, dearest. You must want something to break your fast. Oh, no, that bit of coffee and toast will not do—why, it is barely civilised! I shall have another tray brought to the drawing-room for you, and you and I may sit with Mamma until Sholto wakes from his morning nap. If the weather is fine this afternoon, I thought we could walk to the park. What do you think, Margaret?"

Margaret looked up at last. "I would like to walk," she confessed.

"Wonderful! I think I shall ask the captain to join us, for it was he who said the afternoon ought to be fair. Oh, but Mamma will not wish to come, so that leaves you to walk with Mrs Collins, the nurse. You would not mind that very much, would you, Margaret? Perhaps Maxwell will bring Henry home for tea, for I think they had gone on some errand together. I expect them back just after luncheon."

Margaret made no objection as Edith laced their arms and drew her away. From the corner of her eye, she could see Dixon frowning and clucking over her scattered cosmetics, casting the occasional glance over her shoulder as she left the room.

Mrs Shaw's callers had gone by the time Margaret came below, a fact which did not grieve her overmuch. She had heard enough of sympathy for the loss of her parents, had seen her share of arched eyebrows at the news of her marriage to a Milton cotton manufacturer. The questions they always wanted to ask were silenced behind raised teacups and nervous reticule fans, hesitant smiles and doubtful congratulations, but Margaret could read each, with painful clarity.

A tradesman! Margaret Hale, of all girls? She, who was too poor for this gentleman, too proud for that, and so serious and grave that none could have met with her approval? A hypocrite, that is what she is, she who always spoke so high-mindedly, taking up with a tradesman from the North!

Oh, yes, she could hear each scathing thought, read each sideways glance. They would presume that she had, after all her brave talk of lofty ideals, sheltered with the nearest wealthy protector who would have her. They might wonder what compromises she had made, how far her dignity had slipped… or they might stumble upon the truth and despise her even more for it. Love, vulgar and inconvenient, had smitten her from her high horse and lured her into a match they could only think unwise, sentimental—if not outright shameless—and wholly unsuitable. No, she was not sorry that she had missed the last of her aunt's callers.

The remainder of the morning passed, and the afternoon sky happily obliged Edith's grand scheme for a walk. Margaret returned upstairs to dress for their early spring outing, and when she came below, found that Captain Lennox had, indeed, decided to attend the ladies, as well as his brother. There was no graceful escape; when Henry Lennox extended his arm as the party set out, there was naught else to do but to rest her gloved hand over his coat sleeve. Margaret walked with a sick feeling in her stomach, her eyes ever glancing at the street in irrational fear that John might even, at that moment, drive by in a hired cab and be made unhappy by the sight.

"Are you unwell today?" Henry asked, after several minutes had passed in tense silence. "Or are you simply uncomfortable walking with me, Mrs Thornton?"

A faint smile tugged at the corner of her mouth. "I have always appreciated your candour, sir."

"You have no reason to fear me, Mrs…" he sighed, frowned, and addressed her again. "I used to call you 'Margaret.' Do you think I might still do so, at least between ourselves? I should be sorry to feel I have lost your friendship."

"You have not done so, sir, as I assured you when you came after my father's death. I shall always remember you kindly for that."

"I am glad to hear it. A little sorry, naturally, for it does make me wonder what might have come under different circumstances—"

"Henry," Margaret stopped him. "Please, don't."

He seemed to stifle himself, his lips pressing into an unhappy smile. "Of course, that was unfair. Oh, have no fear, Margaret, for I do not intend to cast blame or false guilt to you. You are content in your choice, and I shall be happy for you." He paused, then looked at her gravely. "You *are* content, are you not?"

She smiled, a little too widely. "Quite so."

"And you have learned to like Milton, for all its hedonism and smoke?"

"I should think London boasts more of the former. Milton is not without its flaws, but the people there are... simpler."

"I imagine they are. When a man works a twelve-hour day for his bread, and his wife and children must work almost as many, why, I suppose little time is left for the sort of debauchery one often sees in London. But if there is little thought or money for vice, there is equally small portion for refinement. Have you missed the culture of London, Margaret?"

"I have missed the finer sights," she agreed, nodding significantly in the direction they walked as the park came into view. "And perhaps the art museum... I do enjoy admiring the paintings, and Milton has precious little in that way."

"Well," Henry comforted, "I am sure it is only a matter of time before that city makes room for more genteel pleasures. Where there is affluence, there are fine ladies, and where there are such creatures, social arbitration ensues, then religious fervour often follows, then education and the arts. Tell me, is it really true that all the children in Milton work from the age of eight?"

"Mr Thornton does not take children younger than thirteen."

"Still! Very young, indeed. And what of education? Why, they could have just learned their letters before they are turned out to work at the mills!"

"Henry, I think you are trying to provoke me. You know the law states they may only work set hours, and that they must attend school the rest of the day."

"Forgive me, Margaret, I had not intended to annoy you. I only wonder how you can justify it. Does it not trouble you to see it all? The suffering I saw, and that only on the streets, I found appalling. But you have seen the mills, and how the people work and live. How do you reconcile it in your own mind?"

Margaret was silent for several seconds, looking thoughtfully at the ground as she sought an answer to Henry's challenge. "I cannot."

Henry glanced quickly to her—she felt his gaze on her cheek—and then looked away. "Well, let us speak no more of such unpleasant thoughts for now. Look, it is a beautiful day for this time of year—I declare, we shall have a warm spring. You and I have always loved Regent's Park. We need not be gloomy here, am I right?"

Margaret drew her mind back from the polluted streets, the dirty children, the noise, the hunger, the smog. She forced herself to look instead at pristine oaks, dazzling in their new spring finery. Brightly dressed Londoners; gentlemen, ladies, and children alike, wandered about with no object but to enjoy the day. Edith and her captain were many paces ahead, taking their son from his nurse to show him the marvel of an early thatch of crocus.

"Margaret?"

She caught her breath, looking with a conscious blush to her walking companion. She smiled tightly and nodded. "Yes, let us enjoy the park."

~

Two more days, and he could see her again.

Thoughts of his wife had not left his consciousness for more than a fleeting second since he had seen her in London, but last evening's dinner had perplexed him in the extreme. Could there be a chance of pardon for Frederick Hale? How welcome such tidings would be, most particularly now!

His mind told him the notion was foolish—dangerous, even—but his heart pounded with fevered hope. Dare he speak to her of it, or would it terrify her too greatly to even consider? Perhaps… perhaps he would write to Hale himself, without alarming Margaret. Perhaps the man would have something of his own to say about these tidings of Fortin's.

John's eyes roved blankly about as his thoughts pressed upon him. It was two o'clock, which set him into his prescribed rounds through the mill. His presence on this day was merely a reminder that he was on site, rather than an investigative tour, but he would keep up the appearance regardless of his conflicted state of mind. He canvassed every corner of the mill, as he always did—the carding room, the spinners, the looms, the washing and drying racks.

He was not blind to the happenings around him, but the sights were all so familiar, his decisions so automatic, that he scarcely recalled the details in his path as he neared his office. Familiar faces had become a blur as he moved from one room to the next. Williams, in his old brown tweed jacket, the women pushing the loom and carefully watching the children—often their own—who set the spindles below the cloth. The same men who stood every day at the shuttles watched him pass, all making a visible effort to step up their pace when the master walked by.

Only one face had the power to give him pause. Higgins, meeting his eye a little longer than the others, smiling just a little where no other had, drew him up. "G'day Master," the fellow touched his cap.

"Good afternoon, Higgins," he answered over the din. He glanced about, feeling not averse to a moment or two of conversation with the man, but it was impossible in the busy mill. At last, he settled upon a quick inquiry. "Are the children all well?"

Higgins shook his head, his eyes darkened by a sudden gloom. "Johnny—'e were too little. 'Tis no good, Master."

John's eyes widened in alarm. "He is not…"

"No' yet, bu' my Mary weeps o'er 'im something fierce. I din'na, Master," he shrugged, his eyes falling away. "There's naught any can do for 'im, like a' th' others. Even th' doctor says so. Either 'e's strong, or 'e's not."

John sighed, his heart sinking. "Margaret will be distressed to hear of it," he murmured, almost to himself.

Higgins could not have heard his words over the clatter of the looms, but he nodded as if he understood. With a weary shrug, he turned back to his loom. "The worst is gone, Master." He gave a forced grin as he resumed his work.

Indeed, the worst was over, but what remained was bad enough. Several of his hands were still out, and those only because they could not stand at their post. Many more came to work each day, coughing and feverish, and all insisting they could not afford to go home… and thus, he must pay them. At least the tide had slowly begun to turn, since fewer seemed to be contracting the illness this week than the several previous.

He returned to his office and immediately flipped to a calendar. The weather was warming, and if new cases had begun to dwindle, and the typical course of the sickness remained two to three weeks, it would be… he groaned inwardly. Still nearly two months—well into May before the mill and all connected with it would have put this trial behind them—if there was still a mill for them all to work at by that time. Barring a miracle, there would not be.

He sank into his chair, rubbing his jaw. How many of the children had fallen ill? And he powerless to ease their suffering or protect them from further sickness. All he could provide—and that not for much longer—was employment to keep food in their bellies and a roof over their heads… but work was not enough for some of them. Indeed, for some, it could be called the very means of their undoing.

His dull vision cast about for some project into which he could fling himself, the better to remove from his thoughts all his helplessness and guilt. His fingers crossed over a note he had missed before, and he recognised his mother's tight hand. She must have sent Jane to his office with the missive, and finding him not present, the girl had left it on his desk. He broke the seal and blinked his eyes a few times until they focused.

John,

The doctor and I were hoping you would take dinner with us this evening. He has been out frequently, as you can imagine, but he expects that tonight he will have some measure of rest. You have been working too late, and do not persuade yourself to believe I have not heard of it. We shall look for you by eight.

HD

His mother's terse, commanding note, complete with a hint of motherly admonition and—most disturbingly—her new initials, found him shaking his head in resigned laughter. Yes, perhaps he could do with a quiet evening in her company. He had not seen his mother since her wedding the previous week, and Donaldson was an agreeable chap.

Perhaps he would ask the doctor about the illness still ravaging the city, and whether he agreed with John's hopes. And, perhaps, he might find a moment to draw his mother aside to solicit her advice concerning the great scandal of the Hale family. What little she could share of intelligence on the matter was unimportant. She was, and always had been, a sympathetic ear, and he was sorely in need of that just now.

He thumbed over a leaf of notepaper to pen a reply, but before he could begin it, someone knocked at his door. Thinking little of it, he scarcely glanced up when he summoned his caller, until some sense alerted him that it was not Williams or Higgins who stood before his desk.

John looked up again, catching fine grey twill and shining buttons. His eyes travelled the remaining distance to the man's face, and his jaw tightened. "Wright. I thought we had no further business."

Wright tossed his hat upon the peg. "Good afternoon to you, too, Thornton. You might spare a moment before throwing me out again."

"The moment would be wasted. You can have nothing of interest to say."

"Well, one detail at least might interest you. I thought you would like to know I am now on the board at the bank. I was already invested heavily there, and I decided to deepen my relationship. The board agreed. I heard you stopped in yesterday?"

John did not lift his head but glanced up through a raised eyebrow. "I did not know customer transactions were public knowledge."

"They are if one of our best customers goes away dissatisfied and possibly in search of another alternative. Members of the board hear about these things."

"And you came to be certain I received adequate service? You may inform your colleagues that I was shown to a comfortable office and was even offered a cup of tea. I believe that concludes our business for the day."

"Au contraire, old friend. We have no wish to see one of our best clients suffer economic hardship due to circumstances beyond his control. That damages the bank as well, for if such a pillar of our base fails and he cannot honour his debts, why that hurts everyone."

"I have no history of neglecting my debts."

"And no such accusation was meant, but if repayment is to take years, we would be wiser to find some compromise to keep up your cash flow during this season of lean times. All the better to ensure a promising future for us all, do you not agree?'

John crossed his arms. "Do you mean the bank is willing to ease the terms of my current contract?"

Wright began to pace the office, picking up random items to weigh in his palm, then replacing them to examine something else. "No. I have not the authority to change any existing contracts. I speak more of a personal loan, such as I offered before. Through the bank, I have access to funds of my own for the express purposes of investment, and I would like very much to see my old friend prosper. My relationship with the bank is such that I believe something could be worked out regarding your collateral. You put your looms and some of your other equipment up against your loan, but you have repaid a respectable portion of that debt. Therefore, the bank holds an interest in collateral that is worth far more than your remaining balance."

"And again—" John levelled a frown at the other man—"you would write the contract to place yourself in first position. Therefore, should anyone be in the position to call in my debts, you hold everything."

"Thornton! How did you get so far in business being such a pessimist? You know very well that I cannot lay claim to that which is justly held by the bank, but yes, I suppose I would hold a good portion of your assets. What does that matter? They are bound up anyway, even without my assistance. There is no expectation you would fail, is there?"

"Many things are unforeseen in business. You may apply to your father for his experience if you are curious."

Wright shook his head in disgust. "Good lord, man, will you never let that go? You are like a dog after a bone that has long since decayed. I am not my father any more than you are yours. Helping you is good business sense, and that is the end of it. I would have thought a man such as yourself would understand that."

"I understand you have been trained since boyhood to exploit opportunities. I have no intention of making myself the next one. I believe our business is finished here."

Wright stepped back, lifting his hands in defeat. "As you wish, I suppose. I cannot force you into something for your own good. It is a pity, for I believed you had changed. Married? Perhaps a family man soon? One would have thought your interests would take a more practical direction."

John turned gravely to the window, his teeth set and refusing to answer.

"I understand Mrs Thornton is a lovely woman," goaded the other. "Mrs Wright was most taken with her and hoped to continue the acquaintance. I do hope that relations between our families need not always be strained, Thornton."

"That is up to you, Wright. I've no intention of accepting your offer, but know that I am watching your other dealings with interest."

Wright smiled. "I trust you shall find nothing to reprove. I will bid you a good day for now. Do send word if you decide to reconsider. I am in Milton for another fortnight before returning to London, and my dear Mildred speaks often of having you to dinner."

As Wright turned away and opened the door, John resumed his seat and his work before he had even left the room.

Nineteen

He was late. Margaret had dressed and come below by five o'clock, expecting at any moment that John would walk through the door. The train was scheduled to arrive at half-past four, and surely it would not take him long to find a cab to Harley Street. Five, then six o'clock came and went, with no sign of him.

"Perhaps Mr Thornton took the seven o'clock train," suggested Edith. "I do not know how you manage with a husband who must work all day. Why, I should go distracted! Is it not terribly lonely for you when he is away?"

Margaret was seated on the sofa, her hands folded in perfect composure. "Of course, but he is never far away. It is not as if I cannot go out to see others, or even walk to the mill to see him if I wish." She refused to meet Edith's eyes when she gave this reassurance, for she dared not confess how very far such a rosy portrait was from the more recent reality.

"Margaret! You do not go into that filthy mill? Why, it is no wonder your hems are stained! No gown would be safe in such a place."

Margaret blinked innocently to her cousin. "Why should I not? Nearly half the people working at the mill are women."

"Yes, but not ladies. Surely the true ladies of Milton avoid the mills? Oh, do not tell me the other tradesmen's wives dare go. You do not associate with the workers, Margaret!"

"I have some good friends among them."

Edith gasped, fanning herself as if she would faint, and caught Mrs Shaw's gaze.

The elder lady clucked, shaking her head. "I do not like to think of a young lady brought up as you were walking about the mill, Margaret. I cannot think it would even be safe for you! Surely your reputation—"

"Aunt, I married a cotton manufacturer. I am, therefore, safely secured of my reputation, and Mr Thornton could hardly object. How could anyone think the less of me for walking among my husband's operations and speaking with those in his employ?"

Edith sighed. "Pray do not tell our friends here in London of your wild ways. I am sure they would not understand, and many would even think you had lost your head! Please, you must act your usual self at dinner tomorrow night. And you simply must wear that gown we decided upon, for you did look so ravishing in it."

"Edith, I thought we had agreed that you were not planning a large dinner for tomorrow. Mr Thornton will be here, and I would prefer—"

"Oh, do not be silly, Margaret! So many of our friends want to meet your new husband! They are all curious about him, and Mr Crenshaw, one of Henry's friends and a very influential person, they say, has a great interest in industry. I know he will want to ask Mr Thornton a number of questions."

Margaret suppressed a low groan. "It is a little too much to join a dinner of twenty-four. It hardly seems fitting."

"Twenty-four!" Edith scoffed. "I did trim down the guest list after you complained so. We shall only have eighteen."

"I do not feel proper at all about attending such a large party when I am still in half-mourning."

Mrs Shaw graced her niece with an affectionate smile. "You are a good girl, Margaret, to continue honouring your father and my poor dear sister so, but no one expects a newly married woman to hide away from society for an entire year for the death of a parent. Six months suffices for the blackest mourning, which not everyone even does, and you have completed that. We shall not have dancing, so you need not be left out of the enjoyment of the evening."

"I wish we could have dancing," lamented Edith, "but of course for you, Margaret, we will forego it." She patted her cousin's hand. "I know you have never liked dancing anyway, and I suppose your Mr Thornton does not dance at all."

Margaret did not answer, but she narrowed her eyes for an instant. She did not know if John danced! Mrs Wright had claimed that he did, long ago. She had never seen him do so in their acquaintance, but most gentleman did… although she had to remind herself that he was not a gentleman by birth and his formative years had been rather different from her own. How had he even learned? Needled by the realisation that another woman knew a detail about her husband that she did not, Margaret lapsed into another unhappy silence.

By half-past six, the family had decided they were weary of waiting for Mr Thornton's arrival and adjourned to take their evening tea. Margaret was listening every moment for someone to announce him, but the tea service was cleared away without ever seeing John Thornton.

"Captain," Margaret asked once they had settled again in the drawing-room, "what were the other arrival times for the Milton trains tonight?"

Captain Lennox glanced up from his paper. "Seven and ten. But sometimes the ten o'clock runs late. Last of the evening, you understand."

Margaret nodded silently, then her eyes found the clock on the mantel. It was already well after eight, and still John had not arrived. She began to fret, but then stilled herself. John rarely returned from the mill in the evenings until late, and he still had a train to catch. It was likely that he would have taken the last train, but the note he had sent with Dixon had said he intended to take the earlier one. She could only assume that some unexpected circumstance had arisen to keep him from returning to her when he had planned.

She amused herself with a book for the greater part of the evening. Ten-thirty. Eleven. Edith grew weary of her needlework and implored her to join her at the instrument. Exhausted, she nevertheless agreed rather than to retire, for she was determined that when her husband did arrive, she would be the first to greet him.

By midnight, she was truly beginning to worry. Was he not coming, after all? Had he sent a letter that had not arrived yet, telling her of some change in his plans? Her fatigue and aching for him conspired to invent irrational fears in her heart. Had there been some accident? Had John, the healthiest man she knew, at last worked himself to exhaustion and contracted the fever? Or had he found better amusements than visiting a wife he thought dull and fragile, among relatives who disdained him?

Sick with dread, she did not realise that her fingers were white on the music she turned for Edith. It was not until she accidentally tore one sheet and dropped the rest on the floor that Captain Lennox cleared his throat, causing all eyes to raise from the scattered pages. "Well, I am done in for the evening. Shall not we go above, my dear?"

"Oh, yes, let us retire, Margaret," Edith pleaded. "Surely, he will be here in the morning, you will see! Mamma has already gone to bed, and I fear I shall be of no use tomorrow preparing for the dinner party if I do not rest."

Outnumbered by the forces arrayed against her, Margaret gathered the piano music and surrendered. "I suppose he will," she mumbled half-heartedly.

~

The house was dark when John finally arrived. Someone had posted a manservant to watch for him, but even he seemed surprised to find the awaited guest arriving after one in the morning.

"Sir," the manservant spoke in a hushed tone as he took John's hat, "Mrs Thornton and the rest of the family retired well over an hour ago. Did you wish me to wake anyone?"

John's spirits sank. He would have given anything to gather Margaret in his arms just then, to seek her company after his travels and to allow her sweet voice to soothe his ragged heart. "No," he sighed. "I presume I am for the same room as before."

"Those were my instructions. Do you need me to show you the way?"

"No, thank you." He allowed the manservant to help him out of his coat and dragged himself wearily up the staircase, pausing at the second floor. He could see Margaret's door from where he stood.

How many times had he joined her in bed when she was already asleep? And she always turned to snuggle next to him, waking only enough to kiss him before slipping back into her dreams. How delicious it would be to cradle her to him after this long week, to sense her beside him as he slept, to listen to her soft breathing when he woke!

He lingered for another moment, allowing himself to drink in the temptation of going to his wife. But those memories, they were from the Time Before… those fleeting days of heady paradise, before life with its griefs and cares had stripped the joy from his love's eyes. Before she had begun to regret…. His hand dropped to the balustrade again, and he climbed the next flight of stairs.

~

"Mr Thornton, it is a pleasure to see you again, sir."

John was caught off guard, his sleep-starved eyes not even looking ahead as he came down the stairs the next morning. He glanced up, felt the creases etch into his own forehead, and hesitated for just a moment before answering. "Mr Lennox. I had not expected to see you here."

"Yes, my brother and his wife wished to walk to the park again this morning, so I came to escort the family. It is my great pleasure that they often invite me on their outings."

"Do they? You are a fortunate man, indeed."

"If you are looking for Mrs Thornton, I do not believe she is come down yet."

John swept Lennox with a quizzical look. "You also were waiting for her?"

"Well—" Lennox smiled self-deprecatingly—"I purposely arrived early to place myself at the family's disposal. I am never quite certain when the ladies will be prepared to go, so I always ask when I enter the house."

"You are a very enterprising fellow. I do not know any ladies who take their constitutional before eight in the morning."

Lennox laughed. "You have caught me! It is true, although I have known Mrs Thornton to be ready before nine. I came a little early to break my fast at my brother's house, for my own housekeeper desires a day off, and as a bachelor, my household is not deeply staffed. You know how it is, Thornton, we must give way now and again to those in our employ?"

"Indeed."

Behind him he heard a faint intake of breath, and both men turned to see Margaret standing at the top of the stairs. Her eyes bore a strange sheen, but she was smiling faintly. John postured himself to welcome her, his hand extended. Her fingers slipped into his, but when she raised her eyes, she was not looking at him.

"Good morning," she spoke softly, as much to Lennox as to himself. He tightened his fingers around hers, in his best approximation of a warm greeting.

"Good morning, Mrs Thornton." Lennox was smiling broadly. "You are looking well today. Will you please excuse me?" He inclined his head to John once more, then wandered towards the breakfast room where other voices could already be heard. Only then did Margaret look him in the face.

"I am sorry I was late, love. I had to catch the last train, and there was a stoppage at Leicester. I thought I would never arrive!"

"We were all worried for you."

"Well, it is no matter now, for I am here. I hope you passed the week pleasantly? Surely your cousin was happy to have you here."

Margaret seemed to hesitate. "She was very happy." She pressed her lips together and drew in a small breath. "Yes, it was a good week. But I missed you."

She looked up to him again with those clear, sincere eyes, and every instinct he possessed cried out for him to carry her up to his room for a proper reunion. But no… she had not been receptive of that kind of intimacy of late, nor would he be wise to embarrass her in her family's home. It was better this way. He gave her a gentle smile and pressed a soft kiss to the back of her fingers, then led her towards the breakfast room.

"John—" she stayed him—"how is everyone in Milton? Are they improving?"

Oh, how he hated to answer this question! "Not as quickly as we might wish, but yes, matters are somewhat better. There are still new illnesses each day, but not so many. Margaret... the youngest Boucher child is faring rather poorly."

"Johnny, the littlest? He was his poor mother's pride and joy! Oh, it cannot be."

"I am afraid so. Higgins says it is a serious case, but they are doing all that can be done. I asked Donaldson to look in on them and take them a basket of fresh apples. There is so little any can do."

"I could go to him! I wish to bring them some comfort. John, you must let me, as soon as we return home, for I know it would encourage him."

"We will speak of this later," he interrupted, but there was a defiant spark in her eye that promised that she would not yield happily. He tried to will away any discord with a warm smile and a touch to her cheek. "Come, I have not yet greeted the rest of your family."

She nodded, fighting back the argument simmering in her bearing and looking now at the floor.

"Has...." He hesitated. "Has Lennox been here often?"

"Nearly every day. He often takes meals here."

"Indeed. He seems to be rather close to his brother." He stopped, trying to catch her eye, but she would not look up.

"John... I may as well tell you that Edith has planned a dinner party for this evening. She wished for everyone to meet you. I asked her not to, but she insisted."

"It is her house, and we are guests. Why do you seem so troubled? Did you think I would be displeased?"

"No—" she lifted her shoulders uncomfortably—"it is just... they are not the sort of people you are used to, that is all."

He touched her chin, lifting her eyes to his. "I think I can handle it. Come, let us go in to everyone."

~

"We need not walk all the way to the park if you are too weary, Mrs Thornton." Henry Lennox paused solicitously at the door as the family were donning their outer clothes. "I understand you had a late evening, and we shall have another again tonight."

Margaret glanced at Henry in slight confusion as John drew near to take her arm. "I am quite well, Mr Lennox." She looked away quickly, hoping John would do the same, for he was beginning to glare at her old friend.

Henry backed away in surrender, but Margaret could see from the corner of her vision that he did not stray far. John's jaw was clenched as he buttoned his own overcoat. He had moved to help her, but the manservant had already done so. He stepped back and offered her his arm to lead her down the steps of the house.

"Henry means no harm, John," she reassured her husband as the family's steps separated them along the walk. "And he was always very considerate."

He jerked his head to glance at her with a look of consternation. "Yes," he agreed through clenched teeth. "I imagine he was."

She glanced up at his profile, and could see the muscles in his cheek working, even his nostrils flickering, but he kept his eyes straight ahead. Perhaps she ought not to have used Henry's given name in John's hearing.

"Mr Thornton—" Henry fell back from the larger part of the party to walk beside John. "Have you been much in London?"

"Often enough," he answered evenly.

"Excellent. I do not know if you can have been to Regent's Park before, but it is a favourite among our family. Is that not right, Mrs Thornton? I believe we have been coming here for two or three years now as a regular thing whenever we are all together. Have you seen it before, sir?"

"I have."

"A fine thing it is, that all in London may now come whenever they choose. Why, when I was a boy, it used to be that only…. Well—" he stopped himself, looking somewhat abashed. "I suppose that it is a new world we live in, is it not Mr Thornton?"

"How do you mean?"

"Why, you remember how it was, surely. Only certain days were open to the public, but the classes mingle more freely than they have ever done before. This industrial era of ours has seen the rise of a large middle class of persons, and the distinctions have become rather blurred. I think that a fine thing, do you not?"

"I think a man's worth ought to be determined by his merits, not his birth."

"Truer words were never spoken, sir! Do you know, Mrs Thornton and I were speaking of this very thing just a few days ago. How do your workers stand in Milton, Mr Thornton? Is their status somewhat higher than the common labourer?"

Margaret tightened her grip upon her husband's arm, wishing she could warn him off from some harsh comment he might regret, and equally frustrated with Henry for provoking him. But John was annoyed and would not now step back.

"The experienced weaver has employable skills. He will always be in demand because he knows how to do something that others have not learned. Naturally, his pay is somewhat higher."

"So, his wages are better than a common dustman or farmer? Do not they work equally hard, and does not each occupation require some expertise? What then of judging a man by his merits?"

"The workers in the factories are paid better than other trades because the profit potential in manufacturing is greater. I would recommend it over many other positions, particularly for the women. A woman can earn half again in the mills what she might as a seamstress or a domestic, and she still has some hours to herself after her work is done for the day."

"Most interesting. Are the women paid as well as the men? I do not see how they could be, for a man could do two or three times the work, and for longer hours, according to the law."

"I have not implied that they are, but as I have said, they are paid better in my mill than the gentry pays for household service, and they do not rise to their work so early as your own kitchen maid."

Henry laughed. "Very well, Mr Thornton, I see you have an answer for all my questions! I hope someday to tour one of the mills. It is fascinating what you lot have done for England."

John lifted his chin in acknowledgment, but he glanced to Margaret. He did not speak a word to her, merely offered a tight smile then raised his eyes again to the park they neared. For Margaret, it was an ironic moment. Only a few days ago she had walked the same path and had such a similar conversation with Henry, all while missing John. And now he had come, and so little was different!

"Ah!" Henry was behaving nonchalantly now, and he gestured ahead. "There is the tree! I have always loved looking upon that old oak. Do you remember, Mrs Thornton, I believe it was two summers ago, just before my brother and Mrs Lennox were married. We came here for a picnic, and it was such a hot day—do you recall? What a nuisance the squirrels were! I had not known they were so bold, demanding little bits of bread and titbits of fruit. Yet you continued to encourage them, Mrs Thornton. My, how cross Mrs Lennox was with you for that!"

Margaret smiled hesitantly, chuckling at the memory of Edith's frustration, but then she looked up at John's face. He had gone quiet again, his jaw tense and his gaze fixed straight ahead. Margaret cleared her throat and fell silent.

~

The visit to the park lasted a great deal longer than John would have expected for such unreliable weather. He had become agitated by the colour in Margaret's cheeks, concerned by the cold rigidity of her hands despite her gloves, and frustrated by the oblivious Mrs Lennox who thought only of her own delights. He was most greatly annoyed, however, by Henry Lennox. The man seemed ever at his left hand, always eager to make some witty remark calculated to make Margaret smile and to imply a former intimacy—or worse, to impress upon him his own status as an outsider to their previous revelries.

Margaret did not engage Lennox more than superficially, but the fact that the pair had once enjoyed a vibrant fellowship was apparent to anyone. That Lennox felt free to speak to Margaret about her opinions on a wide variety of subjects unnerved him. At one point, the man even lamented that the weather was still too cool for Margaret to bring her watercolours, else she could have captured the pond and the early ducks that walked so determinedly about its perimeter, searching for new sprigs of grass.

This caused John to stop and stare quizzically at his wife. "I did not know you painted."

"Only landscapes, and occasionally flowers," she admitted. "I am not skilled at painting faces, although I have in the past had some success with very young children. For some reason their faces were easier for me to capture."

"Indeed, and you have not lost your talent, Mrs Thornton," Henry agreed. Then to John, he explained, "Mrs Lennox at last persuaded her to try painting little Sholto two days ago, and the painting does credit to both the artist and the subject. I have often thought Mrs Thornton really underestimated her own talents. Perhaps one day soon, she will have ample opportunity to practice in her own home." Lennox was distracted just then by his sister-in-law, and he walked away after dropping his innocent remark, but the darkness fell once more over Margaret's face.

John watched her in concern. When she spoke nothing for several minutes, he turned her to face him and noticed that her eyes had regained that peculiar sheen. "I am afraid this week has not been as restful for you as I had hoped."

"Do not be troubled, John. I am well—" she drew a shuddering breath, and then nodded jerkily. "Truly, I am."

He continued gazing at her, unconvinced, but she looked away without granting him another opportunity to ask more questions. The party returned to the house after that, and upon their arrival Margaret went above stairs to change. He saw little of her through the afternoon, as the ladies of the house retired to rest before the evening's dinner party. John kept to his room, preferring his own company to that of the Lennox brothers.

Some hours later, after a most dissatisfying and forgettable afternoon, he found himself standing in the dinner receiving line beside his wife. She was attired in a gown he had never seen before—a silvery grey masterpiece of silk which was brightened only by her powdered cheeks and a dusky pink rose in her dark hair. She was... breath-taking. Married to her though he was, he had been parched for words when he had first beheld her.

He still felt the oafish fool, a brute standing beside a queen. She looked stately and elegant, the very image of the untouchable, but it seemed to him that the icy colour of the gown had drained the life from her beautiful features. Cool and serene, that was the sense she projected, and perhaps it was fitting, after all. A woman who yielded little in the way of warmth gave little of vulnerability, little of herself to strangers. And it was for him to stand beside her and attempt to be her match in the eyes of these London folk! He straightened his shoulders, smiled only when she did, and held his breath.

Henry Lennox introduced to him to a friend of his, a Mr Crenshaw and his wife. He also met a Mr and Mrs White; a widowed Mrs Harvey and her son Sterling Harvey, a man about his own age; and three younger couples whose names he did not remember. Regrettably, the social strictures of the evening forbade him to escort his own wife to dinner or to sit beside her at table. Before that, he was permitted to remain near her, but compelled also to mingle with people who spoke guardedly and surveyed him under arched eyebrows.

When the dinner bell rang, he offered his arm to Mrs Harvey as he had been instructed to do. Margaret walked ahead of him with Henry Lennox, just behind Edith Lennox and Sterling Harvey. She glanced over her shoulder once as she was led away, but she was speaking amiably to her dinner companion. It seemed she had no objections to the arrangement.

Once seated, he noted in dismay that she was far down and on the same side of the table as himself, so he could not even claim the pleasure of admiring her from a distance. He could hear her voice, though, and it burned his ears at every moment. For the first time in... a long while... she sounded light and gay as she spoke with the man she must have wished in his place. John forced a tight line to his mouth—hardly a smile—but he scarcely heard other voices and his dinner held no flavour.

After the second course was carried away and several bottles of wine had flowed, Crenshaw raised his glass from across the table, drawing John's attention. "Mr Thornton, this is a most fortuitous meeting. I have been eager to speak with someone of your profession, and your reputation precedes you. I am hoping you can help me to understand a bit of your trade."

John tried not to hear the tinkling of Margaret's laughter down the table in response to some jest of Mr Lennox's. *How long since he had heard her laugh?*

Aloud, he simply said, "I would be happy to oblige, sir. Of what did you wish to speak?"

"Well, a very good friend of mine has a seat at Parliament, and he has asked me to assist him in gathering information for a new law they are considering regarding the factories. Unfortunately, my experience has all been in tobacco, so I confess that I know very little of textiles or the mills. I wonder, sir, can you tell me about a typical day at your mill? What time do the workers arrive?"

"We have two shifts, but before the day begins, the engineer arrives to stoke the fires for the steam engines. Work begins at seven because that is when the overhead line starts, and everyone must be at their place. We have a half hour dinner break at eleven, and then the women and the children from the first shift go home by one-thirty. The second shift of women and children come on, with a supper break at five. The mill shuts down for the evening at eight."

"And the men work the twelve hours? Do they not grow tired of such a long day?"

"If I were to ask any of them to shorten their shift, they would be angry with me for cutting their pay. In fact, if the law permitted, many of the women would wish to work more hours as well."

"And what of the children, how old are they? I have heard they work as young as eight."

"In some mills, perhaps. I see no benefit in working with children who are so young. There is nothing a child of eight can do that a child of thirteen cannot do better, and I find they grow up healthier if they do not spend so many years of their youth inside a mill."

"How very interesting! I am curious about something you just said, regarding the health of your workers. I have heard much of this horrible brown lung disease. What can you tell me about it?"

John glanced around, becoming aware that several of the other diners had ceased their own conversations to attend his. He was the curiosity, he supposed, the only member of the party who had laboured for his bread. He paused for a moment to gather his thoughts, then replied.

"It is a wasting disease. There is nothing that can be done, and it is still all too common. It was worse five or ten years ago, and there remain those who contracted the disease in their youth."

The guests had quieted even more, and his ears could discern no conversation from Margaret's end of the table. Undoubtedly, she was listening.

"But what is being done now? You say it was worse. How has it been improved?"

"I am certain you have heard of the wheels which many mill owners had installed in their sheds to blow the fluff away. I did so six years ago, though not all my workers approved, and certainly they came at no mean expense. There was no immediate benefit, but since that time, we have had less disease. That, coupled with refusing to hire very young children, has done a good deal to improve the health of my workers in the last ten years. There is little that can be done for the humidity and the temperature because the sheds must be kept warm and damp for the weaving process. There was some doctor a few years ago who suggested that all the workers wear a light cotton mask over their faces to protect them, but in such humid conditions, they all refused."

"Mr Thornton—" this came from a voice a little farther down the table. John glanced to Harvey, who was seated directly opposite Margaret. "What of the influenza outbreak? Is it really spreading to the other cities?"

"I have not heard it has, but we have seen such things before."

"How has it impacted everyone in Milton?" asked Crenshaw. "Has it crippled your mill? I keep hearing of how many are afflicted."

"It has done no one any favours. My mill was working at half capacity this last month, simply because so many were too ill to work."

"That must have been an economic windfall for you!" observed Crenshaw. "Half the labour to pay during a time of slow trade, without the bother of inciting a riot?"

John gritted his teeth. "I would far rather have all my workers at their stations, sir. However, I believe we are slowly mending."

Mr Harvey spoke up again. "I heard there have been a number of deaths. Most of them were the working class, too poor for good food and proper care. Is that true?"

John drew a bracing breath and placed his hands upon his knees under the table. "It is."

"I, for one, who would like to hear a lady's impression of the epidemic." This could only be Henry Lennox, down at the far end.

John leaned forward and found that Henry, at the opposite end of the table, was doing the same—looking at Margaret but frequently glancing up to make certain that John saw the intimate way he was leaning towards her.

"Mrs Thornton, you have many friends among the workers, do you not? How do you feel about their conditions? Has their situation been worsened by the way they live and work?"

Margaret touched a napkin to her mouth, refusing to look up at anyone. "I know those who have suffered."

"But have the mills worsened their circumstances?" Henry Lennox insisted. "Do you think they would be faring so poorly if they were say, farmers in Hampshire?"

John watched his wife swallow carefully. "No. I think it is a good deal worse for the factory workers."

This brought a loud murmur from around the table, and several knowing, condescending glances in John's direction.

"How so, Mrs Thornton?" Crenshaw asked.

She looked up, still reluctant to meet John's gaze. "Their close living conditions. Sanitation is not what it is here in London, or even the country. They work for so many hours, and in such hard conditions, I cannot help but think that increases the spread of disease. The mills, do you see, are dreadfully stifling, and many of the houses are damp. And—" she bit her lip, still looking down—"their income does not stretch so far in the city."

"Oh, but we spoke only today that mill workers often make better wages than other employees. Is that not true?"

"Everything costs more in Milton than it does in Helstone, to use your example of a farmer's situation. Factory wages have raised the general price of living. Many families find it difficult to support themselves as they wish. I think of the families where a mother struggles to raise children on her own, or where one family has seven or eight children all too young for factory work. That is very common. Those years until the oldest children begin earning a wage can nearly starve a family."

"So, do you not hold with Mr Thornton's belief that the children should not be employed until they are older?"

John watched as Margaret surveyed Mr Crenshaw, bristling at the trap neatly set for her by her questioners.

She hesitated, her eyes flitting about the table at every person but himself. "I am not in favour of children working at all," she answered in a low voice.

"But Mrs Thornton, you have just said yourself that until a family's children begin earning a wage, they may suffer extreme hardship. What do you propose as a remedy? Higher wages? Forgive me for imposing myself upon a lady so, but I am earnestly interested in your opinions, Mrs Thornton. You are in the unique position of one who came to know industry rather intimately from the original perspective of an outsider."

Margaret inclined her head. "As you have said, sir, I was an outsider. I do not imagine I have the answers you seek."

"Mrs Thornton—" Crenshaw spoke to Margaret but glanced to John with an apologetic smile—"I beg to differ. You seem to have rather deep opinions on the matter, and I would wager they might be more objective and informed than the perspectives of many others. This point interests me very much. Do you think last year's strike could have been prevented, had this matter been resolved somehow?"

She hesitated, blinking those dark lashes. "Naturally, it would have… but I am sure that such a solution is beyond my powers to offer, sir."

"But you were sympathetic to both sides, were you not?" Lennox put in. "Surely you did not condone the way the masters had been treating their workers?"

"Of course not, but neither can I approve of violence and open rebellion in the streets," she answered quickly. "I can only summarise by stating that there was provocation on both sides."

"Was not Mr Thornton the man who gained a reputation for not bargaining with the unions when he brought in Irish workers?" Crenshaw laughed. "Provocation, indeed!"

Margaret's cheeks deepened to a crimson blush, and she glanced guiltily in his direction. John leaned back in his chair. It was not his place to answer, but his expression was calculated to intimidate Crenshaw and Lennox into silence, if possible. It was not to be—in fact, his growing irritation only seemed to fuel their improper curiosity.

Margaret fingered her glass. "I think all sides learned a great deal from those strikes," she faltered. "And all are still paying the price."

"What can you mean by that, Mrs Thornton?" Mr Harvey asked. The rest of the table seemed intent upon the subject as well.

Margaret risked another glance down towards John, who had leaned forward again to catch her expression. She paused, and looked as if she would make no answer, but Harvey spoke up again.

"Perhaps I should ask more specifically regarding my own question, Mrs Thornton. Mr Lennox asked earlier if you thought the general living conditions in Milton have worsened the influenza outbreak. Do you think the lingering effects of the strike and the poor pay of the workers have exacerbated the issue?"

"I..." she shook her head again. "I do not feel it is my place to speak on that."

John could contain himself no longer. "I must correct one point, sir, as Mrs Thornton has demurred. These questions have no basis, for we have already established that my workers are better paid than others, and the strike, as you have said, was a year ago."

"Forgive me, Mr Thornton, but I spoke in reflection of Mrs Thornton's statement about the cost of living in the city in comparison to such pay, for they must live where they work, is that not correct? Mrs Thornton, you mentioned extreme privation—have you indeed seen cases where a family was close to starving?"

John's face heated in anger. What sort of gentleman openly interrogated a lady at dinner and then cut off her husband when he attempted to speak in her defence? And what sort of host did not redirect the conversation?

Margaret was staring at the table now, blinking as if she wished she could refuse to answer. Every eye was on her, however, and John could say nothing without making matters even more uncomfortable.

"I... have seen it," she confessed. "The wife and children of a man driven mad with desperation during the strike—he despaired and took his own life."

A few voices hummed indistinctly.

"Good heavens," Lennox murmured in sympathy. "The children did not starve, did they?"

"They became orphans—the mother did not long outlive her husband."

"But surely, someone must have been in a position to offer some aid!" cried the gentleman. "Who is it to take an interest in the orphans of factory workers? What of the mill owners or the Union?"

"In the end, it was neither," she answered, a hint of pride glowing in her cheeks. "A neighbour, a kind soul who had neither liking for, nor responsibility to the dead man, took all six children as his own."

John watched as a few heads shook—some in gloomy doubt, but some in clear approval.

"I take it this is a friend of yours, Mrs Thornton. The man is to be commended," Lennox smiled, even raised his glass slightly.

"Indeed," Crenshaw agreed, "but this is a great wrong! Why was there not someone of better resources to take up the task? What of their precious Union? What is it for, but to see to the workers? And what of the bosses, who were certainly making their own fortune off the dead man while he lived? Have they not the responsibility to look after their own workers?"

Margaret gazed back in silent attendance, not fluttering even an eyelash. Crenshaw tilted his head, but when she seemed as if she intended no answer, he sighed and drained the contents of his wineglass.

"Do you not agree?" Lennox prompted softly at Margaret's elbow.

She swallowed and looked to her companion. "Yes… I mean, no… perhaps another could have… it is not so simple as you say."

"Who was the man's employer, Mrs Thornton?"

She glanced up, then her gaze fell to the table again. "Mr Thornton."

~

The last of the guests finally received their coats and bade their hosts a good evening. Margaret rested her hand on John's arm, but it was stiff and unreceptive to her touch. She had puzzled over his behaviour all night, but there was no opportunity to ask what had troubled him. There was an indignant set to his chin as he made his short bows. His manners had been abrupt after dinner, his attitude speaking clearly that he would rather be anywhere else in the world than in the same room with these Londoners.

For her own part, she had forced a smile and made light of his dry quips, as if it were his natural caprices surfacing rather than a simmering resentment towards some unknown object. She had so wished for everyone to be impressed by him—his manners were always impeccable, his intelligence and good sense unparalleled among his peers. With ladies he was always gracious, with gentleman always witty and clever. Why should he alter so materially in the presence of Edith's guests?

He was no longer looking at the door as it closed. Neither was anyone else, for everyone had sensed a growing discomfort among the residents of the house. The party all made paltry excuses to retire at once, claiming fatigue or some grand schemes for the morrow.

Margaret, eager to speak with John alone, bade her cousin a good evening as gracefully as she could, and asked her husband to escort her up the stairs. He gave her his arm, still refusing to meet her eyes. At her door, he released her with a tight, "Good evening."

"John, will you not come in? I have not seen you all week and we have hardly spoken today."

He looked down the hall towards the stair, raised his hand in a gesture of acceptance, but stopped just inside the door. She smiled in welcome and reached to touch him, but he put his hands stiffly behind his back, as if he were a martyr waiting for the pyres to be lighted.

"John, what is troubling you? I have seldom seen you look so unhappy."

His eyes widened incredulously. "You ask what troubles me? Do you not know?"

She shook her head. "That conversation at dinner was unpleasant, but—"

"I had little idea that you thought so poorly of me, Margaret."

"Poorly? What can you mean? I spoke only the truth in response to their questions. I did not intend any of it as a condemnation of you."

"Did you not! You cast every recrimination you could think of in my direction. I had forgotten, I suppose, and I should not have. Boucher's death was my fault, as was that of your friend Bessie Higgins. The union was right to revolt, their children are all mine to look after, and I deserved what I got. I am a hard-hearted tyrant, bent only upon profit, and I care too little to do anything for anyone! That is what your friends all think of me after this evening."

She cringed in pained reflection. *Oh, dear. Not this old debate again!* She began cautiously, attempting to soothe him. "They are not *my* friends."

"Are they not? What of Henry Lennox?"

"Henry? He is a friend, and has been for a long time."

"Yes, a good deal longer than you and I have known one another."

"John! Surely you are not jealous of him! I told you once before that I would not marry him when he asked me."

"You did not marry me the first time I asked, either. I wonder, would he have had the same results as I upon a second attempt? Are you sorry you did not wait a week?"

The fire erupted in her core. "How dare you accuse me of changeable sentiments! I misunderstood you before and then came to see my own error. That was not the case with Henry, and you know it very well!"

"I understood from the beginning that he wished to have you for his own. He has done well, cultivating the seeds of discontent while I was away. I daresay he found fertile enough ground for it."

She clenched her teeth, her fingers knotting. "If he has, it is because you have done the ploughing yourself! I have never seen you so insolent as you were this evening. At least Henry never lost his countenance over something so silly and humiliated me in public!"

"'Silly!' If that is how you and that leech perceive the insults done my character tonight, then perhaps he is not a true man, and your esteem not a thing to be desired after all. You prefer a whelp who performs well at dinner parties to a man who has earned the right to his self-respect?"

Her jaw fell. "Insults to your character! We only spoke of facts. Are they so difficult for you to hear? Listen to yourself! You sound like a puerile braggart who deserves his bruises for provoking a larger fellow. Can you really be so insufferably small-minded that you must strut about as a cock claiming his territory?"

He spun towards her and hissed, "Aye, and do I not have the right? You are my *wife*. If Lennox has forgotten that fact, perhaps I may remind him!"

She restrained her impulse to cry out his name as a frustrated epithet. Seething, she clenched her fists and sought the last shreds of his tattered reason. "That will not be necessary! Am I not my own person, and do you have no faith in my dignity? This is not about Henry Lennox, whatever you have persuaded yourself to believe."

"No, I suppose it is not." He turned sharply and paced by her door. "I think I am beginning to understand my own place better than I have ever done before. I was a fool, but no longer."

"What can you mean by that?"

"I mean that these are your people. I never shall measure up in their eyes. Oh, they will ask me all manner of questions, perhaps even find my experience and knowledge useful to themselves, but I shall always be a dirty tradesman who dared to step over the lines of class."

"You are wrong!"

"Am I? Was your family so eager to embrace me?"

"I... well, not at first, perhaps, but only because they did not know you as I do. I had hoped you would make a better impression upon them, but tonight you showed yourself to be an easily offended, taciturn, and imperious capitalist who thinks solely in terms of trade. I know that is not the truth!"

"Do you?" he crossed his arms in contempt.

She shook her head, pleading with him to understand. "Why could you not show them the intelligent, thoughtful man I know?"

"Perhaps he does not truly exist. Besides, that is not what they came to see. They desired a spectacle, and I suppose I performed as they expected. And you, my own wife, played right into their hands!"

"I had no such intention. How could I fail to respond to direct questions? I spoke only the truth."

He scowled. "And you enjoyed the opportunity to air your opinions, as you could not do in Milton of late. Opinions you may have, I would not begrudge you that. I know we do not agree in every particular, but I never expected you to disrespect me, and everything I have ever done, in so public a setting. I suppose I should have!"

"Disrespect you! How have I done so?"

But he would not heed, for his temper was already high. "Poor Margaret Hale, the victim of her careless father and unfortunate timing," he snarled with derision.

"John! How dare—"

"You never liked Milton, you were never comfortable with my position, and there have been few enough pleasant times in our marriage to smooth the way."

"That is not the whole truth." She tried to reach for his arm, but he pulled away. Her hand dropped, and she stood awkward and alone. "It is true that there are certain matters on which we do not agree, but—"

"Why did you marry me, Margaret? Was it a moment of weakness? Sentimentality? Fleeting passion?"

She drew back, the blood draining from her face even as the fury tumbled in her heart. "How could you say such a thing to me?"

"Can you deny that you have been unhappy?" He turned to glare at her, his face pinched in pained laughter. "I thought we would do well together. I had even fooled myself into thinking we had something that might endure, that I could love you enough to raise you from all your griefs. But now I understand it was a mistake, nothing more than a trick of timing and vulnerability on both our parts."

She was shaking her head, tears spilling over her cheeks. "A mistake?" she whispered.

"And there is nothing we can do about it now. It is too late, and we have known one another too well to reverse what is in the past. I cannot give you your freedom, but I can give you what you wish—a life in London, free from the stink of the factories and the harsh reality of poverty surrounding you. You may live comfortably among your relations, well supplied with funds even, so long as I have work."

Her throat was burning now, and she could scarcely make out his twisted visage for the sheet of sorrow clouding her eyes. "What are you saying, John?"

"You know very well what I am saying, Margaret! I will keep our vows to my death, but I will not require you to live with me. Stay here with your simpering cousin and her foolish husband. Take tea and walk to the park with that snake Lennox. I suppose it is as well that our child did not survive, for that is one less thread binding you to me. Enjoy the company of another and think as little of me as you wish. You may have everything else but his bed and his name, but as you have shown little inclination for a man's company of late, and even less for honouring the same man's place in your life, I doubt those constraints will trouble you."

This accusation broke the final regret in Margaret's heart. Until that moment, she had been ready to plead, to cajole, to fall to the ground and kiss his boots in supplication, but that bitter allegation, the fury snapping in his eyes, kindled a defiant passion in her own. "You think so little of me? Then perhaps you should go, sir. Free yourself from all responsibility regarding me, for I will not accept a farthing of yours in support!"

His chest heaved, and his fists balled as he glared back at her. "Very well! I leave in the morning, and you need not fear I will be visiting you often."

Twenty

"**M**a'am," Jane bobbed her curtsey before Hannah's sewing chair, extending a note to her mistress. "Mr Thornton is not receiving visitors. He sent it back."

Hannah took her own note, still sealed just as it had been when she sent it, and gazed up to the girl in confusion. "You could have left it, as you have done before."

Jane's eyes widened in helpless appeal. "He wouldna' allow it, ma'am! I made to drop it on his desk, an' he bellowed somethin' fierce! I were afraid to go against wha' he said, ma'am."

Hannah scowled. It had been over a week since John's latest return from London, and still he had not acknowledged her repeated requests to join them for tea or dinner. In fact, the only greeting she had from him was a short note explaining that he was too unwell to attend services on Sunday, and not to risk sickness herself by calling on him.

That was a thin bit of fiction, for everyone said the master of the mill was certainly not lying abed sick. Word had it that he had been a raging despot all week, and even Williams was judiciously avoiding any contact with the awakened tyrant.

"Very well, Jane," Hanna muttered. "I will call on him myself. Please see that the doctor's tea is ready when he comes home."

Hannah wrapped herself in her new lavender cloak—a gift from Robert, as she now called him—and ventured the ten-minute walk to Marlborough Street. She entered the gates just as the break whistle blew and stepped aside to allow the greater part of the throng to pass. The machines were quiet, and the sounds of voices and feet were the only clamour reaching her ears.

As they scuffled by, she realised that most of the workers fleeing the mill doors for their break had their heads down, hands stuffed into pockets or crossed over chests. They did not speak to one another, so the shouted words she could hear from within were not theirs… she sighed. She had drawn near enough now to make out the words and recognise the savage voice, boiling from her own son's throat. She shook her head as the last of the crowd filed out before her.

When she was able to push her way inside, she found him. John had kept back some of the weavers and was storming about a bad lot of cloth, now ruined because a machine had been run when it should have been stopped and mended. Heads hung universally low, eyes darted from one man to another, save for the worker who stood nearest John. Higgins, his face red, was giving answer for accusation, defending his lads the best he could against the master's fury.

"I do not care if the line was running!" John barked. "I see a dozen yards of ruined cloth!"

"Only one edge!" Higgins shot back, his own stance squared for combat. "'Tis more than suitable for piecework, and 'twould'a made a bigger fuss to shut th' line down twenty minutes before th' dinner break!"

John rounded on the man, his eyes spitting rage at the piquant old fellow who would dare defy him. He opened his mouth, and Hannah did not doubt that his next words would have dismissed Higgins and that entire crew from Marlborough Mills, but he stopped just before uttering them. His face hardened when he noticed his mother, and his shoulders dropped.

"Go, then," he hissed at the men. "Make your repairs so this does not happen again, or I will sack every last one of you!"

Hannah arched a brow and waited for him to thread towards her. She set her jaw grimly, and without a word, turned and led the way to his office. Once inside, she waited until he had closed the door and then demanded in an icy voice, "John David Thornton, what has got into you?"

"Me? What of you, waltzing through the mill, Mother? It is not a lady's place."

"As if I have never been inside the mill that fed and clothed me all those years! As if I did not know its workings nearly as well as you do!"

"It has never been yours to manage, and even less so now, when you belong to another. The mill is no place for a lady."

"You mean, rather, that a conference with your lessers is not a place for a woman to contradict you! That is what really troubled you, is it not?"

"If I must be brutally honest, yes. What business can you have in searching me out and glaring at me as if you were scolding a mere boy, and that before my hands!"

"John, what is troubling you? You have been a recluse and a monster of late, and that is not the son I know."

"Is it not? Have I not always been a beast at work and a cur at home?"

She rolled her eyes. "John Thornton, you are speaking nonsense. Tell me you have not quarrelled with Margaret."

He clipped out a short, bitter laugh. "What makes you suggest that? I am her humble servant, as always."

"And your hackles raised the instant a woman dared to stand up to you! What have you done, my boy?"

"Nothing I should not have done long ago. I was a fool, but I am not a doormat."

"So, she has thrown off your care and protection, or was it you yourself who withdrew? Is that why she remains in London?"

He turned away. "It is not your affair. Go on back to your home and leave me to my own business."

"You are my business. Tell me, what was the substance of this ridiculous little spat?"

"Do not—" he whirled back—"do not attempt to make light of it! We were mismatched from the beginning. You were right to doubt my wisdom in that matter. Would that I had listened then! But the damage is done, and now she regrets that she ever heard my name. Would that Hale had kept his sorry place in Helstone and I never had the misfortune to look on her!"

"Don't be such a fool," she snapped, in a tone she might once have reserved for Fanny. "That girl answered for a part of you, and you for her. I had never even believed such a thing possible outside the realm of some ridiculous poets."

"And that is where it should remain. You were right to marry sensibly, without confusing the matter with feeling. All such folly has brought me was the stripping back of whatever defences I might have possessed."

"And she thrust her sword into your heart with relish, did she not? I always thought she would do so one day."

He turned his head to peer at her quizzically. "What do you mean?"

"The pitiless jade!" she sneered. "I knew how it would be. Once returned to the bosom of her fashionable relations, she would renounce any feeling for you and persuade herself that she had been badly used, pressured into a marriage that was beneath her!"

His brow furrowed, but he did not speak.

"Aye, I suppose she demanded a generous allowance to replace all the gowns that are filled with the stench of coal smoke. She will be gracing the finest houses of London, no doubt, distancing herself as far as she might from trade in general, and you most particularly."

"Mother—" he shook his head—"she is not a social climber. I pray, do not spin matters to look worse than they are."

"As if I could! She played her hand well, the heartless baggage. She would know that you will fund her lifestyle handsomely, and she may live as she pleases without the stigma of spinsterhood."

"Mother! This is not your affair!"

Hannah tilted her head. "It is only a pity she waited to display her true colours. I wonder that she bore your attentions so long! I might not have felt compelled to marry and leave the house myself, but I suppose it is just as well that I did. It will make matters easier on you when the mill fails."

He was staring, his mouth agape. "*When?* It is a surety now, and you do not even have faith enough in me to doubt the demise of all I have laboured for?"

She shrugged, a calculated gesture foreign to her usual mannerisms. "Did I not witness you only moments ago tearing your work apart with your own hands? Let it burn to the ground, and then you may be free to move on. Perhaps you might sail for America if you cannot make a go of it here."

He had narrowed his eyes. "Mother, if you think I am behaving wrongly, tell me plainly to my face rather than abusing me with your ridiculous fancies until I lose my temper."

"From what I understand, you have been losing your temper all week, so I should not be surprised to see you do so now. What are you going to do, John?"

"What can I do? No amount of hard work on my part will restore the mill to profitability. It is beyond what one man can do."

"I ask what you are doing regarding your wife."

He raked his fingers through his hair and began to pace. "What would you have me do? I cannot force the woman to respect me, nor to wish to return to my home."

"So, you have given up already? I had thought better of you than that, John."

"You just finished telling me she was only acting true to her character!"

She snorted. "And you allowed me to persuade you? You are worse off than I imagined. Where is my son who never backed down from adversity? Where is the man who was made new when he found love with that woman?"

"What good has that brought me? It was all a lie, a futile effort. I have wasted myself in trying to hold on to something that should never have been mine."

"You would so easily surrender, then? You do not try to mend whatever is broken, so that she who once cherished you so well might forsake this London foolishness and return to you? Or was the fault yours alone, and you are too stubborn to apologise? Serve you right if she stays there."

He was shaking his head, his shoulders bent away from her, but she was not deceived by the tightly controlled voice when he did speak. "I would not persist in tormenting her. If she wishes to remain there, if she is so ashamed of me, there is nothing more I can do. I have made fool enough of myself."

She emitted a disgusted sigh. "There is no more brittle thing on earth than a man's witless pride. Very well, then, sit in your empty house and watch your business fail alone, with none to share your burden. I am no doubt wanted at home, so I shall leave you to your own self-pity."

He spun round in genuine surprise as she made determinedly for the door. "You would go, too? Have you no sympathy for your own son that you would hear his troubles and then leave without so much as a kind word?"

She pursed her lips as she gazed back at him. "My son is a man grown, and has been for many years. He does not need his mother to pat his head. What he has got himself into, he must find his way through. But he is welcome to stop by for tea, if he can behave civilly."

Then, deaf and blind to his sputtering and his offended astonishment, she swept from his office and walked home.

~

"Have you seen the paper today, Margaret?"

She did not respond at first... could not respond. It seemed all her movements of late were burdened by leaden weights, her vision clouded by a film. It rendered all she did sluggish and painful, and so she blinked her aching eyes and deliberately turned towards the source of the question, her head tilted almost as if she did not understand.

"Margaret, did you not hear me? I thought you would recognise this name." Henry Lennox spared a confused glance at Edith over their morning repast, then addressed her again. "Do you not know a Mr Watson from Milton?"

She blinked again. "Watson? My... Fanny's husband?"

"Yes, I thought you had some connection to him. It seems he has done rather well for himself. Look here."

Margaret accepted the paper, but her eyes refused to focus on it. She stared at it for several uncomfortable seconds, not comprehending the printed page, until Henry's finger pointed to the place he desired for her to read.

"It says he has been exceeding fortunate, he and his partner Wright. I remember meeting Wright once or twice; a shrewd fellow, and a wizard in the financial world. Of course, this business at hand is hardly complete, but if all goes as they expect, both Wright and Watson will be poised as some of the leading rail tycoons in the country. So long as they continue to have the funds to finish the work, that is."

Margaret tried to read the page, but the words blurred. She touched her fingers to her forehead and closed her eyes as the pounding behind them intensified.

"Oh, dear Margaret, have you got the head-ache again?" Edith set aside her saucer and Margaret could hear her summoning a maid to bring something for her comfort.

"No," she objected lamely, "it is nothing, Edith." She swallowed and forced herself to look on the page again. The words swam, but eventually took shape from the haze, and she could make out at least a dozen of them.

"Ten thousand pounds!" She squinted, shook her head faintly to be certain she had read properly, and looked again.

"Oh, at least, and that only the final stages. It costs a great deal to fund such a project. I should say they have invested many times that already. Certainly, it is not only Watson and Wright supplying the funds, for they will have found several smaller investors as well, but you know, it is always the men of vision who reap the greatest rewards. They will be paid back handsomely for their trouble."

Edith was leaning close enough to read over Margaret's shoulder. "Was Mr Thornton invested in that, Margaret? It would be a lucky thing for him if he were."

Her throat filled suddenly, and she had some trouble in forcing herself to speak. "No," was her hoarse reply, and she thrust the paper roughly back towards Henry.

"No!" Henry's brow wrinkled in condescension. "Why ever not? It seems a sure means to security if he could do without the capital for a short time. Perhaps that was the reason."

A sob trembled in her breast, but she caught her breath and found an answer. "He does not believe in chance speculation, nor does he trust Mr Wright."

Henry glanced again to Edith, almost a pitying resignation writ over his face. "I should not like to grieve you by calling your husband a fool, but... well, Margaret, you see how little chance there is of failure. And Wright! Why, his family is well-regarded for their genius at matters financial. Were I a man of business—" he smiled and spoke the word as an amused slight—"I would have thought it the opportunity of a lifetime. I wonder what Mr Thornton could have been thinking to refuse the offer."

Margaret felt her cheeks burning. Indeed, what could John have been thinking? Blinded by pride and the past? For she could not argue that Henry seemed to be correct, but... she closed her eyes and struggled for an even voice.

She remembered that day... all those days... when Watson had worked upon John. How it was then; how she had been crippled by the depths of grief and pain, and John had scarcely left her side but to face difficulties with the mill and public derision for his refusal to cooperate with Wright. And she had found no blame in him then.

How time and perspective could alter! For if John possessed a fault, it was an arrogant satisfaction in how he had overcome his past. The deeply personal man he had once revealed to her was calloused by a brittle shell of scorn for any who would presume to disrespect him, and a fierce, almost maniacal jealousy towards any outsider who would claim a share in his success. Had Wright truly wounded him so badly as he had come to believe? Or had John been rather too ready to assign his father's folly to another?

"Margaret? Darling, you look positively ill. Do try a little more tea, surely it will soothe your nerves," Edith persuaded.

Her eyes were stinging, that dreaded precursor to shameful tears. Margaret forced herself to steady her breath, to turn her thoughts, and to make a calm reply. "Yes, thank you, Edith," she mumbled dutifully. She tasted the bitter amber, realising that she had forgotten to sweeten it. Well, she would not today. Better gall and vinegar than honey for one of her dark spirits!

"I say, Margaret! I had almost forgotten to ask if you had any word of Cousin Frederick. When did you last write?"

"I wrote to tell him I was visiting you and had seen your son. I expect he received the letter last week."

"Do tell him how I miss him when he replies!"

Margaret's voice was unsteady. "I do not expect he will write to me at this address...."

"Oh, then you must write to him again, and tell him you had decided to stay on a month or two. When you do write, I should like to include a note of my own. I cannot wait to tell him all about Corfu, and my darling Sholto."

"He has been to Corfu, Edith."

"But he has not seen my boy, nor even the captain. I think I shall begin this very hour, for I know it would please him to hear all my news. What do you think, Henry, for you met my cousin? Is he not an amiable gentleman?"

"Indeed. I think any brother of Margaret's could not help but be... agreeable." This he said with a curious inflexion, and Margaret looked up in time to catch a lingering glance, a strange heated interest.

She coloured and looked down at her hands. "I miss him so."

Henry nodded in sympathy. "I should think you would! A pity he had to become wrapped up in that foolishness."

Her gaze snapped up once more. "Frederick was only defending his crew. He had no choice!"

"Oh! I did not intend to slight the man. I only meant to say... well, circumstances could have been improved with a bit of discretion, a little care for the future. He might not have been lost to you."

Margaret's neck stiffened. "You are suggesting that he should have lied?"

Henry and Edith exchanged glances again. "There are things he could have done, surely," Edith soothed.

"Nothing that would not have betrayed his comrades. You think perhaps if he had given himself up, offered the names and where to find each of his fellows, that the Navy would have been lenient?"

"We did not intend to distress you, Margaret," Henry protested. "Of course, that would have been out of the question. Here, let us turn to more pleasant topics, for I would not see you troubled by any useless talk."

"Yes, indeed!" Edith seconded. "Forgive me, darling, that was silly of us to mention. Do you know, Margaret, there is to be a symphony concert on the sixteenth of next month, and I asked the captain to secure tickets for everyone. I know how much you love listening to the music. You *are* staying that long, are you not?"

"I…" she wetted her lips and that helpless, choking feeling threatened to smother her once more. "I do not know," she whispered miserably.

"Oh, surely Mr Thornton may do without you for that long. He has his business to run, after all, and there can be nothing of pleasure in that dirty, smoky town at this time of the year. You must stay, Margaret."

The throbbing had returned, piercing her temples and squeezing her chest until she thought her heart might burst. "I… oh, please excuse me, Edith!" she stuttered. She lurched from her chair, toppling it over with her thick skirts, and did not even slow to set it upright. Edith's and Henry's voices blended in affronted concern, but she heeded them not, nor did she acknowledge any other she passed as she fled up the stairs.

"See here, Miss Margaret!" Dixon ejaculated as Margaret pushed into her room.

"Please leave me, Dixon!" she begged, and then stumbled headlong into her bed. She wrapped her arms up over her head and allowed the tears to flow, shaking the frame and gasping. She pressed her face heavily into the mattress. What mattered breath? Perhaps she would be in less pain if she smothered herself there!

"What for are you cast down like this? I can see your drawers plain as day, Miss. Have a care for your skirts," Dixon chided, and then reached to tug Margaret's hoops herself, preserving something of her mistress' modesty.

"I do not care, Dixon! Please, just leave me in peace for a while!"

"It's that brute Lennox, isn't it?" Dixon accused. "Has he touched you?"

"Please, Dixon, just go!"

"Nay, Miss, for what am I to do? It's you I'm concerned for. Mr Thornton told me, 'Watch over Margaret, see that none distresses her,' he said, and that's what I'm to do."

At John's beloved name, the sobs shook her until she could make no reply, her own throat betraying her until she could not breathe. She refused to turn over, hating her own weakness and mortality, and the first lances of dazzled light scorched her blackened vision as her body struggled for air.

"Miss," scolded Dixon, "you will faint like that, and then you will have the head-ache again." She bodily heaved Margaret's inert form until she lay on her side, still trying to cover her face and weeping.

"Now, what is this? You have been like this all week. I think it is time you went back to Milton, for you were never like this there!"

Margaret tried to curl herself into a protective ball, away from Dixon's prying fingers and eyes, but her stays were laced too tightly to permit much movement. "I cannot go back, Dixon. Please do not ask me more! Just go, leave me for an hour!"

Dixon made a disdainful clicking sound with her tongue. Margaret could fairly hear and feel each roll of Dixon's eyes, each daggered glance towards the door and the relations who lay beyond it. "I'll write to someone, I will, Miss Margaret," she threatened. "I'll write to the dragon herself, and she'll set you right."

"Write to no one!" Margaret pleaded. "Dixon, this is a private matter. Please, just go. I only require a bit of rest."

Grumbling and fiercely reluctant, Margaret heard Dixon's lumbering steps leave the chamber. She held her breath until the latch clicked, and then she permitted herself to give way. She tried pressing into the counterpane again, so she might only see blackness, but he would not cease tormenting her. John, with his roughly groomed face, his cravat loosed, and his eyes warming gently for her, beckoned.

She could almost feel his hands, cupping her waist, his breath tender and welcoming against her neck, and her heart reached for him… but the moment she pleaded his name, his face hardened, his arms crossed over his chest, and his figure dissolved as so much smoke. And then she heard the words that shattered her heart.

"I never knew you."

May 1852

"A mill fire, Thornton, is the most horrific thing a man can see, short of eternal damnation. Pray it is never your lot to count the dead."

Kramer's words, uttered long ago in his early days at the mill, had plagued John's thoughts all this dreary morning. He peered steadily out the window of his carriage at the spring deluge from the heavens and could only mourn that the rain had come a day too late.

An accidental flame, that was the suspicion, but none were certain. Though young, he was already a respected magistrate—and a mill owner himself—therefore, he had been summoned to investigate. A man from the Milton Examiner paper, Mr Smythe, had ridden in his carriage with him to take his own part. Their eyes met now, across the darkened space, in soundless dread for the sight that was about to greet them.

John stepped down first. If the acrid pungency of the ruined building, the mouldering ash of incinerated cotton, and the sickening aroma of scorched hair had not been dreadful enough before the door opened, it was a hundredfold worse when accompanied by the spectacle that met his eyes. A green hillside sloped away from the river, standing sentry between what was once a bustling cotton mill and the pristine country fields beyond. In better days, it would have been decked with May flowers, but today....

"Good God!" Smythe exhaled. "How many were employed here?"

John sucked the breath between his teeth, trying not to smell the scorched air. "Over four hundred. Most of them did not make it out."

"But how? Surely they must have seen and heard the blaze."

"Of course." John cast his gaze over the neat lines of bodies, all arrayed face-down in the trampled and sodden grass. "That only makes it the more hideous. Doom was upon them, and they were helpless to do anything but watch it come. There is nothing like cotton for a hot, instant inferno."

"Instant? How long had they?"

"Two or three minutes, at most. Those who did not burn at once would have been trampled or smothered by the smoke. This mill was built in the old style, too few doors and no way down from the upper floors but wooden stairs that pass through the worst of the blaze... or the windows."

Smythe uttered another cry of dismay and began jotting down his notes. "I would never have thought of it! Thornton, if you do not mind, I should like to stay close during your investigation."

John nodded heavily and moved towards the inspector who came to greet them. "Mason. What have you learned?"

Mason touched his cap. "Mr Thornton, sir. Sorry to take you from your work today. We were hoping you could hear testimony from a few of the survivors and see for yourself the place where they say the flame began."

John cast his eye again over that morbid hill, the rain cascading from his hat brim and already soaking through his shoes. Even in the downpour, he could still smell the smoke. "How many, Mason?"

"Three hundred and sixteen, sir. Not all the bodies could be recovered, but we counted the missing as deceased. Two hundred thirty-two men, thirty-eight women, and forty-four children."

He huffed an astonished breath. "They got most of their women and children out first. They must have been working on the lower levels."

"In part, Mr Thornton," Mason agreed, "but some of the survivors are wives of the deceased men. Many of them have testified that the men stayed to help them escape. They had only moments, but I understand the men barred the doors for them, and a few even dropped ropes from the upper windows for their women to climb down while they stayed above to help."

"Good Lord!" Smythe exclaimed. "Can you be in earnest, sir?" He looked quickly to John. "Why, such a thing… it is inconceivable!"

John thinned his lips, but it was Mason answered. "Not so, sir. I have seen it time and again in my work. You would not credit, had you not witnessed as I have, but it seems there is nothing a man will not do to save a woman. Be it throwing himself before a train or bearing the punishment for her crime, he will sell himself cheap to save her life or honour."

Smythe raised his brows, then wrote furiously. "Well said, sir," was his distracted praise. "Very pretty—yes, that will read well in the papers."

John was still staring at that stricken hill—a charred bit of cloth here, a child's blackened cheek there.... One man lay, his arm stretched out as if agonising in his last burning breaths, his blistered hand reaching towards the limp form of a woman nearby.

Tears formed in his eyes… what man could not weep? So much death and waste, so many futures stolen, yet in the moment that mattered most—when death raged before them, a handful of brave souls had taken that horror upon themselves rather than let it fall to another. He could only pray that if ever he were so blessed to call a woman his own, he would do no less for her, if given the choice.

Mason was beckoning now, and John cleared his throat, steeling himself for his grisly task. "If you will follow me, Mr Thornton, we have gathered a few witnesses in the old shed. It's the only building still standing."

John drew out a small notepad of his own, prepared to take down his observations in as cool and detached a manner as if he were making a report about stolen vegetables. But his neck prickled as he walked, his throat grew tight, and he knew the truth of it. This day, as had so many before, marked him for some purpose, some impression of tragedy and heroism he was meant to remember.

John threw down his coat and hat upon entering his own chamber, then yanked at his cravat. Every day of late seemed to add fuel to the inferno devouring all he had built. Today, Williams had given notice that he had taken other employment. He had lost the last of his supporters, save Higgins—who was likely still too annoyed with him to speak a word in his favour.

John could not help but acknowledge Williams' wisdom in leaving, but it had taken him four hours of bad temper and anger-induced mishaps to confess it. He growled down at the dark ink stain which had ruined his shirt sleeve, and the fresh bruise on his thumb from his own foolishness with the drawer of his desk.

A knock sounded at his door, and he heard, "Master Thornton, sir, did yo' wish to take supper in yo'r room?"

He opened it more roughly than was warranted and felt a second's remorse when the kitchen girl jumped in fear. She gestured hopefully to the tea cart the cook had loaded with good things to tempt him, but nothing roused his interest. He began to shake his head and close the door again, but decided better of it and took a bit of bread before he dismissed her. It held no flavour, but it would banish the hunger pains.

He sank down on the small couch by his own darkened fireplace, balancing the dish on his knees, and was reminded uncomfortably of those early days in Weston when they owned no table upon which to take their meals. But they had one another! Try as he might, he could not think himself worse off then, when misery was borne with companionship.

He choked down half the serving he had taken, then consigned the rest to the cold fire grate. There was little left to do but to retire for the night, so he moved to the dressing table and unbuttoned his waistcoat. As he did so, he noticed in the mirror that some letters had been placed on his side table sometime earlier in the day. Turning in interest, he rushed towards them as if afraid they would disappear. Only personal letters would be brought here to his room, which could mean….

He covered the remaining two paces quickly, his heart thumping and fingers trembling, but when he took up the topmost and held it to his lantern, the pit in his stomach deepened. It was not Margaret's elegant script which addressed him, but a hand he did not recognise. A woman's hand, surely… he ripped it open and found it to be addressed by Mildred Wright. A dinner invitation, very prettily worded, for himself and for Margaret for tomorrow evening. He was welcome to come alone, the invitation assured him, if Mrs Thornton's strength had not recovered. He snorted and cast it into the grate.

The next appeared no more hopeful. It was a tight, purposeful hand, one that reminded him a little of Mr Hale. It was certainly not from Margaret. He sighed in disappointment—what else could he have expected?—and almost tossed that letter aside as well, but some stubborn hope, some deep loneliness shook him. At least someone in this world cared enough for John Thornton to write to him personally, and it was better to read than to writhe sleepless on his bed.

Expecting little of interest, he tore the seal, and then his heart began to burn.

Dear Mr Thornton,

I confess how greatly surprised I was to receive your letter. The motive you professed was, you must imagine, of the most profound interest to me, for I had given over all hope of redemption. Is it truly possible that this Captain Fortin of whom you spoke is willing to testify against Reid? For he is correct, that Reid had been declared unfit, but that the Navy would not hear of his condemnation at the time. I have little hope they shall do so now, but I heartily endorse any efforts in seeking justice.

We had been told that cooperation with the prevailing narrative would improve our situations. As the only officer listed among the condemned, it fell to me to protect my men, and so I agreed. I said nothing of the captain's betrayal, even in private letters, for that was to be our means of salvation and I wished to convince everyone— not least myself—of it. Admiral Trenton sent word pledging liberty and pardons for all, but alas, it was not to be. I have attached to this letter all the particulars of the incidents described, and I hope that the detailed testimony may be of assistance in the case.

I shall not bank all my hopes upon it, but sir, you have given me a gift you cannot comprehend, the nature of which is likely not as you would assume. To once again set foot on English soil with impunity would be the culmination of all my father's wishes and my own desires, but even if it should never come to that, I am satisfied. To know that one in this world, whose face I have never seen, holds me blameless and worthy of a defence, is more than I can deserve. There was another who endeavoured to assist with the law, but his efforts were less sincere, I think, than those of this Captain Fortin.

Yet it is not even Fortin's willingness to exonerate me, but your own goodness in bringing it about in such a way that gives me the greatest pleasure. I thank you for communicating openly with me while doing all with discretion to shield me from harm. Well do I know that no husband would wish to grieve his wife, but you, sir, have shown me your character in a manner that months of acquaintance could never have done.

I am assured now that you cherish my dear sister in your deepest affections, and that you number among the handful of men on this earth who could have deserved her in my eyes. You will forgive a sentimental brother who holds his young sister a paragon of every virtue, for perhaps I have been less aware of any faults she might possess. I am in no mind to learn of them either, and I am both privileged and pleased that I may now accord some of those fine qualities to yourself without reservation.

I enclose a letter in reply to Margaret's last as well, but I wished most principally to address myself to you. Whatever the result of the testimony offered by Captain Fortin, you have my gratitude and my confidence. I shall hope that one day I may have the honour of greeting you in person.

Sincerely,
Frederick Hale

John's arms fell slack, and the letter dropped to his side as he stared at the empty wall before him. Frederick Hale was more generous in his estimation than was warranted. How to tell the exiled brother that the man in whom he had placed his faith was so far from worthy that the mere assumptions in his letter gave pain? He could not allow such warm opinions to persist when he was so undeserving.

Margaret would have known how to answer. It was a bitter thought, but one he could not banish. She would have strengthened him… perhaps persuaded him that her brother's praise was not wholly unmerited… would she? Did she still see anything in him worthy of admiration? Worth encouraging?

He carelessly flipped the opened letter to the desk and snagged his fingers through his hair. Only she could answer that, and he had no expectation that she would still speak to him. No! Not after his scathing insults, his foul temper… not after the way he had attacked and reviled her, her family, and everything she was. Even had she any notion of being in the same room with him again, looking into his face and sparing words for him, that tender regard was a thing of the past. Whether it had been only imagined, had never been strong enough to survive, or had been destroyed by his own hands, this was the mystery which kept him from sleeping at night.

Not knowing what else to do, he found himself staring at the door to her room. The chamber had stood barred and cold for nearly three weeks, devoid of its mistress and a terror to its master. He could deny his craving no longer— his trembling fingers touched the latch, and then the door swung on silent hinges.

Her fragrance washed over him at once and nearly proved his undoing. It was no heavy floral perfume, but the simple, clean allure that was uniquely her own. Her clothing somehow always smelled to him of fresh rain and sunshine, of grassy meadows and musty books. Where the fragrance originated was a mystery to him—like enough, it was his own imagination—but it was as real and tangible now as Mrs Hale's old quilt over the bed, or Mr Hale's rustic settee by the fire.

He could not restrain the aching gasps escaping him when he looked on those furnishings, both so blessed and made sacred to him by the many hours he had loved her there… hours which had defined his life and reshaped his purpose as a man. He was formed to love her, and no other destiny would satisfy what the heavens had set before him.

If only she returned his passion, his depth of regard! They were bound for life, but he would not force her back to his side. What better way to destroy any generous feelings she might have left! He could beg… and raise her contempt for him. He could send tender letters and little gifts, but the mocking eyes and scornful words of her relations in response to his humble sentiments did not bear thinking of.

His hollow gaze swept the room, detecting here and there all the little changes wrought by her presence in his life. A jewelled hair comb left haphazardly on her dressing table; the new house slippers he had bought her tucked neatly beside the bed; a small worked rug that had belonged to her childhood bedroom in Helstone.

He closed his eyes against the stinging torment and nearly left the room, but the prospect of returning to his own empty chamber was too sickening. He shook his head in mute denial, holding an argument with himself, and swung heavily back to face her chair by the fireplace. Whether it was a magnetic attraction or his own weariness, that was the only place in the house that held any welcome for him.

He stopped before it and nearly dropped to its old comfort, but something was still wanting. He crouched and found enough coal and match for his purposes. His fingers were cold and the room dark, rendering the task far more difficult than it should have been. Stubborn and cold and dark... how very like his marriage!

The sandpaper was almost worn through, and only a few matches had remained in the box when he had begun. Most of those he had ruined, and he nearly gave up the deed as hopeless. One last attempt, he determined, and he would either be warmed this night or return to his own room defeated.

He folded the sandpaper once more in a new place, struck the match with deliberation, and his squinted eyes were at once dazzled with the brilliance of the flame. He stared at it in disbelief and awe, nearly forgetting to kindle the rest of the fire until the heat licked near his fingers. Within a very few minutes, he had a comforting blaze crackling in the grate. He caught himself just before turning to share his triumph with the empty settee... and sighed.

He pushed up from his knees to sink into his side of the seat, feeling like a fool when his arm naturally fell over the back. As if she would come and nestle there! He gazed forlornly at the place that should be hers, remembering every sumptuous detail, every articulate look, every whispered affection. The realisation struck him with the crushing force of a blow; he could not live without her.

Oh, he would continue to breathe. His heart would function, and his limbs would carry him forth... for a while. But how long before even his spirit blackened and gave up this pitiful shell of his? To live, to thrive, he needed *her*. At least he must know that she could be won, that he was not beyond all hope as a man. But how to restore the flame once it had gone out?

The one answer which seemed to shine most brilliantly in his agonised mind was the letter lying on his desk. He still had his book of seaman's regulations, the law of the Navy... he could fling himself wholeheartedly into the defence, organising the facts and sorting the details as only a man who knew the law could do.

Even if nothing could be done for Frederick Hale, it would do his heart good to try. It would honour the father who had believed in him, the kindly man cold in his grave these many months who had lost hope of ever seeing his son again. It would please *her* if she ever learned of it.

And perhaps that was something. Every act, every word, every motive must be sifted and weighed against her esteem. He might never prove to himself that he was worthy of her, but she would have no more cause within his power to be ashamed of him.

The master of the house on Marlborough Street remained there, curled in a neglected mistress' chaise before a weak coal fire, until the cold fingers of dawn crept through the window. When he arose, he was no less distressed and despairing than he had been the evening before, but one thing, at least, had changed.

He had a purpose.

Twenty-One

20 April 1856

Margaret hastily scrawled her name at the bottom of the note, then wiped her eyes on her handkerchief before the tears could ruin another sheet of paper. Sniffling, she blotted the letter, and read it over to herself before sealing it. The forced cheer, the inane ramblings, would not fool the recipient, but it was the best she had to offer.

She dared not confess anything of consequence to her mother-in-law, lest the reply be more bitingly truthful than she could presently bear. She grimaced at the superficial small-talk she had written to the woman who had come to know her as well as any other. No, Hannah Thornton… Donaldson… would not be deceived for a moment and would likely roll her eyes and snort through the entire banal missive. It was better than not writing at all, after weeks away and a new marriage for the other. Hannah had written twice to her in that time. She must send *something*, so long as she took care to pen nothing defamatory about the mother's son.

As if she could! Margaret coughed slightly—a lurch of her heart, once again—as she folded and sealed the note, then composed her features. There was nothing ill she could say of John, even had she desired. Throughout this sleepless sojourn, it was her own conviction which had gradually shone through any residual anger she felt for him.

Nothing he had accused her of had been in error. For his temper, his pride, she could fault him, but had hers been better? In the presence of those who would slight him, he had perceived insults she never intended... but had she, even once, spoken in his defence? The casual disregard for his delicate position, the misplaced affinity for her spoiled cousin and the deranged sentiment which had led her hence; all were deceit, conspiring to rob her of the happiness that had been in her own grasp. How—*how*—had she become such a careless, heedless wretch?

She cast the letter, now ready for the post, down on her desk and laid her head back against her chair. Her hand brushed consciously again over her middle—that void from whence all her griefs had sprung. Why had she placed all her hope of joy in that one denied blessing, when the lover of her heart had been before her with outstretched arms? How easy it had seemed, in those dark weeks of danger and grief to blame herself, him, Milton... even heaven itself for all she had longed for and lost? What a selfish little fool she had been!

And yet, the damage was done. The unjust words had been spoken, the tender advances rebuffed, and the very foundations of his character dismissed. How fragile had been the dignity he had entrusted to her, and she had never known! What manner of wife could behave so unworthily?

So many times, she had thought to write to him, to beg his forgiveness and ask to come home to Milton. Would he hear her avowals of love? Or would he assume she was taking a stand against his authority, demanding to return to the city he had sent her away from? Did he even see anything in her that he still desired?

Blinking against the threat of more tears, she withdrew a sheet of notepaper and stared at it. Would he believe she loved him desperately, could not breathe without him, or had he persuaded himself that she was utterly beyond redemption? She dipped her pen once more, then gazed out the window for a moment before she had summoned adequate courage for yet another draft.

~~My beloved~~ Dear John,

~~I have missed you so~~
~~I was hoping to return to Milton~~

The weather here has been fine enough for walking. Twice Edith and the captain~~, together with Henry,~~ have persuaded me to short outings in the park, but ~~I fatigued quickly~~ I found it did not interest me. The park always looks the same as it did on a previous visit, and I confess, I have come to prefer somewhat livelier sights.

Margaret paused, reading over what she had written. It was an inoffensive beginning, perhaps. She dipped her pen again.

> *My aunt has been showing me some of the mementos she brought back from her travels abroad. Paris sounds a romantic, fashionable place, ~~and she assured me I would love it dearly,~~ but I think it would prove a deal too fashionable for my tastes.*

She found herself staring blankly at the page again, fumbling with her pen with one hand and resting her forehead on the other. As if John would care about the weather in London or the fashions of Paris! But it was something, a tentative olive branch. Whatever she managed to write would certainly undergo at least two more drafts.

> *Sholto has been talking quite fluently this last week. He makes us all laugh when he tries to say my name. He pronounces it 'Mawgwet,' for his 'r's sound rather like a 'w'. ~~He remembers you as well, and only yesterday he asked me where 'Jown' was.~~ I attempted another likeness of him, this one a miniature, but it did not bear much scrutiny. I am not so skilled as I was when in practice. I did not even bother to show it to anyone, but I will include it for you to laugh at my bungled efforts. Please cast it into the fire once you have had your amusement!*
>
> *I have had two letters from your mother. ~~She writes most kindly, in hopes that I am enjoying my stay in London, but~~*
> *~~She sounds satisfied in her marriage.~~ I believe Dr Donaldson has been very busy. She says the sickness is beginning to abate in Milton. I am glad to hear it. ~~I was so hoping to~~*

Margaret stared at her letter in disgust. What a thoughtless ninny she sounded! Nothing of import could be said in safety, obliging her to offer only the most trivial of expressions. This would not do!

Frustrated, she shoved the paper away from herself and drew another from the stack. Perhaps she ought not to rush into writing to John. Perhaps she might try her hand at writing to someone else first, someone who could give her news without varnish or delicacy. She sighed, rolling her eyes up to the ceiling, and dipped her pen again.

> *Dear Nicholas and Mary......*

~

22 April 1856

The latest meeting with Captain Fortin had come off rather well... except for the excruciating discomfort of having to journey to London for it. He had tried, without success, to forget that Margaret was a mere fifteen-minute carriage ride from the house in which he sat. No, he could not forget that! Not even when old Kramer's kindly daughter bestowed on him her gentle woman's smile, nor when the business at hand attempted to pull his mind from more personal matters. *She* was ever foremost.

The captain was deeply pleased with Lieutenant Hale's testimony, for it corroborated his own in every way. Even more so did he seem impressed with John's efforts. A proper barrister might have done more than a mere magistrate, but John would be damned before he turned to Lennox with a case that viper had already given up as hopeless. He was not without abilities and understanding of his own, and could write a legal opinion as eloquently as the next man. What a naval board would do with it was beyond his control, but the arguments and citations he had composed would, Fortin assured him, go far in the eyes of the Admiralty at Whitehall.

"Public opinion rules land and sea, my lad," Fortin grinned as he poured John a drink. He leaned conspiratorially close. "Now, with what ye have writ here, if word leaked to the papers that a crew had suffered for the captain's crimes and the Navy itself were responsible for the cover-up...." Fortin allowed that statement to hang, accompanied by a crafty wink.

John leaned back in his chair, an inspired twinge warming his face. "Then when next you come to Milton, allow me to introduce you to a certain Mr Smythe who works for the Examiner."

"There, me boy! Ye learn quick. I'll speak to some of the lads. There's many who've borne this on their conscience for far too long. If the Admiralty won't hear us when we whisper in their ears, we may have to shout in the streets."

"You remember my conditions. Hale is not to be compromised. He understands the risk in signing his name to the testimony and revealing that he still lives, but I'll not divulge his location."

"Aye, lad." The captain stood and extended his hand. "I'd not expect any less."

"So, John Thornton," Mrs Fortin asked when he accepted his coat to leave, "have the two of you saved the world yet?"

"That is for tomorrow," he winked with forced bravado.

"Do you go to Mrs Thornton now? She is still here in Town, is she not? I am sorry she could not come this evening."

He froze. "She is. But I think... no, I shall not have an opportunity to visit her this time. She has been rather occupied with her family, and I must return to the mill."

He began to turn away when her hand stayed his arm. He looked back curiously and found the lady regarding him with sad contemplation. "Is something wrong, Mrs Fortin?"

She shook her head gently. "You look weary, John Thornton. Do not do as poor Papa did, working himself to an early grave."

Her words checked him, and he stared for a moment. "I shall remain above ground some while longer, Mrs Fortin, if only to please you."

She smiled and stepped aside so he could shake the captain's hand once more. The man had the grip of a bear, and an equal measure of enthusiasm as he pumped John's fist. "I'll send ye word, lad, though 'twill be some while."

"Of course. I am only curious why you should exert yourself at all, for a case so long considered closed. Will you not cause yourself significant trouble?"

The captain merely offered a twinkle of the eye, and a cryptic, "A matter of justice. And also, Mrs Fortin speaks well of ye, lad. It is a wise man who pleases his lady."

Sunken and buoyant at the very same moment, John had gone to his lonely hotel to await the first morning train. He had done some little in his way for Margaret's brother, but how deeply he longed to tell her of it! If only he dared go to her now, bursting with the hope which might make her smile on him once more! To see her again... the thought both made him quiver in anticipation and made his stomach twist in terror.

He had almost told her everything, last night in a letter. And the night before... every night this whole blasted week. Each draft had been discarded with contempt. Surely, she would assume his pitiful ramblings little more than a pathetic plea for approval, and his dignity could not suffer for her to think any more meanly of him than she already did. She was well enough entertained, with her cosseted cousin and that coxcomb of a captain and... and that wolf Lennox, who had not the decency to respect the sanctity of a married woman!

His fists curled even now as he thought of it. So many nights of late he had awoken in a boiling sweat, crying in rage and preparing to lunge at the man who would dare to claim intimacy with his wife. And she had permitted it! Whether blinded by sentiment, wilfullly ignorant, or a receptive party to Lennox's obvious ploys for her notice, it was himself she had rebuffed for his natural jealousy, rather than the bastard who was responsible for it!

In his more wrathful moments, he wished he could see her suffer the consequences of that choice, but then his heart bled, and his foolish passion won out. All he could do was to play the gentleman, remaining at a distance until such time as she made some request of him. Let her believe he was well enough without her; that he was sensibly focused on, rather than obsessively consumed by his work; that his feelings were clear and orderly, not battered upon the seas of bitter jealousy. Let her think he was not merely half a man.

It mattered little what she would have thought of him anyway, for he knew it for himself. Moreover, everyone in Milton seemed to know it. His hands all stared behind his back, traded whispers about the master and absent mistress. "She is visiting family," was always his terse reply whenever anyone stopped him upon the street to ask after Mrs Thornton.

How long, precisely, did most ladies stay away for such a visit? Was a month too long? Two? At what point would everyone know the truth? Or had they already guessed because his face was too haggard to be answered by any other explanation?

The mill was quiet when he turned into the gates at midday. The workers had nearly all gone to their meals, and only a few stragglers remained, finishing up odd tasks before they, too, could eat. He grunted dismissive greetings as he passed, his head down and his collar shrugged up near his ears as he walked. Any rational worker would know better than to trouble him.

"Master?"

John hissed in annoyance and raised only his eyes while his chin remained tucked into his coat. "What is it, Higgins?"

The man approached, almost shyly. "We got tha' loom fixed for good. I tho' yo'd like to know."

Another grunt, and John gave a short nod before trying to walk on.

"Master?"

John sighed and turned.

"I set th' lads to shifting the bales in th' warehouse, since Williams isn't here. There's room now for th' next shipment, when it comes."

John stared at the ground.

"There's a shipment of new cotton coming tomorrow, isn't there, Master?"

"No," he heard himself reply. "Not this week."

Higgins' eyes, already pale and anxious, grew large. He drew a manful breath, though, and nodded smartly. "Well, we best see none is wasted. I think we have 'nough to carry us 'til next week, sir."

John at last met Higgins' eyes. Their look held for long seconds, and it was the master who looked away first. "I will speak to the hands tomorrow," he mumbled huskily.

"Sir." Higgins gave a steady nod and seemed to step back. Then, as if remembering another purpose, he raised his cap to catch John's attention again.

"We'd a letter from th' mistress yesterday. She sounds as if she were doing well."

John halted, the breath dead in his lungs and his vision darkening. Slowly, he turned, and fastened hungry eyes on the only person who could give him word of her. "She is well?"

"Well, it sounds like she misses home."

"Home. I wonder what you can mean by that."

Higgins looked confused. "Why, here, of course, Master."

"Surely she meant Helstone, where she came from."

Higgins shook his head stubbornly. "She mentioned Mary and the childer. Asked after some o' th' spinner girls she knew, and one or two of th' littler ones who were ill."

"She is thoughtful," John answered with as much diplomacy as he could summon. "What did you tell her?"

"I'm not much hand for writing letters," Higgins confessed with a slow, guilty smile. "Mary, she said she'd answer. I know the mistress'll want to hear th' news."

John closed his eyes, risking his first long, steady breath in some minutes. "I am sure she will."

"But yo'll be goin' to see her soon, Master? Yo' can carry a letter and tell her everything."

John tightened his jaw. "Not… with matters as they are. I shall remain here this Saturday."

Higgins sighed gently, defeated as John turned to go. "Don' let it go too long, Master. There's mills all o'er the city. There's only one o' her."

John checked his stride, not glancing over his shoulder. "Good afternoon, Higgins."

~

28 April 1856

"No!" Margaret whispered in dread. "Oh, I feared it would come to this, but I had hoped…." She turned over the rumpled note, squinting to comprehend the crabbed, irregular penmanship of the author, and shook her head again in denial. "Not the mill… oh, my John!"

Tears burned once more, and she started when Dixon thumped into her room with a basket of freshly laundered garments. "What a thing this is!" she exclaimed, heedless of Margaret's intent, distracted posture at the escritoire.

"Those wash girls in Milton come dear enough, but I never saw such a thing as these in London now! Why, they must think they're washing the Princess' gowns, and they have not even so much soot to wash away as in Milton. Here, what's this?" she demanded, noting Margaret's face.

"The mill," she answered in a trembling voice, holding the note aloft. "Mary Higgins writes that the mill has failed and will be shut down as soon as all the cotton is gone. A few more days—a week perhaps—and it is finished!"

Dixon's eyebrows raised. "Is it now?"

Margaret bolted to her feet, her entire being quivering, and swept away the scattered, blotted papers on her desk. "And this letter is already three days old.... Oh, why did he not tell me? I must write to John at once! I...."

She turned, swallowing and blinking back a new rush of tears. "Do you think he wished me to know? Surely, he would have written if he had. Oh, but I *must* write! I cannot hear of his troubles and not make some answer."

Dixon blew out a weary huff and dropped the basket with a roll of her eyes. "I'd say it's the mistress' place to know of something like this. Have you not the right to address him? You'd have found out anyway, I daresay."

"But I would not wish to offend him by writing prematurely. I ought to give him the justice of telling me himself."

She wrung her hands in uncertainty, her breath quickening until her nervous excitement thrust her feelings over the threshold of decision. "Yes, yes, I shall write! Oh, I must speak with Edith at once, and have someone ready to carry this to today's post before it is too late!"

Margaret rushed from the room, Mary's note still clutched in her hand, and sought Edith in the drawing-room. She was not there, and Margaret determined to look in the nursery, but heard her name called as she passed by the library. She stopped impatiently, almost bouncing in her desire to speak to her cousin, but Henry came out.

He had been in the habit of availing himself of his brother's hospitality, claiming that the library on Harley Street was far more comfortable than his chambers, when he could choose where he worked. Such he had been doing today, and a thin cloud of sweet tobacco smoke hovered in the room behind him.

He called her name again, his brow furrowed, and he spoke gently when she stopped. "Margaret? Is something amiss?"

"It is nothing," she insisted, denying her words with her eyes as she glanced down again to her note. "I must speak with Edith."

"Certainly not. You are in no condition to be rushing about the house. Why, your face is quite flushed, and your hands are shaking. Come, you must sit down, and I will send one of the maids for her."

"Oh, no, I am well! It is a matter of the gravest import, really. I must ask a favour of her."

"I believe she is with her child just now, is she not? Surely, she should not be disturbed. Will not another suit?"

"Perhaps Captain Lennox—" she hesitated—"I must beg one of their errand boys to carry a letter, and it must go straightaway!"

Henry's eyes fell again to the note in her hand. "To Milton, I presume?"

"Yes. Oh, do please call for someone so they will be ready to take it the moment I am finished writing! I shall not be more than ten minutes."

"Of course, Margaret, of course! But I do not like to see you so distraught. Has something happened? Am I not a friend, that you cannot tell me of your troubles?"

"Yes, yes, indeed, but this is something else entirely. Forgive me, Henry, but I really must write my letter. You will send someone to me, or ask the captain to?"

"Margaret—" his voice deepened, and he caught her hand even as she tried to spin away. "Stay a moment, please."

She stopped, looking in some bewilderment at the serious expression, the uncomfortable manner so foreign to him.

"You will laugh, Margaret, but your disposition just now frightens me terribly."

"Frightens you? You have nothing to fear. The matter is a private one."

"Nothing that unsettles you so greatly can be only your concern. Do you not know that others would share your distress? That in seeing you so, none who calls himself your friend could be easy until all is well?"

She had no answer for this and gazed back in mute confusion.

"Moreover, there is a sense of foreboding in your manner. I fear—can I be wrong to do so?—that this agitation is only a herald of sadder things to come. You are not thinking of leaving us here in London, are you?"

"I... I do not... perhaps. I have received some news I cannot ignore."

"About Mr Thornton, naturally?"

She looked down to her note, dragging the fingers of her other hand across the edge of the paper, then raised her eyes. "He is my husband, Henry."

"Ah! And therefore, he receives the lion's share of your devotion, while we who care for you must wait upon the crumbs of your regard."

"Have I offended you somehow? Is it not right that I should sometime go back to him?"

Henry looked away with a sigh. "Only if such a one is deserving and can properly appreciate the gift bestowed."

She stiffened. "What do you mean by that?"

His lips thinned, and he was silent for a moment before he met her eyes. "Margaret, though you have not spoken of it yourself, I have heard something of your disappointment of a few months ago. I heard how your very life was on the edge of the surgeon's scalpel; how afterward, grieved though you were, you were scarcely permitted the comfort of friends to visit during your recovery."

Margaret's cheeks flushed hotly. "You take great freedoms with my private affairs!"

"Again, I ask you; can they truly be private? Is your trouble any less my own, though I was not the man at your side to share in it? Would I be any less stricken, had death or despair claimed you?"

She shrank somewhat, looking down in mortification at the floor. "Sir, you forget yourself."

"I think, rather, that I was late in coming to my senses. Would I not have spared you what you have suffered? Would I not have given you every consideration, brought to you every cheerful thing to lift your spirits? Is it possible even that the matter would have been brought to a different conclusion if you were not suffering in that dreary city?"

She shook her head. "Henry, you must not do this! I chose Mr Thornton, and it is a choice I will honour all my life."

"Even in this, you deceive yourself. Your heart is not in it, Margaret. If it were, you would not have stayed so long in this house."

"My heart," she repeated, very softly, as if testing the words. "I have been blind and foolish."

"Do not speak so harshly of yourself! I will not hear it. You have regrets, it is true, but you are not without a means to happiness." As he spoke, he extended his hand, a hopeful smile beckoning.

She narrowed her eyes, and her tones became brittle. "I *have* been blind, but no longer. Henry, I will thank you never to speak to me in such a way again. It is an offence against all that is natural and right, an injustice against the laws of God and man, and a violence done to my own feelings."

He shook his head, a beseeching expression crossing his face as he reached to clasp her hand. "Margaret, you cannot hide behind such simplistic ideals. You are upright and noble, but the world is not so. You must see—"

"Mr Lennox!" She drew back, and her head raised in that old genteel grandeur of hers. "Pray, do not touch me again, or I shall be forced to strike you. I shall spare you the humiliation of discovery, for your incautious words I will keep to myself, unless it is right to share them with the one I am bound to by law and by affection. I hope one day we shall meet again as casual acquaintances, but I must now quit your presence."

She whirled in a sweep of her dark skirts, but his mournful cry gave her pause. "I never intended to offend! Please, Margaret!"

She froze, and her tones were hard when she replied. "My name is Mrs Thornton."

She could not—would not—look on his face, but she could imagine it well enough. "We are friends, Margaret! Please, accept my humblest apologies!"

She tilted her head but did not turn back to him. "Perhaps one day I shall. I have valued your friendship, but this I cannot accept. However, your professions today have enlightened me to a conviction which has too long lain dormant. I know now what I must do."

He was silent, but she heard his pleading gasp, and had some little mercy. She turned to look him full in the eye, the haughty grace of old flooding into her limbs. "I bid you farewell, sir."

No further protests did she care for, and she threw back her shoulders as her determined, even steps carried her to her own room. "Dixon!—" she commanded as soon as the door had closed behind her—"we must pack at once. I should like to change into my green travelling suit now—yes, the new one—for I shall be on the Milton train this very afternoon."

Dixon started from her chair, her round cheeks flushed with awe. She blinked, swallowed, and then closed her mouth. Then, for the first time, she bobbed Margaret a curtsey and answered, "Yes, Missus."

~

He was of positively no use at the mill. What good was one who managed the forward progression of a business that was even now heaving its last gasps? He had enough put by to pay everyone—just—but after that, there was no point in striving. And he was weary.

It went beyond the mere bone fatigue of a long day. This was months, years perhaps, of cumulative exhaustion, held at bay by the hope of ambition and the lure of success. That being a vain notion, and without his mother to daily lift his head or Margaret to soothe his anxious heart by night, he was a beaten man.

He stood at the scaffolding from which he had observed countless hours of productivity, his clear eyes discerning every nuance of his mill. Today, however... he blinked and drew a long breath. It had been several minutes since a conscious thought had passed through his mind. What was the use?

He turned, and without purpose, trod his slow, measured way down the steps. He avoided Higgins' gaze, a wave of his hand sufficing to inform the other that he was stepping out. The only trouble was that he was uncertain where to go.

Five minutes saw him aimlessly wandering back into his own house in the middle of the afternoon. His arms sagged at his sides as he took in all the work which must now be done; the sorting and selling off of possessions he could no longer afford to house, the packing up of those essentials he would keep, and the removal to... somewhere. And sometime in the midst of all that, he must tell his wife that there was nothing for her to come home to, even if she should wish it. He released a long, ragged breath, and sank into the nearest chair to rub his eyes.

Some while later, he heard a woman's voice in the passage. He would have paid it little enough notice, but he had dismissed all but his man of all work and one kitchen girl only two days before. That light, youthful voice could not have belonged to either of them, and there was none present to answer the door to anyone else. Could it be...?

He jerked to his feet, irrational hope beating in his chest that perhaps Margaret had come at last, without sending word or requesting his escort from London. In a mere two strides, that hope shattered when Mrs Wright's slender form appeared in the passage. He stopped, bewildered.

"Oh! Mr Thornton!" she laughed. "Forgive me, sir, I had not expected to find you here at this time of day. Mrs Watson was resting this afternoon, so I came to call on Mrs Thornton."

He narrowed his eyes in confusion. "Mrs Thornton?"

"Why, yes, of course." She approached nearer, still smiling. "I was fortunate enough to make her acquaintance on my last visit to Milton, you must recall. I hope you will forgive me for simply entering, but no one was answering to my knock, and the door did not seem quite closed. I thought perhaps I might be pardoned for my eagerness to meet her again if I came in."

He shook his head, his voice low. "She is not here."

"Oh, dear," she lamented. "Then I have indeed trespassed. I beg your pardon, Mr Thornton. Might I call upon her later?"

"She is in London."

"Ah." Her eyes then swept the room behind his shoulders, then fell about the lamps, the sofa back, and at last rested on the small table near him and lingered for several seconds. Unable to help himself, he too glanced down, but could see nothing remarkable save a fine layer of dust already settled upon its polished surface.

"I had heard a rumour," she murmured, "that you are intending to sell off and leave Milton. I should be very sorry to hear it is true."

He turned away, not caring if he seemed rude to a lady. "Why should that trouble you?"

"Why should it not? Come, John Thornton, we were friends in our youth, were we not? I would like to hope we are still so. I dearly hope your resentment towards my husband and his family does not extend to me."

He stopped, turned slowly back, and stared, but no words came.

"Ah! It is as I expected. You do not despise me, but you will think of me only as Harold Wright's wife. I do have my own thoughts, of course. I believe every woman does."

"And yours are?"

She trailed her fingers over the back of the sofa, admiring its burnished wood and luxuriant fabric. "I think it all a waste. It is a hard circumstance, very hard, which would see the ruin of such a fine man as yourself. I am not so modest and shy as I was when a girl, and I suffer no qualms in saying as much. I never saw a man with more right to success, John Thornton, but fate has been most cruel."

"Right to success! You speak as if reward were measured in equal proportion to merit."

"Should it not be?"

"I once thought as such. You are wrong, Mrs Wright, for success and achievement are not given where they are due. They are stolen by the unjust."

She looked hurt. "There you go again, assuming I would be your enemy. I wish to befriend you once more, John Thornton. The years have been kinder to you than you will confess, for the man I now see has been shaped and hardened by struggle, and his character sifted and refined by bearing up with honour when others would have cast him aside."

Her words stoked some ember in his breast. They were the only words of affirmation he had heard spoken over what he felt to be his virtues in... far too long. His lips twitched involuntarily into a hesitant approximation of a smile.

"The... the years have been kind to you as well, Mrs Wright," he answered roughly. "It was good of you to call." He turned away again, backing once more behind the sofa.

"Are you so ready to dismiss me, John Thornton?"

He glanced back in surprise. "Was there another purpose to your visit, apart from calling on my wife?"

A guilty blush stained her cheeks, and she looked down. "Everyone in Milton knows she has been away in London these many weeks, and that Mrs Donaldson has not called in almost as long."

His ears burned in humiliation. "Then, I do not understand."

"And you must be longing for some company, is that not so? The comfort of a friend?"

"A friend would not be unwelcome, but—"

"Do you suppose," she interrupted, "that those who marry must remain happily in that state? Or is it more common that discontent enters into their union?"

"Mrs Wright, I will thank you to not enquire into my personal affairs."

"It was not *your* affairs of which I spoke, but my own." She had begun to slowly circle the sofa, closing the distance between them, but in such a calm, unassuming way that he was not startled back.

"I was too young for marriage, and so was Mr Wright, but it was... convenient at the time. Our families desired the alliance, but had I the choosing of my own destiny, I would have waited." She lifted her eyes to him, a significance in her expression that sent shivers down his spine.

"Do you remember, all those years ago, when we saw you in that draper's shop?" she asked, her tones so low he almost had to lean close to hear her words.

"No."

She gazed up in faint disappointment, then smiled. "Sly creature. Yes, you do. I recall how embarrassed you were, as if it were yesterday, but you had no cause to be. It was then that I began to regret, and to wonder what sort of man you would make of yourself. Imagine how sharp my frustration when I saw you had become all that a woman's heart could have hoped for!"

His skin was prickling now, his pulse beginning to race. "Mrs Wright, take care. Your words are heedless and provocative. What is more, they are deceptive. I am no paragon, and I will thank you not to beguile me with your assumptions. I am not worthy of such unguarded esteem."

"You think so little of yourself! I suppose it is Mrs Thornton who has taught you this. She would not be pleased by a working man, I expect, but the error is her own."

"Mrs Wright, you go too far!" he protested, seeing with some alarm that she had drawn within inches of him and was even now reaching to touch his hand. Yet he was too stunned, too horrified to move away. That Woman, whose sex was the keeper of virtue and modesty against the devices of fallen Man, could approach him with so blatant intent to bewitch, astonished and troubled him to his very marrow.

Her hand closed over his, but she pressed him no further. "I meant no insult, sir. I only think it regrettable that a man such as you would not be appreciated in his own home by someone who *would* offer him the respect he is due."

For one brief, stabbing instant, his heart trembled. For so long had he felt inadequate beside all to which he had aspired. To hear another salving his wounded pride was nearly intoxicating. It would be so easy to listen, and he longed so achingly to believe.... He felt his eyelids drift lower, could sense the feathery breath as her face tipped up.

His eyes closed, and he could see at last the cold, brittle darkness he had struggled so long to check, as the rocks hold back the tide until the storm rages. It washed over him, scoring and eroding the last vestiges of his own strength, and he verily shook at its might. Then it was gone, the waters still roiling about his feet, leaving him bared and helpless. He gasped, his figure began to stoop, and he felt gentle fingers begin to trace the lines of his face.

As if it truly were the sea and sand crumbling beneath him, he felt unsteady. The tide was drifting back, and his deceived eyes drew his body along with it... until the shoals fell away from the precipice, and only a small, bright shard of light remained behind.

Like a gem hidden in the sand, it shone through his despair. It alone would not be taken in, and it alone lodged steady in its place. Whether it was his last glimmer of hope and dignity too long hidden from view, some angelic salvation in the moment, or his own tortured imagination, he could not know. But it was enough.

"No," he whispered.

Her hand stilled but did not fall away from his cheek at once. He would have to fight for his victory.

"What was that?" she asked softly, a hint of affectionate laughter in her tones. "Are you now become modest?"

He opened his eyes. "No," he repeated, in a full voice this time.

Her brow puckered in dismay. "It would not be so very shocking, you know," she purred. "Why, in London—"

"*No!*" he thundered, offended that she continued to tempt and press what he had already rejected. "Leave at once!"

She drew her shoulders back, frowning. "And this is why you are failing, John Thornton. You will not take what opportunities are offered you. Do you not know what a fool you look before everyone? But surely, you are no such creature."

She drew his hand up, almost as if she would kiss his fingers, but he angrily snatched it from her grasp. "Indeed, a fool perhaps I am, but I belong to another, and so do you."

"To your rival! I would have thought, John Thornton, that you would not refuse an opportunity to best Harold Wright."

He snarled, disgusted at her corrupted beauty and the twisted allure of her offer. "I need not bed his wife for that. Get out!"

All traces of desire and temptation now vanished, leaving her breath-taking features cold as marble. "I was wrong, then. I thought you were a man worthy of my trouble, John Thornton. A bulldog, that is what everyone used to call you—one who savagely clings to his object; but I see now you are but an obedient pup, called to heel by a woman who does not want you." She spun and stalked away from him, towards the door.

He let her go, refusing to allow himself to rise to her bait. More words would only endanger him further, and his strength, after all, was flagging. He crossed his arms and glowered darkly after her until she had disappeared round the doorway, then listened to each hasty stride down the corridor.

He heard the door open and dared to breathe again, his arms falling to relax at his sides. It was over, and he had passed the test. Yet… was that the harlot's voice again in the hall?

The door creaked, and he could still hear her tones, though her words were indistinct. Oh, this would not do! Goaded once more to anger, he strode to the hall and commanded in his best master's voice, "You must leave, before—"

The words died in his throat. Not even breath escaped him, for he stood frozen, transfixed at what he saw.

Mrs Wright turned from the door, a conscious look of affected innocence contorting her handsome face into something grotesque. "I did not expect the pleasure," she stammered, then bowed her head slightly to the figure which had just entered the house. "I am glad to meet you again, Mrs Thornton."

Margaret spared her but a glance. Her features were hard, her eyes sparking indignation and fury. And all her ire was focused upon *him*.

Twenty-Two

"Before *what?*" Margaret dropped her satchel with a loud thump for emphasis.

John winced, his face a brilliant scarlet and his mouth still somewhat agape. Mrs Wright had fled without another word, but it only made the situation look all the more suspicious. Dixon, who had been standing behind her with her bags and a porter, had abruptly vanished to seek some other entrance.

It was just the two of them now, alone in the dimly lit entryway. Annoyed by his mute astonishment, she determined to punish him for the mortification of finding Mrs Wright opening her own door.

"She must leave before you were caught?" she demanded. "Before someone discovered your indiscretion? Tell me, Mr Thornton, what caution were you giving Mrs Wright when I so inconveniently appeared?"

At last the anger sparked in his glare and his fists balled at his sides. He answered her with an equal measure of outrage, his voice hardened to a brittle edge. "Think you that I have philandered with *that* woman? That I have broken faith, cast aside all sense of honour, simply because you were not here to secure my lead string?"

Margaret shivered, realising that the door stood yet ajar behind her. She whirled to slam it closed, then stalked a few paces nearer. "I believe I deserve *some* explanation, do I not? What possible reason could you have for entertaining a woman alone, in this house, in the middle of the day?"

"She was not invited! She claimed to be seeking you, and once assured of your absence, she presented an offer which disgusted me, and I sent her away."

"Then it *is* my fault," she retorted icily. "Had I been present, you would not have been tempted, is that it?"

"I never claimed I was tempted!"

"You must have been, for her to stay long enough to have a closed door between you and the rest of the world."

He stormed a short distance away, raking his fingers through his hair as he always did when distressed. He did not answer at once, even seemed to tremble in some expression of anguish.

"And perhaps I was! For but an instant, but I'll not deny it. The words she spoke were as honey to a starving man—words I might have longed to feast upon from you but have not even caught fragrance of in these many months."

He cast his eyes to the ceiling, heaved a pained groan as his shoulders sagged, then turned back to her with a faint snarl in his voice. "But I will have you know, I yielded not. I sent her away! When I heard her tarry in the hall, I came to reprimand her, to demand she take herself far from me!"

"And this is what I am to believe? How simply you explain it all! Why have I heard no word from you these weeks I was alone in London? My husband wanted nothing to do with me, sent me away against my wishes even, and when I return to my own home it is another woman who greets me!"

"And have I had word from you? If you so longed for my company, what was stopping you from writing?"

She felt her brow flush, then begin to perspire, and the words with which she might have struck a blow faltered in her throat.

He was quivering, that same righteous fury evident that had so provoked her the first time he had proposed. "Margaret, have I ever given you cause to doubt my fidelity? Can you think so meanly of me as that? I have failed, indeed, if you can cast such upon me!"

She shook her head, dumbfounded and infuriated. "How shall I know what to think? You have sent me away—you, who once claimed to love me as man had never loved any woman, yet you turned your back and gave me no opportunity to make amends."

"Because I thought you were better pleased without me! Because the only life that came to your eyes these last months was because you had a chance to go to London, away from me."

"That is only half true, but you will not hear the rest."

"And what is that? That you were eager to escape this house? My mother? Was it the trappings of our marriage which bore you down, or was it I myself, the dirty manufacturer?"

"It was none of these," she returned flatly, crossing her arms. "I begged you, I pleaded for some companionship, some purpose to my life, but I was no more than an invalid you would coddle as if I would break."

"A temporary situation! Do you forget that you nearly died? That disease could have posed an additional risk to you? Was I wrong to shelter and protect you, even against your wishes?"

"John—" her jaw set and her teeth clenched in rage—"I was grieving! I never mourned Mother or Father properly, and then...." Her voice choked, and she blinked hastily. She covered her mouth with her hand and tried to control the shrieking, gasping breaths that shook her.

He moved towards her in some concern, but she bore up, her long-repressed indignation blazing. "Do not touch me until you have heard me out!"

He shrank back, chastened.

"When I...." The panic rose in her breast again, and she was terrified of bursting into a sob. She put out her hand, gasping. "When I lost the... oh good God!" She broke, her voice crumbling and the sobs she had held at bay racking her, but he was too wary to approach and offer comfort.

She stifled a gasp with her fist and tried to continue where she had left off. The words were little more than a whisper. "When I was so sick, I was...."

Again, she clenched her teeth and breathed through a shuddering tremor. "I only wished for a friend! I wished for some reason to exist... I wished for you, but you turned your grievances into work, and I saw you not!"

"Did you think I abandoned you, Margaret? Was I not at your side, praying, begging for a miracle that would restore you? Did I not try to comfort you? But you would have none of me!"

"None of your platitudes nor condescension for the sickly. No, I would not have it. Can you not see, John? I was once your partner, your companion, but I became nothing more than a burden. Do you not know how badly I wished to tally one single sheet of invoices, just so I might have felt I could do some good in this world—some good for you?"

"And I was to bring bookkeeping duties before a wife who would scarcely eat? You had not even the strength to look out a window, much less hold a pen!"

She shook her head. "I—I was not weak, but numb. I could not feel. I did not want to feel! For if I did, I was certain I would die."

"And do you think I felt less? Do you think that watching you endure such agony, knowing there was nothing I could do to save you, and nothing I could bring to coax you to remain in this world did not crush me anew each day? Do you think I did not blame myself for each of your sufferings? Aye, I felt the full measure of guilt! And then later, when I knew you would survive, I wished to rejoice... but you refused to live! I could do nothing to cheer you. It was as if you were no longer yourself, and I did not even know you."

Margaret's stays felt too tight and her eyes were cast to the floor. "Yes. It felt that way to me, too. I did not know myself, even." She looked up again, and her gaze hardened.

"So, is that it? Were you so disappointed in me that you could not bear my presence? So willing to grasp at anything that was not your wounded wife that you listened to the lies of a temptress because she offered what I did not?"

He had begun to soften somewhat, but at her accusation his spine stiffened, and his eyes glittered once more in offended pride. "And what of Henry Lennox? I daresay I have less guilt on my head regarding Mrs Wright than you do with him!"

"Was I to abuse what friendship might be offered and reject any sort of companionship I was permitted? Was I to speak to no one since you were not there?"

"A little respect, of the sort a woman ought to reserve only for her husband might have been in order, but that was too embarrassing for you to consider. I know very well that you are ashamed of me, but you could have taken some care to hide that, at least a little."

"Ashamed! I have never been prouder of anyone in the whole of my life than I am of you, John Thornton."

This seem to shake him, and he paused, tilting his head in wonder. "That... cannot be true. I do not believe it."

She dared a step closer to him. "I have never known a finer man than you, nor one whose esteem I desired more, but I have lost you. You have been consumed by work and worry, striving in fear of losing control. I have not seen that competent, clear-headed, gentle man I came to love, but merely a petty, desperate shadow of him. However—" here, she sighed and dashed a stream of tears from her cheek—"I have done little better. I never wished for you to be disappointed in me. You were right about Henry, about Edith, and I too foolish to see it! I wished to give you joy as your wife, but I have only brought trouble and regret."

"No!" He had stepped softly closer, his figure trembling and expanding with new vigour. When he spoke now, his voice was vehement and forceful, and he closed the distance to capture her hands.

"Never think that! You have been my life, the joy of my heart, since the day we married—nay! Long before that, almost from the day I first set eyes upon you, you defined all I ever hoped, and your love was a treasure I thought I could never win. I had never known such happiness, nor such completion as when you took me as your own. I thought I would burst; I could not comprehend how I could love you more, but so I have done each day since. No, love, never think for a moment that I could regret our marriage! It was I who proved inadequate. I could not satisfy—I was not enough!"

Margaret tipped her head up and gazed tenderly into the earnest eyes she had learned to adore. "You are more than I deserve."

He stared in rapt astonishment, his breath ragged. She held his eyes, wishing to assure him in every way of her sincerity. Without warning, he leaned down and crushed her lips, demanding and pleading all at once.

He pulled back almost instantly, resting his forehead on hers and gasping. "Forgive m—"

She did not permit him to complete his apology, for the next moment she was pulling him down, kissing him hungrily, in a manner she had never done before. She felt his breath, hot and shared in her own lungs, and his throat rumbled, whimpering as a creature who has gone too long without water. He was drinking her in, in heady, lingering draughts, his kisses deep and savage.

She reached again to stroke that strong jaw and soft, stubbled cheek she loved so, and found that his face was as wet as her own with tears. She broke away, only enough to whisper against his lips, "John, may I come home?"

He raised his head to look at her, a wavering sob escaping him. "I have no home for you."

She placed her hand over his heart, then looked up. "*This* is my home. It is not in London nor Helstone. There is no home for me but wherever you are. I shall never leave it again if you will let me come back to it."

His eyes were brimming and full when he choked, "You have never left, love."

She pulled his face to hers and kissed him lightly, but in the space of a heartbeat something far different blossomed than the sweet reassurance she had at first intended. Rapt kisses fell over her face, her neck, and pleading hands pressed her against his chest until his very heart-pulse thrummed in her ears. And when, only a moment later, he began tugging her towards the stairs, still kissing her with every breath, she followed with an eagerness that matched his own.

It was she who chose his door, then bolted it behind them. It was she who tore at his clothing; first the cravat, then the waistcoat. There was a primal urgency to her desire, as if some part of herself had been dying all these months and was even now grasping desperately for a purchase on life.

He tried, for half a moment, to guard something of that modest reserve a man was expected to bestow upon his wife, but she would not tolerate such gentle civility from him—not now. How rapidly she was able to overcome him, and how little he objected! He was as a creature starved, his hands stroking and claiming all that was his own, aching to nourish his famished soul.

It was not until one of the buttons of her bodice fell to the floor that he checked himself. "I am sorry. I should not… will not rush you," he panted.

Margaret rested her hands on his chest as if she were staying him. She looked full into his face and smiled—a mischievous, ardent smile that caused his breath to hitch beneath her fingers.

"You are not." With both of her hands she ripped, and the white fabric gave way, falling in little more than ribbons about his shoulders. She caught her lip in her teeth and looked up in half-apology. "I hope you have another shirt."

In that instant, she received the medicine that her heart had craved all these months. Her John smiled. And then he laughed—that keen, hearty, full laugh which betrayed all his earnest delight echoed again in her ears.

"Love! You truly have come back to me!" He swept her up and twirled her, waltzing her through the air until her feet again touched the floor.

He had not yet done—though his eyes were closed, his lips engaged, he swayed and stepped her all round the room as if to the pulse of an orchestra. Margaret was weeping and laughing all at once, her hands tangled in his hair, his clothing, and kissing him back whenever his frantic caresses brought him to her lips. The only tempo their feet kept was their shared breaths, the only melody moving their bodies swelled from jubilant spirits, but they spun until the room was too small and there was nowhere else to dance, then tumbled, in a riotous tangle of limbs and petticoats, into his bed.

She wrapped her arms about his head, so he might never escape till he had satisfied her longing. Knowing what she wished, he kissed down her throat while his hands caressed through her clothing. A moment later he paused, and pressed a sweet, gentle endearment to her forehead as he had done in former days.

"Are you not afraid? For your health? I could not bear if something else were to—"

"I am afraid of nothing. What can be worse than being apart from you? Love me, John or this life is meaningless to me, anyway."

He was not gentle. Neither was he violent. There was some majesty in him in this moment, inspiring all the greatness in his character to express itself in the tender ferocity of lovemaking.

Never before had she felt the full measure of his strength, nor seen what he was capable of when driven half mad with passion and loneliness. It was as if all his frustrations and fears were exorcised in this one exultant moment. She felt his anger, she felt the bitterness and the pain, but most of all she felt his need—a need to be desired by none but her, and desired for who he was; a flawed, noble man who pledged to her with every kiss, every caress, that his life would be spent in devotion to her alone.

He cried out in agony, all those months of anguish threatening to darken and snatch his triumph from him even as he gloried in unity once again. She cradled him, her body pleading for more. Their voices harmonised as one, travailing and rejoicing until they could bear no more together, and the same force shook them both in waves of pure, blissful relief.

He lay gasping in her arms, the demons banished at last. She turned her face to kiss the underside of his jaw, then closed her eyes. Trials they must yet endure, but it was over. All the heartbreak of separation, all the uncertainty of one another and doubt of themselves—such torments were things of the past.

She was *home*.

~

She was stronger than he had remembered. Perhaps it had only been the impression of grief, how it had ravaged her inner being, but it had been so complete, so oppressive, that the force with which she now clung to him was like a new creature.

And was that…? He peered out of one eye at the rumpled clothing they had cast aside. Soft green, just the shade of spring in the country. She looked breathtaking in colourful clothes again… and even more so out of them.

She was peaceful now, her eyes closed and her breathing light, but she did not sleep. A little wrinkle played at the corners of her mouth, her fingers tickled the base of his neck, and her nose brushed against his chin—an affectionate reassurance that they still held one another close.

"Margaret?" he ventured after some while.

She answered with a soft hum, tilting her head closer to his.

Having called her attention, he then struggled to voice what lay on his heart. "Are you… do you still mourn?"

He felt her lashes brush his cheek as she opened her eyes, but she did not draw away to look at him. "I believe I always shall, but it is… different. You said something like that to me once. I will never cease to think of Mother, and Father, and our child. Never will come the day when I do not wish they were here, nor regret the sorrow and pain inspired by their loss, but… it is well."

He tipped his head down to look into her eyes. "How?"

Her fingers played along the edges of his ear as she thought. "I suppose I realised that I was losing that which I *did* still possess, the one I loved above all the others I had already lost. I had to decide to live the life I was given, and I knew I could not do that without you.

"I see now that I must have wounded you terribly—oh, how ungrateful I was! I will own the truth; there was a time when nothing you could do would please me because I was so determined to make myself unhappy. It was not because I wished to be so, or that I relished the distinction of grief, but because I did not feel it right to be otherwise. If I had turned to you, truly leaned on you… it would have seemed irreverent, somehow. I do not know how better to explain it."

"I was grieving as well, Margaret. Did you think I did not? It was more than seeing the pain I had cost you—I could not share the burden of my own loss. You already carried too much grief and refused to release it. I would have helped you bear that."

"And in the same way—" she brushed the hair that lay over his brow—"you would not share with me your troubles at the mill, when I would have rejoiced at the prospect of caring for you in that way. We are two stubborn, prideful people, John. How shall we ever learn to go on?"

"I imagine we will stumble often, but I hope we never again require such a painful lesson. I am stronger with you than I am apart from you."

"What are we to do now? Where to begin again?"

He sighed. "I shall have to find work. We may need to remove to another city. After that... I do not know. Everything seems a loss before me now; all those years of building and working forward—simply gone. I can hardly recall what it was to start from nothing, nor what it was to have a vision for the future, but I thank heaven I am not alone." He kissed her meaningfully on her forehead and released a long breath.

"I wished...." Her brow pinched, and she caught her lower lip between her teeth as she began to blink.

"You wished what?"

Her shoulders lifted, and she offered another faint smile. "I had wished to give you a family. Something else to build, that would stand as a testament to our lives, years after we had both gone. I could not help but think what satisfaction that would have given you, and what comfort it would be now, to know some part of us, at least, shall remain."

"Love, it is not the machinery standing in that building, nor is it a daughter with your beautiful eyes or a son with my rather less beautiful nose which will be our legacy. Can we not stamp our imprint on all those others around us? Leave this world somewhat better by our passing? We have not been idle, for we have already begun on one another." He smiled, a mirthful spark kindled once again. "Why, only think how clever you have become at business, and is that not my influence?"

She laughed, low and melodious—music to a man who had heard none in far too long. "And are you not so much more the refined gentleman than you used to be? I understand you are quite the Classic. I believe I can claim the credit for that."

"No, indeed. That was your father's doing. You, my love, have made me happy. None other has done that."

She seemed to hesitate. "Have I, John? That was always my desire, but I feared I had failed."

He splayed his fingers over her flesh, revelling in the simple pleasure of feeling her body close to his. When he spoke again, his voice was deep and hoarse. "Love, my happiness was never your responsibility, and you must not assume so much. Had I chosen to remain a solitary ogre and nothing more than an industrial magnate, it would have been my own fault, not yours. Blessed was the day Providence saw fit to give me you, and to open my eyes to all I lacked. In you, I find my joy."

A tension seemed to drain from her chest, a breath she might not have known herself to be catching. "There is nothing dearer to me than that." She stiffened again, her hands tightening over his shoulders. "John, I believe I owe you one more apology before I can be easy."

"You owe me nothing, love."

"But I do—an explanation, at the very least. I wounded you in London. I see that now. I knew it then, but I could not seem to change my actions. My family… they were determined to be displeased in everything about our marriage, and I had not the courage to stand against them. I had never lacked that before! Though I was often uneducated and perhaps even wrong, I was never hesitant to defend what I thought was right, nor to speak what I believed when first I met you."

"You have suffered more of late, and they are your family, after all—not strangers lately brought to your notice who confronted all you had ever held dear."

"That was what made it so much worse. My own relations refused to accept a reasoned, conscious decision; a choice for life that cannot simply be undone by their expressions of displeasure. They only spoke of what they had wished for me, and I was too much afraid to confess my true feelings. John! You must know—I would have you know—I never cared for Henry Lennox."

His chest rose sharply beneath the steadying hand she had placed there, his breath feathering unevenly through the silken crown of hair under his chin. It was a moment before he found his voice, but when he did, the cracking of his tones betrayed more of his insecurities than he would have liked. "I am glad, love."

"Oh, what a fool I have been!" she whispered, and slid her arms tightly round him again to burrow her head into his shoulder.

"Come, Margaret," he soothed, "let us put this in the past. I do not care to think on it longer. You should know I have ever been one to look ahead rather than behind."

She sniffled, attempted a light laugh, and drew back enough to wipe her eyes. "And what is before us? The mill you have spent your lifetime building has failed, we shall never have the children we longed for, and both your family and mine are put out with us. Precisely what are we looking forward to?"

He lifted her from the bed, caressing her cheek and drawing her under his arm. "Everything."

28 June 1853

"Margaret, can this be real? Are we truly leaving Helstone and all we love behind? Oh, what can your father be thinking?"

Mrs Hale had not ceased trembling for a se'nnight, causing all about her to tend her with a concern which might have been better applied to their present troubles. Margaret, in particular, had felt the burden of her mother's grief, for it was she who had most earnestly wished to be of some comfort, but her assurances which had been found the least desirable by their object.

Mrs Hale quaked now as they neared the train. The iron behemoth belched out a cloud of coal smoke and hot steam, and the press of passengers all about drove them relentlessly forward. She sought Dixon's arm, but Dixon was occupied in demanding the services of a porter to take their smaller luggage.

"It will be well, Mamma. You know Papa has spoken with Mr Bell, and he has recommended a place for us—and he has a tenant in Milton who has pledged to help Papa."

"But to leave Helstone! Oh, it does not bear thinking of. I see it now, though it is too late, what a haven it has always been! I never thought I should have to leave my home for an industrial city. Could we not have gone anywhere less horrid? Oh! Is the entire journey to be like this?" She shook anew as the great steam whistle cried out for passengers to board and grasped Margaret's arm at last.

"Mamma, hold my hand," Margaret soothed. "We will see that you are well settled and comfortable. And you know, Papa had set aside a sum for you and Dixon to take a few days at the coast while we look for a house—will that not be like a holiday? I am sure it will do you good."

But her mother was shaking her head. "Nothing good is to be found in this, Margaret. It is all a waste. Your father has been a fool, and he has ruined us all!"

Margaret made no reply to this accusation. She could not so readily abuse her father's object, nor fail to applaud the sense of dignity which had forced him into this decision, but there was that lingering sense of disquiet. Once having settled his choice, he did not appear satisfied with it, nor confident in his direction.

He passed by them now, his eyes on the ground rather than the door of the train, and his mouth fallen into that habitual melancholy which bespoke his reluctance to do the thing he had determined. Margaret wished to stop him there and again ask if this was truly his desire, for if it were not, might not he speak again with the bishop? Might not some other situation be found which would not require her mother to spend her later years in a noisome black hole of a city? But Mr Hale appeared no firmer in resolve than his wife and only kept up the motions out of a seeming sense of pride.

Margaret tried to smile back at her mother. "Papa has gone ahead to take our seats. We shall have our own private little box, and you can sit beside me, and we will look out on all the sights as we pass."

At this moment, Dixon reclaimed Mrs Hale's other arm, and Margaret's mother pulled away her hand so that she might draw out a handkerchief. Into this article she wept as she mounted the train.

The journey north was broken into stages; they took a London hotel, but there was no visit to their Harley Street relations to comfort Mrs Hale or to mortify her husband. Margaret had gazed longingly out at their usual stop as the train rolled away north. Edith would be in Corfu by now, and her aunt on her way to Italy. She sighed and stared down at her own rose-embroidered handkerchief, held ready in her lap in case her mother had need of an extra, but Dixon had kept Mrs Hale well supplied.

At last, the engine steamed into Heston, and the family took their lodgings for the night. Mrs Hale and Dixon had a small room not far from the shore, but it did not overlook the ocean.

"Mamma, see how close it is? It is only a short walk. I daresay you could be there in less than ten minutes."

"Oh, Margaret, how could you think of it? I cannot walk so far. Am I not at least to have the pleasure of seeing the water before I spend the rest of my life looking at smoky, dirty city?"

Margaret could say little more, but she again offered her mother her handkerchief and was refused.

Dawn of the following day found Margaret and her father already on a train bound for Milton. Their ride was short, a mere half hour, but the scenery was that of another world. Margaret leaned close to the window and stared in silent awe. Cities, she had seen, but there was something to the raw, earthy quality of Milton which rendered it somewhere between the grit and mire of a destitute farm and the dark hopelessness of a coal mine, all splattered upon tall buildings that blocked the horizon. It looked to her like… like the fourth circle of Dante's Inferno.

"Papa—" she nudged him gently to rouse him—"we are here."

Mr Hale twitched—he had not truly found the comfort of sleep, but a pitiless daze had claimed his consciousness, in which he had no rest but a constant sense of helpless dread. He roused himself now and his gaze took in the charred buildings all round as the train drew into the station.

He did not speak, but Margaret was watching his manner, hoping to draw her courage from his resolve. She found instead a certain frailty of expression, in the slight twinge about his eyes and the nervous workings of his mouth. Perhaps in that moment, she understood. The course he had set upon terrified him as much as herself, and though it had been his determination, it was she who must carry him to it.

"Come, Papa—" she patted his arm—"the doors are starting to open. Where shall we go first?"

He looked down to a bit of paper drawn from his pocket, worn and soft from countless perusals and re-foldings. "A hotel on New Street. There is a room reserved for us."

"Already? Mr Bell must have sent word?"

"No, it was the Mr Thornton I spoke of. I expect we shall meet him today. Mr Bell speaks highly of him and says he will prove a valuable friend in the city."

She smiled and took her father's arm, rather than waiting for him to offer it. "A friend would certainly be welcome."

Yes, any friend, if it gave her father hope. Even a... what was Mr Thornton? A cotton manufacturer, if she remembered correctly. A shabby little king in a filthy little kingdom. She wrinkled her nose as they made their way to a cab.

Christian charity aside, the figures she saw lining the streets were ragged, dismal, and grey... everywhere she looked, from the stone buildings to the drab clothing and the colourless expressions on the faces of the people, it was all one shade of coal-blackened ambivalence.

"It seems a pleasant enough city," she lied, squeezing her father's hand. "We ought to do well here, Papa."

29 April 1856

There was no fanfare announcing Marlborough Mills' last day. No crowds of mourners lined the streets, no fellow mill owners commiserated with the failed master. The same workers came, and when the cotton ran out, they collected their final pay and went.

Had Margaret not come to know each face so intimately, she might have missed the darkened countenances, might have presumed them for a general malaise rather than blighted prospects. But she did know them, and her heart broke in pity as she looked on. They left in family groups, with husbands seeking out their wives and children clinging to their mothers.

Higgins, as something of an acting overseer, would not leave his post until the final, bitter moment. Nor did Mary, for John had insisted that on this last day, what remained of the food purchased for the yard kitchen be cooked up and served, and no one paid for their meal. Margaret had looked on Mary's frantic haste with fascination and had finally persuaded the girl to allow her to help in bringing bowls of stew to the hungry workers as they left Marlborough Mills for good.

Not one worker pushed his way in front of another. Strange, how human nature often inspired a rabid quality in its bearers when something was offered without cost, but it was curiously absent on this occasion. Perhaps it might have been her own presence, the master's wife, which gave them some pause, but all were reserved and gracious. Margaret could not help but marvel.

At last, the food ran out. Margaret went away with the larger group, but her steps carried her not towards the gates, but up to the master's office. John had sunken into his chair, his elbow propped upon his desk and his weary eyes hidden in his hand.

She observed him a moment in concern as she hung her bonnet and shawl. "John?" He raised his head when he heard her, and she hungrily sought his expression for any symptoms of despair.

"Love," he sighed, and rose from his desk. "That is the end of it. The last worker paid—I have but to wait on payment for the final orders, and then find someone to take the remnants, and we are finished." He extended his arm, and she came to nestle into his embrace, leaning her head close until his breath tickled her hair.

"I found a house we might take. It is not so large as yours in Crampton was, but there is a place for Dixon. It should serve until I have secured another permanent position. I am to speak with Slickson tomorrow, for his nephew has a new mill in Leeds and is seeking an overseer. They have offered me the position, but I have not yet accepted it."

Margaret pulled closer into his arms and rested her hand upon his chest. "An overseer."

He stroked down her back. "Are you now affected by pride, Mrs Thornton? Shall it distress you to be an overseer's wife?"

"No—" she twisted to smile up at him—"but I wondered about you."

"I do as I must and thank heaven for the opportunity. I will confess, however, the prospect seemed all the more daunting yesterday than it does today." He tightened his arm around her and rested his cheek upon her hair. "I only wish I could have done something more... look at them, Margaret."

She looked to where he had gestured and could see that Nicholas Higgins and his family trailing through the yard, on their way home at last. Mary leaned upon her father, and the eldest of the Boucher children, who had recently come to work at the mill, held his far hand.

"Do you know where else they will find work?"

He shook his head. "I told Higgins I would have him on if I should go to another mill. Margaret! You have not seen this." He pulled from her and turned to his desk, drawing out a long sheet of paper.

"Higgins brought it earlier. It is a round robin, signed by most of the hands; all stating their wish to work under me again, should I ever be in the position of hiring. This—" he scanned over the page, pride gleaming in his eyes—"this is something of a victory, I believe. I can think of no failed master who has received such a resounding endorsement of his labours from his workers."

Margaret took the paper into her own hands, smiling at each name she recognised. "A victory it is—it is just right. You have not failed, John. You are simply going on to another opportunity."

She returned the page, and he carefully put it aside to form the beginning of a stack of items he intended to carry away from the now useless desk. Margaret watched him with a growing swell of affection. Every movement was clear and determined. The set of his face, if not optimistic, was far from morose. She observed in silence, her heart full of memory and resolve, and so invested was she in his labours that she started when the door opened behind her.

John looked up before Margaret could turn. "Mother." His face flickered in an instant of pain, then pleasure.

Hannah Donaldson's grave expression swept over them both. Margaret's presence she acknowledged with a faint softening about her eyes, a twitch of welcome upon her lips, but her concern was all for her son. "What is to be done?" she asked, with characteristic brusqueness.

He went to her and took the hand she extended. "It is not the end of all things, Mother. I am looking out for another position, and I've an appointment with Slickson tomorrow to discuss an opportunity. Mr Bell's attorney is coming from London later in the afternoon, to sign papers granting a sublease until mine expires. If I can find someone willing to take it on!"

"And where will you go? Where are you to live, John? Would that the doctor's house was large enough—"

"Mother—" he stopped her—"Margaret and I will manage. You are good to be concerned, and I am grateful that your situation is secure, but you must not fear for us."

Hannah glanced to Margaret, and a peculiar thought seemed to edge her mouth upward. "Then I shall not. You, the pair of you, are too stubborn not to succeed in some manner. Heaven help any who stand in your way."

Twenty-Three

The study would be the hardest.

John released a low sigh as he stood in the centre of the room, daunted by the stacks surrounding him. They meant to sell most of the other household items, and a man from Harper's was coming on the morrow to give him a price for all of it. Margaret's old writing desk they would keep, and Mr Hale's settee, which held so many sweet memories for them both.

But his study... all those books, some of them treasured as his earliest purchases when he could afford them, others cherished as Mr Hale's belongings... they could not keep them all.

Margaret had set to work industriously at his side, and he had nearly wept. Not for grief—no, not in any sorrow, but in relief and pride. It pained him to see her carefully sorting her father's things, pierced him anew each time she smiled wistfully and added another to the stack to be sold, and threatened to undo him when she would look up with that sheen in her eyes. There was no accusation, no regret, but satisfaction, fellowship, and faith. What had he ever done to deserve her?

"Do you think we have space enough for Papa's sermons?" she wondered, her fingers grazing down a stack of handwritten journals. "They are so many... I wish I could have sent them to Frederick, for he would have treasured them."

He crouched again beside her. "Keep them, Margaret. I have read some of them myself, and it is like hearing your father's voice again in my ear. Do not discard them, by any means. I will forego a chair if I must, to make space."

She turned, her nose brushing his cheek. "I have thought of something else we could do to save space."

"Have you? Pray, tell."

She kissed the lower edge of his ear, then whispered, "Let us keep only your bed. I never liked sleeping alone in mine, anyway."

"Or better yet," he murmured back, his tones suggestive, "let us sell mine as well, and buy a smaller one. Then you could not evade me so easily."

She sputtered in laughter, leaning on his shoulder until he could see nothing else for it but to draw her into his embrace and kiss her as she deserved. The tower of journals was soon scattered by her skirts as she shifted to return his affections, and her arms looped possessively round his neck.

He laid her back, supporting her with his arm, and only forsook the pleasure of gazing at her for the tempting, soft kisses she brushed over his lips. He closed his eyes and felt the sigh of her breath, her fingers in his hair, and the even drumming of her heart against his. What need had a man for anything but her? His was a wealth that could not be counted in pounds, shillings or pence, and he meant to revel in her as a miser did his gold.

"I... hope I am not interrupting," came a voice from the doorway.

Margaret gasped and straightened, and John cleared his throat. They were both still splayed on the floor, and he scrambled to his feet to help her before he turned to identify their surprise visitor.

It was Margaret who recognised him first. "Mr Bell!"

"Well, Margaret, my dear, it *is* you! I had wondered for half a moment," he chuckled, seeming vastly pleased with himself. "Would you prefer that I came back at another time?"

"No!" John had recovered some of his dignity and extended a hand. "You are most welcome, Mr Bell, but we had not expected to see you. I thought you still in South America."

"Did you? I am quite certain I wrote of my intentions to travel back in the spring."

"You mentioned something of it last autumn, but we had heard nothing since."

"I did not think you needed to," Bell retorted with a wry twinkle to his eye. He turned then to Margaret. "Well, my dear, let me look at you. I see that married life has not, after all, been the death of you."

John arched a brow. How much had Bell been informed of in her letters? For there was a time when it almost had been....

"Quite the opposite," she assured Bell with a smile, which she then bashfully bestowed upon John. "I am most content."

"And your husband has not been too tiresome? I understand such creatures can be, but of course I could not speak on that point."

Margaret laughed and lifted her hand for John to take, as the fine lady she was. "You would not believe me if I told you that Mr Thornton is without fault, but our mutual flaws are well suited."

John glanced down in guilty confirmation and found her smiling up at him with such affection that he forgot, for half a pulse, the presence of their visitor.

"Well, my dear—" Bell coughed politely—"I believe you may be the first person to accuse John Thornton of some deficiency and manage to provoke him to smile at you for it. I always suspected him of some sense, and I am glad to see I was not, after all, entirely wrong."

"Even a fool knows when he has been given a treasure," John answered, regretfully tearing his eyes from the amused sparkle in hers. "Mr Bell, may we offer you something? I am afraid the cook has gone, but we've some cold provisions. You must have been on a train all day."

Bell shook his head and waved a dismissive hand. "No, no, just a chair, please. This dratted gout—ah, that is better! Thank you, my dear." Bell sagged heavily in the chair Margaret had led him to, and his eyes began to wander about the room as John and Margaret settled into a sofa facing him. His countenance changed, and he sighed.

"I heard about the mill yesterday when I arrived in London. I am sorry, Thornton! I'd no idea you were in such straits. Margaret, you have married a taciturn, hard-headed fellow. Somehow, he can contrive to honestly lay out his circumstances, concealing nothing of fact or import, and yet in so confident a manner that none could suspect he did not have every expectation of success. Thornton, I did not like to lose you as a tenant, but for Margaret's sake I was even more troubled. It simply will not do! Naturally, I came myself instead of my solicitor to see what might be done."

"What might be done?" Margaret repeated with arched brows and a note of suspicion. "Had you some particular thought?"

John felt her glance in his direction, and a shiver of concern washed over him. Her hopes for him were everything generous, but perhaps she did not understand the cost of accepting charity!

"Why, naturally, child. Although, I would not like you to think I might prove the answer to all the mill's troubles—my pockets are not so deep as that just now. A month—nay, a fortnight even, will tell."

"Mr Bell—" John shook his head—"I must thank you for your concern, but we will ask nothing of you. We had settled it between ourselves that we were to go elsewhere, and go we shall."

"And where will you take my god-daughter, Thornton? Have you work yet? A situation? No! It will not do. You must remain here, for I am not impoverished, after all. I can at least grant you a month or two of rent on the house, or as long as it takes to determine your course. I'll not have Hale's old books feed the fire—" he gestured about the room—"simply because you must remove in a hurry and can scarcely put a roof over them."

John and Margaret glanced at each other. "I do have a situation secured for us, sir; another house, already taken under contract, and one or two sound prospects for work. I would hardly describe our circumstances as desperate."

Bell studied him for a moment, then turned his attention to Margaret. "I see how it is. All the foolhardiness of young lovers, not a care in the world save one another. Well, let me be the last to disrupt your happy poverty, but I will be satisfied on certain points. Margaret is still my god-daughter—well, you are, my dear, or at least, I have taken you as such. Since Frederick was christened as my god-son, I've taken a fancy to claiming both my old friend's children. Surely I must be permitted some dignity regarding her provision."

Margaret leaned forward and took his hand between hers. "You are generous, Mr Bell, but you must look for another tenant for the mill, and the house will likely be desired by the same."

"If it is, what matter a month or two? They can wait to take possession of the house if it is not ready. My real reason for wishing to do something now, Thornton, is that I expect to be in a fine way rather soon. You must have heard of that rail speculation of Wright's—indeed, I believe he must have approached you."

John felt his face twitching, and Margaret was now shifting her gaze towards him. "He did, but I refused."

"As I expected you might, but no matter, for my man had invested a fair sum of mine there. We should begin seeing the pay-out at almost any moment, and then I shall have the power to be of real use to you. Meanwhile, Thornton, what do you say to a loan of three hundred pounds? I am afraid it is the best I can do at present, but it would go some way, would it not?"

A lump tightened in his chest, squeezing round his throat, and he felt, once again, Margaret's eyes on him. How could he disappoint her with his refusal? And yet, how could he respect himself if he accepted?

His teeth clenched, and he risked one regretful glance at her face, but rather than hopeful pleading, discovered resolve. Her look was grave and quiet; trusting and speaking of a will united with his own. He began to breathe a little.

"I thank you, Mr Bell—" he slid his eyes from her and back to the gentleman—"but I cannot."

"What is this? Not even to save your business? What could you do with three hundred pounds in the short-term?"

"Nothing but inspire false hope, sir. I am afraid it would take at least double that to set matters right—enough to purchase cotton and time. We had orders we were never able to fill, but I found other mills to take them on, and now I have no buyers at all. Additionally, I would have to approach the bank again to take out another loan on my own machinery, as it is all forfeit—and at present, I have not the credit to do so. I mean no slight against your generous offer, for it is indeed kind of you. Three hundred pounds would put us in cotton long enough to begin, but we could not sell it quickly enough to go on."

"Yes, but three hundred is only the beginning. I mean to do more, and I shall be able to soon. You would not refuse an old man the pleasure of being useful to his god-daughter."

"I would not place the mill in a situation which depends upon circumstances beyond anyone's control. My men deserve better than false starts and uncertainty. It is a matter of proper timing, sir."

Bell narrowed his eyes and touched a finger to his lips. "Then, indeed, I am being scolded for my reticence when I first heard of your marriage. Had I offered the same then, you are telling me, you might have done more with it? You had sufficient cause to expect something then, did you not?"

"Mr Bell!" Margaret's cheeks had flushed. "Do you mean to imply that Mr Thornton had mercenary motives when we wed?"

"Thornton? You married a manufacturer, Margaret. Do not they all require capital? I confess, I noted some fascination between the pair of you last year, but I never thought you would have him. The timing, as Thornton says, gave me pause, for I knew he was in some difficulty after the strikes, and I was just contrary enough to think perhaps it was no more than a business arrangement on both your parts. The little scene I witnessed earlier proves to me what a fool I was in that regard, but I was not entirely without cause for concern, was I? I wished to see you content with my own eyes, Margaret, and your letters had each sounded rather despondent."

"Mr Bell," John broke in, the heat rising in his face, "I had no expectations of you, and cannot now accept what you might consider as charity, granted with one hand, while the other dictates terms. Dignity, honour, even my feelings for my wife object. You think I married Margaret for what advantages I might have gained? Indeed, perhaps I did, for I have gained in every possible way, but I care nothing for your money or your support. I am already more blessed than I deserve, and I will not bear the injustice of hearing her, or myself, suspected of anything but the sincerest attachment or the noblest reasons for marriage."

Bell gazed up from his chair with a crooked smile, shaking his head. "I was attempting to apologise, Thornton. I was wrong, and I would make what amends I can. Sit down and let us speak of this rationally. You are too intelligent to bear a grudge against a man because you were once thwarted! I speak both of myself and of Wright. Is my money tainted because I was a stubborn, grieving old goose who could not wish you happiness when I first heard of your marriage? Does it have blood on it because I have invested with the son of the man who swindled your father?"

The tension began to drain from his shoulders, and he looked again to Margaret. "Mr Bell," she explained in her sweet, sensible voice, "let it all be forgotten. The conversation can have no purpose save to agitate those who are meant to profit by it. Mr Thornton was quite correct when he said before that a loan would only delay the inevitable, and therefore it would be unfair to accept."

"Did you not hear all I said? I shall have more than I know what to do with inside a month. Can you so readily allow your husband to pass up this chance, Margaret? I should have thought it enough of a comedown in the world for you to become a manufacturer's wife, but an overseer, a common shopkeeper? No, no, I recall how calmly you removed from London and Helstone to come here, and I see you have settled well, so that is perhaps an unreasoning fear. I shall have faith that you, my dear, might content yourself almost anywhere, but your husband would run mad within a week, having so little to do after having once found such success. He would drive you to distraction, I will warrant."

Margaret laughed softly. "It would not be the first time he has done so, nor the last, Mr Bell. I have become rather fond of anticipating how he will shock me next. I do know, however, that he is quite determined, and I am in agreement with him. It might harm more than it could mend, with so much that remains uncertain. Surely, you must also know that his reluctance to enter into a short-term loan is out of concern for you as well as for himself."

"Ah, yes, I see it. You are cynical because Wright was involved, and you think I shall be left holding nothing but my hat. That is it, is it, Thornton? Well, you may set your mind at ease, because I invested nothing I could not afford to lose, though others might have done more. It was enough that the return shall see to all my own wants and then some. Thornton, you would truly pass up an opportunity to start the mill back to work the sooner because you doubt so strongly? Prudence has its place, of course, but I think this excessive caution must be unwarranted."

"Be that as it may—" John slipped his hand over Margaret's shoulders, drawing her close and caring little for the teasing twinkle in Bell's eye when he did so—"we must respectfully decline, sir. We shall proceed with our plans to remove so the house may be let by another. If you must exert yourself on our behalf, I would be most appreciative of any contacts to whom you might forward a recommendation, as I have not yet found a situation which presents itself to me as suitable to our wants."

Bell sighed, and his look passed from John to Margaret, and back again. "Well, suit yourself, Thornton. But you are going nowhere today, and I should prefer to impose upon you for lodgings, rather than taking my chances at a hotel. I know Mrs Thornton's rooms will be well-aired and comfortable—" he spared Margaret a wink—"and the company is the best in Milton."

~

Mr Bell remained with them only one day, for the presence of a guest when one is removing to a new residence cannot be welcome. He did not go far, only to a hotel three streets from the mill, but Margaret felt keenly the loss. That night he had stayed with them, the old stone house on Marlborough Street had rung with more laughter than she had ever known it to do. It felt to her so very much like the old days in Crampton that she almost expected to see her father reclining in a fourth chair by the fire, and to hear her mother stirring in the next room.

The next day brought a sad recollection of their true circumstances, for after their most immediate belongings were packed into a drayage cart, she took her husband's arm and they walked the half mile to their new residence. Many a face greeted her on their route. Some looked on in pity, others in disdain, but more with lost hope. John Thornton had been the idol upon whom they had placed their faith, and he had fallen as any other mortal man.

She squeezed her arm through his and glanced up to him; read the tightness behind his eyes and the grim line of his mouth. He would face them as a man, as one who could stand proudly knowing he had done all with honour, but he did not do so without sorrow and regret for what he could not complete.

Their new residence was, indeed, much smaller even than the Crampton house. It boasted two bedrooms, a small area that could be termed a sitting room on each of its floors, a respectably sized utility closet that might do for a bedroom at a scrape, and a kitchen which Dixon instantly pronounced to be abysmal. With so little space to fill, they were settled quickly.

Hannah found her assistance unnecessary when she arrived to help put things into order, but her presence was welcome to Margaret in more meaningful ways. That hour they spent over tea while John was out on a business call served to christen the little abode and make it into a home. When her guest had gone away again, she could look about the humble walls and feel that this, now, was her place in the world, and it was well with her.

A fortnight of relative peace slipped away in this manner. Mr Bell remained in town only a few days longer, then returned to Oxford. He wrote more often, though, and frequently referred to his expectations, which would surely be answered any day. Margaret only replied in the vaguest of terms and refused to vex John by continuously showing Mr Bell's letters to him.

John, with his characteristic decisiveness, agreed to work with Mr Hamper for a month. Hamper desired to glean some of John's expertise to tighten his own operations, and within only a few days, John's advice and oversight were already doing much to improve circumstances at Hamper's mill. What he was to do after this arrangement had been completed, he did not yet know, but he departed early each morning with a spring in his step and returned at the same time every evening with a smile on his lips for his bride.

"Do you know," he confided to Margaret over dinner that second week, "there is some charm in knowing what hours are to be my own. I shall not say I prefer working for another to being my own master, but for the present, I am quite delighting in my ability to walk away from my work when the day is over, and not having it haunt my evenings with you."

"Even when Mr Hamper ignores your suggestions for improvement?"

"Particularly then, for every time he has done so, I have been proved correct. He is learning to heed my advice the first time I give it rather than the second or the third. I even persuaded him to take Higgins back today, and that was an accomplishment of which I am rather proud."

"You did! I thought Mr Hamper swore he would never have Nicholas enter his mill again."

John raised his glass with a spark of mischief in his eye. "I will admit to a little sleight of hand. I told Hamper I knew of a fellow who could keep the line running more efficiently than his present foreman, and who could turn out the finest cloth on any type of loom of any man I had ever employed. I led him on the whole of the day with mysterious compliments to the same effect until he insisted that I track this man down and bring him on at eighteen shillings per week. He only coughed for a moment when I gave him the name of the man I had hired for him."

Margaret laughed and rose from her seat to put her arms around him and kiss his cheek in both gratitude and amusement. "My dearest John, you have achieved the impossible!"

He raised his brows in interest and pushed back his chair from the table, the better to receive her attentions. "The impossible, you say? My love, I did that long ago, when I persuaded you to have me."

Margaret lowered herself to his lap, her arms still round his shoulders and her lips hidden somewhere just below his ear when she answered. "That was far from impossible. Rather, I would call it inevitable. You captivated me from the first, and even before I loved you—even when I heartily disliked you—I measured every other man by you. So, do you see, there was little hope of any other outcome."

"Then," he frowned pointedly, "I am not quite so gifted a miracle worker as I had thought. It is a hard thing, to discover that my opinion of myself was entirely unjustified."

"Shall you require some comfort after such a revelation?" She tightened her arms around his neck, preparing for what she knew he would do next.

"Indeed," was his ragged answer. A moment later, he had lifted her from the table, and his steps scarcely faltered when he carried her up the steep little flight of stairs.

~

28 May 1856

John's month at Hamper's mill flew by for Margaret. By the time he left off his advisement, Hamper was seeing a better return on his labours, had hired thirty-five new hands—all former workers at Marlborough Mills—and John had secured more permanent work.

He had turned down an offer from a wealthy Londoner who wished to "dabble" in cotton, purely as a side investment, as well as Slickson's offer to work under his nephew. In the end, he accepted a lower position as an overseer at a small mill just acquired by the Browns on the outskirts of Milton. When his mother asked why he would have accepted such low pay as the Brown brothers offered when he could have made twice as much in Manchester, he merely smiled, kissed her hand, and stated his loyalty to the city of his birth.

Margaret learned the leisure of a husband at home for the first time in her marriage. It was four days before he was to start working again, for there had been some delay in the first shipment of cotton to the new mill. Everything else was in order, and John had nothing whatsoever to do.

She watched him in some amusement as he tried to appear at ease with the wait. He had muttered gloomily about the short holiday his father had once taken them on to the coast when he had been a boy, but she cheered him with something far more delicious than salt air. He confessed later that he would much rather cradle his wife in the comfort of their own home than distress her with travel and expenses they both well knew they could not afford.

Thus, it was that on this first day of his brief liberty, he did not rouse so early as had always been his wont, and Margaret was glad of it. She had been feeling slightly unwell, perhaps owing to her labours of the last weeks or the dust of the new house, and he made it his stated object to keep her off her feet for at least another hour of sweet repose. When they did come below, the morning was half done, and Dixon had gone out.

"I should not make a habit of mornings such as these," John confessed over tea, "but I begin to see what pleasures I have missed. I was always up before the sun, even on days when I needn't have been."

She caught his hand and held it tenderly, but no response could she utter before there was a frantic pounding on the door. Margaret watched John's face alter—the protective instincts of a husband warring with concern for whomever demanded entry to their house in such a desperate fashion. He motioned for her to remain seated as he rose to investigate. Before he had even opened the door, however, they could both recognise Dr Donaldson's voice from without.

"Thornton, are you at home? In the name of heaven, man, let me speak with you!"

Margaret heard a low curse from John as he struggled with the stiff latch, and then the door was wide, and Donaldson stood there, covered with blood.

"Mother!" he cried. "Donaldson, where is my mother? What has happened?"

"No!" the other hastened to assure him. "Your mother is quite well, or as well as she might be. Close the door, Thornton."

"My mother is well?" John repeated, a little insensibly. Margaret had arisen, and it was she who closed the door while John collected himself.

"I left her with Mrs Watson. Thornton, Watson has killed himself."

Margaret's knees weakened, and she sought a chair before she grew faint.

"Watson!" John, too, fell into a seat.

Donaldson was less unsettled by now and declined a chair due to the state of his clothing. He stood instead by the fire grate and drew out a handkerchief which looked as though it had already wiped his hands once.

"About an hour ago, I understand. Mrs Watson was not in a state for explanations when we arrived. Her housemaid came to beg my help, but there was nothing I could do for the poor bastard. He shot himself, Thornton. Just the same way...."

John was nodding weakly. "I remember."

"Doctor, what of Fanny?" Margaret rose again, unsteadily, to place a hand on John's shoulder. He, too, looked urgently to the doctor.

Donaldson shook his head. "She heard it all from another room and is in a fit of hysterics. Your mother fears for her, in her condition. Thornton, you must go to her."

John nodded, numbly, and laced his fingers with Margaret's hand. Both men looked to her, and she bore herself up with a courage she did not feel. "I will come, too."

~

They found Fanny Watson half dragged to a fainting couch and slumped in her mother's arms. Hannah was rocking her as she used to do when her child was very small, cradling her and stroking her hair with an overt affection she had not shown in many long years. Fanny's swollen body shook with deep, shrieking cries, and she did not notice their entry until John knelt at her side and rested a hand on her shoulder.

"Fanny?" he called gently.

She raised her head from her mother's bosom and turned bleary eyes on him, but it was not his face she ultimately sought. She tried to rise, stumbled and scarcely noticed when he caught her fall, then flung herself headlong into Margaret's arms. John could only stand back and watch as Margaret embraced his sister.

Margaret looked as baffled as he for a moment, but she accepted her charge with steady grace, crooning comfort and tender words to the sister who had so often disdained her. John turned his attention next to his mother. Donaldson had arrived behind her chair to take her far hand, but she turned haggard, stricken eyes to her son.

"Mother!" he sat beside her and took her other hand. "What has happened? Has Fanny told you anything?"

"She did not, but there was a telegram from London on his desk. The maid says a runner brought it just before Watson shut himself in his office."

"What did it say?"

His mother glanced up at Donaldson. They shared a significant look, then directed their gazes back to him. "I did not read it. It was not my chief concern."

"Of course." He sighed, raked his fingers through his hair, and rose. "Has the body been carried away?"

The doctor only nodded and assumed the seat John had just vacated, draping his arm over Hannah's shoulders in a shocking display of tenderness. John hesitated only a moment, struck for the first time by the look of peace in his mother's face as her new husband shielded her from the horrors which could not help but remind her of darker days.

He glanced to Margaret and Fanny, now seated together on another couch. Fanny was clinging to his wife with the strength born of despair and terror, and Margaret bore it all with gentleness. For a moment, at least, he was not wanted.

Watson's study reeked of that same metallic tang, the same earthy pungency he had tried for almost eighteen years to forget. His hand caught on the door latch, and he felt it tremble. His eyes, he forced open again, and a sick, helpless feeling overcame him. He was fourteen once more, standing in the midst of carnage and longing to push back the reality before him, to undo what was done.

His steps faltering, he shuffled towards the desk. The blood—oh, good God, it was everywhere! John's stomach twisted, and he nearly gagged. He pulled his handkerchief from his pocket to cover his nose and wished to heaven he could blot the images from his mind as well.

Watson's desk, typically so meticulous, was scattered all over with bloodstained papers. John drew near, blinking back the sting from his eyes to make them out. The telegram was thrust to the left of the desk, and half covered in red. John squinted, tilted his head, and read what he could.

"... *accident. Stop. Three thousand more needed. Stop. Remit... recover the debt... Stop.*"

The rest was darkened with Watson's blood, and John could not bring himself to pick it up, tilt it in the light, and decipher the impressions in the paper to read more. He turned his attention instead to the documents scattered over the desk, the open drawers, and, most particularly, the document which lay on top of all the rest. Pen marks slashed over it, and it had been ripped in two.

John turned the remains of it over, his fingers extended delicately to avoid the drying blood splattered over it. It was a contract, or what was left of one, signed several months earlier by Watson... and Harold Wright.

~

Margaret followed her mother-in-law softly out of Fanny's room and closed the door. "Should we not remain close, in case she wakes?"

"The doctor assures me that the draught he prepared will see her resting for hours." Hannah passed a hand over her eyes, then sought Margaret's grasp as they turned away from Fanny's door. "My poor girl! I am afraid it has only begun for her, and in her condition, she will need her strength. We will look in on her later."

Margaret steadied the older woman on the stair, for Hannah swayed a little as they neared the descent. "Are you well?" she asked in alarm.

Hannah winced, then released a low groan. "I am no longer young, Margaret. I have seen this before, and I know what lies ahead for her. I will do all I can, but I am afraid—" she turned to Margaret as they reached the landing on the stairs, "—I am afraid most of it will fall to John, and to you."

Margaret forced a brave smile, clasping her mother-in-law's hand a little more tightly. "We will do all we can for her, I promise."

"Margaret...." Hannah hesitated, glanced down the stairs, then looked steadily back. "I wonder if you realise yet what you have promised. Fanny must go elsewhere. The house will be confiscated, as it was a suicide. All her other possessions, whatever remain, must be sold to cover the debts. The doctor has already assured me that, if necessary, we could make a place for her, but I do not think it will be her preference. It was not my arms she ran to when she sought comfort, but yours."

Margaret looked to the carpet. "I am certain that was only the impulse of the moment. I cannot think what could have made her do so, other than the confusion of all her feelings. She will long for her mother when her time draws near, and she must raise a child without a father. She will look to your expertise, for I have none."

"What she will long for is one of her own age, who is experienced in sorrow and can whisper encouragement. I have never been such a one for her. For John, yes; his character is made of sterner stuff than Fanny's. I could admonish and exhort him, but Fanny—" her eyes misted for a moment. "Fanny was always more like her father. I have tried to be tender with her, all her life, but I have misunderstood her. You will succeed where I cannot."

"Surely, it is still early for such fears. Of course, John and I will welcome her if it is her choice to come to us. I am afraid our house is rather humbler than what she is accustomed to, but we can find a way."

"And when the babe comes, Margaret?" Hannah arched a brow and held her for what seemed an interminable stare. "Her confinement is near—less than a month, most likely."

Margaret looked down again. "Dixon and I can help."

"That is not my concern. What of your own disappointments? Will you not nurse some bitterness for a sister you hardly know, thrust into your house and interrupting your peaceful home? What of when she dandles a child upon her knee while you have been denied the same?"

Margaret swallowed thoughtfully, then raised her eyes again. "No," she whispered, but with a firmness which sent a shiver through her core. She meant it, and would choose that resolve daily, for so long as this duty was asked of her. "I will not. Has not Fanny suffered more greatly than I? I still have the husband I love, and I shall ever content myself with that. I will love her child and care for her as they deserve—as my husband deserves. Unless Fanny marries again someday, John will be like a father to his sister's child, and I will rejoice with her who takes comfort in her babe."

Hannah's eyes had filled with tears—the first time Margaret had ever seen her so. She cupped Margaret's cheek with one knotted hand and sniffed back what seemed to be more feeling than she could contain without breaking.

"God love you, my girl! 'Tis a deal for me to say, but you may as well know; you have become as my own flesh and blood now. I bless the day my son lost his heart to you."

Margaret trembled herself, blinking back a tide of unexpected emotion, and captured her mother-in-law's hand as it caressed her face. "And I, who lost all my own family, have found a home with yours. You have given me far more than you can ever know… Mother."

Hannah blinked, sniffed again, and composed her features. She lifted that square chin of hers and then laced her arm round Margaret's waist as Margaret reciprocated. "Come, then, my girl. Let us see what John has discovered, so we may learn all that lies ahead."

~

John had scarcely dropped into a chair in the sitting room, opposite Donaldson, when his mother and Margaret appeared at the door. They walked with their arms wound about each other, closely as he had seen sisters do—heads tipped towards one another in quiet confidence, strides matching, and skirts blending into one green-grey swirl.

He rose, and Margaret broke away from his mother to come to him. Even in the presence of the others, she nestled under his arm, looked up into his eyes and, quite easily, read all the horrors he would not speak. He saw her complexion pale, felt her small hand tighten where it had gripped the back of his coat, and he stroked her shoulder in comfort. "You had best be seated," he advised them both.

Margaret settled herself beside him, and all eyes fixed on his face. He squeezed his wife's hand. "It is as I feared. Watson had invested everything of his own with Wright, and then more. I found promissory notes for six different creditors, and I suspect there may be more I have not yet discovered. I daresay he imagined it would all come right, and he would handily pay back whatever was owed, but the telegram this morning spoke of some misfortune he had not foreseen. I could only make out that he was expected to render another large sum, for most of the telegram was... damaged. And then, the paper came."

Donaldson was casting haggard eyes to the ceiling by now, but Margaret and his mother leaned forward intently. "Has the speculation failed?" his mother guessed.

"Catastrophically, it would seem. There was an earthquake, and several miles of new rail line were destroyed. Two new engines fell into a chasm that opened below them, and the fireboxes exploded when they were smashed. Nearly fifteen hundred pounds are now smoking ruins, and I've no idea the cost to replace the broken lines or purchase and ship new materials, but that is not the worst of it. Six men were also killed trying to back the engines away from the danger, and the blame for their deaths has been cast—unjustly or no—to the shareholders."

"Good heavens!" Margaret cried. "It is everything dreadful! But—" her brow clouded, and she tilted her head up to him—"I still do not understand what would lead him to... what would cause Watson to despair so."

"He was already in debt beyond what he could ever hope to recover, unless the speculation came through... and quickly. I found correspondence with his creditors and, most importantly, a contract with Wright, which I believe will answer for that. Watson had nowhere else to obtain funds, for he had depleted all his credit with the bank and tapped every other man he could persuade.

Some of these were already growing impatient for repayment, and none would have been willing to invest more.

"The terms of Wright's contract were likely what drove Watson beyond reason. If at any point Watson could not uphold his share in the partnership, all would revert to Wright. It is precisely as his father used to do—lure men with promises of grand pay-outs, but if the costs went up and they could not meet the increased demands, they forfeited everything. Watson must have been searching for some way out of his contract, for it was marked up and shredded when I found it. He was ruined, utterly and completely, and too distraught to bear the disgrace."

"What now?" his mother demanded tightly. "What of Fanny?"

"I've no notion what Watson could call his own before all this. I expect that whatever is not confiscated will be leveraged to some degree—I cannot say how far. For a certainty, all that he invested with Wright is lost."

"And Wright himself?" Margaret asked, her jaw rigid. "Serve him right if he is ruined as well!"

He looked down into her flashing eyes and nearly kissed those stubborn, indignant lips which even now drew up into an outraged scowl. "I do not know. Nor, I find, do I care."

She arched a brow and tilted her head sceptically.

"Very well," he conceded. "I doubt Wright is ruined. He must recover his losses and will naturally be in search of another partner since he cannot claim more support from Watson. At worst, I expect he will see a delay to his fortunes. Perhaps his own investors might grow impatient, but if anyone can mollify such men, it is Wright. A year from now, it will be to Wright as if this had never happened, and poor Watson will be as forgotten as my own father."

She was shaking her head angrily, her body quivering in boiling fury. "But it is so wrong! How can you accept this so calmly, John?"

He touched her cheek, smiled affectionately, and then looked to his mother's raised chin and glittering eyes. He held her gaze for a moment, then turned back to Margaret. "Because I have come at last to recognise what is worth caring about, and it is not Wright. Come, Mrs Thornton, we still have a family to look after."

Twenty-Four

2 June 1856

Hannah Donaldson had been correct in all her assumptions regarding her daughter's immediate disposition, save for one. The distress of her present circumstances, the shock of removing from her home to live with her brother, and the physical exorcising of her emotional state in constant pacing, all conspired to bring Fanny to childbed only five days after her husband's death.

It was a hard case from the start, and Margaret and Dixon took their turns through the night—soothing the labouring mother's brow, quenching her thirst, and clasping her fevered hands, until the doctor and would-be grandmother arrived the next morning. Doctor Donaldson made his examination, shook his head, and confided to those standing by the bed that it was too soon, that it could go ill for both mother and child.

"However," he reassured them, just as their faces grew ashen, "the babe is presenting well, so perhaps it may yet come right."

John had not the luxury of remaining at home to watch over his sister, nor would he have been permitted to be of any use to her if he had stayed. He went, therefore, to his new post, and when he returned late that evening, he was rewarded by a sight that caused a joyful, excruciating pang through his heart. Margaret, bathed in radiant exhaustion, rocked near the hearth with a swaddled bundle in her arms.

She looked up at his entry, smiled the weary triumph of one who has agonised in sympathy with the sufferer, and lifted the bundle. "You have a niece, John."

He drew near and hesitantly touched the blankets to draw them away from a wrinkled face. "How is Fanny?"

"Well, but quite done in, as you might imagine. It was a bad time for her—harder than most, I understand. Your mother is sitting with her, and she asked me to bring Patience down here so that Fanny might not be disturbed for a while."

"Patience?" he asked, one brow lifted.

Margaret smiled. "I can only presume her name has some special meaning to her mother."

His fingers grazed the blankets one more time before tucking them close to the pointed little chin, the ruddy cheeks, and the pale streaks of hair. "It is too early to make any suppositions, but I believe Fanny will come through it all stronger than she has ever been. I have never seen her so thoughtful as she has been these days, and I am glad to see her confiding in you."

Margaret snuggled the child again to her body, rocking her protectively and bending her cheek to catch the infant's soft breaths. "Fanny is a Thornton, and if I have learned anything about them, they are a stubborn lot; hard to defeat and even harder to ignore once they have determined their course. I have complete faith in her."

He laughed and brushed a curl back from her face. "Shall I tell you what I have learned of the Hale family characteristics?"

"Oh, I do not dare ask. I am certain you will tell me how frightfully self-righteous and impulsive I can be, and I shudder to think how my own stubborn nature compares to yours. I fear you may have found one more stiff-necked than yourself!"

"And a lovely neck it is," he murmured as he bent low to kiss her ear. "May I hold my niece?"

Margaret surrendered her willingly, shifting from the old rocking chair she had kept from the Marlborough house garret to allow him to take it. He accepted the babe with a hesitant grin lighting his face. "It has been twenty years since I held one so young."

"Mind her head," Margaret cautioned him, but her concern was unnecessary. He settled himself, then smiled confidently. "You must need a rest, love. We shall be well enough—shall we not, my princess?"

Margaret laughed gently and accepted his offer of a respite. She returned only a short while later with an easel and an old box of watercolours and proceeded to situate herself only a few feet away.

"So," he teased, "you really can use those? Oh, I must see this."

"I shall only show you if it turns out," she informed him archly. "And I will begin straightaway, so I might master her face while she is still an infant. Hold her up just a little."

~

After the immediate crises of Watson's death and Fanny's labours had passed, the Thornton family were naturally concerned for Mr Bell's interests. Margaret had written him, hoping to learn that he, at least, had not suffered unduly in the recent setback. Three days later, a short reply came.

The letter was cryptic, as Bell's correspondences often were, but by no means despairing. Bell spoke of a small property he owned that he was able to pledge towards his own share, thus meeting the unexpected demand for payment before the prosperous enterprise could be concluded. There were others, however, who were not so fortunate, and Wright was "knocking on doors" to secure the additional funding needed to save them all from ruin.

Bell made some veiled hints about another contact of his, a secure businessman who might be well disposed towards him. It was a chance, he said, but a chance for what, Margaret could not guess.

She showed the letter to John, who shook his head. "Would that Wright could be taught a lesson in this," he sighed. "Perhaps he would think a second time before luring others to their ruin, but I suppose that is too much to hope for."

Margaret turned the note over again. "Perhaps… but did Mr Bell not sound rather smug to you? I am certain he knows some secret. Do you think he has some scheme of his own at work?"

"If he does, perhaps I ought to pity Wright! I would rather not think on it now, as it would be pure conjecture on my part."

Margaret put the letter away, then bent to tickle Patience in the cradle beside her chair. "Whatever it is," she crooned to the child, "it shall be none of *your* concern. What do you say, little dear, shall we persuade your uncle to hold you once more while I try to paint your pretty face?"

John laughed and obliged her before Patience could make any answer of her own. And thus, Harold Wright was never meant to be spoken of in their house again.

~

The sale of all the possessions remaining to Watson at the time of his death took less time than anyone could have expected. John naturally managed the affair, and a fortnight after the birth of her child, when Fanny had just begun to stir from her small bedroom, he presented her with the final details.

She sat beside Margaret, one hand clasping her daughter, and the other reaching for Margaret's reassurance. "What is left?" she asked tremulously.

John glanced between them. "Nothing. In fact, there remain over five hundred pounds to repay, but I have pledged myself to that. You have nothing to fear, Fanny."

She nodded, a silver tear slipping down her cheek, but she lifted her chin in that way of her mother's. Her throat trembled, and her lashes fluttered, and when she spoke, there was a choked sound to her voice. "I do not deserve your kindness, Brother." She turned to Margaret then, before John could utter his denial, and said, "nor yours, Margaret. I have been careless, and I daresay even wicked."

"It is forgotten." Margaret squeezed her hand. "Do not trouble yourself over the past, Fanny."

"But I must! Do you not see, Margaret? When you grieved, I triumphed over you. When you were near death, I coveted the concern that was shown you. And now, when it is my turn to walk through misery, I look and find only you at my side." She shook her head, then turned tear-filled eyes to her brother.

"And you, John—how often when I was a child, and you were little more than one yourself, did you soothe my hurts and suffer my indulgences? How many hours did you bend your back, so I could be kept in little comforts? And when I was grown, still I could not see beyond my own desires. How often did I sneer at you for not taking me to London, or for chastising my behaviour when it was unbecoming? How much did I require you to spend on my wedding to a pompous, short-sighted fool who was too arrogant to heed your advice when he ought to have?"

"Fanny," he cautioned, raising his hand, "do not do this."

"Do what, John?" she asked innocently. The tears fell more freely now, but her voice was curiously steady. "Recognise my own faults? Has it not been your wish these five years at least that one day I would do so?"

"Not in this way. Not in a manner which will only grieve you further and insult the memory of your husband."

"His legacy was destroyed by his own hands," she retorted. "And now you, who were not at fault, must accept responsibility for his folly. I'll say nothing kind in his defence. Had he not been such a weak-minded buffoon, he would have—"

"Fanny," John's voice rose, "you only harm yourself by abusing Watson!"

Her eyes clouded in annoyance. "There, you see! Even when I try to apologise to you, I fail!" She sniffled, her lips puckered to stop herself from sobbing aloud as she raised a hand to cover her mouth. "Am I never to be good enough, John?"

"Fanny," Margaret soothed, reaching again for her hand, "what John is trying to say is that he would not see you injured by bitterness."

Sullen eyes fell to the floor, and she pouted stubbornly. "I do not know what you mean."

"I mean, Fanny—" he rose and paced the room—"that for over seventeen years, our mother carried that same burden. It robbed her of her joy, stole the light from her, and cast a shadow over both of us. I was forced to become the man our father never was, and you grew up in constant want of approval which was never given—not by the one you desired it from. I came to be respected, and you pampered, but neither of us were permitted to forget the betrayal of our father. I would see you do better for your daughter."

Fanny glanced to the bundle in her arms, then back to her brother. "That is the closest I have ever heard you come to criticising Mamma. You always worshiped her, and she you, until I was scarcely an afterthought."

"That is where you misunderstood. I have never been blind to our mother's faults, but I forgave her them. It took me three years to discover that I must also forgive our father, and only lately have I at last succeeded."

He swallowed, then cast a significant look to Margaret before resuming. "You must do the same for Watson, Fanny, or his error will colour your child's life as well as destroy your own."

Her shoulders rounded, and she clasped Margaret's hand more tightly, then raised it to her forehead to weep softly against it. "How am I to do it?"

John came to kneel before her, drawing her head to his shoulder. "One day at a time."

∼

16 June 1856

The letter arrived just as any other did. Bound in a stack—a thinner stack than the Thornton household had used to receive every day—and dropped innocuously on the desk, it could have been mistaken for a casual correspondence, and thus, Margaret assumed it to be when she first discovered it. Not recognising the hand, she set it aside in preference to one from Mr Bell, which had arrived at the same time.

Mr Bell's letter itself held the power to unsettle her to such a degree that she could not remain quietly at the house to await her husband's return. After a quick word to Dixon and Fanny, she wrapped her shawl about her shoulders and hurried the twenty-minute walk to the small mill where John now spent his days. There was no gallant Nicholas Higgins here to escort her into the bowels of the cotton mill, so she wandered in alone, anxious and set upon her quest.

"Margaret!" The voice behind her betrayed his surprise and chagrin, but when she whirled—almost upsetting a young spinner at her work—the intensity of her own expression impressed upon him the importance of her errand. He caught her elbow at once to lead her from the workrooms to the warehouse where they could speak.

"Is it Fanny?" he demanded at once.

Margaret shook her head, still breathless, and extended Mr Bell's letter. "You will never credit it! Oh, but I shall not try to tell you all. You must read what he says!"

Regarding her curiously still, he took the letter and Margaret watched his features slacken, then kindle in shock as he read.

My dear Margaret—and Thornton, for I expect you will read this as well,

All your gentle concern for my financial well-being you may now lay to rest. I have in my hand a telegram that will answer for the fortunes of many. How many, it remains to others to determine, but I've no doubt of its universal benevolence. The report will be spread more generally by the end of the week, but you will both be curious how it came about.

As you recall, each of the investors in the rail speculation were required to put up some additional interest or lose all. My portion was but small and was little difficulty to procure. However, as Watson was, until his death, one of the largest shareholders, many others began to lose faith. After one disaster, and facing what seemed insurmountable odds, Wright seemed to feel rather insecure of himself.

I was not the first to entertain a visit from him that week, but I fancy I was among the most receptive. I did mention to you that I had a smallish property I was able to pledge? My dear Margaret, that was only half true. Marlborough Mills was the property, and with it, I obtained a large enough mortgage to cover all the support lost with Watson's death. I would never have done, had the mill still been in operation. I am not so fearsome a rascal as that, to endanger men's' livelihoods, but since your husband so stubbornly refused any attempts to keep it open, what I did with the mill and the house was no one's concern but my own. It is a blessed thing that your husband saw fit to maintain and improve the property so well as he did, for it was valued at far more than I even dared hope. Remind me when next I have the pleasure of taking tea with you both that I owe Thornton my heartiest gratitude.

You may well imagine with what pleasure Mr Wright received my offer of support. It was not enough, however, to restore all that was lost. Many other supporters had fallen away—smaller investors all, but they found it preferable to limit their losses and seek other opportunities. After a few days of more refusals, and with a dwindling amount of time to procure what was needed, Wright came back to me, as I had proved obliging and had now a rather large stake.

'Well,' I told him, 'it seems that you are bled dry, old chap. Now look here, I am an old man, and I've no children to concern myself over, so this is all something of an amusement to me. Should the investment fail tomorrow, I might be obliged to cease my consumption of my favourite Havanas, but it would be no crushing blow. However, I imagine to you, it might not be so easily forgotten. Tell me my good man, what incentive might I look forward to if I, or perhaps a partner, should find it possible to put up the remaining thousand pounds you require?'

Well, my dear, he paced and fretted, and at last offered to me a hefty share in his own profits. I suppose it was better to part with some rather than all of what he expected to receive in the end, and so he offered, and I agreed. I sent a telegram at once to a young chap I know, and as he knew of my connection with your Mr Thornton as well as yourself, he was more than eager to oblige. The money was wired and transferred in tidy fashion, and the rail enterprise saved. The work nears completion now, and the contract to build the line shall be satisfied in a matter of days.

I do apologise for the length of this letter, but I do not anticipate traveling to Milton for at least a fortnight and I knew you would eagerly wish to know the truth of the matter. By this time next week, I shall in earnest have more money than I know what to do with. Wright will scrape by with just enough that he will be able to claim a profit—though not a handsome one. I expect it may be some while before he attempts anything of the kind again, or has enough credibility to sustain it, but then, it matters not to me.

I send you my fondest greetings, my dear—and you as well, Thornton, for I expect you have read the entire letter over Margaret's shoulder.

Yours & etc
A Bell

John's eyes were fairly starting and sightless by the time he finished reading. He passed the letter back, and his fingers were cold where they brushed Margaret's hand. "I cannot believe it," he muttered under his breath.

"John? John! You are not well!" Margaret clutched his sleeve, trying to catch his attention, but he still looked blindly about the room, shaking his head. After a moment he froze, a strange smile growing, and then he startled Margaret with wild, awe-struck laughter.

"Do not accuse me of seeking revenge, love," he gasped after a moment, "but I never thought to hear anything so satisfying come of all that business! Fancy that doddering, mischievous Mr Bell besting one of London's craftiest financiers at his own game! And not just besting—forcing him to become a dependent! Why, he could have ruined Wright if he had desired, for he could have let the whole thing fail. As he says, it would have mattered little to him if it had, but our Mr Bell is nothing if not fond of his games."

"But who is this person he speaks of as a partner, who helped him because of his connection to us?" Margaret was re-reading the bottom portion of the letter, and John leaned over for another look.

"It sounds like a phrase exactly tailored to pique our interest," he snorted. "Whoever the fellow is, I am certain that Bell will find some dramatic way of telling us when he is quite ready."

"Do you really think it possible that Mr Wright will be forced to a more conservative approach in business now? Mr Bell says his reputation has suffered because of all this."

John was still shaking his head in wonder. "Perhaps. It would be a much-needed caution to others, and for that, I am content. It was not my hands that humbled him, so I might not suffer pride or the indignity of personal retribution. I am glad for that."

"Yet your reputation and the work you left behind at the mill made it possible. Mr Bell was quite clear about that. But I am pleased that *your* hands are clean, John."

"Indeed. And now let that sorry chapter rest, for Wright is none of my concern." He pressed her hand and seemed aware of his surroundings once more. "Shall I walk you home, Margaret?"

She tucked the letter into her reticule. "I would never turn down your company, but I can manage, if you still have work. Stay, John, I am no stranger to Milton's streets and therefore quite safe."

"I ought to insist on walking with you, but I know better. I will see you tonight, love." He smiled, his blue eyes twinkling in that way of his that always sent a shiver through her. She returned his look with an impertinent one of her own and left him to his work.

~

Many hours later saw them nestled quietly on their favourite settee before the fire in their own room. Fanny and Dixon had long retired, and at last they had leisure to again marvel over the day's revelations. Their inclinations, however, were so very far from curiosity over the affairs of others that Mr Bell's name only crossed their lips once, and Wright's not at all.

John had drawn Margaret's hand over his knee and was gently kneading her palm. She seemed to find his ministrations soothing, for her head draped over his shoulder, her countenance was suffused with a mellow warmth, and her fingers spread invitingly. She sighed, rolled her neck to better meet his gaze, and graced him with one of her more eloquent, doting smiles.

"Have you considered," he asked at length, "that we are likely to hear more from Bell very soon?"

Her brow quirked. "I have."

His thumb pressed and traced the deep groove stretching the width of her hand, and he blinked for a moment. "You believe as I; that he will make us some offer—a loan or some such—that would be nearly impossible to refuse, or at least imprudent given our present circumstances."

"I cannot think why else he would have taken such pains to give us the earliest intelligence of his affairs unless those were his intentions."

He swallowed. "Margaret... I am not inclined to accept. At least, I would not do so without much deliberation." He raised his eyes again to hers. "I would be sorry to displease you, but—"

"Displease me?" She lifted her head from his shoulder. "John, what do you believe my wishes are?"

"I..." he bit his upper lip and scowled thoughtfully. "I believed you wished me to regain what I had lost."

"And what, precisely, have you lost, John? Honour? Wealth? Position?"

His fingers stilled along the ridges of her hand and he tilted his head, leaning forward to look at her better. "Perhaps I ought to mourn those things, but I do not. I am sorry to have lost what I felt was the progress of my own labours."

"But they were not lost, John. Your labours served their purpose in the time they were given. People had work. You made a product that others then traded and used. You were a large part of the force of this city, bringing many together to create something that was necessary and tangible, and to repay them with a livelihood. Your efforts made that possible, John."

His mouth tightened to the side. "The former Miss Hale, who once disdained all such enterprises! You are not the same woman I met two years ago, love."

"I should hope not! She was a naïve and foolish girl, that Miss Hale, though she did nurture one or two admirable notions. I hope they have found proper expression in the somewhat wiser Mrs Thornton."

"It is that wise woman's advice and opinion I now seek. Would you account me a thoughtless wretch if everything were offered to us—a painless and extravagant solution to our present difficulties—and I refused?"

"I suppose—" she answered slowly, her fingers curling to cup his own in a feathery caress—"that it would depend upon your reasons for refusal. You would prefer to rely upon your own dignity and hard work rather than permitting another to do you a service that will likely give him as much pleasure as he would think to give you?"

He leaned back, smiling a little. "You suspect me of too much pride?"

She pursed her lips. "I believe pride, the twisted, blackened sort of pride, could ensnare with either choice. You could just as easily be accused of it if you leapt at the chance, simply to shake from yourself any taint of disgrace. What is a month or two of a closed mill in ten years? No one will speak of a failure quickly recovered, but they will remember a generation of your oversight and management."

"And in which circumstance do you feel I am in greater danger of this mortal sin?"

Her smile returned, a teasing sparkle to her eyes dancing in the firelight. "The first, certainly. John—" she tipped towards him, placing her free hand upon his cheek and drawing close—"let it not be about you and your preferences. Let it instead be a decision made after considering where you can do the most good."

He caught her hand, turned his face into her palm and kissed it. "Do you know when I first knew I loved you, Margaret, beyond reason or hope?"

She laughed softly but shook her head.

"It must have begun long before, but I knew myself lost on the day of the riot. You told me, in rather blunt and forceful language if I recall, that I was being an arrogant blockhead and failing in my duties to others. Excessive hubris, I believe that was the root of the accusation."

"Was I any less guilty of that same vice? What a fool I was! But I thought the moment of decision for you would have been when the rock struck me."

"No, love. That was the moment the world as I knew it ceased turning, and I knew I could not live without you, you glorious, wilfull creature. I am in earnest when I beg you now—speak to me from your heart. All that I ever aspired to be, it was all a waste until I saw myself in your eyes. I must answer to my own conscience in the path before me, but before I take some fateful step, show me the path as you see it so that I may hope to hold fast to that vision."

Her thumb traced his cheekbone, her eyes misting with feeling. He waited, threading the fingers of his other hand through hers. She wetted her lips, and a glistening pool formed at the corner of one eye.

"John, I am no longer a girl that I should fear hardship. I have seen it destroy, and I have seen it inspire. The chaff might be burned away, but the gold remains to flourish, pure and vibrant and unhindered. Who is to say why sorrows and difficulties come? But I am my father's child, in that I believe with all my heart that we are being shaped for a purpose."

"Do you know, my mother said something very like that to me once—long ago, when my faith was weak."

"And what else did she say?"

"That we cannot always know what that purpose is, but that such times are sent by a wise, loving hand."

She drew a deep breath and her smile returned, her glittering eyes now alight with fervour. "John, do you not see? Every trial has, in truth, been a gift that strengthened us. All that we have seen and endured, every tear and each moment of pain—we would not have chosen them, but we would have been weaker without them."

"I cannot deny you that. So, are we to remain stubbornly rooted in difficulties, believing them to be sent to profit us, or are we to consider opportunities?"

"Are they not also gifts? But I would not wish away what has been sent to us for good and holy purposes simply to pursue what appears to be an easy path, freely granted. If it be a test of our faithfulness, let us not fail. But if it be right and proper, just in every way, then let us not hesitate."

John ceased toying with her hand and wound his arm around her. He leaned close, tipping her back against the seat. "And how are we to know which path we should choose?"

Her fingers tangled in his hair, sending a shiver down the back of his neck as her eyes narrowed thoughtfully. "As I said before, it will be the one where you can do the most good. Perhaps it has not yet been revealed. Until then, John, simply be the man I know you are, for you are already a gift to me."

A tightness squeezed his chest, and his held breath came as a choking laugh. "Good heavens woman, I love you!"

Her response was not in words. She tenderly kissed his brow, then drew him to her, pillowing his head on her shoulder and tightening her arms possessively about him. Her heartbeat, full and even and strong, pulsed against his cheek until he felt his own breath and heart steadying to keep time with hers. They remained thus, intimately twined and stirring not at all, for a long, hallowed silence, until the fire cooled and his fingers began to tingle.

He sighed reluctantly and raised his head from her soft embrace. "Have I ever told you—" he nuzzled a kiss to the flesh just below her ear—"how much fonder I am of this room than my old one at the Marlborough house?"

She sighed luxuriantly and leaned against his arm. "Because you at last have a fire in the grate?"

"I am certainly warmer, but that is not the reason. What a capital idea you had about saving space."

"Ah, yes." She captured his chin with her forefinger and drew little circles round it, tormenting him with that teasing, bewitching smile she employed so well. "I have become quite clever at matters domestic, have I not?"

She blinked then, as if recalling something. "Oh! How silly of me. It seems that I am not infallible, after all, for another letter came for you today that I had quite forgotten. It was addressed in a bold, dark hand, and I presumed it for something of consequence. I had intended to show it to you hours ago, but I am afraid Mr Bell's letter distracted me."

"And other matters are presently diverting me," he whispered against her throat, winding both arms about her waist until her body arched willingly into his embrace and she allowed him to lift her from the settee. "I have had enough of letters and business for one day."

Her eyes had acquired that delirious, glassy look, and her breath hitched as he carried her towards the bed. The words were almost lost on a sigh as she relented, "Tomorrow, then."

~

"Margaret?" Fanny Watson's voice wavered uncertainly into the kitchen where Margaret and Dixon had been engaged in some menial task. "Were you expecting callers?"

It was late in the day, and in fact John would return at almost any moment. The evening meal was prepared, Patience was crying out in a manner not at all befitting her name, and it was the last moment any would have expected to receive company. Nevertheless, the knock sounded at the door again.

Margaret tilted her head in curiosity. Dixon was more busily occupied than herself, so she whisked away the apron she had worn, touched her hair self-consciously, and gestured to Fanny that she would wait until the fractious child had been removed to another room before she opened the door.

On the step, she encountered a pleasant-looking couple she had never seen before. The gentleman was possessed of a singular appearance—broad of shoulder, deep of girth, and boasting the sort of countenance which could be best likened to a bearded lion, with its capacity to intimidate or reassure in equal measures. Beside him stood a lady perhaps ten years Margaret's senior, with gentle features and glowing smile. Her hair was the same shade of nut-brown as Bessie Higgins' had been, and her manner, it could be seen at once, was genial and unassuming.

Margaret could not help but to smile at this strange couple, although it seemed they held entirely the advantage of her. "Good evening," she greeted them cautiously, "may I assist you?"

"Mrs Thornton!" boomed the gentleman. "A pleasure, and no mistake." He cast a quick look of appraisal up and down Margaret's person, then, as an aside to his wife, commented, "The lad did not mention that he had wed Andromeda herself!"

Margaret's eyes widened, her brow furrowing in some confusion, when the lady laughed and bestowed a scolding look upon her husband. "Pray, pay the captain no mind, Mrs Thornton. He intends it as the purest compliment, I assure you. It is a pleasure to meet you at last."

"I—I am honoured," she stammered, "but may I know whom I have the pleasure of meeting?"

The captain's bushy eyebrows pinched together. "Why, did Thornton not tell you to expect our call? I imagine he must have wished to surprise you, madam. I had written—he should have had my letter by now! My apologies, madam. Captain Fortin, at your service, and this lovely creature is Mrs Fortin."

"A pleasure, sir, madam—a letter... oh!" Margaret blushed and instantly stepped aside to invite them in. "I am afraid I am partly to blame. Mr Thornton had not an opportunity to read the post last evening, and this morning he was in haste when he rose. He did receive a letter, but it still lies on the desk, unopened. You have just arrived in Milton?" She spoke this as she gestured hurriedly to Dixon to bring something for their guests, then led them to the family's small sitting room.

"Aye, from London. I knew the lad would wish the first intelligence, so we came as soon as could be."

Margaret felt her face crinkling in a furtherance of her confusion, but rather than interrogate her guests, she determined to play the role of a proper hostess. Though they claimed London as their home, the choreographed manners and style she had been taught in her aunt's drawing-room did not seem to suit with this couple. Neither did the rather more austere demeanour employed by the elder Mrs Thornton, whose place it had been for so many years to host John's guests. Margaret found herself, instead, falling back to the simple ways of the country parson's family home, and within a very few minutes, had settled herself and her guests with light conversation and humble refreshments.

"You must be at a great loss, Mrs Thornton," Mrs Fortin confessed after a few moments. "I can see that our names are not familiar to you."

Margaret set aside her cup, sensing that the mystery was about to be revealed to her. "Indeed, I must own that I am. However, it does not follow that the acquaintance must be unpleasant or unwelcome. I am delighted to meet any old friends of Mr Thornton's."

"You are a credit to him, my dear," the lady smiled. "The captain is only lately acquainted with Mr Thornton, but I first met him when my father brought him on as his partner at Marlborough Mills."

"Ah! The Mr Kramer he has mentioned. He told me of you... I believe your name was Brockett, if I recall correctly. Forgive me, I had not known that the acquaintance had been renewed, nor that you had married, madam."

The couple exchanged amused looks, then the captain suggested, "Perhaps we ought not say more, my dear. I expect the lad wished to surprise her, if there were good news to be had, or to spare her disappointment if it were otherwise."

"Disappointment?" she repeated.

At that moment, the door to the house opened, and John himself entered. He turned to shed his coat and hat in the small, partial passage afforded by the cramped house, and stopped when his eye caught the presence of guests in his home. Margaret watched his expression eagerly, hoping it might yield clues to whatever unknown enterprise the captain alluded to. He started, paled, then his eyes widened and sought hers before he addressed the captain.

"Sir! I did not know to expect you. It is a pleasure... and Mrs Fortin, we are honoured. I presume you have already been acquainted with Mrs Thornton?"

"Aye, lad," the captain rose and clapped John on the shoulder, as no one in Margaret's previous experience had ever dared to do. "And a lucky fellow ye are! I ought to call ye Perseus, who won himself a princess! Eh, but let us have done with the sea stories, for I expect ye and yer lovely lady here must be near to burst with curiosity."

John's face changed colours again as he glanced uncertainly to Margaret once more. She watched him then, staring for a long second at the captain's satisfied expression, and saw his posture ease somewhat. "Margaret," said he, beckoning to her with an outstretched hand, "I believe we ought to be seated to hear his news."

She settled tensely beside him, and both instinctively leaned forward. The captain, his face perfectly grave, bent to a satchel at his feet and withdrew a rather impressive-looking document. Margaret could see even from a distance that it bore half a dozen signatures as well as an official seal of some sort. John's hand clamped tightly over her own.

"I have here—" Fortin permitted himself a broad grin at last—"an official pardon from the Board of Admiralty for all persons, living or deceased, previously convicted of mutiny aboard the *Russell*."

The room tipped at odd angles, and the air rushed from her lungs. Her eyes were dazzled, unfocused, and she felt John's strong arm slipping round her shoulders. "Margaret?" his voice called from far away.

She felt herself trembling, blinking but not seeing—much as John had done the day before. "It is impossible!" she murmured, again and again.

"I have the proof here, madam," the captain was laughing. "I should say that many things were more impossible!"

"But... but there was nothing to be done! I have read Frederick's letters, the ones he wrote at the very point of the crisis! Please, sir, do not toy with my feelings... John, can he be in earnest?"

"He is." John caught her fluttering hand and held it firmly, anchoring her in his presence until at last she could perceive the natural colours and shapes of the familiar room clarifying behind him. "I did not tell you before because I did not wish to inspire false hope, but it seems the captain here knew his business. Your brother's name has been cleared."

"I do not understand!" The formal document was now in her hands, the list of the condemned and exonerated men printed before her eyes. "On what grounds could they reverse the judgment? Justified or no, Fred and the others were mutineers! They put off the officers and took the ship—it was in all the papers. There must be some mistake!"

"No mistake, madam, but a lie. A wretched, villainous lie to save face for the Navy, and even some of the crew repeated it because they were promised leniency if they confessed to the crime. Lieutenant Hale must have done the same, but I were there, madam. There was naught I could do then, nor the others who saw the wicked deception played out. We had our orders, and none of us wished to hang beside those poor devils on board the *Amica* when they were court-martialled."

Margaret blinked as understanding flooded over her. "Fred has never told me any more about it, since that first letter to Mother. Last year when he was... when I spoke with him, he said there might be a chance, he wanted to defend himself, but I did not understand.... I thought it was impossible! How have you done this, sir?"

"'Twere not my own doing! Yer husband here is a man of good sense, Mrs Thornton. It were a lucky thing we met. 'Twas a burden we both bore—he in his heart, myself in my conscience. I and others could bear witness, but I had nothing worth bringing before the Admiralty, and had no hope of ever making sense of it all before I met your Mr Thornton here. He made just the proper arguments and won the trust of one of the crew who could testify. The Admiralty found enough evidence that they determined a quiet pardon, without the fuss of the papers, the best way to avoid scandal."

She raised her brimming eyes to her husband, that flawed saviour who had borne with her through so many trials and sought her interests above his own. His cheek was tight, and twitching with a rich conflict of emotions she could read more easily even than her own heart. Proud delight warred with humility, joy with regret, and hope with that old air of confidence, rendering his expression in that moment the perfect mirror for her tumbling feelings. She lifted a hand to his cheek, sniffling and weeping, and touched her forehead gently to his—a promise that she would find some way, however long it took, to properly express her gratitude for all his tender care and devotion.

"My dear," Mrs Fortin's low voice broke them apart as she spoke to her husband, "perhaps we ought to call again on the morrow. Mr and Mrs Thornton must have a deal to talk over this evening."

"No!" Margaret's and John's voices raised in unison. They shared a brief glance, a mutual resolve, then Margaret spoke.

"Please, we would ask you to stay for dinner. This is cause for celebration, and do you not know that the bearers of such glad tidings must be shown the highest honours? I am afraid what we have to offer is modest at best, but we would cherish your company."

Mrs Fortin's gaze moved from John to Margaret, and her face blossomed into a sincere, jubilant smile. She seemed not to care for her husband's opinion on the matter—her mind was clearly resolved, and she answered for them both without taking her eyes off Margaret. "We would be delighted, Mrs Thornton."

"Please! You must call me Margaret. I should like to think of you as a friend, Mrs Fortin."

The lady's expression softened still more. "Deborah," she said.

Margaret inclined her head. "Deborah. I am dearly pleased to know you. Oh, you must meet Fanny—I do not suppose you remember her?"

"Margaret—" John drew her aside—"perhaps you will allow me to perform the introductions while you have a word with Dixon." He narrowed his eyes, a playful suggestion twinkling there, and gestured towards the document still in her hands.

"Oh!" She flushed, made a quick apology, and hurried from the room. She found Dixon seated at a small stool in the kitchen, her forehead resting in her hand in a moment of quiet repose.

"Dixon!" She fluttered the document, startling poor Dixon nearly out of her wits. "Oh, Dixon, it is the most wondrous thing! Fred has been pardoned, he can come home!"

Dixon jerked, then stumbled to her feet. Her eyes rounded, the strange truth of what she heard descending upon her as a glad shock infuses life into the hopeless. No protests did she utter—she merely clasped her hands over her heart, raising teary eyes to heaven, and cried out, "Fred, my boy! Oh, Missus!"

~

20 June 1856

"Yo'r brother, he's to come back, then?" Mary Higgins asked as she passed Margaret a fresh cup.

"I do not know. We have written to him, of course, but he is married and settled in Spain, and his first child was born just a few weeks ago. I doubt they will go anywhere for some months, at least. I am simply relieved that he shall never again be in danger. We may visit each other whenever we choose, and I can even speak freely of him."

"Tha's a' right, then," Mary agreed. She offered a bit of bread and cheese, but Margaret lifted her hand and shook her head.

"Please, nothing to eat, Mary. I mean no offence—" she hastened to explain, when Mary's eyes darkened at the presumed slight—"my stomach has been somewhat unsettled today. I only stopped by for a moment to visit and to see the children."

"Da's to come home soon. Yo'll stay tha' long today, won' yo'?"

"Mr Thornton will be arriving home soon as well, but perhaps I may stay a short while. I was hoping Christine or Joseph might like to read a book I brought."

At that moment, a knock sounded upon the door. Margaret straightened— recognising that sound by instinct and knowing even before Mary opened the door who she would find at the threshold. John's imposing figure cut out the glare from the street, his eyes lightening in some relief when he found her. He ducked his head to enter the room, and his countenance looked grave.

"John?" She rose from the chair. "Oh, what is it?"

He cast round to smile at Mary. "Forgive me, Miss Higgins, but I must deprive you of your guest." He looked then to Margaret, and his expression chilled her spine. Margaret hastened to leave, promising to call again when she could.

The streets were quiet when they stepped outside. Most of those who lived in the neighbourhood were still at work, and only a few young faces loitered about. John glanced about, then clasped her hand more tightly.

"Do you wish for the news now, or would you prefer to wait?"

She shivered, despite the spring day. "Oh, I should prefer to hear the worst now. What is so very dreadful?"

John stopped and drew a letter from his coat. "This was brought to me today. It is for you, but I assume the sender did not wish to distress a lady." He held it for her to take, but her teeth clenched, and she flinched.

"Just read it to me, please. It is not some ill tidings about Frederick again, is it? I knew it was too good!"

"No, it is from Mr Bell's solicitor." He unfolded the letter, assured himself once more that she could bear up, and read.

Dear Mrs Thornton,

I regret to inform you that Mr Adam Bell of Oxford died yesterday. I had been engaged to meet with him that day on some matters of business, and his housekeeper gave me the news that he died without warning during his morning tea. I found a letter on his desk which was already prepared for the post and addressed to you, and I enclose it. I expect I will have more to send you as his affairs are settled.

John stopped reading as her hand tightened upon his arm. She was already wiping tears away with her bare fingers, and he procured his handkerchief. "I am sorry, love. I did not know he was so ill as that."

"He has suffered gout for years, and they say the end can come on without warning, but I did not expect… oh, it is too much to lose him, as well as Papa!"

"It does seem to have been rather sudden. Come, let us return home before you open Bell's letter. Perhaps he has left some prophetic words of comfort for you."

~

She did not wait even long enough to refresh herself when they returned home. John followed her to the nook set aside as a study, where they could speak privately, and placed the letter in her hands before she could request it. She found the letter opener from the drawer, and he drew the chair back from the escritoire for her to seat herself. Then, contenting himself to kneel beside her, he listened as she read with wide eyes and pale lips.

My dear Margaret,

I had intended to come and stay with you again for a fortnight in Milton, but I have been feeling somewhat poorly. It shall pass, I am certain, and then I may again have the pleasure of seeing you and Thornton for some days this summer before I depart again for South America in the autumn.

I write regarding some matters of business. I would have preferred to discuss them in person, but I suppose it cannot be helped. You are aware, of course, that after that business with Wright, I came off rather handsomely. The mortgage I took out on the mill has, naturally, been satisfied, and there remain no further encumbrances. The disposition of the property has been of concern to me, for as you must be aware, a mill that is not operating is worth nothing, and deteriorates quickly.

Thornton is as hard-headed as they come, but he is also a clever fellow. I am depending upon you, my dear, to persuade him to accept some assistance in resuming operations. I am comfortably well off now and have less interest in collecting a lease than seeing the property tended. I would far rather trust your bull-headed husband with the property than some half-witted naif who cannot even tell cotton from linen. If he determines to be stubborn, my dear, tell him I will turn the mill over to just that sort simply to spite him.

I intend to set aside a sum for your purposes. I hope you will not consider it a loan to be repaid, but an instalment against the legacy I intend to leave you, which, naturally, shall include the house and mill property, as well as a handsome bank account for which I have absolutely no use.

Now, spare me your protestations, for I shall not hear them. I have no other heirs but you and Frederick, and your father was my dearest friend. As I understand your Thornton has found some way to clear Frederick, I trust we will see him in England again soon enough, and I may speak with him more particularly about his own inheritance in person.

You may be interested to learn that Wright approached me for a loan two days ago. It seems that one of those to whom he owed money was a Mr Abram Harris, his father-in-law, and Wright is most urgently seeking a means to satisfy the debt. For some reason there has been a falling out between the two—I can only presume it has something to do with the rumour I heard earlier in the week that Mrs Wright has gone to live in Paris. By the by, I was not inclined to agree to the loan, and informed him that I was committed to other interests.

As for yourselves, I have seen my solicitor today. He is to come again on the morrow to collect the last of the documents I have signed, and I hope you may have the mill open again soon. I will close now and write more soon.

Yours & etc,
A Bell

John took the letter from her as she laid it aside, his eyes brushing only lightly over Bell's neat script. His heart was pounding in his ears. In one letter, the course of their lives had changed again… and he could not decide whether the news was welcome or not.

That Bell had been kindly disposed towards Margaret, if not himself, he had never doubted, but for the man to make her—*them*—his heirs... it was too incredible to comprehend. And that he was gone already, with no opportunity for his beneficiaries to protest his generosity, or even to thank him....

Was he thankful? Surely, he must be! But it seemed too easy, too obvious. What effort had he exerted for such a prize? The mill would belong to them, and it was his pleasure... his duty... to return to it. The only difficulty was that he was not certain he still wished for it.

He clasped Margaret's hand and found it shaken and cold. Occasional sniffles betrayed her own heartache, and she wrapped her near arm about him to pull him close, seeking comfort. Another loss for her! Yet in her own quiet expressions of grief, he sensed an equal measure of concern for himself. He felt her fingers threading through his hair and he allowed her to draw his head to her knee.

"Margaret?"

She stroked her thumb over his temples, where his hair had begun to show the first shards of silver during her harrowing illness, and he heard a trembling sigh escape her. "You are to be the master of the mill again, my love."

"Shall I?"

"What would you propose to do instead? Even in life, Mr Bell wished for this. His death must make it even more inevitable that it is to be yours."

"I cannot deny that it would answer for every hope, but I do not like having that choice made for me. I have done nothing to deserve it."

Margaret gave a low chuckle. "Then sell it."

He lifted his head. "What?"

"All of it. Sell it off, take the proceeds elsewhere, and do what you wish."

"But... would that not dishonour Bell's wishes? How could you content yourself with something so mercenary?"

"What were his wishes, John? Do you think he cared about the buildings? About you making cotton?"

"Did his letter not say as much? He could not have been plainer."

"Read it again," she urged softly, tracing the edges of his jaw with her fingertips. "He was concerned for the upkeep of his property while it remained his, but his primary concern was for you—for us. Has he not always delighted in goading you with compliments disguised as impertinence? If he had admired you less or wished to impose his will without regard to your wishes, would he have taken the trouble to abuse your stubbornness or to tease you for your pride?"

He stared at her in wonder, even laughed a little. "And my love, you seem to take pleasure in advising me to do one thing when you truly wish for me to do the opposite."

She leaned down to touch her lips to his brow. "I wish for you to be content in your purpose, whatever that is."

"You would not prefer that we remove from Milton entirely, shed from ourselves the trappings of industry? We could go to the South. You could plant rose hedges, like your mother's, and I could—"

"Go mad? John—" she took his face between her hands—"the North is where we belong. You would suffocate in the South, for you could not take your ease. I know you aspire to more than you have accomplished thus far. Should you not begin again at the mill you know so well? What might you do for your workers, for your family? And when you have thought of a new object and the means, what more might you accomplish?"

"You are suggesting…." His eyes drifted from hers, and a slow smile grew as an inspired breath left him. "Ah. My Margaret, I know precisely what I wish to do. I believe you will be pleased, and Bell's memory honoured as it should be. And… are you well?"

"I hardly know! I never knew Mr Bell intimately, and it has only been since we came to Milton that I have been reacquainted with him. But he was dear, for all that. Of course, I am grieved. He did care so prodigiously for Papa, and he has proved more than kind to us. It is too much, John!"

"I am sorry you have lost another."

"Yes." She pulled him close again, and he gratefully leaned his cheek against her thigh. "It feels unjust somehow, that he should intend to leave us such a legacy as he proposes."

"Not 'us'. *You.* I am merely the lucky man who married an heiress. You always were a queen consorting with a dustman."

"Oh! If I have ever given such an impression—"

"Do you not remember the day we first met?"

"I have tried to forget. I am certain I was insufferable!"

"Irresistible is a better description. You certainly held me in your thrall." He rose up and pressed his lips to hers, cupping her cheek. One hand slid round her, and she leaned willingly into him.

"John—" she caught her breath and brushed light kisses over his cheekbone—"whatever I thought or said, whatever you believed I felt, know this. I am blessed beyond measure in you, and I thank heaven for all the sorrows, all the troubles that opened my eyes to see you. I love you, my obstinate, bewildering, magnificent John."

"Do you?" He tightened his arm around her, nibbling at her neck and pulling her to the edge of the chair.

"More than life," she promised, her voice now a whisper in his ear.

He shuddered, clasping her to his heart. Those words—so sweet, the fulfilment of every hope since he had first set eyes upon her! The rest of his life, gladly would he surrender to hold her close.

Twenty-Five

30 June 1853

"I am sorry, Mr Thornton, but the gentleman has gone out again. I believe he expected to have returned within an hour." The smart, wiry little waiter held himself at tense attention, knowing it would please his employer to show honour to one of the most powerful men in Milton.

"An hour, you say?" John Thornton was no stranger to decisiveness, and it required not an instant's musing for him to draw his conclusion. "I shall call back. Will you please let Mr Hale know to expect me when he returns?"

"Yes, sir!" The waiter touched his forehead briskly, but John scarcely noticed the obeisance. He had many other matters which required his attention and set out at once to see them accomplished. It was fortunate that the hotel he had arranged for Mr Hale was in a central part of the city, and he could easily pay another call he had purposed for himself, either this day or on the morrow.

It chafed him to so employ himself on his market day, running after a "renegade clergyman," as his mother had so succinctly described Milton's newest resident. In truth, he was not entirely certain that this friendship would prove profitable for himself, but at Mr Bell's behest he had pledged his assistance, as well as his patronage. And certainly, reasoned he, it would do no harm to dust off his Plato. What else was a man to do when he had dominated all his other challenges?

If this Mr Hale were half the noble gentleman that Mr Bell claimed, he felt he would stoutly admire such a man. A family man, such as he had heard Mr Hale was, to give up a comfortable living over a principle! He had known few men in his life capable of such determination. Mr Hale might do well in a city such as Milton.

With his typical long, measured strides, he drove down the street to the rail station and found the freight master. It was only information he needed, really, and it was well to gather it now before the storm struck and suspicions might be aroused.

"And you are certain that cargo from Dublin and Belfast are received through Liverpool three days per week?"

"Oh, yes, Mr Thornton. Mondays, Wednesdays, and Saturdays, usually late. It's little enough what comes, unless it's the people themselves! Had a lot of that the last few years, with the famine and all." The cargo master shook his head in pity. "Sometimes fifty to a car they would come—men, women, and children alike. Aye, 'tis a mercy that nonsense seems ended!"

The firm features softened, only briefly, with a sympathetic twinge around the eyes. "That it is. I understand matters are still far from well there, but we have not seen so many immigrants of late."

"Aye, and that's a fact, sir, but see if any of the mills here ever have a turn-out. Why, a man could send a wire and have his factory full of workers again by the end of the week, and the rail company only too happy to oblige with extra freight cars!"

John feigned an easy chuckle. "I know of no masters who would provoke the anger of the Unions so." With a tip of his beaver hat, he thanked the freight master for the schedule information. After a brief look at his pocket watch, he decided he might as well return to the hotel to enquire after Mr Hale.

The man had not yet returned at his arrival, but the waiter assured him that he expected Mr Hale momentarily, and offered to show him his room. He accepted, only wishing that he had with him some means of biding his time more profitably.

He sat, crossing and uncrossing his knees with impatience. After three full minutes, by his watch, he rose and slowly paced the room, surveying the few personal belongings the current tenant had left arrayed over the table. A handful of books, a pair of men's gloves, and a rose-embroidered handkerchief which he assumed must belong to Mrs Hale and had been brought out of sentiment by her husband. She had remained at the coast for the fresh air, from what Mr Hale's letter had said, and he expected that the maid and little daughter he had heard of were there as well.

A moment later, the door opened, and he turned to greet… his breath died in his chest. It was not Mr Hale who had entered the room, but a young woman he had never seen before. She was no Milton woman, that was certain! Her dark silk gown was of considerably simpler style than what he was accustomed to seeing. The fine ladies of Milton would hardly have considered it fashionable, though the weave and craftsmanship were exquisite. Her close straw hat was understated at best, though of excellent make, and her regal features embellished by no strings of jewellery. The modest, tasteful ensemble contrasted sharply with a heavy, luxuriant Indian shawl draped about her shoulders, and she carried the rich, formidable garment like a queen wore her train.

He glanced uncomfortably to the side, thinking that perhaps he was in the wrong room. Who was this graceful creature, who gazed frankly back at him with complete unconcern? Every look and move seemed calculated to impress upon the unfamiliar observer her superior ways. She could not be connected to the humble former parson he had come to see! He tried to open his mouth to apologise for his mistaken intrusion, but no words would come.

It was she who spoke first. She came forward, her fresh, earnest gaze meeting his. She gave no symptom of distress or unease at his presence in her quarters, but rather seemed to have expected him. In this, she held entirely the advantage of him.

"Mr Thornton, I believe!" Her voice, an even, cultured alto, betrayed neither eager welcome nor displeasure. She was simply stating the fact; that she was aware of his identity, and he need not untangle his own tongue to introduce himself. Her name, however, was still a mystery to him.

"Will you sit down?" she continued. "My father brought me to the door, not a minute ago, but unfortunately he was not told you were here, and has gone away on some business. But he will come back almost directly. I am sorry you have had the trouble of calling twice."

He stared for several breathless seconds. *This* was the daughter Bell had told him of? Why, she was no child, as Bell had spoken of her, but the most magnificent woman he had ever set eyes upon! All thoughts of his pressing schedule vanished. Obediently, the master of men took the seat she offered and looked readily back to her. He was as an enraptured scholar once more, hungrily admiring the masterpiece and hoping to learn a little more of how it was achieved.

She had removed her hat and fully entered the room now, her strides so level and untroubled that her elegant carriage scarcely bobbed with each step. She chose a chair near the window for herself, and he could not help but wonder if she had done so specifically for the intimidating advantage offered by the position of the furniture. She stood beside it before assuming her seat, her shining dark head tilted ever so slightly as she waited still for some response from him.

His mouth was verily gaping! Resolutely, he closed his teeth and swallowed. He must think of *something* to say in reply. "Do you know where it is that Mr Hale has gone to?" he managed—though his voice, he feared, was far from its typical authoritative tone.

He took another quick breath and offered the next plausible thought to come to him. "Perhaps I might be able to find him." The suggestion was quite reasonable, though a false one, as he had no intention of stirring from that spot.

"He has gone to a Mr Donkin's in Canute Street. He is the landlord of the house my father wishes to take in Crampton."

These were words which jarred his thinking back to its accustomed stream. "I am familiar with the house."

He came very close to seconding Mr Hale's opinion that the house would do very well for them, but at that moment the apparition before him unveiled her full radiance. She slid the lavish drapery from her shoulders to place it over the back of her chair, and for the space of one hammering pulse-beat, she stood before him—the light from the window seeming almost as a christening on the simple, undisguised lines of her form-fitting gown.

For the first time in his memory, he could not look away. When was the last time he had permitted himself to notice a woman's figure? Hers was a sculpted fascination; long, elegant shoulders flowing roundly to taper fingers; the hands held in quiet repose rather than fluttering nervously as most women's did in his company. They laced gently before her, highlighting all the more markedly the extravagant dip of her waist where her elbows curved away from her body. His eyes widened as they helplessly traced a sweeping arch up, over a figure that was at once generous in its feminine appeal and dignified in its aloof poise.

She cast a faintly haughty glance upon his speechless admiration, as a regent would a subject, then lowered herself slowly into the chair. She settled herself delicately, but without the affected fragility of manner which was expected of fine ladies. Her movements were majestic and fluid—confident in a manner which no lady ought ever to be—and he was at a complete loss for words.

He shook himself. And this divine being was to reside in Crampton? It was as unsuitable a place as any he could fathom! Why, the house was sound enough, to be sure, but rather rough, even for a simple clergyman. Certainly, it was nothing to the ambrosial surroundings which seemed more of a piece with *her*. For the life of him, he could not think of a residence in all of Milton—even his own—which seemed worthy of her.

He glanced down at his person in some heightened consciousness. He had canvassed nearly all the Milton streets today it seemed, and they had left their mark. The dust still clung to his shoes, the creases had all but vanished from his trousers, and his tidy black cravat almost certainly hung lifeless and dull.

Even his hat, where he had set it to rest beside that fine ivory handkerchief, gave testament to his unpolished state.

She, too, bore evidence of her own encounter with the city—but where the grime of his toil seemed common to his coarse figure, he sensed that the unwelcome tarnish would fall from her as naturally as any interloper was evicted from a palace. He shifted uneasily in his chair, and his face, it must be confessed, took on the more commanding and austere expression which he found comfortable, rather than the genial one which befitted conversation with a refined young lady.

She had plucked up a bit of needle work to occupy herself, but she appeared to give it little effort. Perhaps she was weary, as he imagined she must be after all her travel and searching for accommodations. He struggled for some comforting thing to say, something to reassure this Southern beauty that Milton might hold more interest for her once she had settled there. No words came readily to his tongue, for at every moment, when he thought he had perceived a subject upon which he might express himself, that proud curve of her brow declared to him once more what she saw him for—a coarse-hewn fellow, calloused and hard, and scarcely fit to offer her a courtly bow.

At last, she deigned to speak. "I understand, Mr Thornton, that you are the proprietor of one of the cotton mills in the city?"

Here, naturally, would have been his opportunity to impress her. His was not merely *one* of the mills, but the most modern, the most consequential, and he the self-made master of it all! Somehow, though, he felt she would be less than intrigued by such confident boasting—that his connection with the mill made him not a figure of admiration in her eyes, but an object of scorn. His face hardened. "Yes, Miss Hale, that is true." He ventured no further details on the subject.

The ebony contour of her brow lifted faintly, perhaps in surprise at his terseness, but curiosity did not seem to plague her. She returned her serene attention to her needlework. Her expression never altered a few moments later when she asked, "You have been acquainted with Mr Bell for some while?"

"Yes, for about ten years," he answered readily enough. He ought to have offered more—that Bell was his distant landlord; that the old gentleman and he regularly clashed in their social opinions but shared a well-founded working respect; that Bell had spoken with repeated and unabashed admiration of her father. Each statement would have only emphasised further his distance from her genteel position, so he kept his mouth resolutely closed. He could not quite decide that he liked her, for all his gawking at her exotic beauty.

She allowed him to simmer in wordless suspense several moments longer. If it were any disturbance to her, to sit in silence in this rented room with a strange man in attendance, she gave no indication. A most singular being, this Miss Hale! To his own mortification, he continued simply to stare at her, for he was helpless to do otherwise.

"Is it true that Milton has a fine park for walking?" For the first time he thought he detected a spark of interest from her.

"I am sorry to disappoint you," he answered reluctantly. "Our best approximation is the cemetery, just outside town. There are some fine trees, and one or two small lawns to be found there. If you wish a more idyllic scene, you must venture towards the sheep farms, another mile to the west where the workers often picnic, but there are no cultivated walking paths."

A flicker of some disappointment showed in her eyes, but it was quickly tamped and replaced by what he took for disdain. "I expect the city has grown too rapidly to make room for such considerations."

"Indeed." What she said was quite true, but at no point did he detect indulgence or understanding in her tone. No, she had pronounced her judgment over his city: it was beneath her, and the energetic growth that proclaimed Milton's success only presented itself to her as further evidence of its rawness.

Her angelic countenance began to fade in his eyes. Of what good was unspeakable beauty when possessed of such supreme arrogance? Mr Hale could not come quickly enough for his taste, but he now wondered if the father were half so supercilious as the daughter. If so, he ought to rid himself of the burdensome acquaintance straightaway!

She kept up a few random topics out of duty, but never again did those clear eyes brighten with genuine enthusiasm. He was an obligation, no more—oh, yes, he knew the gentry and their ways! His two years in London and his many years among the elite investors had taught him with what disingenuous politeness they dismissed those they deemed lesser than themselves.

He answered her disjointed questions with stilted civility, but as she seemed barely interested in his responses, he gave them little enough thought or effort. Had she enquired about him more personally—which she showed no inclination to do—he might have answered her that he had a mother and sister who might make welcome acquaintances in this new city for herself and the still-unknown Mrs Hale. He might further have had an opportunity to ask after her own connections, and to understand whatever prejudices in her experience he might be able to chip away. If ever a thing seemed worth doing, this was certainly it, but he feared the task an impossible one.

At last the door opened behind him, and a lanky, soft-spoken gentleman entered. Mr Hale was as affable as his daughter was reserved, showing him every courtesy and apologising most earnestly for his delay.

The young lady appeared to have done with him, he observed in some dismay, for as soon as she felt herself no longer needed, she rose and wandered to the window. He spared her one disconcerted glance before turning back to Mr Hale, who was all praise for Milton and his friend Mr Bell.

They spoke for several moments, each man taking his measure of the other by well-chosen compliments and questions. Mr Hale, it seemed, was every inch the classically trained scholar Bell had claimed, though he struck John as rather less firm of mind and deed than he had originally expected.

Still, he felt the man's society might do him much good—particularly if his renewed studies in Latin and Greek afforded him any proximity to *her*. Surely, she might admire him for the effort, as such pursuits belonged to the realm of men of leisure and refinement. The back of his neck prickled as his father's words echoed back to him through the years, but he brushed off the feeling.

Mr Hale turned from him suddenly. "Margaret!" cried he, and he was obliged to repeat himself, for she did not appear to hear him at first.

John Thornton felt his palms ache with a nervous impulse such as he had not known in many years. *Margaret*. So, that was her name. He mouthed it silently—the name which was to become a mantra to him, representing all to which he could never aspire. He sought her composed, granite-like features for some flicker of emotion when she looked back to where he stood, but none appeared until her father spoke again.

"The landlord will persist in admiring that hideous paper," Mr Hale was explaining, "and I am afraid we must let it remain."

"Oh, dear! I am sorry!" she objected, but he could rapidly follow the tide of her thoughts as she turned inward to contrive some amelioration for the blight upon her hopes. In truth, he quite agreed with her opinion—he also had thought the papers in the Crampton house horridly outmoded and garish, but it had not occurred to him that they ought to be replaced in preparation for the house's new residents. His resolve was sharp and decisive—he would remonstrate the landlord himself, and if the dainty pattern he had seen on the handkerchief gave any indication of her tastes, he would recommend a moderate ivory and rose pattern for the new motif.

"Well, it is all settled—" Hale was turning back to him. "I have taken the house under contract, and I hope we shall be installed by the end of next week. Mr Thornton, we have not yet taken our luncheon. Might I persuade you to join us?"

He hesitated, a refusal on his lips, for by the time he returned to the mill, he would have lost well over two hours of his time this day. He could ill afford to lose another. He glanced to the young lady—*Margaret*—to see if by any flicker of receptiveness, she would second her father's invitation. Under no circumstances could he have refused!

It was as well that she did not, but he almost decided in that instant that he despised her for not doing so. It was only the barest level of civility, but she could not extend him even so much. He set his teeth and turned back to Mr Hale. "I am afraid I cannot, sir, but I thank you. I shall call on you once you have settled. I wish you a good day, sir."

He claimed his hat at the little table. Miss Hale gazed once more out of the window, scarcely giving notice of his leave-taking, and certainly not offering to accept his hand as her father did. He shook his head to himself as he marched down from the hotel steps.

One day—one day!—he might pledge his life and honour to a woman such as that, gladly laying all at the feet of such a noble, poised, and commanding figure. She held no fear of him and would never draw back from speaking freely what so many others simpered behind gloved hands. How refreshing such beauty and boldness would be in his life—if only she did not suffer such abominable pride!

30 June 1856

John pushed back from the scaffolding where he had been surveying the empty looms. All would be pulsing and alive again in a few days' time, and a swell of pride surged in his breast. He would be an ungracious wretch to think any of it his own doing—no, it was all the sweet touch of Margaret in his life that had brought him every worldly blessing. By her, he could account all he might ever achieve and all those who might profit by his efforts.

None might have imagined it from such an inauspicious beginning, that he would be looking over all his life and crediting a haughty, impertinent Southern lass with all his present happiness! How provoked and bewildered he had been on that first day he had met her—that baffling, majestic, inscrutable slip of a woman who made him her own with a single glance.

He had not been fully honest, and he realised it now. It was not the day of the riots, nor the dinner party at his house, nor the many delicious evenings he had visited the Hales over tea when he had lost his head and heart to her. It was that very first moment, when she had so blithely assumed command, and he had surrendered his defences without even a shot fired. A private smile stole over his face as he tapped his fingers on the railing. Her prisoner he was, and a most contented one at that. Now, to ensure that her faith in him had been well placed.

"Yo' wanted to see me, sir?"

John turned. "Higgins. I did not expect you to come so soon."

"Well, sir, Hamper's cut hours this week. He says wi' Marlborough Mills running again soon, he wan's to drive up th' price o' his cotton before yo' get back into production. Some o' th' others are doin' th' same."

"He is a damned fool."

"Tha's what I told him today, sir, right before he fired me."

John burst into a hearty laugh. "All the better for me, I shall hope! Will you come back to Marlborough Mills?"

"I was hopin' yo' would ask, Master."

"Let us not have that. Just call me Thornton, Higgins."

The other's brow clouded. "Sir?"

He stepped back and leaned against the railing. "I don't need a line chief, I need an overseer. Williams has a good place and has no wish to come back, but even if he did, I would not have him. He left when you remained. I can think of no better commendation. Will you accept the post?"

Higgins flushed with flattered warmth. "A man would be a ri' fool to refuse. I'm not so arrogant as that, sir."

"I once was, almost. I scorned it as charity, though it was not then, and it is not now. I can use an honest man, and I know of none better."

"Thank yo', sir. When will yo'... we... be running again?"

"I have purchased some small lots of raw cotton from other mills. Most were accommodating enough to sell me a little, and it should all be delivered by tomorrow. The Liverpool shipment begins arriving next week as usual. I already have two small orders—I think those buyers overlooked the closure notice before they sent their letters, but now we shall have the pleasure of filling them. I assume many of the hands will wish to come back?"

"Give th' word, sir, and I'll have three hundred a' th' gate tomorrow morning."

"The word is given, Higgins."

Higgins nodded and made as if to go but turned back. "Sir, it's too soon to ask, but will th' kitchen open again? The men'll want to know."

"As soon as we can have the food delivered, but do not expect it to be in operation long."

Higgins blinked. "I see, sir."

"No, I do not think you do. Mrs Thornton has informed me that the building is wholly unsuitable and insists that it be torn down in favour of something more modern. Perhaps we might apply to Miss Higgins for her opinion on how the new kitchen ought to be built?"

Twinkling eyes met this request. "I'll ask, sir."

"Moreover, the lady insists that we build a school room here on the mill property, so the children needn't walk so far for their studies. She has already procured the name of a teacher and has informed me of her own intentions to assist where she may, so I must see it done lest I displease Mrs Thornton."

Higgins' whiskered cheeks rounded, and he stifled a hearty laugh. "Yo' can tell Mrs Thornton if I e'er get a dog, I wan' hoo to train it."

John crossed his arms. "I am certain there is some insult to my character there, but I would rather not be made to understand it."

Higgins chortled and turned down the steps without another word.

"Here, did you not wish to discuss your new pay?"

Higgins lifted a good-natured hand as he continued his descent. "Can't be worse than what I were gettin' a' Hamper's."

"Thirty-five percent."

Higgins faltered. He turned back, aghast. "What, sir?"

"Twenty-five, if you persist in challenging me."

"But...."

"I find I have too many ambitions, Higgins. Many of them, I confess, were inspired by that vexing woman who has taken over my home. This past month has given rise to all manner of bothersome notions, and I have half a lifetime yet to pursue them. I shall remain here for some while, but I would like to think there are other possibilities. A portion of your share will be invested in the mill, so that you may begin purchasing interest as I did, and my own resources might be used elsewhere."

Higgins' jaw had fallen open, his complexion ashen. "Yo're serious, sir? Yo've na' been down with th' fever?"

"I am in perfect health. Are we agreed?"

Three unsteady breaths shook the man, and he nodded slowly.

"Excellent. If you will excuse me, Higgins, I must return to the house. Margaret is settling our belongings once more, and I am sure she will wish to hear the good news."

~

"I am still surprised he was persuaded to it." Hannah cast a speculative eye about the drawing-room which had long been so familiar to her. It was still almost empty, save for two crates just brought in to be unpacked once more.

"Persuaded?" Margaret flashed a mischievous look her way. "No one persuades John to do anything that was not already his wish."

"Save for you. Legacy or no, he certainly must have made some objection to the whole affair. He is too proud to do otherwise."

"Oh, he did!" Margaret bent to examine the contents of one of the crates, and then directed a man to take it upstairs. She straightened, her cheeks flushed brightly and one hand resting on her hip. "He protested that he wanted no charity, that he was content to work on his own merits as he had always done, but he soon realised that it was a matter beyond himself. He can do more here, and I believe he has already decided on many new objects."

Hannah repressed one of her old snorts. "Vanity and nonsense. I don't hold with some of his new notions, but it will avail me nothing to speak against them."

"I would doubt it. He has been up half the last three nights, writing out all the proposals he wishes to explore. Why, even Fanny has roused at the idea of coming back. Did you know that she plans to spend some of her hours teaching at the new mill school? I do not even think she intends to wait until her period of mourning is complete. She announced it to us last evening and outright dared us to try to stop her. I think it will be just the thing to mend her spirits."

"So long as your school has no place for a music teacher, she might serve well," Hannah retorted drily. "And what of you? You have not worn black since you returned from London."

Margaret drew out a few curios and trinkets that looked like they might have belonged to her mother and carefully arranged them on the mantel. "Nor do I intend to. I have mourned long enough, and I think Mr Bell would not be offended if I chose to honour his memory in a different way. Oh!" she beckoned to two more men who entered the house with fresh burdens. "Upstairs with the crates, but I will take that painting."

She took a rolled and bound parcel from one of the men and returned to Hannah, a peculiar glow about her countenance. She drew close and seemed to hesitate.

"What are you about, girl? Have you purchased some ghastly new art? Well, it is your house, who am I to disapprove?"

"Ghastly it may be, but I did not purchase it, and it is not destined for this house." Margaret's figure tensed, then as if releasing a great coil, she spread the painting open. "Is it very dreadful?"

Hannah put a hand to her mouth. Captured in the soft shades of the watercolours was the image of her beloved son. Every feature was rendered faithfully—the wisps of hair over his brow, the set of his mouth, his father's nose and her own eyes. His head bowed in tender affection for the child in his arms and his expression radiated the peace and contentment she had only recently begun to witness in him.

Her hand shook as she extended it to touch, then drew back. "Where... how? What is this?"

Margaret cast one more loving look at the portrait, then held it out to her. "I have never managed its like before. I could not, do you see, unless I knew and loved my subject so well. I want you to have it, for you first gave him to me."

"I... I do not know what to say." Hannah tried to swallow the lump in her throat. "Why, it is... to think of anyone painting John in such a manner! He has always been accounted fierce—anyone else would have placed him as a tyrant in his mill, arms crossed and glowering at something. In this, you have portrayed the son *I* know."

"I am glad you approve. I did hope you would."

"How could I do otherwise?" Hannah sniffed roughly, blinking back a bit of sentiment, and bestowed a motherly kiss on the young woman's cheek. "And have you spoken to him yet?"

"He has not seen the painting. I did not even tell him I was trying to capture him as well as Patience, for I wanted to show it to you first."

"That—" Hannah shook her finger in the general direction of Margaret's middle—"is not what I meant, sly one. Does he know the rest?"

Margaret paled and touched a hand to her stomach. "What I wonder is how you knew! I only became certain myself a fortnight ago."

"And you thought to avoid having him fret and worry the better part of a year? You may as well spare yourself the effort, for if I can see it so plainly, he will not lag far behind. You have taken to eating little again, and your cheeks look perfectly ruddy. You may expect to be seeing the doctor at your door as soon as John feels the faintest glimmer of suspicion."

Margaret blushed, then laughed shyly. "I did not think it even possible. I thought I could not... surely, the same cannot happen a second time, can it?"

"The doctor has already spoken to me of it, for I was anxious as well. He says your chances are no worse now than they were before, so let us take comfort in that. I presume you are feeling well?"

Margaret offered a braver smile, and a satisfied gleam of her eye in answer. She straightened, however, when footsteps sounded in the passage.

"Margaret, where did you—Mother! I did not know you were here." John strode into the room, his frame alive and sparking with that same driving sort of energy which had long ago defined it. He came to greet her with an eager smile but froze when his eyes fell upon the portrait of himself.

"Margaret!" John stared, almost trembling, his expression softened in awe. "It is remarkable! You... you did this?" He raised wondering eyes to his wife, then turned to Hannah for some sympathy in his admiration.

"It seems your wife is a fine one for surprises."

John frowned, then his questioning gaze went back to Margaret... and the hand she still rested over her stomach. His brows arched.

Hannah straightened her shoulders and raised her head, surveying the son who had been her life and the daughter who had stolen her affections. "I think... you do not need me at present."

Twenty-Six

Christmas 1856

"Love, you act as if we are expecting royalty! Sit, before I must restrain you myself."

Margaret nudged her father's portrait into its proper place and patted down a cushion that had belonged to her mother. She turned to look round the drawing-room once more, almost satisfied… but not quite. Something was… *there*. She retrieved a dusting cloth from a side drawer to polish the glass flower cloche Hannah had given her, tucked her sewing basket farther out of sight, then stood back, her head tilted to appraise her work.

"Margaret! Are you ignoring me, or incapable of settling?" John caught her hand and tried to drag her to the sofa. "I am told this constant flutter over the house is normal in your present state, but you must cease! I will call for Dixon if you force me to."

She relented, but slowly. "I am so eager to see Frederick! Oh, what can be keeping that train? I do hope Dolores has not found the journey too cold. What do you suppose she will think of England? We ought to have met them at the station—"

"Frederick is well aware of why I would not permit you to meet them at the station. You needn't fret, for Higgins will see them safely here. I might have gone myself, had I thought I could trust you to stay off your feet while I was away."

"John, I will not break!"

"Empty promises. I shall believe you in a month's time, not before. Humour me, will you love? You have already made the hairs of my chin turn grey."

She turned and affectionately touched that chin—disappointingly smooth now, as they were expecting company and he had dressed for the occasion—and waited for his smile to return. "I think it lends you an air of distinction, Mr Thornton. How mature and wise you look!"

"And how dashedly exasperated! I would capture you by the waist and imprison you on my own lap if I thought I could get my arms around you."

"And this is the speech of a gentleman!"

"I never claimed to be such, madam." He swept her a playful bow. "And I meant it as no insult. I have never seen a more bewitching creature in my life than you, in all your maternal glory. You cannot know the pride it gives me to look upon you! But if your brother should walk in that door and see you engaged as one of the house maids at a time when you cannot even wear a proper corset, I fear his first impression of me may be less than favourable. And Higgins! I would never hear the end of it."

"Nicholas would understand my plight very well, and it will hardly be Frederick's first impression of you. But there, you have submitted a cause with which I cannot argue." She surrendered at last and attempted to ease herself into the sofa, but nearly fell instead.

John caught her halfway, chuckling. "Do you know, I think I am finally the more graceful of the two of us." He placed a pillow behind her back and helped her to shift to a more comfortable position, but scarcely had she sighed in acknowledged relief when Sarah came into the room.

"Ma'am, th' carriage is just pulled up. Sha' I show them in?"

"No!" Margaret bounded to her feet again—though not without some assistance from her laughing husband. "I shall come. Thank you, Sarah." She tried to straighten her skirts, but she could not see them well enough to decide whether her efforts had availed anything. Her palms ached, and a wild shiver passed through her as they moved to the passage together.

"Love, you are trembling. Take my arm, and you may squeeze it all you like if it calms you."

She rewarded his solicitude with a nervous smile and accepted his offer as the door opened. She felt him flinch—perhaps she had been more troubled than she cared to confess. Nicholas opened the carriage door for someone, tipped his hat to her, and then she saw him no more, for Frederick was coming up the steps.

"Margaret!"

She ran to him and he swept her into his arms. "Frederick!" Tears—joyous, beautiful tears flooded her eyes until she could scarcely make out his face, and she cradled it between her hands. "Oh, Fred, you are finally here!"

He was laughing and weeping in equal measures, and he pulled back, drawing her hands into his. "I am here, dearest, and look at you! I never saw you looking lovelier. *Mi vida!*" He gestured to the petite lady at his side. "I have so longed for you to know one another! Margaret, this is my Dolores."

Margaret was too overcome for a sedate greeting, and it seemed that Dolores was similarly affected. They embraced, long and warmly, and her new sister seemed to be trembling as much as she was. The young woman offered some words in broken English, too muted and emotive for Margaret to understand fully, but the meaning was clear enough.

"Thank you for coming," Margaret whispered into her ear. "You look just how I imagined you would! Oh, you must both meet John!"

She turned, her hand extended to him, and found him standing a little aloof, just at the door of the house. His eyes bore a sentimental sparkle, and he appeared to be enjoying the scene with detached reverence, as if interrupting would break some spell.

"John Thornton!" Frederick ascended the steps and fiercely grasped John's hand in his own. His other gripped John's shoulder, and his eyes welled with feeling. "I know not what to say to you, sir, but God bless you!"

John glanced swiftly to Margaret, somewhat bewildered. "We are pleased to see you safe, Hale. You are most welcome to our home."

"If I am so, it is your own doing. Thornton, you have my eternal gratitude—not least for securing the happiness of my beloved sister."

"The honour has been entirely mine." The two men spared another moment; hands clasped, eyes locked in mutual respect, and at length both turned to her.

Margaret's heart was too full. She wanted to laugh, to weep, to rejoice to the heavens and dance upon the oceans that had separated them for so long. She touched her fingers to her mouth, her body trembling, and could only sob for joy, the tears streaming freely down her face. Tears—she had shed so many this year, but these tasted sweet as they washed away all the past.

John came gently to her, drawing out his handkerchief, and Margaret saw the pleased triumph in Frederick's face as he witnessed the tender gesture. Yes, let him admire her husband! The world should know that her own John had won his place in her heart by every virtue man could possess, and that he would hold it forever.

"Margaret—" he tipped up her chin, stroking it with his thumb and permitting her to compose herself—"shall we invite our guests in from the cold?"

She laughed, brushing the last tear from her eyes and bestowing a watery smile on her beloved, and then took Dolores by the hand. "Do come. Surely, there is much to be said!"

~

"Frederick, you stayed in London last night, did you not?" Margaret had seated herself near Dolores on the sofa, while John and Frederick claimed the straight-backed chairs opposite. Dixon had hovered possessively near Frederick until Margaret had demanded that she also draw up a chair.

"Yes, Edith insisted that we stay with them. I finally met Captain Lennox, but we spoke little enough. I was mostly engaged with his brother, Henry Lennox. He seemed surprised to see me. I think no one had told him the news."

Margaret darted her eyes to John, but his expression remained impassive. "I wonder why that would be?"

"I gather he has been visiting less frequently. He seemed rather uncomfortable—why, he turned red as a cabbage when I asked Edith if she had more recent word than I of your health... er, I apologise, Margaret, I am afraid I may have let slip an indiscreet remark or two, for Edith appeared rather uninformed...."

"It is no matter, for it can hardly be a secret now. I am surprised that Edith seemed to know so little! I had written to her, of course, and more than once."

"I suspect she may not have taken the time to read your letters. Why, they hardly seemed to comprehend how it was I could have been pardoned, so I had the very great pleasure of extolling Thornton's efforts, so they might understand. Lennox nearly lost his temper when he heard, I am sure of it, for he quitted the room in what looked to be a fit of pique. When he came back again, he managed himself tolerably well, and asked how it was he had not been told certain details of my case, for as a barrister he could have done more than a simple magistrate, etcetera.

"I had given him precisely the same testimony as I gave you, Thornton—" here, he turned to John, whose ears had brightened to an embarrassed pink— "but he remained convinced that you had held some advantage, or worked some secret leverage somewhere. Some men simply cannot abide giving credit to another! Anyway, I spoke no more with him, for he went away just after that. But Edith! I am sure you wrote her everything, Margaret, but other than knowing to expect our arrival she seemed perfectly ignorant of every matter of import."

Dixon stirred and made some uncivil noise, but Margaret caught her eye with a warning. "How do you mean?" she asked carefully.

"Why, if we were not talking of travelling or babies, she could not speak more than two sentences together on any one object. I tell you, Margaret I scarcely knew her! When did Edith get so simple?"

"I do not think she has changed. Perhaps it is only our perception, you know—oh let us not speak ill of her, Frederick."

"Forgive me, Margaret. Edith always was more for dinner parties and fine clothes than anything really serious, so I suppose she is the same, as you say. Then it's us that's changed, is that it? Yes, perhaps it is. I shudder when I think what a conceited, vainglorious blockhead I was in my youth. And now look at me! The family heritage I boasted of was lost, and I had only my head and my hands to make my way in the world—and a bit of kindness where I had least looked for it. A proud tradesman I have become, but I would be an ungenerous fellow if I did not also acknowledge the gifts of good fortune strewn along my path." He bestowed a loving smile upon his bride, which was just as affectionately returned.

"You know, of course," he continued, "that Dolores' father has made me a partner. I have nothing to complain of, and every reason to be content."

"What is his business?" John asked.

"Rail."

Margaret blinked and looked at John, who had frozen with his cup halfway to his mouth. "R-rail?" he stammered.

"And textiles, of course. The Barbours started out as wool merchants, and the family's trading house is still among the largest in the country. Barbour saw the need for better ground transport, particularly from Barcelona where much of the wool is manufactured. He was one of the first to raise support for a rail line to Mataró, which finally opened seven or eight years ago. It is a short line, but it allowed for easier transport to and from the Barcelona port for the vineyards—and it proved how convenient such a system can be. It was not the grand network he envisioned, but it was a beginning. It was harder in those days to finance such an undertaking, but of course, since then, the laws have changed and now we have French and English investors. I should think in only ten or twenty years, he will see his vision realised."

John cleared his throat and put his saucer aside, looking significantly to Margaret. His right brow quirked, and he addressed Frederick again. "Our Mr Bell was, at the last, involved in a similar undertaking."

Frederick's lip curled, a sage twinkle shone in his eye, and he tapped his boot in smug restraint. "Was he? The old devil, it was always something for him."

"Frederick!" Margaret was leaning forward in her seat now, and she caught the silent amusement passing between Frederick and Dolores. "*You* were his partner!"

"Indeed, I was—or, rather, the Barbour house was, is that not right, *mi vida*? And profited a rather tidy sum, if I may express such vulgar satisfaction. However, it was not that which persuaded me, but the hope of being useful to Bell, and by extension the both of you, for he told me his intentions towards you. He also told me a bit about that scoundrel Wright and some of his shadier practices. I was only too pleased to lend what help I could. Why, you are laughing, Margaret! Should I not look to the interests of my sister and her husband, a man who had already done much for me?"

"Oh, Frederick! You always did try to look out for me, even when we were children."

"Ah, yes... I recall getting a few thrashings which you probably deserved more than I. Remember when you dressed Farmer Grady's old dog up for Sunday services and brought him right under our pew? It was a marvellous idea, if I do say so, but I never thought you would actually do it."

"You did what?" John straightened, his brow furrowed.

"Oh!" Margaret flushed—"that was not nearly so shocking as our late-night forays into the garden, climbing trees and counting the stars. Do you remember, Fred, the last night before you left for the Navy?"

Frederick's face softened. "Like it was yesterday." He leaned back in his chair, contentment seeming to settle over him as he looked at each person in turn. "I told you, did I not, that the Northern stars would guide me home? Had I only known then that they were not in the heavens, but here, in people—a sister possessed of more strength and spirit than even I could have suspected, and a brother worth more than all the friends and family I ever lost."

Margaret's eyes had grown misty again, and she raised them to John. He had gone quite still, and his voice was husky when he replied. "I believe, Hale, that loss is really only a starting place, a making room for all that is to come. We have gained far more."

~

That evening, the stone house on Marlborough Street nearly quaked on its foundations for all the exultant celebration taking place within its sombre walls. Frederick and Dolores Hale's arrival merited no less an acknowledgment than the company of all those dearest to their hosts. And this evening, Margaret would hear nothing of formalities, for Dixon took her place at table beside her long-lost boy.

Nicholas and Mary Higgins sat near Dr and Mrs Donaldson—who raised her eyebrows but held her tongue. Dolores had quickly bonded with Fanny over the rosy-cheeked babe in the nursery, for she had left her own child home in the care of her family. Even Captain and Mrs Fortin had made the journey to Milton for the occasion, and the gaiety shared by the gentlemen dispersed round the table was matched only by the knowing smiles and gently shaken heads of their ladies.

Margaret had taken her place at the foot of the table, and so often that night her eyes swept the disparate assembly of beloved faces to search out that one seated at their head—the one with the power to arrest her eyes and cause her pulse to still by the sound of his laughter. Each time she sought him, some sense caught his attention—or, perhaps he had been seeking her, as well. A quiet shared smile, an intimate understanding, and they would turn again to their guests. If they imagined their exchanges to be discreet, they were greatly deceived, for not a soul about that table could miss the devotion shining openly between the master and mistress of the house.

It was a home of the sort she had never imagined she might call her own, yet it suited her in every particular. Steady and practical, seasoned by both bitterness and beauty, the house that had once been only a token of her husband's prestige now reflected her touch in every surface. Its very walls seemed permeated by joy, its rooms welcoming and gracious. John had once told her, just after they had come back to it, that never had he felt such a sense of *home* anywhere he had known.

Home. Indeed, it was, but it was not the bricks or the furnishings, nor even the mementos of their mothers which decorated its corners. It was *him*—the lover of her heart who dominated its centre, whose life was bound up with hers and who had given to her all that he was and would ever be. She admired him now as he held sway over the room; the candid honesty of his pleasure, the humble frankness of his wisdom, and even the boyish sense of his humour.

He paused in his conversation, noticing her gaze lingering upon him, and his eyes warmed. She smiled back—an invitation and a promise. When all had departed again, and the house had gone quiet, it would be in his arms where she would take her rest, and nowhere else.

~

2 February 1857

"With this ring, I thee wed, with my body I thee worship, and with all my worldly goods I thee endow: In the name of the Father, and of the Son, and of the Holy Ghost. Amen."

The gold band caught the evening light from the window and shone his reflection over its warm face. Worn now—burnished by pain and glory, all its imperfections smoothed away—it held his eye as he clasped the hand wearing it. Every vow made that day he had fulfilled with his very soul, the blood of his heart, and the core of his being. His life had begun that day; everything that had passed before being only a prologue, a context for the purpose of his existence—the purpose he had found in her arms.

She writhed in pain now, those clear eyes darkened for a moment.

"Margaret? I am here, love."

Her fingers clenched his as another tremor shook her, then she gasped in relief when it had passed. "John," she panted—begged—"hold me!"

"I am, my love. I will not let you go. Not even the doctor will drive me from your side this time. I am here, and I will never leave."

She flexed her wrist, pulling herself nearer so she could bury her tousled head into his chest. Her body shook and trembled, great tormenting spasms racking her, but through it all, she clung to him. She shrieked, moaned, and bore down in gritty silence. His soul nearly split, his own body sweating and agonising with hers. Voices echoed beyond, but his concentration was all for her; for soothing her fears, for lending strength in her suffering.

And then, it was over. With one last, triumphant shudder, she cried out and then fell back, heaving and exultant. He could see nothing but her face, awash in a radiant splendor he had never before witnessed, but beyond the makeshift veil held by the maids, a new voice reached his ears. The cry was lusty and intense, and something broke inside John Thornton's strong heart.

He occupied himself in smoothing her flushed brow, stroking her dark, sweat-streaked hair, and fervently kissing her as she curled again towards him. "Margaret, my Margaret!" he crooned through his own joyful sobs. "You cannot know what you are to me, my life!"

Her eyes opened, a blissful peace now shining forth, and she touched his cheek. She said nothing, only caressed his face, but her weary tenderness was more than sufficient to convey her feelings. He pulled her against him, as well as he was able, and pressed his lips to her forehead. With every restorative gasp, he sensed the intrepid, miraculous power of her travails beginning to ebb, and she was his own once more.

"John, Margaret." His mother was coming round the narrow birthing bed, her arms full and her proud features alight. "You have a son."

Margaret could not yet straighten, so he held out his arms, then lifted his treasure for her to see. No barrier was to be tolerated, and they both eagerly pulled away the swaddling to reveal their son. Fingers... toes... a perfect little body and a thumping heartbeat. Dark hair—thick and shining already—fell over a rosy face, and two bleary eyes opened to them.

"What will you call him?" his mother asked.

John met Margaret's eyes, beheld the faith and trust there. Only one name suited—a name to declare their heritage, to send forth as their legacy. "George. His name is George."

Margaret kissed their child, then lay her cheek against John's. "George," she whispered in agreement. "And may the name be your strength, my son."

One more added to their family. John held his two loves close. For all that had been, and all that was to come, he would look to the future with his head high, his courage by his side, and his hope secure.

Prologue

Regent's Park, London
2 May 1837

The lanky boy with the dark hair stood enraptured before the glorious fountain, sprays of rainbow mist showering over his clothing. Blinking the drops from his eyes and squinting in the magnified sunlight though he was, he could not tear his gaze away.

It was not the aesthetics of the sculpture or the purity of the falling water which dazzled him, although the fountain's beauty was beyond all that he had ever seen. It was the steady, silent pump he contemplated; drawing water from the shattered glass of the pool's surface and forcing it into the explosive steam which dampened his garments. What a marvel of technology!

The pump was nothing new, of course. He had studied the mechanics of it long ago, but back home in Milton, there were not many opportunities to admire such graceful fusions of machinery and art. *This is how it was meant to be!* This was the perfect union of practicality and wonder, of simple principles employed to best advantage.

That such impressive technology could improve the nation, make lives better, and bring something of beauty to the hurries and wants of his world, made the boy's gangling frame quiver in sympathetic yearning. The call was upon his life, and he longed to be about the business of making and doing, seeing the fruit of his labours borne out in the betterment of his surroundings.

He turned his face fully into the spray, closing his eyes and standing far nearer the shimmering mist than any of the more refined park goers. He was not of their kind, and already at fourteen, he knew it. Perhaps it was well, he reflected, that his mother had at last overruled his father's desire for him to remain here in London.

The letters from home had never presented the facts so plainly, but John knew his mother. She was no silent, retiring little wife. More often than not, his father lost to her when she pitted her will against his. Therefore, he would be boarding a train the next morning. This was to be his last day in London for some while, and he counted himself fortunate that it happened to fall on a day when the splendid park was now open to the public.

He stepped back at last, beginning to sense himself conspicuous. It was not like him to display his pleasure so openly—he must take care in the future, or he would be mocked by those whose respect he desired. His enjoyment was honest and intense, but it would sink others' opinions of his self-control, and that he could not have. He briefly shook the droplets from his face and hair and looked about for an empty bench where he might open the bread and cheese he had brought. He found one within easy view of the fountain and proceeded to savour his repast.

Just behind him, in a little grassy area, he could see a fine family enjoying their own day at the park. The gentleman was older, but his wife appeared young and merry. There was a boy, perhaps a year or two younger than himself, shepherding two little girls who were probably about three or four. John draped his arm over the back of his bench, observing with some delight as he ate his meal.

One of the little girls, the one with darker curls, simply would not do as the other desired for her to—wandering near the sparkling fountain, tumbling after a passing duck, or contemplating the squirrels in a nearby tree. The blonde girl remained sedately near the family's picnic and complained strenuously when her counterpart would not do likewise. It was at these junctures that their older brother would retrieve the child, only to become distracted himself as the girl wandered off again.

John was nearly laughing aloud by the time three such episodes had played out. He felt somewhat akin to this curious little girl and thought her vibrant wonder at the world quite like his own. It was with growing amusement that he watched her escape once more, and this time, she ambled near to where he sat.

He smiled cheerfully, not wishing to frighten her. She did not look directly at him at first, her eyes instead diverted to the sprinkling fountain. She paused near his bench.

"It is beautiful, is it not?"

Her little bonneted head jerked in his direction. Clear, green-blue eyes surveyed him, and a plump lip stuck out in thought. Slowly, she returned his smile.

"Do you like it?"

"Yes," was the frank reply. The girl turned her face back towards the fountain—not precisely dismissing him, but not focusing on him, either.

He glanced over his shoulder, wondering if the child's absence had again been noted. Apparently, it had not, as the older brother was absorbed in a book, and the parents were chatting with some acquaintance.

"Does your sister not enjoy it?"

"She's my cousin," the child informed him blithely. "That's my brother. We are visiting my aunt and uncle for a fort… a fort-night."

"I see. Here," he offered in sudden inspiration, "I've some bread left. Would you like to feed some geese with me?"

"Aunt says they are dirty."

"It is not dirty to feed them, surely. Do they not need someone to care for them?"

Doubt creased between those large, bright eyes. She drew near with heightened caution, and quickly, as though she were afraid he might make a grab for her, snatched the piece of bread he had offered.

Still eyeing him with some cynicism, she turned and gave an awkward toss towards a hopeful goose. Several others descended upon the recipient of her goodwill, and amidst a raucous flapping of white wings, one emerged the victor. Boldly, the flock looked back to their benefactress.

The girl turned to look helplessly at him. "They all want some!"

He grinned. "We will just have to share a little more, will we not?" He rose from his bench to kneel beside her, and together they broke the pieces of bread. He quite liked the hearty giggles bubbling from her. It sounded so healthy and genuine compared with Fanny's weak and ailing laugh. If only his sister were strong and vivacious like this little girl!

At length, he ran out of bread, but his new friend did not abandon him at once. He returned to the bench and made a show of checking his empty satchel for more morsels of bread, but of course, there were none. When he spread his hands in laughing remorse, he noted that her eyes had strayed to the book he had brought. She was scrutinising the title with a furrowed brow, tilting her head to read it properly. He watched her in some amusement.

She looked back to him with surprised appreciation flashing in her eyes. "My papa has that book."

His brows shot up. "You can read the title?"

She spared him a withering look, which seemed wholly out of place and comical in so young and innocent a face. "Of course, I can," she scoffed, as if it were the most natural thing in the world that a child of four should be able to recognise *The Iliad.*'

"Papa reads it to me. Helen is my favourite, but I do not think Paris was very nice."

John was laughing heartily now. "No, he was not. But have you thought that perhaps Helen was little better?"

Shock washed over her face at such an audacious supposition. She gaped at him in confusion and horror that he could suggest the lovely Helen of Troy might not have been a fully innocent party to her own abduction. Such was her consternation that he dared cast up any blame to a woman that he began to feel he ought to apologise. After all, it was only conjecture on his part to begin with, and certainly no concept with which he ought to burden a little girl—and a *very* little one at that. As he began to make his amends, however, another voice cut in.

"Margaret! What have you gone and done now?" The girl's older brother at last came huffing up to retrieve her.

John glanced over to the younger boy, noting the look of embarrassment on his face. "She does not trouble me, I assure you."

The boy glared at him in speechless indignation, then bent to collect his sister's hand. "Margaret, Aunt Shaw is very cross. You must not continue to wander so!"

"We were feeding the birds, Fred. The boy is nice." She peered back up at John with the faintest shadow of hesitation crossing her features. She still had not fully erased her qualms about his views on literature, but his initial kindness to her had in some measure founded a basic amenity for him.

"It was a pleasure," John declared. And it had been. Here in London he had been largely without friends, though accompanied by boys of similar age in Mr Wright's house. None shared his spark of quick interest in knowing and doing all he could, and for the second time he wished the little sister he went home to on the morrow might grow into one closer in character to himself.

The older brother, however, wanted none of John's assurances. A smartly attired gentleman's boy, he scowled askance at John. "Margaret, do not meddle with tradesmen's sons." He grasped the child's hand and dragged her unwillingly away.

John stood bereft and empty for more than one reason. Again, he had evidence that he was simply not good enough in the eyes of the elite. The girl—Margaret—looked plaintively over her shoulder as her brother propelled her forward, but she obeyed and left him alone. He watched as the entourage of gentle folk made ready to depart. The only one ever to acknowledge his existence was the dark-haired maid, who offered him one last comradely smile and a wave of her hand.

It was a pity, he thought glumly, that within a few years, even that innocent, friendly little soul would have her views soured on the middle class. What hope was there for one such as himself when those he encountered only sneered at him because his father had a profession? How was he any less worthy than the next boy?

Somehow, someday, he would find a way to make something of himself. He would not bear scorn based on such archaic notions. The will to achieve, to rise above, and the deserving pride in a job well done ought to be the measure of a man—not what he had inherited at birth, without any proof of his worthiness!

Scowling as he stuffed his book inside his parcel, he made himself a vow. One day, he would prove himself so wholly and utterly that none might ever dare look down on him again—not that haughty boy, and certainly not that charming little girl, nor any of their well-heeled relations! It was time to leave behind himself the lessons of a scholar and take up the mantle of industry. He drew a deep, filling breath.

Tomorrow, he was going home to build his future.

The Beginning...

Printed in Great Britain
by Amazon